chasing a starlight

A NOVEL BY
TAMISHA KUENEE

★ · ☆ · ★

To anyone who had a crush so intensified,
it was all consuming.

CHAPTER ONE

Soleil

IT'S LIKE CLOCKWORK. He goes for a run early in the morning before the sun is even up, he comes back home and heads out in a suit, meaning he goes to work, and just like clockwork he's back home, before 5 pm not a second before and not a second later. I sounded like a fucking stalker to know his schedule like this, and it really didn't help the fact that my schedule was probably the exact same, but Reiner Kline was predictable like that, and no matter how hard I tried to *not* notice him, I do anyways. Because he was everywhere. We're neighbors is what I meant. He's probably the first face I see in the morning, and the last I see at night. our schedule was too alike.

I usually wake up and I slurp my coffee while I stare out the window like a sad widow. That usually lasts a while, because I zone out, stressing about things that haven't even happened yet. Then I shower and I'm out before he is because I have morning classes, and I'm back home before 5 pm, unlike him I sometimes arrived late or early. I work after my classes, and on the days I'm off I come straight home, or I try to force myself to socialize.

I have every intention to believe that Reiner Kline fucking hates me.

How did I know? When I first moved in this neighborhood, only a few months ago, I was completely unsure of anything. My father died and left me his house — a house that cost more than all of my paychecks combined. Corbyn Walsh (my father) left behind a nice house in the suburbs. It has three bedrooms, his room, a guest room, and my room — which belonged to me long before he even died. I knew about the house because I visited my dad sometimes, occasionally — rarely. Though I never claimed the room, it was always mine, Corbyn always wanted me back with him, but like any other stubborn kid, I chose to take care of myself instead — barely surviving.

Now I own a nice house in a safe neighborhood at the early age of twenty-three and I could never truly figure out if all of this was a good thing. But with a single parent and no sibling to claim anything, everything became mine, it was a good thing until it became a burden.

The day I moved in the neighborhood was one hell of a day to remember, not because of the happiness and excitement, but because of the embarrassment. I baked a pie, I wanted to be welcomed, even though my neighbors should've been the one to worry about that, but I baked the pie anyway. The closest door to knock on was his, so I did, with a bright smile on my face, ready to offer him the pie I just baked.

He opened the door, and I was still smiling. I think I spoke and I said something close to hello, but he only stared at me then, his jaw ticked — his eyes were judging everything I had to offer. I felt uncomfortable, I did. But it was different, my stomach was turning, and the more he stared my nervousness only increased.

Reiner said four words that day. "I don't like pies." Then he closed his door before I could get a word in.

My skin crawled with embarrassment. I felt silly to even have thought about baking a pie, to feel welcome in the neighborhood, to feel like maybe I do deserve to be here and it should be enough, but the more I thought about that day the more I realized how stupid I had been.

The events that followed after were probably just as bad as the first one, but it could be described as funny if I were to exaggerate. I stopped studying one afternoon — I got bored and I've been growing a little garden which now is presumed dead — but back then I did give it some of my time and attention. I didn't know Reiner was around at that time. I was focused on the flowers, watering them, but I guess he said something behind me and I jumped and when I turned around with the hose in my hand, I drenched him with water. He took me by surprise and since then I've been cringing at the memory.

And like an idiot I apologized a million times and tried to magically dry his shirt while I patted on it, but his jaw only ticked.

8

Biting hard down on his teeth as he pushed my hands away, cursing under his breath. That was that.

It's been nothing but three months, after the first months of kissing his ass, I learned not to care anymore. Instead we played these games, I still don't understand them. *We stared at each other,* although he looked at me like he wanted nothing to do with me. We also race in and out the house quickly just to not acknowledge each other.

Last week was his birthday, I think. People were at his house, car door slamming, cars going off, and I was too distracted to study. I cleaned a lot that night— I only guessed it was his birthday because I overheard someone wish him a happy birthday before the hug — something I didn't think he was capable of doing.

This week, his house was quiet. So was mine, because it always is. I had a neighbor joke about how they were nervous to have someone so young live in the area — they worried I'd be partying every week, like this would be a frat house.

This morning, in that same week, my car broke down, right in the driveway, it didn't even try to take me a few miles out, just right here. Now I couldn't exactly call for a lift, or send it to the shop because I was drowning in student debt and bills to pay around the house. The house was fully paid off, and that was the greatest parting gift my father could ever give me, but bills, fucking light bills, water bills, all that shit still had to be paid. Between college and my waitressing job I was broke every week, barely eating, surviving on coffee, crackers, and noodles. Nights when I treat myself I order pizza.

I couldn't touch the money my dad left me yet. I call it the rainy days stash and as long as I could breathe it was considered sunny to me. But right now I was so tempted to buy a new hot car. Wouldn't have to put up with this piece of shit again. I kicked the car and groaned because that might've cost me my left toe, but before I could hurl in pain, my grumpy neighbor's front door opened. Meaning it was exactly seven o'clock, not a second early not a second late.

I bit my lips looking over my shoulders, "morning." I grumbled, staring at his suited body as he walked down his driveway. I didn't know what he did, for all I know he could be a gigolo. Who knows? The man had a body on him, when I spilled water on him that afternoon, his shirt was practically stuck to his shredded body, and I could quite literally count all of his abs. I didn't but I could've. His suit fitted his body, more than fitted, blessed his body. His dark brown hair was slicked back as always, I didn't know how old he was, and I was so curious because he looked so young yet so. . . Old?

One hand in his pocket, and the other held a briefcase. Now whatever he does has to be important because his house was bigger than mine, he had a fancy car, and that had me questioning how the hell did my dad afford this place to begin with?

Reiner didn't say morning back, because he never did. I just like to be the bigger person and do it anyways, besides I was only out here stuck in the driveway still because my car wasn't working. We never crossed paths in the mornings, only on the weekends, sometimes Saturday at the gym, because my ex and I had this joint membership at the gym and even though we broke up, he was still paying for it and I'd be a monster to let that go to waste wouldn't I? And on those rare days me and Reiner cross paths at the gym. He avoids me like the plague.

I pulled out my phone, scrolling to see who to call that could drop me off to campus, and my options were literally limited.

If I call my ex, it'll be awkward as hell, but I know he'd still show up, and my only other friend besides the people I work with at the diner. She's most likely not even awake, and I'd feel so guilty waking her up so early in the morning simply because I didn't have a ride. Although that did sound like a reasonable excuse, I still couldn't find it in me to do that. I groaned as my finger hovered on his number, *Luke,* my ex. I really wish it didn't have to come down to this, and to make matters worse we just had a record of not talking to each other for two weeks straight, no regret sex and everything.

Fuck, fuck, fuck.

"Car trouble?"

I gasped as his deep voice drilled its way into my head. I honestly thought he left already — he scared me a little.

I sucked in a breath before turning around. "Oh, I'm fine." I wavered.

"I could give you a ride." He offered.

My brows furrowed as I stared at him, like an idiot. I was waiting for the joke, waiting for a laughing soundtrack from the 60s to play. But there was no one laughing. It was only Reiner staring at me with honest eyes. As honest as they could be anyways.

I know I should push my pride aside and accept the ride, but if Reiner — being who he is, offered me a ride I must've looked really desperate. Yet, I still couldn't wrap my head around the fact that THE Reiner Kline just offered me a ride.

I stared, then I blinked. My eyes still felt dry, "to campus?"

I always enjoyed playing with his patience, so it amuses me a little when he released a slow breath, tilting his head to the side as his jaw clenched, "to campus." he said the words like his final offer.

God, I wish I could record this conversation.

"I'll have it figured out," I mumbled as I played with my fingers over the keyboard preparing to shoot Luke a text, "but thank you." I mumbled.

"How will you get there?"

Now I was annoyed, as much surprised I was that we were even talking, I was annoyed. "I'll just call someone."

"Okay." He said, his voice was so eerily calm. "Go ahead."

I looked up, "what?"

"Make the call." His steel blue eyes pierced through mine, and I tugged my lips, forming a frown.

I think if I just stared at him, he'd get bored and he'd finally leave but it didn't work. He was actually waiting for me to make the call. There was this painful feeling in my stomach, I felt sick. Reiner was still far away, his body was stiff. So far away, and I was grateful for that because I was a shit liar when people were too close.

"Okay." I whispered.

Luke better fucking pick up.

I breathed before dialing his number. And I wasn't surprised when it went straight to voicemail; *"Oh, shit I missed your call. I'm not sorry, but call again if you want."*

The message rang in my ears.

But I was stubborn, a stubborn woman. So I cleared my voice, and prayed that this wouldn't backfire, "hey, Luke, my car broke down, I need you." My eyes concentrated on his face, so I didn't miss it when his jaw clenched.

Grumpy old man.

"Yeah," I nodded as I faked a laugh, "okay, that's fine. Thank you." I smiled as I pulled the phone away from me.

He paused for a second, "So, this Luke you called. . ." I could've sworn I saw his lips twitch a little, "received the phone call, after it ended?" He said, his eyes shot daggers, accusing me. "Because from what I saw, before you even spoke your phone flashed me the Home Screen."

If I knew what amusement looked like I'd say Reiner was amused. Having a sick kick at my embarrassment.

I could feel my face heat up, but I know I'd never give anything away, I simply couldn't. So I stared at his neck, avoiding this painful humiliation. This was one of those situations where I wish the earth would just swallow me whole.

"Reiner, I'll be fine."

"Get in the car, Soleil." It was no longer an offer, it was an order and I just stood there for a few seconds questioning what just happened, watching him as he made his way to the car — and his car was *almost* as attractive as him.

I remember the first time when I saw him drive in with his black *acura,* I was carrying a few boxes in and I just had to stop and watch the car move. I stared so longingly at that car I almost bought myself one, Hayley had to talk me out of it.

And that was the first time in three months Reiner had said my name. Something in my stomach stirred. I wasn't even sure he knew my name. I felt like a school girl with a boy-ish crush who didn't even know she existed. My stomach squirmed and I felt a little sick as I walked around the little fence, making my way to his driveway reaching his car as I opened the door.

The smell of a faint cologne hit me, so bittersweetly delicious, I almost closed my eyes as I sniffed some more. I laid my hands on my lap, my bag was near my feet. It was nearly summer, and the degrees got lower and colder by days though. Summer is a blizzard here in Minnesota.

"Thank you." I whispered. Almost choking on the words.

"Hmm."

"Give me your keys, I'll fix your car when I get back." He glanced at me over his shoulder, so quick like he was stealing a glance but I was already staring at him so I noticed.

I shuffled in my seat, "you don't have to."

He doesn't. We barely know each other — he doesn't owe me anything, if anything I owe him.

"I know I don't. I *want* to."

He wanted to. Whoever just wants to fix their neighbor's car? especially one you avoid like a plague. I didn't want to ask why because I was scared he'd change his mind.

14

"Is that what you are? A mechanic?" I said.

He's not — I know he's not, but there were so many more things I didn't know about him, and curiosity was eating me from the inside.

He fixed me a look, "no."

That's it? No answer like; *'no, Soleil, I kidnap kids, or I'm actually the troll under the bridge.'* Or a simple answer of; I help the Grinch steal Christmas every year. *Just no.*

I nodded, completely out of things to say. Completely out of place, because I was inside of his car, nothing felt familiar, and the air was thick with tension and the raw aroma of awkwardness was fuming out of me.

"So you actually know my name?" I blurted out.

I stared at him, patiently waiting for him to say something, *anything.* I knew he was not a man of many words, and he'd always find a way to shorten every sentence, but I was still waiting for him to *say anything.* I say the dumbest things without thinking, hoping it would help him realize that he doesn't have to calculate his next sentence when he is talking to me.

He stared straight ahead but his lips twitched a bit. Was Reiner fighting a *smile*? I can't fight the uneasy feeling in my stomach, nor my amusement.

"How could I not? Each time you talked to me you introduced yourself." He sighed, almost overwhelmed by saying more than a *'hmm'.*

I was no longer amused.

"I only do that because you act as if I'm not there."

"Hmm."

I clamped my mouth shut for the rest of the ride casually glancing out the window — watching the trees go by. My brain is still wrapped around the fact that I'm sitting in Reiner's car — Reiner Kline offered me a ride, and I still haven't decided if this is a dream or a nightmare.

Not only that but he is interested in fixing my car, and I'm not interested in turning down the offer because I hate giving up an opportunity. I might be stubborn but I'm not stupid. A lot of people do stupid things like turn down help just because they think it makes them look stronger or independent.

But giving up a free opportunity can only make you one thing; *stupid*.

I was trying to imagine a time in those last few months where Reiner might've been this helpful or nice, but I just couldn't see it. Seriously if anyone told me, soon in the future I'd be getting a ride from Reiner. . . I'd laugh in shock.

I didn't know him well enough to make any kind of assumptions but I do know he was an awfully private person.

It didn't take long for us to reach campus, after he pulled to the curb, I grabbed my bag thinking of a way I could possibly say thank you without literally saying those words.

"Soleil, your keys." He asked again, his hand brushing the side of my shoulders, and I nearly jumped out of my seat because his touch felt so alarming.

There was my name again, rolling off his tongue so easily. Like he said it millions and millions of times before. Like it was his national anthem. My name never sounded so entertaining coming from his mouth.

My brows shot up as I dug into my pocket fishing out the key and handed them to him. I opened the car door glancing at him one last time before hopping out, mumbling another thank you under my breath.

CHAPTER TWO

Soleil

I COULDN'T BELIEVE MY EYES. I blinked again as I stared at the man in my driveway, my car hood was up, and he was practically shirtless. Outside of his suit, showing so much skin — too much skin — skin I'd never seen before, not even at the gym.

I gathered my bag and water bottle that was in the car trying to make this as quickly as possible before Hayley screams any sexual innuendos and scare the poor guy away — her eyes are wide open and I know she'll never let this go.

Hayley whistled and I swear Reiner heard it because he looked in our direction for a brief second. "Woah, who's this babe in your driveway?"

Hayley was my only friend outside of everything, I truly think she's the one person I could always rely on, but she had a knack for embarrassing me, only because I come off quiet, and she was always unapologetically herself, which is great. . . until it isn't.

I rolled my eyes, "shut up." I grumbled out before opening the car door, desperately trying to make her drive off, the longer she sticks around, the risk of her brutally embarrassing me goes higher.

"Just make sure to reward him for his hard work." She popped her tongue in, pushing it to the other side of her mouth as she used her hand to fist air. She rolled her eyes back as she gave the air a fake blowjob. and I flipped her off as she drove away laughing like a maniac.

I released a breath turning around, walking towards Reiner, a little mortified that he might've seen...*everything*. But he didn't, he was haunched down in front of my car, twisting stuff. His back was sweaty and his muscles flexed with each movement, my eyes are like a magnet, following his every move. I swallowed, clearing my throat in the process, but I am aware that there's moments like this where I have to fix myself because once again I am forced to remember that Reiner is a *man*.

I walked closer towards Reiner, close enough that if I spoke he'd hear me. "Well I'm glad you beat me here first because I was an idiot giving you my keys. I forgot that those are the same keys that open my door," I awkwardly laughed. I'm used to laughing at my own jokes but I don't usually have such a dense audience.

"*Hmm.*" He replied. That one sound answer. *I really hate it.*

I stretched out a hand, "can I please have my keys back."

I watch him shift his body to the side digging for the keys, the silver chain around his neck coming to view.

A cross.

My breath was caught in my throat as I blinked for the third time, getting a better view, my eyes were glued on the silver necklace around his neck, the cross dangled against his wet sweaty skin. *Fuck me.* Reiner placed the keys in the palm of my hand, without even sparing me a glance — in matter of seconds he was back to twisting and turning what whatever the hell he was fixing

Goosebumps pricked my skin, and that sick feeling in my stomach was back. I glanced at him one last time before walking to my door, opening it as I shoved myself inside. The second I closed the door, Blue rubbed his body around my feet, doing his greeting ritual. I smiled before crouching down to pet him.

"How's Blue today?" I cupped his face and he meowed, probably complaining about me not coming home soon enough. But without a beat Blue wagged his tail making his way to the kitchen, and it's my job to meet him there.

I adopted Blue after I moved in, the house felt empty. I felt lonely enough to not want to feel lonely. And Blue got his name because of his fur. It's so dark it looked like it could be blue. It was that or Salem.

When I reached the kitchen, Blue was on the kitchen counter, one jump away from his food bowl. I placed my bag on the counter, shaking my head as I grabbed the cat-food from the pantry and Blue was standing near me before the food even reached his bowl.

I took a shower, put on some comfy clothes, completely unsure of what to do, Reiner was still working on my car in the driveway. Just a few minutes ago I filled up a tall, cold glass of water and brought it to him. I handed him the glass of water and he chugged it in a matter of seconds. I smiled to myself because he groaned out a thank you. I glanced out the window every five seconds because the sun was about to go down soon, which only meant he was going to leave pretty soon.

I sighed, "Should I feed him, Blue?" I stared out the window with the cat in my arms, "will that keep him happy?" Blue purred but only because I rubbed that special spot behind his ears, definitely not because he wanted me to bring Reiner in for food.

I nodded when Blue meowed, "yeah, I'll go talk to him before he leaves." I placed blue down, finding my shoes before going outside.

Before I even reached him, Reiner spoke, "I'm almost done, but it looks like I'll be working on it tomorrow too," he used a towel to wipe his hands, those same large hands that were covered in grease. My eyes lingered on them for too long I think.

I sucked in a breath, "okay,"

"You should get your oil changed."

"*Hmm.*" It was my turn to do the on sound response. I took a mental note to change to oil soon, but I dreaded watching the money leave my pockets. It sucked watching it go.

A bead of sweat rolled down his neck down to his shoulders, that feeling was back again — I looked away staring at his large hands. But my eyes found their ways back to his face before even catching a glimpse of what he was doing.

His brown hair was barely slick back, pieces of it started to fall down his forehead. His brows furrowed as he concentrated — at

21

least now I know the look on his face when he's focused. His full lips were nearly pouted, so pink. It made me wonder what other intimate places could be pink.

I felt my cheeks flush at the thought. I really shouldn't be thinking that way. But staring a little longer wouldn't hurt.

His jaw clenches and unclenches a lot, his defined cheekbones made it difficult to not notice. But for as long as I looked at Reiner his eye lashes were my favorite. He has the eyelashes that could make every girl jealous. They're so long and straight. It fits him perfectly because his eyes are downward yet rounded.

Not a day in my life has I ever seen Reiner look anything but perfect. Even now with the car grease all over him he still looked perfect. So well presented, organized. He was the type of organized I wish to be. I am organized but I'm also really messy.

I sucked in a breath watching his eyelashes flutter each time he blinked. "Are you finally going to tell me what you do for a living?" I asked, the air getting caught in my lungs as I waited for him to speak.

His shoulders tensed as he huffed, wiping the wrench, "I'm a lawyer."

My brows shot up with amusement, "and here I thought you were the grinch who stole Christmas."

He blinked, pausing his actions to glance at me, his brows coming together in confusion, "What?"

I sealed my lips shut, "nothing." I mumbled as I shook my head.

I stood there still awkwardly staring at him, my eyes would

drop to his bicep for no more than three seconds, how do I know? I counted those seconds. Then my eyes are back to his neck, the only safe place I know I can stare at for as long as I want to.

The little voice in my head smacked me.

Be polite, Soleil. He is fixing your car, he is spending more time outside than he has ever spent outside, it's hot out and you're hungry. He might be too.

"Do you want to— uh," I paused, awkwardly pointing at the house, thinking about all the words to say. "Join me for Pizza? Today is my cheat day." I mumbled. Already playing the cheese pizza commercial in my head.

"Cheat day?" He mutters under his breath in question. His eyes were still glued to the pieces of my car.

My shoulders sagged at the need to explain, "well, I have this bad habit for cheap junk food, and pizza is the closest to healthy food I'll ever get." The second the sentence left my lips, spoken out-loud, I realized how unhealthy my routine really was. It honestly sounded better in my head.

And that jaw of his ticked again, his eyes refusing to leave mine, it never does, when I'm not staring I always find him staring instead.

"Thank you for the offer, but I'll have to pass." He said.

"Oh, c'mon, just one slice and I'll send you away to your humbled home." I lifted my index finger up, almost close to his face, and I'm pretty sure I was doing something weird with my eyebrows. "of course if you want to stay for more that's completely up to you." I smiled. This whole conversation will be burned into the deepest core of my memory for the rest of my life. This level of cringe should only be punishable by death.

He blinked and his chest waved, "just one is enough." He said.

"Good, because I was afraid I might've had to sneak into your house just to bring you that slice myself."

The horror on his face almost made me laugh, "kidding." I added, before turning around going for my house, "I'll call, I hope you like cheese." When he didn't answer I decided he liked cheese.

Moments later, the Pizza came and I placed it on my living room coffee table. I'm also grateful because of the furniture my dad left behind because if it was up to me I'd have my cardboard boxes as furniture — I'd be sleeping on a single mattress eating and drinking out of plastic plates and cups. But I am blessed with a house full of furniture. And thanks to Blue I get to vacuum almost everyday.

By that time, Reiner was long gone out of my driveway. And I figured he bailed anyway, but that much didn't matter because it just meant more pizza for me, and I'll get to save some to feed myself for two days straight.

Sure leftover pizza is nasty, but when you're financially struggling barely surviving, it's everything, I feel like royalty ordering pizza once in a blue moon.

There was a knock at my door, that — and because the doorbell broke, and I refuse to spend money on it if you can easily knock. Blue jumped off the couch, probably going to hide somewhere. *I spend so much time alone I've managed to force my cat to be introverted.*

I opened the door, and those steel blue eyes greeted my brown ones again. Reiner didn't greet me, he only stared.

"Hi. I thought you bailed on me, I was already celebrating the amount of pizza I'd saved."

"I had to shower." Was all he said.

And my eyes raked his body, noticing the gray sweatpants he wore, a light white shirt glued to his body but not so glued. The cross was no longer visible around his neck. And his hair was still wet from the — *however*— long shower he just had. He ran a hand through his hair and I realized how long I've been staring.

"Cool," I mumbled, moving out of the doorway, "come on in." He hesitated before his foot passed the threshold and I felt the need to put him at ease.

"I have a cat named Blue but I'm a very clean person." That I am. I might be stingy with money but I'm clean. Scarily clean. Even though it was up to me I'd have a cardboard home, but it would still be spotless.

"I didn't know you had a cat."

I nodded, "Blue's a homebody."

He only sent me a curt nod as he followed me in. I led him to the living room, and I just couldn't help but feel threatened by his height. I'm five foot seven, not a inch higher, not a inch lower, and this man looks like he was boosted up by another foot.

"Oh-" he huffed, "I brought beers, if that's okay." He said as he brought the tiny pack of *Bud Light* into view.

"Thank you." I mumbled grabbing the pack of beer. "You

didn't have to."

"It's cheat day." he said with a small smile on his face.

I sat on the couch watching him take his seat on the other couch. The TV was on the Olympic Channel and two figure skaters were skating. So passionately and romantically, I've always wondered how they managed to keep it professional. I opened the box of pizza wider, pushing it towards him.

"This entertains me." I mumbled when he stared at the TV for too long. He hummed, his gaze still glued on the TV.

"Do you want me to put on something else?" I shuffled trying to find the remote.

I didn't even know why I was offering something else because our option was down to live TV only. My Netflix account got canceled, and I'm too proud to ask Luke for the login to his account, and I'm not sure I even know where the remote is.

"This is fine." He wavered.

I nodded as I grabbed a pizza from the box, and I stared at him until he grabbed a slice too. He opened two *Bud Lights,* handing me one as he took a sip of his.

With a mouth full of pizza, I spoke. "How old are you?" I asked, and I'm praying that age isn't a sensitive topic for him, because I am not trying to offend him, I just want to know because I'm tired of the guessing game.

His brows furrowed as he stared at me, "thirty-two." he mumbled, taking a long sip at his beer.

He *just* turned thirty two. He could fool anyone if he wanted to. He didn't look a day over twenty-nine, his clean shaven face makes him look even younger — I wonder if he grows out a beard how much different he would look — how much older.

And I don't know why I blurted out my age but I did anyways, "I'm twenty-three" a smile formed on my face. And I took my first sip from the beer. He sent me a curt nod and I wanted the earth to swallow me whole because how much I've already embarrassed myself.

The room fell quiet again, and I spoke before things could get awkward. "How long have you been practicing the law?"

"*Ten* years."

There's a pattern with Reiner: he will answer the questions asked but that's it, just the answer, he's never interested enough to share more about the answers he gives. He doesn't care enough to return the favor. If it's a story I want out of him, I wouldn't even know how to get it.

"What is it like?" I asked as I took another bite of the pizza, it's starting to get cold.

He only stared at me, "What is what like?"

"Being a lawyer."

He shrugged, sipping on his beer, "well I'm no criminal lawyer so I can't say it's dangerous, I just sue people, or at least I help people get sued and suck all their money like some money thirsty vampire." he paused, "but it's never fun when one of my clients is the one getting sued."

God, I think this is the most he's ever said in three months.

I propped myself and tucked my legs under me. One thing I wasn't stingy about was the temperature of the house. It has to be cold, so cold that I won't like the feel of my cold fingers. And right now I was cold, so cold that I have to tuck myself. But Reiner, who is just in white T-shirt and wet hair, didn't even seem fazed by the temperature of the room.

"So, this is what I know." I raised a brow. "By all means correct me if I'm wrong."

"Your name is Reiner Kline, you're thirty-two and a lawyer." I said, frowning at the lack of information.

"And you're a catholic."

Reiner stared at me in disbelief. His blue eyes are so empty. "*Soleil*, what are you doing?"

"What?"

"Why are we having this conversation?"

I sucked in a breath, preparing my long list of reasons but instead I just came up with the only logical explanation. "Look what you did, I don't know how to repay you. I don't have anything valuable and I thought—"

"Friendship?" he cut me off, "You want to repay me with your friendship?"

Before I could speak, the words choked me when I heard his laugh. I bit my lips savoring the sound of it. The smile reached his eyes, *Reiner Kline had fucking dimples* — and his chest rumbled as the sounds fought its way out of him.

His eyes softened when he caught a glimpse of my expression, and my shoulders tensed under his gaze.

He formed such a polite smile on his lips, his eyes brightened when he told me, "I don't *ever* want to be your friend, Soleil." his jaw clenched, his gaze flickered down to my chest which was now rising and falling.

"*Oh.*" was all I could form into words.

The sentence hit me like a slap on the face. And I took a while to recover and realize how stupid I was being. And how deluded my brain leads me to be. Reiner, my neighbor who's never said more than two words to me until yesterday, the same one who probably has so many bad assumptions of me — I actually thought he'd be open to starting a friendship with me. The interaction between us has been radio silent for months, and I thought we'd finally get somewhere after today but I guess not.

I nodded as I stared at him, "Okay, um— my mistake for ever suggesting that. I'm sure I'll find another way to repay you."

"You don't have to."

"I know I don't. I *want* to." I fed him the same words he fed me the other day.

Before he could speak I took a bite of my cold pizza staring at the TV in front of me watching the couples do a *triple lutz,* "I got an early class tomorrow."

He sucked in a breath, understanding the subtle meaning behind my words "yeah, I get it," he mumbled as he stood up.

"I could drop you off again, your oil still needs to be changed."

"It's fine," I wavered — looking up to meet his eyes, "I'm getting a ride from my *friend* Hayley."

"Oh." His shoulders tensed as he swallowed, he paused for a second like he might apologize, but he didn't. "Thank you for tonight."

"*Hmm.*" I mumbled, I'd say anytime but he's not my friend so instead I told him he can show himself out. Later that night I drinked a can of beer and fell asleep on the couch before they even announced the winners.

CHAPTER THREE

Soleil

THERE'S A ROOM IN THE HOUSE THAT I RARELY GO IN. My father's old office. It's filled with old empty cardboard boxes that I was too lazy to recycle, his desk and a few things were still lying around in that room — even before then, the room was never truly empty. Not when it was filled with bad memories I had of my father. Corbyn Walsh was a workaholic, he worked and drinked — I never learned which he loved to do more. My father died from a seizure alone at night — in his sleep and I can only hope it was painless. And I can only pray he's somewhere better. Hoping he found some sort of peace, at least his version of peace.

He was all I had, and this room that I barely stepped in is all I have left of him. Half of his stuff was donated, and the things I couldn't give away are somewhere — hidden in the cramped room.

I kicked a box the second I stepped into the room and made room for myself to walk in. I kept saying I'd organize the room or fix it a little, but it got postponed everytime. It's always something, too tired after work, a school assignment due long ago — I didn't like to admit it, but the bigger reason was always because I didn't like facing the reminders of my father. But it looked like I had to today.

Hayley wanted a box, and she refused to let me back in the car without one, she's almost as stubborn as I am, which meant she was really not going to let me back in that car if I came back empty handed. The first box I kicked was ripped.

I turned on the light and Blue was already in the room, wagging his tail as he walked further into the room. I didn't pay him any attention as I walked towards the stacked boxes. The first one was full of books, no doubt written by my father. I lifted the heavy box, placed it on the floor and pushed it near the desk.

"Blue, out of the way." I wavered my hand, trying to get him to move, but he just sat there, staring right at me. I rolled my eyes as I moved on to the second box, it was filled with papers. The box was light so I threw the papers on the desk, making a mental reminder to properly store them away later. Even if that's probably never.

I untapped the box, flattened it, and folded it under my arms as I grabbed my phone from my back pocket to check the time on my way out.

I pushed my foot against the door, "c'mon Blue, we're done

here."

With that, he wagged his tail and pushed himself out of the room. I closed the door and made my way downstairs, praying to God that Hayley didn't leave without me. We were already late for classes, and she sent me back inside the house for a stupid box.

The second I walked out of the house with the box in my hand Hayley pulled down the car window with a smile on her face, "You got it!"

"I got it." I whispered under my breath, I threw the box in the back seat the second I sat in the car, "now let's go, we're late."

"I want a page on the recent accident." Professor Daniel said. I turned to face Hayley, "what accident?"

She wasn't frustrated that I was asking because I never keep up with the news. That's why I was freezing my ass off today, I didn't know the weather would change so drastically overnight and by the time I stepped outside in my skirt going back to change would only have me late for class.

Apparently a storm is on its way to Minnesota. We won't get the most of it, just a little. More angry wind to ruin our summer. That's what Hayley said. She's a journalist at heart because unlike me, she does watch the news, read articles, and she does know things like which celebrities ate a pizza for breakfast.

"The car accident was like a hit and run, but they found the guy." She explained.

"Oh," I pondered a little, still confused.

I nodded. Sometimes I wonder if this is my true calling. Half of the time I sit here and listen to lectures, I do the silly assignments, but I find myself confused about my purpose — I know in my heart it is, and I know for the longest that this is what I've always felt like I needed to do. But there are times I wonder about the way I robbed myself from any other careers.

The thought of being able to still start something new is what comforts me at night — so I study, I try to pay attention — I try to prioritize this more than anything else. Because I want this and I'll take it.

"So we're supposed to write what?" I asked, my voice booming through the class, some students who weren't paying attention faced the professor now.

He only stared at me, "you're a journalist, Miss Walsh. Write me a story." he pushed his glasses on his nose. Still staring at me — waiting for any signs of agreement from me.

Murmurs erupted in the classroom, everyone whispering to one another all complaining about the assignment. This is ridiculous because we're journalists — or atleast studying to be, we shouldn't be complaining over light work.

Professor Daniel sighed, obviously frustrated with his lazy students. "And the paper I like most gets an automatic pass on the exam."

Everyone gasped, the murmurs came to a stop, all of them shuffling to their phones and laptops pulling up the article — some of them already began to write. *What could they possibly be writing?*

I turned to Hayley who was one of those people who were already writing. Her laptop was on a blank screen she was already filling up with information that left me curious.

"What the hell are you writing?" I mumbled peeking at her laptop but she was only typing out names and dates.

"Just the basics." She spared me a glance, "you clearly want to take the exam."

My laptop was still on the log-in screen. And I blinked before finally putting in the password, "don't worry," I mumbled as I pulled up the article, "I'll have it done."

I swear I'm passionate about this, but without Hayley I'd be way behind because I tend to get distracted a lot.

Hayley noticed me in class — I asked too many questions, half of the times I am confused. That's not too difficult to miss. She has a good heart, she might put on a charade and be this sultry person with countless innuendos but she has a heart of gold — that's why she helped me in the beginning, she doesn't like to admit it because that'll ruin her cool appearance.

She's easily the best person in my life.

"You want to go to Josie's for drinks after this?"

I shook my head, "I can't, I got work."

"*Luke* will be there."

I grimaced, "and I'll still have work."

As I walked down in my driveway I watched Reiner get out

of his car. His hair neat as ever, the black suit on him looked never better. And I walked a little slower watching him open one of the back doors and a blonde little girl hopped out of his car, she couldn't be an age over six, so small and kind of tall.

I've never seen her before in the span of three months I've been his neighbor. She's never stepped foot in the house, I didn't know Reiner had kids, could be his niece — I could imagine Reiner as an uncle, a little uptight, but a good uncle. Maybe he's babysitting, I told myself.

But then I did the worst thing possible. I waved at them, "hi guys!"

I could almost hear the groan Reiner was fighting inside, but he placed a forced smile on his face,

"*Hello*, Soleil." He stared at me with those dead eyes that only seemed to come alive for anyone else but me — only one thought was bouncing through my brain.

He said my name again.

"This is my *daughter* Anna — *Anna* this is my neighbor, Soleil."

I looked at the little girl in front of him, then back at him. When she looked in my direction, I noticed the small similarities, she had his blue eyes, and Anna smiled and waved at me. I realized she had his dimples too.

"Hi, Soleil!" she beamed.

"Hey, Anna!"

She looked at her dad before turning to look at me again, "are you my dad's friend?" she tilted her head at me, clutching on what looked like her iPad

I close my mouth shut, glancing at Reiner for a quick second, "I think so." I said with a small smile.

She smiled at me too, one that could easily be appreciated. "The mean neighbor wasn't daddy's friend, he was mean."

"Anna—" he began.

I stared back at him, "well, he's gone for good now." my eyes landed on Anna again, her pale cheeks growing red.

"And you won't be mean to us?"

I shook my head, "of course not."

I smiled again and it's silent. Reiner was uncomfortably shifting, clearly impatient to get inside, he stared at me, then Anna, then at his house. Without Anna this conversation wouldn't be happening in the first place, this is not the first time we've crossed each other in our driveways — we just have never acknowledged each other until now, until today — because of Anna.

I decided it was time to put him out of his misery, so I cleared my throat, "it was nice to meet you Anna."

"Nice to meet you too, Soleil." she bubbled out.

Reiner stared at me for only a second, his eyes took a quick raking at my body before he turned away watching Anna walk. Her backpack on her shoulders as she walked closer to the door, Reiner right behind her with another backpack in his hands, a suitcase in the other hand.

I watched Anna reach for the doorknob, she wobbled it once, twice before she finally spoke, "I want to open the door."

"Hold on, Princess." he said, as he switched his briefcase to the same hand that held the backpack — his now free hand fished out the keys in his pocket, and I realized how weird it was that I was still looking.

I opened my own door and before I went inside I glanced in their direction one last time — the smile on Reiner's face was so different from the one I saw the other night. And I grew curious about this side of Reiner.

The one that smiles at the simplest thing, the one that's easier to please.

My phone pinged before I got in the shower, and I flipped it to see the screen because usually Sylvia does schedule changes at the last minute, even if she does get lots of complaints for it, not to mention, it messes with our personal times, and it's just unprofessional.

My brows furrowed when I read the text from Luke. *"you up?"* It was a simple text but I knew what it meant. And it was not the first time he got drunk and texted me late at night like I was some booty call, but I usually wait till the morning to reply back — sometimes I don't reply at all.

CHAPTER FOUR

I WALKED INSIDE THE RESTAURANT. Quick on my strides to reach the back room. I opened my locker as I waved at Sylvia, our manager. I was only a few minutes late so I rushed myself with the uniform. I didn't realize I had such a big head until moments like this. Me struggling to get my head through the shirt. After struggling for what seemed like a while, I slipped myself into the black dress pants, and the white dress shirt was hard enough to deal with — it was the skates. Instead of shoes, we wore skates. It was like *Sonic*, but worse.

I frowned, tying the lace of my skates. This was a decent restaurant, so having to wear skates was beyond my understanding. I tied the skates, glancing around the empty locker room, until my eyes rounded on the person I was looking for, the second she walked in — I grinned. "I thought you asked for today off." I laughed, because I know asking for a day off without at least a week's notice is like asking for snow in Florida.

Mara rolled her eyes, "Sylvia wasn't in a good mood."

"Is she ever?" I frowned, "I swear I don't think I've ever seen her laugh." I shook my head in disbelief.

Sylvia is hardcore — like a math teacher, she makes almost everything complicated, and when we do find a loophole to un-complicate things, it rubs her off in the wrong way. We've decided that her bad moods are just *her* moods. There's a reason why she doesn't take orders or deal with customers at all for that matter.

"No one has," Mara replied, "wait, her husband, maybe her husband."

My eyes widened, the evident shock ripping through me, "she's married? Sylvia is *married?* She has a husband?" I repeated the words, but they were hollowed.

Mara's eyes rounded on me with disappointment, "she wears a wedding ring."

I frowned, "So?" I grabbed my apron, wrapping it around my waist, "a lot of people wear those nowadays, and it's often promise rings."

Mara only shook her head at me as she opened her locker, more disappointment.

Mara's about the only co-worker I can get along with, she's an easy person who doesn't outshine my personality and with her something clicked almost immediately with her, there was never any need to force our conversation or anything. She's short, full of life and has really great tits. I accidentally saw them. *(Twice)*

Before I could say anything else, the bell attached to the door rang alerting us we have customers. The restaurant was pretty dry when I walked in and that's only because we're a few minutes after lunch and hours after breakfast. Half of the morning crew is gone, the ones left are the ones who work the kitchen — unless I want Sylvia to scare our customers away with her *moods* it's my cure to go out there.

A group of men sat at one of our four chair tables, their brief-cases each by their feet. I skated my way to the table greeting them with a large smile on my face. Smiling and looking pretty gets me a satisfying tip — satisfying tips pays for my pizza.

"Welcome to *Bavaria-*"

My voice fell flat, almost to a whisper when my eyes met his. I blinked a few times before turning my attention elsewhere, but I could still feel his cool gaze on me. Reiner was here, but he wasn't alone, he's surrounded by three more men and there was this awkwardness between us that I couldn't get rid of and it feels like the whole table caught on because everyone was just quiet.

I tried not to meet his eyes again, waiting patiently for them to order whatever they mind find in our four page menu. I glanced over my shoulder watching Mara welcome the new people inside a booth, when her eyes met mine as she scanned the people on the table behind me — Mara did a face, grinning a little.

When I noticed how everyone was still struggling reading the menu I suggested what I always suggested, "are you guys open to a few suggestions?"

They all looked up at me, eyes softening, "yes, please." One of them says, his eyes were so soft to stare at. So much light in them. He had his locs neatly pulled back into a nice man bun and everyone else looked so well dressed, this must be his colleagues.

I checked the watch on my wrist. It's nearly four, lunch was ruled out of the menu for them. I cleared my throat, "the pasta here is really good," I paused to stare at their suits, "but I'm sure there's other classy things on the menu."

"I don't mind getting a little dirty." One of them said, I raised a brow, a smile forming on my lips because I could understand the heavy meaning behind his words.

I shook my head a little, "for the steak here, I suggest medium rare, if not that you'll be chewing for days."

With that, they laughed — well almost all of them.

I pulled out the little notepad taking everyones order one by one, the guy who said he was fine getting down and dirty ordered one of the pastas, and another one ordered the steak with mash potatoes — what surprised me was the fact the guy with the locs, the one with those puppy dog eyes ordered a burger. The messiest thing on the menu.

I only smiled, taking the notes down.

After taking everyones order I turned back to Reiner, the only person who hadn't said a word.

He's been staring.

I pointed my pen at him, "Reiner?" I asked and everyone at the table turned to Reiner. Who only clenched his jaw.

"You guys know each other?" Someone from the group said

with laughter.

I cringed a little, "we're neighbors."

A grunt growled out from one of them, "Reiner, c'mon man why didn't you introduce us?" the blond one said.

Still waiting for Reiner to say something, but he said nothing — his eyes were suddenly busy staring at the —*fascinating*— menu. I don't mind this now because I know they will never stop giving him shit for this.

The one with the soft eyes stretched out a hand, "Ian." He introduced himself.

My eyes softened as I placed my hand in his, "*Soleil.*" And I noticed when Reiner's nose flared at the sight of our hands touching, something flashed in his eyes, so quick and so dark. I paid him no mind because everyone was taking a turn to introduce themselves now.

"Ryan." The blond one said but he didn't offer me a hand.

And the quiet one, who is even more quiet than Reiner, just sent me a curt nod. "Nico." He said.

I nodded after everyone introduced themselves, plastering a kind smile on my face as they stared into my bare soul, my cheeks were starting to hurt. I want to move to the next table and beg someone else to take this one. They were waiting for Reiner to say a word to me, because apparently they're all in on a secret and I have no idea what it is they're hiding.

All eyes were sharp on me.

"So...Reiner." I danced around his name, "what would *you* like."

He licked his lips, his eyes finding mine, and I had no option but to swallow, suddenly uncomfortable under his stare. "The creamy chicken pasta soup."

I wrote it down, I looked up, "And for drinks?"

"Water."

"Water."

"Water's fine."

"Apple juice."

Now that caught my attention, I smiled the second Ian offered me an apologetic smile. "Well at least it's not *orange juice*." I shrugged before skating away, and their voices grew loud as they began to argue.

As I skated to the back I placed the order next to a line of other orders, and the second my eyes landed on those bouncy brown curls, tanned skin — I smiled as I skated towards her.

"Oh, Mara. My sweet, sweet, sweet Mara." I shook my head, pretending to be in some sort of agony.

Mara only rolled her eyes, she placed her little notebook into the pocket of her apron, *"ay,"* she moaned in frustration, "let me guess, Luke is here and you want us to switch tables?" she said in a bored tone.

I placed a hand over my heart, faked a gasp. "I am hurt." I whispered, "You think so low of me."

She raised a brow, tilting her head, *"entonces*... is he here?"

"No, this is so much worse, this is *code blue*."

She blinked a few times, "since when did we start doing codes?"

"Since now." I breathed, trying to be more quiet, we're supposed to be out there right now, taking orders. If Sylvia notices we left tables unattended she'll flip.

"My neighbor, Reiner, is here." I whispered, ashamed of the words. Heat rising on my skin.

"*And?*"

"You don't understand Mara, he *really* doesn't like me, and it's always so *weird and awkward*, it's even worse when it's just the two of us talking."

"Fine." she huffed.

I was hugging her the second she agreed, kissing her cheeks all over. "Oh Mara," I sang, "my sweet, sweet, Mara."

"You owe me." she whispered against my hair, but I was already nodding agreeing to whatever she may want in the future.

Mara loaded a tray of their drinks, skating over to their table, and I skated away to a different booth, taking a new order. Two elderly who want nothing more than a plate of spaghetti to share, just to recreate *Lady and the Tramp* as their 20th anniversary. Usually when people talk my ears off instead of just placing the order it pisses me off, but I found myself gushing over what those two old people have.

I never looked at my romance life that way — thinking of growing old with someone, I never thought this far into any of my relationships. Even with Luke, I *loved* to a point — I think, but I never looked that far into our future — it was always about what we had in the moment, never more. Maybe that's why we were doomed from the beginning.

I only saw those kinds of happy endings on TV — shows, movies. My dad never settled down, he was heartbroken until he died — his entire heart was shattered, he was even scared to love me. I never knew my mom, and all my desire to meet her withered away watching my father apart everyday, because if she was capable of doing that to him, someone she might've loved for a long time — God knows what she'd do to me, someone she didn't even care to know. All my boyfriends… Well, I only dated people I thought I deserved.

When I skated back to the prep area, Mara was already waiting for me and she just leaped in front of me, scaring me. If I didn't know how to balance on these skates I would've fallen on my ass.

"Ohmygod" the train of words blew out of her mouth. "You didn't warn me about how good he looked." her shoulders sagged, pushed up again, her cheeks flushed and I wondered what he could have possibly said to her.

"Ay dios mio." she breathed.

I pointed a finger at her, "you said that already… but in english." Mara only fixed me a look.

I placed both hands on her shoulders, trying to match her breathing, "breathe, Mara. Breathe." her face was red, the more she struggles to compose herself the more I want to ask about their conversation.

"He's like fucking Henry Cavill, but also Chris Evans?" she gushed.

I wanted to laugh but I frowned, "he's too old for you, Mara." I tried to say it like I cared about who she dated, but it only came out as a warning. It felt like I was asking for her to back off. If anything he's too old for me, Mara was only two years older than me.

Her tongue only clicked, tsk, "he can't be that old."

"He has a daughter." I added. That seemed to shut her up.

Mara stared at me long and hard, a creepy smile spreading across her face. "You got the hots for your neighbor."

I grimaced, "I do not."

"You should see the look on your face just now when I talk about how good he looks, I'm surprised you haven't dragged my ass yet."

"I mean it, Mara. I'm *not* attracted to him." the words came out so bitter, even I couldn't believe what I was saying. But I didn't want to feel any more guilty than I was already feeling so I just grabbed the tray of drinks that were ready for my table and skated away.

Little as three days ago, he closed all of my windows, laughed in my face for even thinking we could possibly be *friends*. So no, I will not be ridiculed, or laugh about how nice his hair looks, or how *blue* his eyes are. They are not pretty by the way, they are *creepy.*

I gave the elderly couples their order, and just as I skated towards a new table, my name was shouted in the middle of the restaurant.

"Soleil, *Oye.*" Mara waved me, motioning for me to come to her. My shoulders sagged, because she was making a scene and I couldn't exactly ignore her.

"Just one moment please," I whispered to the blonde lady that was dining alone, before she could set me straight I skated away towards Mara.

I reached their table again, another painful smile plastered on my face, my cheeks were really working off any fat that was on them. Ian was the only one that was staring at me, everyone else was too busy reading the menu to even look up.

"The boys here are very curious about dessert, and Ian wanted to ask you for a few suggestions." Mara explained, and I can hear the amusement in her voice.

I slowly nodded, taking a light breath thinking about what to suggest. "The apple *pie* is really great."

His gruff voice rumbled every emotion out of me, "I don't like pies."

"Right…" I bit out. that same day playing over and over in my head again. I baked my sweat and tears and he did nothing but reject it — the worst ways you could reject something.

I stared down at him, "Well, I suppose you could always help yourself with some ice-cream."

Or nothing at all. There's no rule that declares you must have dessert after eating a hot meal. But of course, I couldn't tell him all of that, Sylvia would have my tongue before I could even tell Reiner to fuck off.

When he said nothing I stared down at the rest of the table, "that's about all I know about this side of the menu fellas," I forced on another smile, "Have a good day."

★ · ☆ · ★

After my shift today, I showered and got in bed with Blue. I made the effort to at least open my laptop and started reading for the assignment. It's hard to find in the local newspapers because when a small accident like that happens, no one cares — especially if it has nothing to do with them.

And it's messed up that we live in a world that classifies accidents and other gruesome things as nothing. No one is phased until it's something horrible they've ever heard of before. It's like a competition, who has it worst. Who can make it on the news? No one wants to hear about the local hit and run because who cares? And as a journalist, it's my job to use my voice to make sure they're heard.

Blue meowed, crawling on my chest, needy for some of my attention. I smiled, running my hands over his body, he purred as his tail waged a little, pushing himself into my hand.

"You missed me?" I whispered as he brought his face close to mine, rubbing it against mine. He just laid there completely, laying on my chest with his little paws around my neck.

"I missed you too."

CHAPTER FIVE

Soleil

THE LITTLE WHITE CLOCKED TICKED, and my eyes kept bouncing from Hayley to the little white clock, watching the minutes tick away.

"So he was in here?" Hayley asked for the third time as she leaned forward on the counter.

And I was constantly checking the oven for my pie. I was at the store today and the pie expired days ago, which means it's free. I didn't even have to argue with the cashier, they just let me have it. Today must be my lucky day because it's an apple pie.

"Yes, he was here. In my house. Eating pizza."

"How old is he?" Was her next question.

I close the oven turning around to meet her mischievous gaze. *God, no Hayley.* "Thirty-two." I replied, watching Blue walk in the kitchen, going straight for his bowl of food. He usually hides when I have people over, but I guess Hayley isn't anybody.

Hayley's brows pulled together, masking this confusing look on her face. "Really? He's young, but he looks...younger, he could lie and say twenty-six and I'd believe him."

I bit my lips, the same thoughts flowing in my head, "yeah, I know. It's the body."

"I bet." she smiled, "I'd be all over that if I were you."

I laughed at the thought, "good thing I'm not you." I mumbled enough for the both of us to hear. Before Hayley could make a face I turned around facing the oven as I grabbed the oven mitt as I slid my hands inside of them.

I opened the oven just in time to hear the apple inside the pie sizzle a bit. I can already taste the crispy edges of the pie on the tip of my tongue — the crunchy sounds are nearly as good as an orgasm. I pulled the pie out of the oven, and the smell of those cinnamon apples was enough for my eyes to roll to the back of my head.

"You're an easy woman to please, you know?" Hayley chimed in.

I huffed as I placed the pie on the island, "I know, all it takes is food."

I lifted the pie again only to place a knitted mat under it. I have no idea what the difference could be but I'm afraid to find out the hard way. I gave Hayley a plate, I didn't bother to grab myself one because I know I'll eat straight from the pan.

Hayley grabbed her fork, hesitant to touch the pie, "you're

sure we won't die from this?" she asked, and the concern is evident in her eyes.

I rolled my eyes. I'm sure there are some possibilities, but there's always possibilities, "it expired only a few days ago, we'll be fine...I think."

She tilted her head to the side, staring at the pie closely, "every famous last word."

I shrugged, "don't eat it if you're not sure." I mumbled as I took my first bite.

I've never eaten an expired pie, so I had no idea about what the pie was supposed to taste like. I was expecting something like a foul taste or smell, something that could warn me that the pie is expired, but the more I ate, the more it tasted like nothing. I took another bite glancing at Hayley in the process and she was still examining her pie, she still hadn't tasted — I don't blame her, not everyone is always thrilled to eat expired food.

"Leil..." she began, and I almost groaned because I was expecting her to make a sly comment about the pie, but her voice only grew quiet.

"Why is your neighbor staring at us?"

"What?" I choked out, forcing myself to swallow the food in my mouth.

I stared at Hayley's blank face as I followed her gaze — the second I looked out the kitchen window that hovered above the kitchen sink, I understood her surprise. Reiner's face came into view, he was standing on his porch gaping in horror. I thought his eyes were on me but the more his brows furrowed the more I realized he was staring at something entirely different.

I dropped my fork from the pie, taking a sip of water, "give me a second," I whispered under my breath but it was meant for Hayley.

I walked outside and I was only blessed with the hot humid weather, the wind was slightly blowing. And I know the only reason the air feels so sticky and humid is because a storm is coming.

After speaking to Reiner at the restaurant which was as little as two days ago — we haven't spoken nor acknowledged each other since then. While his daughter seems to have disappeared too, because I haven't caught sight of her. Unless she's being kept locked away in a room in his house like some abandoned princess, but I doubt it.

I made my way to the back of the house, gaping into my own kitchen window, instead of finding Hayley in her seat, she was dumping her pie into the trash, I shook my head in disappointment — my whole body shook when he spoke, his presence caught me off-guard, I forgot the fact that he was the reason why I was outside in the first place.

Reiner was only a few feet away from me, he stared at me like something was amusing, "your hose is on." Was all he said. My brows furrowed as I searched a few steps ahead until I grimaced feeling myself step into a very wet part of the grass.

There goes the water bill. My money. My hard earned money. My sweat and tears, my future. *Everything*, because God knows how long this fucking hose as been on. A low blow of profanities escaped my lips in a quiet whisper.

Staring wouldn't make it go away. I marched further towards the water and miserably tried to twist the spigot to shut off, but it didn't budge.

Reiner on the other side grows impatient, "it's overwatering my lawn,"

I rolled my eyes as my palms reddened, "there's no such thing." I hope not, it sounds ridiculous.

As much as I wanted to laugh at Reiner's dramatic outburst over his regularly fresh cut lawn, the spigot wasn't closing — it simply doesn't budge, and now I'm grunting as I placed two hands over the material trying to push it to the direction that could close it.

A thunder clap in the sky, and I look up just to notice the lighting that follows after, the weather is getting darker and darker by the minutes that goes by. I am so desperate to get this thing close so I can go back inside to send Hayley back home. The only reason why the storm would possibly catch her on her drive back is because she is too caring to not supply me with an endless amount of canned food and other supplies just to prepare me for the storm.

I grunt as I ground my feet into the —*now*— wet ground, trying to twist with more force. But I'm only slipping as the mud paints my feet.

"I'll fix it." His voice spoke as another thunder clapped and I jumped, unsure of which one scared me the most.

The moment was just so cinematically creepy. It felt like in the movies when the creepy character kept popping up in the strangest way possible. This was it.

My hands were still wrapped around the spigot, my chest rising and falling — trying to catch my breath from both the scare and the efforts I've put into this stupid hose.

"You're a plumber now?" I mumbled out of breath, my voice sounded hoarse, but I spoke loud enough for him to hear me, and my back still faced him.

He let out a long, bored sigh before answering, "It doesn't matter, all this water will be ruining my lawn."

I didn't respond to him, I just moved to the side letting him take over the spot I was previously in. It was my turn to watch him struggle to turn off the spigot now — I thought I'd enjoy him struggling but it backfired the second I watched his bicep flex each time he tried to twist.

His muscles taut. The grunts escaping his lips made it so much worse. I swallowed the last few tastes of the apple pie that lingered on my tongue.

"Soleil!" he called, bringing back to earth. The way he called for me made it seem like he's been calling for a while.

I licked my lips, "yeah?"

"Get me a wrench."

It took me two steps in the direction to my house to realize I don't have any sort of tools, I paused in my steps, "I don't have any."

"Of course you don't,"

I was about to ask what he meant by that but he started talking again, giving me a list of instructions.

"Go to my house, straight in the kitchen, open the cabinet

under the sink and grab a wrench from my tool belt." he paused, staring at me dumbfounded, "do you even know what a wrench looks like?"

I scoffed, "of course I do,"

"Go." he fixed me a look.

I ran towards his house, only to realize it'll be my first time in his house. The house is dark, almost all the light were off, the only light that was on was the dimed light coming from the kitchen, I didn't have any time to be noisy because the house was practically dark — I walked into the kitchen, surprise to see the place spotless, well decorated and organized. I didn't know what I was expecting, but I knew it wasn't a spotless house.

I ran a hand on the island, *no dust.* And his house had this fresh laundry smell, I could just melt by the scent of it. Before I could march towards the sink, the fridge caught my attention. I walked closer towards it, finding a whole schedule on a magnetic board on the fridge with a erase board marker next to it. I smiled as I read the schedule, it was a messy handwriting and I could tell it wasn't his.

Daddy day with Anna, on wednesday.
Daddy day with Anna, on friday.

And under it was a much better writing, one I was sure be-longed to Reiner;

Anna's wrestling match on friday, @4

I looked at the rest of the fridge to find pictures of Anna, or pictures with him and Anna — just the two of them. Anna's first day of school. Anna with her first tooth out. Him and Anna on her fourth birthday. A really old picture; him looking younger and holding what looks like baby Anna, he was in the hospital still, and a hand reached for them but I couldn't see whose hand it was because the picture was partly ripped.

Then there was this hideous drawing that caught my attention;

Happy Father's Day!

Then there was this deformed stick figure with an arrow at the top that points at, *Daddy.* Anna was right next to him as another form of deformed stick figure with her own arrow saying, *Anna.*

My heart is full, so full of these pictures. Reiner is obviously an incredible dad, which is so hard for me to wonder what happened with Anna's mother. I can tell it was something really bad because Reiner doesn't strike me as a deadbeat dad.

I blinked as the realization of my true purpose here hit me. I moved fast towards the cabinet under the sink. I was taken aback by the big tool belt, they were organized from smallest to biggest. And like an idiot, I couldn't tell the difference between any one of them. I knew what a wrench was, but here under the dimmed light there seemed to be a smaller wrench and a bigger one — I have no idea which one he wanted.

Fuck. I was overwhelmed by the amount of tools that were in his belt so I grabbed the whole thing.

I ran back outside only to find it raining. I sucked in a breath before running under the rain. *There goes not getting my hair wet until next week.* I reached Reiner with a pained expression, feeling the rain fall on my scalp. The sky is much more angry now. It'll only get worse soon, I have to send Hayley home.

I handed him his tool belt and he looked at me in amusement. Heat crawled from my cheeks to my ears, "I figured you might need something else," I shouted over the rain.

He chuckled under his breath, "of course you did."

I smiled, only a little — because my stupidity amuses him.

I watched him grab a familiar silver tool twisting the spigot close, the water growing smaller and smaller, the only water that was pouring down on us now was the rain.

"Thank you." I huffed, my clothes were already starting to stick to my skin. My eyes flicked to his body, his own clothes drenched too, the outline of his abs was starting to come into view.

I forced myself to look elsewhere, "where's Anna?" I asked as he regained his posture, stuffing the wrench back into the belt.

"She's staying with her mother."

"Where is her mother?" I asked before I could bite my tongue to hold the question in.

Curiosity will get me killed — but at least I'll die knowing what most don't.

His jaw ticked, "What are you doing, Soleil?"

"Making conversation."

My answer was an innocent one but bullshit nevertheless. I seemed to have hit a soft spot because he decided he can no longer stand the sight of me. He walked only a few steps away from me before I spoke again.

"We're having pie. Do you want some?" I don't think people should be allowed to offer others expired food, but for some reason I find it hard to leave Reiner alone.

That seemed to have caught his attention, his hard back was still facing me as his muscles flexed under the white wet shirt, "we?"

"Yeah, my friend Hayley is over, I know you have no interest in being a friend of mine, but I'm starting to run out of ways to repay you."

He started walking again, "I don't *like* pies."

Right.

"It's expired anyways." I blurted out.

He turned around, his fist clenching around his tool belt. "It's expired?" He hissed.

"I got it for free."

His eyes softened as if he remembered something, "*please*," he hissed the word like venom. And I wince, "do not eat the pie." He said, "you'll get food poisoning."

I stared at him, blinked once, blinked twice. "Okay."

He sent me a curt nod, still hesitant on my obedience.

I figure arguing in the middle of the rain about eating expired pie wouldn't do us any good. I said okay I wasn't going to eat the pie, but I ate half of it before he told me not to — eating the rest won't do much harm. I thanked him again with a soft smile as I walked back towards my house.

When I went back inside, Hayley was lounging in the living

room with a big bowl of chips and I had to shoo her out of the house because of the storm getting closer and closer to us. As much as I want her here with me, her sisters need her more.

I pulled down all the curtains as I reheated my last slice of apple pie. The rain was only coming down harder and harder — I closed all the lights, limiting myself with the light coming from my open laptop. Taking a bite of my pie as I dive into my web of search. Blue, who can't seem to stay away from me, ended up joining me on the couch.

CHAPTER SIX

"HOW'S ANNA DOING? IS SHE WITH YOU?" My mother asked, as she moved around attempting to peek beyond the view. I'm not sure she understands how FaceTimes works.

"She's with Noa, and yes, she's great — growing up really quickly."

She smiled, "I know that feeling, I had a total breakdown when you turned one, Tom thought I was crazy."

I laughed, leaning against my chair, "you cried because *I turned one,* and dad thought you were crazy?"

"Your father always thought I was crazy, even now. He still does."

My brows furrowed, "you guys talk regularly?" Though, I doubt that's possible, there's only a certain amount of time until they stop tolerating each other.

With the camera so close to her face, I saw it when she rolled her eyes, "not much, he's been busy traveling with Constance."

I threw my head back, laughing at her jealousy, "Her name is Connie, mom."

She glared at me through the screen, "I know." The death stare seems to have put an end to my laughter.

I don't usually keep up with who dad dates but Constance—Connie has been with him for over a year now, which explains my mothers irritation. My parents have been divorced since I was thirteen, and mother has never approved of who my dad dates — none of them ever stuck around for long which is why she was always pissed, getting word that dad was seeing someone again. She used to scold him about it, telling him it would confuse me — but the older I got the more ridiculous the excuse sounded, now she has no reason against Connie except for the fact that she might be dad's longest relationship since his divorce.

Mom calls me often since dad started traveling with Connie. I often feel for her, but then she starts to pry for details in my life, the divorce with Noa, the attempt of the custody battle for Anna, she just nags and nags everytime the opportunity presents itself. I just think she misses dad, and she's a little jealous things are working for him. I'm not entirely sure she thinks it's fair that she gets to watch Connie have the happiness she always wanted with dad.

So because I felt bad about all of this, I always answered when she called. Sometimes.

"I've been keeping an eye on the news, you okay down there?"

I nodded, running a hand through my hair, "it won't be so bad but I think the heavy wind might knock out our power at some point."

She frowned, "see this is why I keep telling you; just take Anna and move back here, to Canada."

"Mom, you can't keep advising me to move back to Canada everytime something bad happens. I have a life here, a career, and I can't just *take* Anna."

"Of course you can, you're her father." she scoffed, "and didn't Noa practically do the same? She disappeared for months with her, Reiner I told you to report it to the police—"

"Mom."

"She shouldn't have gotten away with it Reiner, what she did—"

"Mother, *please.*"

She sighed, moving her phone from one hand to the other as she rubbed her forehead. "I just don't understand why you're protecting her." she mumbled under her breath.

"Because I love Anna." I replied in defeat.

A divorce is one thing, but taking away her mother? I couldn't do that to her. My mother keeps telling me she'll understand later in life, but I don't want to raise her resenting me. And Noa came back, eventually and that's all that matters. Anna is finally starting to adjust with the divorce, seeing me again, and a huge part of that has to do with Noa. I can't take her away from Noa without her hating me in the process.

The call went quiet. My mother was quiet on the other line.

Sometimes she calls me at night crying after she had something to drink, and I listen to her blaming herself for my failed marriage. She believed she could have stopped me from marrying Noa from the beginning, Mother's intuition, she says — she never liked Noa.

"You'll be okay?" she asked, and I'm not sure if she's asking about the divorce or the storm coming.

"I'll be fine." I went with the safe answer, "I have a back-up generator, I'll be okay if the lights go out."

"Will Anna be okay?"

"She's with Noa, visiting a cousin out of town, they're far away from the lightrain that's coming."

The lights flickered as it rained harder outside, it was raining since yesterday afternoon, but it was a very light rain, now I can hear the rain fall down with a brute force all the way in my office.

I stared at my phone, running my hand through my hair as I sat up straight, "okay, mom I have to go."

"Okay, call soon, or I will, to make sure you didn't die in Minnesota instead of canada."

I laughed a little, "I'm only allowed to die in Canada?"

"Yes." She replied with no hesitation.

"Okay bye, mom." I hung up before she could even talk anymore. I dropped my phone on my desk, taking a breath before I grabbed my computer — I tried not to think about Noa but sometimes I always wondered how things would have turned out if I reported her, and at least tried to get custody of Anna.

And with every outcome, there was only one feeling I cared about, and it's Anna's.

64

CHAPTER SEVEN

★·☆·★

Soleil

★·☆·★

EVERYTHING HURTS. But the pounding on the door had me wanting to claw my eyes out. I closed my eyes, trying my breathing exercises for situations like this. The second I opened my eyes, I was in pain. The rain hasn't stopped, it only got worse I think. The wind is blowing very harshly and it worries me a little, the last thing I want is a new window, or house.

A groan escaped my mouth as the ponding grew louder and louder. I managed to slip out of bed without falling on the cold floor. My stomach was *screaming, stabbing, hurting*. I wrapped an arm around my stomach as I flipped the light switch but I remained in the darkness.

I rolled my eyes because out of all fucking days today is the day that my lights want to go out.

By the time I reached the stairs, the impatient person behind the door decided it was a good idea to pound on the door again. Now I wish I fixed the door bell, because it sure would've been nicer to my ears than this aching loud pound.

"I'm coming, you dickwad!"

I opened the door, only to greet a half wet Reiner in a gray raincoat. It's so early in the morning. And my eyes have been blessed so heavily with the sight of his unhappy face.

Speaking of morning, where's the sun?

Reiner held what felt like the sun in the palm of his hands close to my face. Glaring a flashlight to my face. The light was so close to my face I winced as I brought my hand over my face. Reiner lowered his flashlight, only stared at me. I grew self aware — I just got out of bed to open the door, and he's probably staring at the dried drool on my cheeks.

My subconscious took over and my hands reached to wipe my cheeks, "shit," I breathed. "I look like a gremlin, don't I?"

Reiner only tilted his head to the side. Flashing his flashlight on my face again, a faint smile on his face, "you just call me a dickwad?" There was a small sound of disappointment in his voice.

I did nothing but blink at him, ignoring his question in general.

"What's up with the lights? Or is it just mine, because I could've sworn I paid the light bills last week." My brows furrowed the more I thought of it.

"Power's out." He explained.

"Oh." Was all that left my mouth, and before I could question his visit, he spoke again while I struggled with the sharp stabbing pain in my stomach

"I have a back-up generator, if you want — you could just stay with me until the power comes back on." He says the words very patiently, like there isn't a thunderstorm behind him, the wind blew very harshly and he barely budged.

The word *"Oh."* Left my mouth again.

I thought of a couple of new words to say to him besides "oh" but the sharp pain in my stomach had me clutching my stomach gurgling on a moan. The need to hurl felt stronger than ever.

A wand wrapped around my waist, securing me. I wasn't about to fall, but I guess he thought I would because the grip he had on my waist is the same grip that should be saved for people who are actually going to fall — and maybe it was because of all the pain I was in — but something else entirely pricked my skin. A sensation that demanded to be felt.

My skin felt hot. Heat rushing down my stomach to my thighs. My hand held his arm as I felt his cold finger brush against some of my exposed skin. And the thin material of a shirt I was wearing did me no favor when his wet coat stuck against my skin.

"Reiner." I whispered, but it came out in a wheezing sort of way. His grip on me didn't feel like it'd loosen anytime soon.

"Reiner?"

His hands slowly unwrap around me, and a deep exhale leaves his throat. I took a few steps back shoving myself inside the house, and Reiner was right behind me — showing himself in.

"You do look like a gremlin." He said as he gripped on my

waist dragging me to the living room.

I rolled my eyes as I sat down on the couch, holding a hand on my stomach trying to settle myself. But the pain wasn't going anywhere.

"Can you stop?" I hissed at him when he flashed his light in front of my face again, my irritation was boiling. Blue came to my side, wagging his tail he brushed his body against my arm but once he realized I was wet, he stopped and just hopped off the couch.

Reiner sucked in a breath, "you look sick."

"I'm not sick."

For a second I tried to inhale more oxygen than my usual dose, but my heart rate only increased, as the sick feeling in my stomach surfaced again. This time it needed to be released, drained out of my body.

Before I knew what I was doing — I was sprinting for the bathroom. Sweats breaking all over my face, as I hurled over the toilet — grateful, for my hair that was already all wrapped up in a bonnet.

I felt the rush of cold air that greeted my back as the door creaked. Reiner's probably right behind me, watching me spill acid out of my mouth.

What a fucking day.

I felt my stomach twist as I vomited. And no matter how hard I tried to stop vomiting, it didn't work. When it did finally stopped, every muscle hurt, my whole body felt drained. I was too tired to even be embarrassed that Reiner just witnessed all of that.

"Are you going gloat?" I asked before running water through

my mouth, shaking the bitter taste out of my taste buds.

I felt him shift behind me, "why would I gloat?"

I shrugged as I split past him, walking out of the bathroom with a hand wrapped around my stomach, his light steps followed right behind me, the flashlight in his hands lighting the path for me. I should probably find my phone, I'm praying I did remember to plug it in last night before falling asleep.

"Remember when you said not to eat the pie?" I spoke when I finally took my seat on the couch.

"Yes. I specifically told you *not* to eat it." his voice dropped an octave.

I awkwardly laughed, "you're *not* gonna believe this..."

I wish I could see the frown on his face, but I could tell he frowned by the way he sighed, it was a *very* disappointing sigh. "You ate the pie."

"I ate the pie." I repeated. Even I was disappointed in myself, now that I'm in pain. My head feels heavy and my stomach is still in pain, even after vomiting.

"You have a weak immune system."

I'm not sure if it was meant as an insult or not, but it still felt like it. "I don't think food poisoning cares if your immune system is weak or not."

"I'm not sure if you're aware of how the immune system works."

I groaned very dramatically, "why do you care?"

When he didn't say anything else I moved to find my phone, and it sat perfectly next to my dead laptop. When I tapped on the

screen praying for a good battery percentage. But I was disappointed when the screen dimmed showing me the dead screen, I never
realized how much I took my electricity for granted.

I dropped the phone in my lap, throwing my head against the
cushions, "my phone's dead."

Reiner cleared his throat, "like I said, I have a generator on,
you can charge your phone at my house…" he paused, "if you
want." He added the last part, as he set the flashing on the coffee
table, facing the ceiling, and very little light poured in the room —
I could see him much better now.

I know he thinks it's a choice, but it really wasn't. I stayed quiet, trying to think this through, but really I'm trying to recover, my
throat is bone dry, my stomach is empty and everywhere ached.

I cleared my throat but my voice was still hoarse, "can Blue
come along?"

He laughed very softly, "yes."

I did a lousy job at wiping the sweat on my forehead, my
breathing felt shaky and shallow, the air growing cold around me
— if I'm in this horrible state, I wonder how much of it did I slept
through? and how can I keep sleeping through it?

"It's cold," I murmured, wrapping the blanket on the couch
around me, "I'm cold."

It took him two strides to reach me. I didn't know what to
expect when he came so close to me, but I winced, feeling the back
of his hand on my forehead. His breath fell against my cheek when
he exhaled, "Fuck," he whispered, and everything in me vibrated
with the words, my stomach somehow hurt even more. I sat

there, patiently, squirming in pain, waiting for him to speak.

Reiner pulled his hand back, brushing his thumb against his palm, "you're coming down with a fever," he explained.

Then he talked about how much throwing up I'd be doing today until the bacteria is out of my system — how much body fluid I'd end up losing. All the electrolytes would be leaving my body and I'd find a new way to gain them back because I need them. And the massive weight loss that comes with all of this.

Reiner kept talking and talking about all the symptoms I'll be going through, and how critical my situation can get — all that worse case scenario talk.

"Would you look at that," I smiled up at him, "you're a doctor too."

He chuckled under his breath, "no, I just have a daughter who loves seafood." I smiled at him, wishing he would smile more because Reiner has the world's cutest dimples. It makes him look so damn charming.

His eyes met mine, and the look on his face was so soft and warm, it made me want to melt in his hands.

"How much pain are you in?" he asked.

And I glanced up at his hand, which was —*still*— on my forehead, his hand was warm now, no longer foreign. His eyes flickered on my forehead, finally realizing his hand was still on my forehead — Reiner released a ragged breath as he retrieved his hand, camping it shut, fisting it, unfisting it before shoving it in his pockets like some foreign object.

I swallowed, "enough." The air was thick with something unfamiliar, daring. We were somehow closer, when I finally gained the courage to meet him in the middle, he stood up straight again.

"Where's your room?" He asked.

I cleared my throat, "upstairs first door on the left."

After a while, and I don't know how long that time could've been because I was too focused on the pain in my stomach, but he came back with a duffel bag. Filled with what I assume to be my clothes.

When he came around the couch, he stared down at me before grabbing his flashlights, his arm going around my waist, he gripped my waist, hoisting me up. "Let's go."

"Wait, you have to grab Blue." I protested, attempting to search for him in the dark.

"Give me your keys, and I'll come back for him and lock the door."

★ · ☆ · ★

Reiner had lights in his house. The lucky bastard thought of everything. I thought he'd drop me at his couch, but he dragged me all the way to a room upstairs, a sad, sad, empty bedroom.

Reiner laid me on the bed, my eyes met his when finally let go, he reached for the cover at the end of the bed, throwing it over my body, he tucked the cover around my waist as he let out a ragged breath, "get some sleep," he whispered.

I grabbed his hand when he turned around to leave, I stared at him as he stared at our hands, "you'll grab Blue?"

He nodded as his soft gaze met mine. "I'll grab Blue."

My eyes felt heavy as I yawned, feeling the pain in my stomach boil again, "promise?"

Again, he nodded, "I promise." his hand clutched around mine with the words, and it felt good.

"If I die, could you please give Anna Blue—"

His shoulder dropped as he chuckled, *"Soleil."*

I nodded, letting go of his hand as I flipped to my stomach, feeling my eyes glued shut. I wasn't too eager to stay up and bear this unbearable pain — or throw up everytime I ate something.

CHAPTER EIGHT

Reiner

"GET SOME SLEEP," the second her head hit the pillow, she went out. I dropped the duffle bag by the bed before grabbing her phone from her hand, plugging it in charge.

I moved out of the room quick enough not to do anything stupid like watch her sleep, I closed the door before going back downstairs — turning off the unnecessary lights. I may have a backup generator but I have no idea how long this storm will last. I grabbed her keys from my pocket making my way outside through the rain again.

I have no idea why I offered her a room. I was thinking about what my mom said the other night, that I should fight for Anna, but between me and her I know that I know more about the way the trial works, it's not as simple, and with Noa who's financially stable, and who appears to be a great mother, the chances of me getting custody are low.

There's another part of me that's just scared of the resentment that will come after. And if Noa wins, I know she won't make it easy for me to see Anna, she might actually flee the country with her as my punishment. I think, Anna is happier with both of us in her life — whether we're together or not, she wants both of us present. For her I'm willing to try and forgive Noa, to brush my own feelings aside.

When I thought of all that, my mind thought of her as an escape. The power was out, I wondered what she was up to. And when I saw her, she didn't look well, and I wouldn't be at peace with myself if I didn't help.

I shook myself a little before stepping into her house, flashing my flashlight as I looked for the cat. I'm not sure if I should call it out or not. I walked around the couch for a third time, before I sighed.

"Blue?" My voice was uncertain and almost quiet.

"Blue?" I tried again but this time louder, but I heard nothing.

I moved to the kitchen as I opened the pantry, grabbing cat food for him. If he wasn't going to step forward now, hopefully he'll come when he hears the sound of food.

How am I going to carry the cat, his food, and the litter box?

With Blue missing, I managed two trips to my house, one for the big litter box, and the other one was for his food, and more litter. I closed the door behind me when I came back to the house, it's eerily quiet, all I can hear is the rain from outside. I used the flashlight to get upstairs because there's no way Blue could still be downstairs after all these noises I just made.

I checked her room, and sure enough, there lies Blue, all balled up in her sheets — the poor thing is probably scared and missing her. I reached to grab him but his claw sought for my skin first. He just pressed his whole paw against my skin, digging his nails into my skin. I hissed, but made no effort to move him. I learned that with cats, you have to earn their trust. So when the threatening and the hurting comes, you're supposed to just take it.

Blue growled, bearing his little teeth.

I laughed in pain, "you little–*mhmm...*" I used my other hand to stuff the flashlight into my mouth, as I bit on it, then I used that free hand to hold onto Blue, finally lifting him off the bed. His claw was still deep into my skin, and I'm sure I'm already bleeding. I clenched my lips around the flashlight as I held onto the cat, making my way downstairs.

Blue made a run from me the second we made it to my house. I guess he's excited to see light, and his bowl of food apparently because he wagged his tail as he found the kitchen, going straight for his bowl.

I finally winced, feeling a certain burn on my hand, I clenched my hand under the light, watching the back of my hand bleed from Blue's claw marks. Three little slashes, and I can tell it was deep. I sighed under my breath, making my way to my office.

I didn't want to be too dramatic, so I just cleared the cut and let it be. I sat down in my office, the dimmed light coming from the lamp reflecting on the papers in front of me. I grabbed my glasses — placing them over my nose. Revising through my latest case.

The storm outside was still raging, the air blowing impossibly strong. I bet just standing out there in the middle of the storm with the wind blowing so hard I'd rock — the wind would rock me completely no matter how hard I try not to.

But I didn't mind a little storm. The harsh sound of the rain hitting my roof is my favorite thing to hear. I am very satisfied at night, listening to the sound of the rain. Find things easier to manage without the constant pressure of interaction with other people. Well, I do worry a little because Anna isn't here with me right now — and with the really crappy signal, I can barely make a phone call.

I rubbed a hand on my face, *"what the hell are you doing Reiner?"* I asked myself, because the question needed to be asked.

A storm is happening and I know she could've done more than handle herself without me ever knowing she was sick, but why was I at her door already — giving an invitation to my house?

I do stupid, *stupid* things to keep her away only to bring myself back into her life again. There is nothing more I love than being sure, and being near her clouds my judgment and I end up being anything but sure. I'm anything but myself around her.

Blue was at her feet when I walked in the room with food and a cup of ice in my hand. The cat didn't even bother to glance at me, he's just on the bed wagging his tail as he slowly blinked. I released a breath as my eyes met Soleil's. She woke up a while ago, and I figured it was time she ate something but by the way she was staring at the food in disgust — she doesn't agree with me.

She pulled the pillow over head, "Idon'tlikebannas." she muffled out all together.

I placed the cup of ice on the nightstand, already peeling the banana, "you have to eat *something*." With that she groaned, taking the pillow off head, glaring at me.

"Here," I poked the content to her lips, "eat the banana."

She only scowled, "*you* eat the banana."

I frowned, "if you're as stubborn as you are right now, you'll only get worse and I'll have to drive you to the hospital in the middle of the storm, do you know how bad hospitals are in the storms?" I asked, but she didn't answer so I spoke again.

"It's horrible, it's crawling with sick kids and people seeking shelter, people injured from car accidents, and let's not forget about the long-ass wait until they finally decide to treat you." I paused.

"And the treatment will just be them prescribing you what to eat because you can't hold anything down but banana, oatmeal, crackers, rice, and applesauce."

She only stared at me with this weird expression on her face, like I was the alien invading her world. But it's been six hours, so I came up to check on her. She was thrashing non-stop on the bed, mumbling nonsense, her stomach growling even in her sleep.

Her eating wasn't even a choice on the table right now, she is obligated to.

I sighed, trying this one last time, "you need the gluten if you don't want to end up at the hospital, so eat the banana."

"All I wanted to hear was '*please*'." She murmurs as she grabs the banana from my hand, taking an aggressive bite.

oh.

I released a breath, my shoulders falling down as I relaxed, "thank you."

God, I *hate* hospitals. They are crawling with bacteria and sick people, I can't stand the sight. And it bugs me that I pay the emergency room a visit often. Anna wrestles, she often ends up with a nose bleed or a fractured bone. A small price for her happiness.

I awkwardly stood there and watched her eat half of the banana, I could see the discontent look on her face and I didn't want to push her too much so I didn't press when she didn't finish the banana all the way. I offered her a small smile, one that was supposed to be encouraging but I think it annoyed her altogether because her eyes shifted from to the glass of ice next to the banana on the nightstand.

I grabbed the glass, "it's for you." I explained as I grabbed an ice cube pressing it against her lips, my eyes dropped on her full lips as I swallowed, finding her gaze again, my throat was bone-dry. "Suck on the ice ship."

Her eyes met mine, and the innocent act of her batting her eyelashes twice at me has my head light, *"Soleil,"* I spoke her name like a prayer, so soft and quiet. *Full of desperation,* "please, suck on the ice."

She shuddered, fucking *shuddered.* She licked her lips before she could take the ice from me, her lips brushed against the tip of my fingers and my whole body seemed to ignite. I could feel my ears grow hot, the tips of my fingers are still burning. There's something in the air, something we're not ready to find out about.

I shook my head but my whole body felt light, "don't chew the ice, just suck it."

Her eyes never left mine, and it made the whole situation feel *wrong.* I've thought about taking a seat next to her on the bed, keep her company, tend to her needs, but being near her would have me thinking about *my needs,* and that's the last thing I want to do.

Soleil pushed the ice on the side of her cheek, "what is the ice for?" Her voice came out raspy, grabbing my attention from her lips.

I cleared my throat, as I looked away. "To keep you hydrated, you can't drink water right now."

"The less you vomit, the sooner you get better." I took a step back away from her. I don't trust myself enough to stay here any much longer.

"There's more ice in the cup," I pointed a finger at the cup on the nightstand and her eyes followed the movement as she slowly nodded.

I looked at Blue who was starting to purr as he stood up, stretching his paws, obviously tired from all the sleeping. "Blue was fed a while ago, and he knows where to find his litter."

She smiled very softly as she glanced at Blue who was still at her feet, "thank you," she whispered when her eyes met mine.

I nodded, I couldn't decide if it was even necessary to thank me, all I was doing was showing basic human decency. I glanced at her one last time before walking off, "the bathroom is down the hall, I'll be downstairs, try to sleep," I said as I reached for the door.

The storm has calmed down a bit. The rain stopped falling so hard it's barely sizzling, but the wind never stopped blowing. I barely got any work done when I reached my office — I was so hungry I couldn't focus. All the things I found in the fridge were either expired or too frozen to taste good.

I decided to cook the easiest thing I could possibly cook, sweet chili chicken with brussel sprouts and white rice. Took about forty minutes, nearly burned brussel sprouts. I decided to air-fry some potatoes last minute because I don't trust myself at all when it comes to cooking. It's always a surprise.

Blue hopped on the counter when I grabbed a half crispy brussel sprouts, I can tell he's judging my cooking just by the way he wags his tail, staring at me, waiting for me to finally taste what could possibly be my last meal.

"I followed a recipe." I mumbled in defense, but Blue just stared at me because after all, he's just a cat.

I finally threw the brussel sprouts in my mouth. I think I could've done a better job with other veggies, but the brussel sprouts looked a lot better than all the other frozen stuff in the freezer.

It didn't taste bad at all and that left me surprised, because of the brussel sprouts I have hope for everything else. I grabbed my spoon as I glanced at the rice.

"How can anyone fuck up white rice?" I chuckled as I grabbed a spoonful of rice, blowing over it.

"I'm feeling a little better." Her voice boomed from across the room.

The spoon of rice was still in my hand and before I could even think about anything I shoved the spoon in my mouth. She stepped closer into the kitchen as I chewed, her body coming into view, her outfit was changed, and her hair was out of the bonnet, but still up.

She only slept for two hours, her fever went down within the first twenty minutes she fell asleep. She's getting better and I'm glad, but I just didn't expect her to be up and about so soon.

My eyes raked her body, taking in her outfit, her eyes followed my movements and she looked down at her outfit. "Um, I took a shower, I smelled like vomit."

I nodded, finishing the food in my mouth, "you're only feeling better because you have an empty stomach right now."

I lifted the sleeves of my tee — it never felt more attached to my body under her glare. I grabbed a towel before I opened the oven pulling out the chicken, holding it as far away from me as possible as I placed it on the counter. The chicken looked golden and it smelled good. I smiled, obviously proud of myself because it looks almost identical with the one the lady in the video I watched cooked.

I looked, meeting her heavy gaze, the fact that she was already watching all of this happen, makes me feel like I should be embarrassed, but I'm not.

I pointed at one of the stools, "sit."

I watched her tuck one of her loose baby curls behind her ear, as she walked towards the stool. For the first time in a *long* while, there's a woman in my kitchen. A barefooted, sick woman.

I grabbed a bowl, plated it with rice, then the potatoes, then the chicken with brussel sprouts, she never complained so I just assumed she liked all of it. I could feel her gaze burning holes in every inch of my body, and I find myself slightly glad because of how well my clothes fit me.

"Thank you for charging my phone," she paused, clamping her mouth shut before opening it again. I handed her the plate of food, "and everything else." she said in a low hushed tone.

Handed her a spoon, "don't mention it."

"Try it," I mentioned the food, "hopefully you'll keep it down."

She made a face as she poked the chicken, "do you really know how to cook?"

"Yes. Eat."

"You're bossy, I don't like it."

I shrugged, "I'm not so fond of your stubbornness either."

I made myself a plate as I sat on the stool next to her. We sat so close, her knee brushed against mine and I released a small breath — When I finally tasted the chicken, I realized I shouldn't have served it. The chicken was bone-dry, with little to no flavor.

She took a bite of chicken first, and watching her try to eat was more painful than witnessing her vomit. She just looked so miserable — her slow chew only confirmed her lack of appetite. It reminds me when Anna tries to eat after vomiting so much.

She finally swallowed the small bite that she chewed on for what felt like five minutes, "thank you." She mumbled.

I pinned her with a look.

Soleil rolled her eyes, "right, not mentioning it."

It's hard to *not* stare at Soleil. I could describe her beauty in a thousand different ways and I would still not be able to grasp the concept. I sat on the edge of the bed staring down at her, it wasn't much of a choice really, she asked me to stay for a few minutes. How could I not?

She sighed, "how long does it last?"

"Food poisoning?"

She nodded.

I shrugged, "A day or two, not too long because the body flushes itself pretty quickly."

It's when she stares at me with those brown eyes I often find myself speechless. The obsession I feel when she does is primal. I find myself strangely wanting to be the only one to be able to get lost in her eyes.

Thirty minutes after eating the food, her fever went sky high, but at least she managed to keep the food down — that's some sort of progress.

Her head was on the counter, earlier — whimpering in pain. I had to help her get back in bed — trying to ease her pain, or at least bring down her fever, with a few cold damp towels on her forehead, and for a while it helped cool her skin down, and because she was able to keep food down now she was able to drink an advil for the headache.

Now, Soleil is staring up at me with those brown eyes. A color I recently adopted as my favorite color. I leaned closer towards her, reaching for the damp towel on her forehead to flip it. Her fingers hooked a finger around my necklace, my lips formed a thin line as my muscles shifted under the small brush of her finger, and I leaned a little closer towards her as she tugged the necklace. I'm starting to sense that whatever she asked I'd give.

She looked up, finding my gaze, "you're a Christian?"

"Catholic."

"Oh." And her lips remained parted as she released the necklace from her hold. I swallowed as I fixed my posture again.

She smiled a little, cradling her head down, "what's your biggest sin?"

A dry laugh escaped my lips, "I can't really tell you..."

"Right... this whole sinner and priest confidentiality thing."

"No, it's more than that." I didn't care to take my explanation further because it'd be like talking to a drunk person. She's sick and half asleep — half of the things I'll be saying probably won't even make any sense.

I could see the sleep in her eyes, but she's so stubborn, refusing to get any. I took the damp towel off her forehead, dropping it in a small bowl of water. Her eyes softened a little, so tired. If I don't leave soon, she'll force a conversation out of the both of us.

I placed my hand on her forehead, feeling her temperature — the fever went down, just a little. I thought about removing my hand, but curiosity got the best of me the second I ran the tip of my fingers down her face, everything felt safe, the sound of her breathing echoed as my thumb stroked her cheeks. My eyes followed my hands against her skin instead of meeting her eyes.

I ran a finger under her chin, and her eyes *fluttered* close.

She released a *devastating* breath, her eyes still closed, "you're so much nicer than you let on." She whispered, "you're spoiling me."

I smiled at that, "good night, *Soleil.*"

CHAPTER NINE

Soleil

I SLAMMED THE DOOR SHUT BEHIND ME, my hands shook as I placed a hand over my mouth, silently gasping in horror. My heart was racing so fast it felt like I ran a marathon. I think my brain is still processing but it's having a hard time finding the proper response to the situation.

I can't stop thinking. "God, I'm so sorry!" I wanted to drown in my own pool of embarrassment as I stood behind Reiner's door.

What happened wasn't supposed to happen. I shouldn't have seen what I saw. He hasn't said anything, even after my dramatic apology, he doesn't even seem to mind this awkward situation, it's all weird. I want to leave now and hide until I can go back home, but I already feel bad as it is, and it feels wrong to pretend it didn't happen.

I'm still having a hard time processing the fact that I walked in on him — naked. I walked on him naked. Naked?

I didn't think, I just did. And now I feel so stupid. He didn't pack my toothbrush, there was no other toothbrush in the guest bathroom, so I thought I could ask him, by just marching in his room like I own the place. *Why didn't I knock?*

My head is spinning with new lewd information. It can't be so bad, I only saw his ass. He had a towel but he was drying his hair with it, and I walked in on him while he was butt-naked. I saw his ass. And it's not a nightmare, just embarrassing.

"Reiner," I called his name behind the door.

He's not answering. I don't blame him, I'm not sure I'd answer to someone who walked in on me either. I walked in, I noticed, I screamed and closed the door shut. Now I am standing behind the door furiously apologizing and he's not responding.

That's it, I think. He's gonna come out, and he's going to kick me out of his house and I'll be damned to go back to my house; where there's no electricity, no AC, no warm food, or anything. I don't plan on protesting if that's what happens because I saw him naked. It's only fair.

The door pulled open, and I stood up straight —*straighter*— my spine is doing this weird salute standing stance.

Reiner didn't look angry, in fact I didn't know how he felt because his stoic expression was the same as all the expressions he's given me lately. But I do enjoy his hair. It's wet and messy, the thought of running my fingers through his hair is a passing thought. My eyes squared on his lips before I even realized it, and when I did I focused on his eyes.

"Knocking would be a good idea next time." He said over his shoulder as he walked past me.

I blinked as my shoulders sag in relief. I've been such a bad guest, laying in bed all day, siphoning his energy. But I'm glad he's showing me some sort of niceness, because I woke up today and I felt better already.

"Of course, I should knock, I wasn't thinking, I'm really sorry."

I was told once I apologize too much. I was also told, I do that because I am a *woman*. Constant apologizing is a *nasty* habit. Even when things are my fault I apologize, I don't know why the words just leave my mouth without a drop of consent.

I could be walking, and someone bumps into me, I'll be the first to apologize. It's a habit. *A nasty, habit.*

Reiner stopped to turn around facing me, "Are you embarrassed?" He cocked a brow. Reiner held my gaze like a challenge he knew he'd win.

I stopped walking, the question taking me aback, "*I-* what?" I could feel my cheeks flush, the heat crawling to my neck, oh yes I am very grateful he won't be able to witness how my skin betrays me.

"Were you embarrassed? seeing me naked."

I cleared my throat, "well I didn't see anything." *Liar, liar pants on fire.*

You saw his taut back, his gorgeous —perfect— ass.

He fixed me a blank look, "you saw my ass." The words sounded like an accusation leaving his lips.

I've been denying it this long haven't I? What's a few more times?

A dry laugh escaped my lips. "Did I? Did I really?"

"Soleil."

I froze. I tensed. My name alone on his lips was enough warning.

"I saw your back…" I paused to stare at him, but his gaze was so intense I looked away in shame, "and *apparently* your ass." I squeezed my hands, worrying about my confession.

"I might've squinted a little," my shoulders sagged, before tensing up again, I should really be ashamed of the words that left my mouth.

"Are you embarrassed?"

"No." I lied. "I'm just… *sorry.*"

"Good. Because I'm not embarrassed if you aren't."

I forced a fake smile so wide, my cheeks felt sore. "We're both not embarrassed!" I chirped, "now that's settled, I wanted to ask you for a toothbrush, you didn't pack me one."

"Although you did pack me a couple of lingeries."

At this his skin flushed, his cheeks tinted pink. I, for one, think it's *cute.* Reiner cleared his throat, scratching the back of his head. And I'm enjoying this so much it should be a crime.

"I don't remember— it was dark, I had zero intentions—"

I let out a laugh, interrupting his little apologetic speech. Holding my stomach in the process as I grabbed onto his bicep for support, "I'm messing with you." I laughed again, "God, you should see your face." I patted his arms for a second before realizing how my laugh died out when his whole body *tensed* under my touch.

His whole body *froze*. Tensing up. His breathing ragged. The whole playful dynamic froze over our heads and this new chilly air laced with something tempting was breezing around us. *I didn't like it.*

When I pulled away he huffed, almost in relief. "Funny." His words fell flat.

It took me a second to realize I was teasing him earlier. My head is light, filled with things that happened just a few seconds ago. I touched him. His arm. He froze, tensed. I stopped laughing because nothing was funny, nothing was ever funny.

I looked up at Reiner. Nothing about him seemed shy, he was tall and muscular, but almost lean. It was weird at first because I was nearly the same height as Luke, and I thought It was cute for our current generation. But now I'm standing in front of Reiner, who is so much taller. I found it weirdly comforting. Like if a tornado happened he'd be able to wrap his body safely around mine. *Weird.*

I swallowed, gaining the courage to finish our conversation because standing awkwardly under these dimmed lights in the middle of the hallway won't get us anywhere.

Half of my statement was true though, but he only grabbed a few thongs, but I can't really blame him, it was dark and he was in a hurry — half of my drawer is filled thongs and I can't imagine him taking his time to pick them out, even if he did have time for that it'd be weird.

"So you needed a toothbrush?"

I nodded.

Reiner got me the toothbrush, we didn't say much after that. I don't know his boundaries. Maybe he doesn't have any but everybody does. Either way I always end up tiptoeing around him all the time, I let him have the lead — because then, when something awkward happens it'll equally be both of our faults.

The rain calmed down yesterday night, but before the night could be over it came back again. It's not as bad as the first time, it's been on and off all day, but still strong and colder this time. I can't imagine trying to survive this at my house. I probably would've been passed out somewhere in the bathroom near my own puke. *No lights. No TV. No fridge. Nothing. I'd have nothing.* And poor Blue would be cold and starving because I'd be too sick to get his food out.

I found nail polish in the bathroom. It was another reminder that Reiner has a *daughter.* After brushing my teeth I snooped, I was feeling better and I was bored, Reiner had disappeared into his office. I went back downstairs, taking a comfortable seat on the couch. I stared at my toes, the old white nail polish, nearly gone. I was so clearly bored out of my mind, even Blue was hiding so adding another layer to my toes was the least I could do.

I'm only doing this out of boredom. Reiner failed to bring my laptop. I can't work, and I still haven't got any good signals on my phone, and when I do get so much as a bar I shoot Hayley a text, she hasn't replied, but it could also mean I can't receive shit because of the bad reception.

I could be writing right now. Instead, I'm painting my toe-nails white.

I felt his silhouette linger near me before he sat on the couch opposite of me. He's staring, gawking. Whatever it is he's doing, seems to have been fascinated enough to talk.

"Are you hungry yet?" he asked.

I shook my head. I was actually starving, but admitting to that would somehow feel desperate. Yesterday's food was not as awful as I thought it would be, or maybe because I was sick, half of my tastebuds weren't present.

"Do you want anything specific, or are you okay with the same thing again, we didn't eat much of it yesterday."

I turned to stare at him, my throat was bone-dry when I looked at him. Reiner wore a white dress shirt with the sleeves rolled up, and the first few buttons, loose, and dark dress pants. I'm not sure when he changed from this morning, but he clearly did.

He looked down at his own body from head to toe, scratching the back of his head, "I had a virtual meeting with a client earlier when the rain calmed."

I nodded, swallowing, "can I help?" When he looked at me confused, I realized I never answered his question, "I'm okay with food from yesterday, I just want to help."

"Sure."

I don't like the words sure much, it always felt like an unwant-ed answer. I followed Reiner in the kitchen, where he just worked his way around the fridge, grabbing things. I know I'm supposed to be helping, and I was trying to, but I just couldn't stop staring.

I blame myself for not getting laid any sooner, and all the medicine Reiner has been giving me. It's making my brain all gooey and horny — all of a sudden Reiner is becoming a sex symbol.

I think I stared so hard to the point even my cat caught on. Blue rubbed his body against me as he meowed. I reached down to pick him up but he moved his body away. His cries only grew louder, and I understood those kinds of cries. He's ready for food.

I watch Blue claw the cabinets, trying to jump the counters, *he's so dramatic.*

Reiner glanced at us, and I could see the stress on his face. He softly dropped a bag of brussel sprouts on the counter, "is he... okay?"

"He's hungry." I mumbled, going around Reiner, trying to brush against him as little as I could.

"It's over there," he pointed to the corner of the kitchen, near the backdoor.

I grabbed the cat food and before the food could even hit the bowl Blue was already around my legs, nuzzling his face into the bowl.

"Blueee." I groaned, I didn't want to dump the food on his head. I moved my hand around, away from his direction as I slowly poured the cat food from the side.

The room fell silent after Blue got his food, and I awkwardly walked back to Reiner's side, he pushed the cutting board in my direction and handed me the knife. When I looked up at him he offered me the world's softest smile. My shoulders sagged as I grabbed the knife from his hand, staring at the brussel sprouts on the cutting board with my heart beating out of my chest.

It hurts so much I want to place a hand on my chest, take a few calming breaths.

I'm constantly nervous around him, and I thought the longer I hang around him the more used to him I'd be, but the more time we spend together, the more my stomach boils, the more unsettling my mind gets. The thoughts I have of him sometimes are nothing but torture. I want to make it stop, but I don't know how to do that when he looks at me with the softest smile on his face.

It's not very asshole of him.

We're seated at the table this time, it's not so big. It only has four chairs. But it's a nice table. I've been exploring this house the whole day and the decor is pretty impressive, and everything is so. . . *neat.* Anyone would guess he has a *wife.*

My thoughts died out at the mention of a wife.

Reiner is seated at the head of the table, and I'm seated on his right side. He shuffled for a while after finally placing his napkin on his lap. Turning to face me, and I shuffled under his gaze. I feel like I should've done the same. I cleared my throat as I grabbed my napkin, placing it on my lap.

I looked at him before I grabbed the bowl of diced potatoes, "you still go to the gym?"

He swallowed, nodding. "When I have time, but when I can't I run."

Ah.

"Do you still go?" He asked.

I shook my head, "I used to, but I think Luke canceled his black card, and just got the regular one." I pushed a few potatoes out of the bowl and onto my plate, "I don't go anymore." I mumbled.

I don't think I'm allowed to be angry at Luke for doing that because we've broken up. And using his gym membership felt kinda like using him. We barely talk anymore, so it was starting to feel weird to have access to his account.

He grabbed the bowl of potatoes from me, "Luke?" He repeated his name. "The guy that was supposed to help with your car that morning?"

I nodded, "but I never called, remember?"

He laughed, tilting his head back, "oh, I remember."

Awkwardly laughed, trying to not remember one of the most embarrassing moments in my life. My embarrassment seems to bring him joy. Like now, he's relaxed, laughing with me. Something I never even thought about, but it's happening. Being sheltered in the house, away from the rest of the world, makes him... *different.* Or maybe he was always like that, but never with me.

I don't ponder on the thought too much as I took a bite of my potatoes, my taste buds weren't deceiving me after all yesterday. It tasted even better today. I added some brussel sprouts on my plate, along with some chicken. Because of the potatoes I have faith for the rest of the food.

"Are you guys still close?"

I glanced at Reiner as I placed the plate of chicken back on the center of the table, "what?"

"You and Luke. . ." He cleared his throat, "I'm sorry, I just sort of assumed the two of you dated."

"We did."

A variety of expressions fleeted across his face.

"And no. We're not so close anymore, it's just. . . awkward."

Reiner nodded as he stabbed a chicken breast with his fork, dropping it on his plate. I shuffled before finally cutting into my chicken, taking my first bite of it. It took every bit of my strength to not cough the food out. The chicken tasted sad, tasteless. If chickens could get depressed, I'd say this one was and we're eating a sad, depressed chicken.

"You look in pain." He swallowed, reaching for the glass of water. Sipping some. "Are you feeling sick again?" He turned to face me for a second before cutting into his chicken.

"No," I brushed. "Too excited to eat solid food again."

I took another bite of chicken. It's painful to eat it, really painful. How can he eat the chicken without choking? I have to fight off all of my survival instincts in order to restrain myself from gulping all of my water down.

He stopped his movements, his fork and knife dropping on his plate with a clank. "How bad is it?"

I laughed, a terrible dry laugh, "oh, no, yea the food is great!"

His face danced with amusement "I've heard that one before." He smiled.

Someone else lied about the food, or did they actually think it's great?

"huh?"

"My daughter." He smiled, "only, she says it out of pity, or guilt," he looks at me, a full smile on his lips and I feel like melting into my seat. Reiner has dimples, gorgeous, *gorgeous* dimples, and he doesn't smile very often so I always end up forgetting.

"You have that same look on your face when she lies about my cooking." He leaned back in his chair, still smiling.

"Pfftt, no. This is actually really great."

"Soleil."

I grabbed my water, drinking half of the glass, feeling that nice relief deep in my chest. "yeah it's terrible." My hands flew to my mouth, shocked by the words that left it.

"Not terrible, it's just... dry. Too bland." This is me sugarcoating. I'm being nice because I need his hospitality right now.

He laughed, "It's okay, you don't have to spare my feelings."

"The potatoes though," I shoved some in my mouth, "are *amazing!*"

That was in fact, true.

"Is that so?"

I nodded, eager. "It is so." I stared at my plate, frowning because I didn't realize when I went through my potatoes this quickly. I looked at the kitchen longingly, "are there any more potatoes left?"

"Yes." He said before standing up, grabbing my plate with him. I offered him a smile watching him go to the kitchen.

Reiner returned with my plate filled with potatoes, he must've trashed the chicken because it was no longer on my plate. Either way I was happy. The potatoes must've been air fried because they were both soft and crispy and the light taste of garlic was everything.

I was into my third bite when I realized there was nothing in front of Reiner, he was simply watching me eat. I tensed, with a mouthful of potatoes.

I used the fork to point at the empty spot in front of him, "where's your food?"

"You were right, the chicken was dry, I couldn't go on."

I pushed my plate of potatoes in the middle, "have some of my potatoes." I stabbed the contents while eating another cube of potato.

"It's fine."

"Reiner," I scowled, *"eat."*

The command had his eyebrows raised for a mere second, then he grabbed his fork stabbing the food for a bite. I smiled, then he smiled. We both faked a smile.

I helped Reiner with the table when we finished eating. We didn't talk much after, we just stared at each other while we ate — well, he stared at me eating with zero ounce of shame, while I cowered under his gaze, trying not to meet his gaze as I ate.

I've never had an issue with people staring at me, I've always liked the attention, from Luke or anyone else for that matter, but the way Reiner stares at me, has always been different — even when I thought he hated me, he always stares at me differently.

The way Reiner stares at me makes my palms sweaty, it makes

my heart beat irregularly. *Nervous.* I get completely nervous when he stares.

I placed the last plate in the sink, "I'll clean up." I turned on the faucet, already in search of the sponge.

Reiner grabbed my elbow, causing me to stop moving altogether. I swear I felt a small electric shock. The side of my body nearly pressed against his chest.

"It's fine, I got it. Just to go to bed." His voice is tired, *hoarse.*

I shook my head, a little breathless. "No, really I'm happy to-"

"I didn't know you had *chores.*"

My brows furrowed as I yanked my elbow free as I turned to face him. "I didn't know I had a *curfew,*" I cock my head to the side, the odd amusement look on his face had my blood boiling. I was a fool to think he makes me nervous.

No. Reiner makes me angry.

I don't usually argue about cleaning up — In fact I usually rejoice when people offer to do stuff for me. But he's done so much for me lately. It would make me feel a whole lot better if he just let me do something for once.

"Let's have wine."

It's random, but when I looked up at him, I could tell this was him trying to compromise, and it worked because my anger settled.

I nodded, "as long as you help me clean up." I offered him a polite smile.

"Okay." He whispered as his eyes met mine, but only for a second because they dipped to my lips. Subconsciously I liked my lips, and his eyes darkened with the small action.

I stood by the sink watching him grab two wine glasses. He placed them on the island table before strolling off in the direction of the living room, I'm guessing it's where he keeps the fancy wines.

I ran a hand through my hair only to realize it's still stuck on that messy bun and I'm no longer interested in touching it because I can realize how tangled it is.

I was wearing a long skirt. With a white rib tank, I didn't have any bra on because Reiner failed to pack me that. So the swell of my breast was damn near visible to anyone gifted with eyesight. safe to say I look like a hippie. Before I could even attempt to fix myself. Reiner came back into the room with a bottle of red wine, and I'm tempted to ask if drinking wine is some sort of sin.

He opened the bottle, pouring wine into both glasses. He sets the bottle down, turning around to face me with both glasses in his hands, handing me one.

"Thank you." I whispered, taking the wine in his hands.

After a glass of wine, we agreed on cleaning up together. Reiner said I was stubborn, and I said he was bossy. Now we're loading the dishwasher, after wiping the counter tops, and believe it or not Reiner actually fought me for the broom. I'm starting to think he's a clean freak.

I groaned, cursing under my breath, "your dishwasher doesn't like me very much."

"Yeah, there's a trick to it," he huffed moving towards me.

I tried to turn around to get a peek at him, but my eyes widened when he stopped behind me. I turned around with my temperature spiked up a little.

Reiner's body brushed against mine as he stood behind me, his scent was the tip of the iceberg, my head was already light and having him this near made it impossible for me to ignore whatever's been growing inside of me these past two days.

I let out a small breath feeling his hard chest against me, his warmth, his scent was so familiar to me. My fingers tightened around the edge of the counter, bracing myself.

"You have to really push it until you hear the click."

I gasped when he pushed the door closed, his body shoving mine forward. My heart was beating out of my chest when his arm dipped around my waist reaching for the counter top for a quick support. Something hard pressed against my ass and before I could feel it again he pulled away. My chest was rising and falling, my brain still trying to register what just happened.

My head was spinning, my mouth was dry, my heart was beating two beats faster than usual.

"Is it working?" I nearly jumped feeling his breath tickle my ear. Reiner was still behind me, his tall height hovering.

"Yea—" my voice was small, *small and weird.*

I turned around, because I'm curious. I'm very curious about what I've been feeling all day. And maybe it's the glass of wine I just had. Yeah it might explain the funny feeling in my stomach.

I took a hesitant step forward, closing the small gap between us. When I looked up his eyes were the darkest shade of blue, his plump lips parted. I sucked in a breath as I licked my own parted lips. The air was crispy cold around us and I could feel his warm body near mine as an armor.

His Adam apple bobbed when he swallowed. He raised his hand, cupping my cheeks. His hand glided to the side of my face, goosebumps decorated my skin. Everything felt so uneasy. I tilted my head back for a second. I closed my eyes feeling his thumb brush cheek.

The single touch, the single action was *everything*. I felt his touch with all my six senses. Whenever he touches me, I feel it *everywhere*. Reiner touches my skin, my soul. *Everything.*

I relax, I come undone.

His other hand cupped the back of my neck with such urgency, my eyes snapped open, finding his cloudy ones. He's freaking out, I can feel it. He's trying so hard not to do this, it hurts. *He's not sure.*

My eyes softened as I placed my hand over his, *"Reiner."* I nearly whimpered, my needs are so desperately obvious. I truly hope this provides him clarity.

He lets go. Reiner withdrew his hands away from me and I *almost* missed his touch.

He drew in short breath as he scratched the back of his neck, meeting my gaze again. "I have *Tangled* downloaded, if you want, we can watch it."

"You have *Tangled* downloaded?"

He smiled, "It's my all-time favorite movie."

I stared at him in disbelief, as he casually confessed his love for a *Disney* animation, "*Tangled* is your favorite movie?"

He looked at me like it was the only logical answer, "I have a seven year old daughter, I'm basically a *Disney* fan. Besides, Anna said I kinda look like Flynn."

With that information, I snorted. Shaking my head as I tried to hold in my laughter, "she lied to you. . . *bad*."

Reiner laughed, nodding along with my statement. I drank the rest of my wine, and he watched me empty the glass. I placed it against the marble counter. "Maybe next time?" I yawned.

Reiner let out a devastating breath, closing his eyes for a mere second. "Right. . . *you* should go to sleep." there's a look on his face I can't describe.

I nodded. I clench and unclench my hands. Nodding some more. "*Goodnight,* Reiner."

CHAPTER TEN

Soleil

I DREAMT OF REINER LAST NIGHT. I woke up breathless, my mind full of questionable thoughts. This feeling I thought would pass because I was foolish enough to think it was a result of drinking *one* glass of wine.

Only, it wasn't a hazy thought or feeling. That funny feeling lingers in my stomach still, even after waking up from the impossible effects of a single glass of wine.

I shuffled in bed, this empty room that somehow became familiar — I didn't want to say goodbye yet. I leave for home today. I'm going back next door. The storm finally passed, well at least it calmed down. The lights are back on, and I woke up to great signals. Multiple texts from Hayley are rolling on my screen, some that threaten to kill me because of me going *AWOL*. But most of them were just happy to hear that I wasn't alone.

It's a blessing Hayley didn't catch the food poisoning, God knows how'd she'd be able to take care of her sisters. I plan to see her tomorrow.

I haven't seen or talked to Reiner since he sent me to bed last night. I wish I could find a way to leave the house without ever seeing him, but not only that would be impossible but also rude — I just don't think I have it in myself to see him today and look him in the eyes after the dream I had last night.

Dreams I shouldn't be having about my nice, uninterested neighbor.

But I realize the sooner I leave, the sooner I get to hide in my house and avoid him for days. And maybe, *just maybe* — the attraction I feel towards him will go away. It has too. Reiner doesn't seem like an available man, he has a serious career, a kid, and an ex-wife, if I am correct. Nothing is ever simple with a combo like that.

I brushed my teeth and showered. I was merely rushing, packing as I got dressed. It didn't take long because the only things I had to collect were my clothes. After packing the bag, I made the bed. I'd change the sheets completely but that requires talking to Reiner — a small thing I can't afford to do right now. I'm scared he'll see right through me, or stare at me so intensively I'll end up saying things I shouldn't be saying.

I threw the bag over my shoulders as I exited the room, not sparring it glance as I closed the door behind me. My hair was all around my face, and the thoughts of stuffing it back into a ponytail was simply tempting. I love my hair so much it aggravates me sometimes.

I thought about relaxing it straight often, but I see these distant pictures of my mom with my dad at the house and we have the same hair — theres this fucked up little voice in my head that somehow convinced me to think my mom would've loved my hair as much as I do, and she'd wish for me to keep it as it is.

Sometimes, it drains me to take care of my hair.

But I only brushed a strand of my hair behind my ears as I descended the stairs — praying not to run into Reiner. I know now that's only wishful thinking because it's his house. And I'm the one who's attempting to sneak out like a thief in the night.

All my prayers ceased to an end when I spotted Reiner in the kitchen, a white mug in his hands, and for a second I thought of just walking past him, and somehow pretending to not spot him, but that would just be too cruel, and he's been really nice.

My body went still as my chest heaved as I took in the looks of him in front of me. His hair is wet, but this time he seems to be sweating. My mouth grew dry as I marveled at his body. The tight black shirt on him revealed *every* muscle on his body. Reiner is still too busy hydrating, still recovering from his morning run to notice me undressing him with my eyes, and I'm taking advantage of that. I continued to stare at him, hoping his clothes would just melt off as my heart raced out of my chest.

I swallowed the feelings.

Pushed the dreams in the back of my mind.

I cleared my throat, gaining the attention of my target. Reiner looked in my direction with curious blue eyes, a small smile was on its way to his lips but when his eyes landed on the bag at my side, his smile was quickly replaced with a subtle frown.

"Good morning." I smiled, watching Reiner finish his water with one last swallow. I want to laugh at this because it reminds me of the weeks he would stare at me until I said good morning, and even now, he still won't say it back.

Reiner sets his glass of water down, his body heaved with a sigh. His eyes found mine again, "you're leaving." He said as he crossed his arms, leaning against the counter.

I nodded, trying to keep eye-contact with him, but it's taking all of me to not stare at the rest of him. "The lights are back on."

He pushed his body off the counter and my eyes followed the movement like instinct. I want to scold myself but I'm amazed with the way his muscles flexed under such small action. I blinked collecting my thoughts — now realizing that Reiner was walking towards me.

He's an oxygen thief. He robbed me of my breath the second he stood in front of me, the dreams I was *not* supposed to have last night were playing more and more vividly in my head. *His hands.* Oh, God. His hands were reaching for me.

My eyes followed his hand as my chest heaved. My whole body tensed when Reiners fingers brushed my shoulder as he hooked his fingers under the straps of my bag, pulling it off my shoulders. His hand softly dropped with the weight. My body is still burning from the small touch. The weight of the bag was replaced by his light touch.

I glanced at my shoulder, his fingers are long gone, but I can still feel them linger against my shoulder, goosebumps threatening to rise on my skin. I released a soft breath as my gaze focused on his again, "Reiner—"

He swallowed, he blinked, *swallowed* again, "I'll walk you home."

I had no words for him, I could only nod.

I followed him outside, walking over his precious lawn as we made our ways towards my house.

When we reached my doorstep, I turned around to face him. A half force smile plastered on my face. "Thank you for taking care of me."

He nodded, didn't say a word, just nodded. I reached for my bag in his hands but he only pulled away. A small polite smile on his lips, "I should drop it off inside."

My brows pulled together, "what difference does it make?" I whispered, cocking my head to the side. "It's not heavy, I can carry it."

Truth. I didn't want him to invade anymore of my space, thoughts, anything. I was at my breaking point, and the more I interact with him — the more I break. I need to be quarantined with my feelings until they fade away. Until I'm able to look at Reiner and not feel my stomach curl every muscle.

His eyes bored into mine, "I'm well aware, Soleil."

I huffed in frustration. It's like he was already set on this, and no matter how many excuses I come with, he'd just dismiss them. I turned around to shove the key into the keyhole, twisting the lock open along with the door. I rolled my eyes one last time as I walked in the house, and an old smell of rain filled my senses.

I turned on the lights. It was a small victory for me that I have a little while left before paying the bills again. I head straight for the kitchen. Everything is still clean which is a good thing but I can imagine all the food I've lost because the fridge wasn't running for days.

I opened both the fridge and freezer. They both seem to be recovering just fine, the freezer is freezing things again, and the fridge is at the right temperature.

I released a breath as I turned around. Reiner walked me home. But the gentleman took the liberties to bring my bag inside for me. I imagine how incapable I must be. He dropped my bag on the couch a while ago and yet, he's still lingering over my shoulders.

Has the grumpy man grown attached? Funny of me to think such things. It requires *care* to grow attached to something. One of the qualities Reiner isn't fond of when it comes to me.

I could almost feel the heavy air around us, so *many thoughts*, so many unsaid things.

"This is ridiculous," I awkwardly laughed at my thoughts. Reiner however, was more lost than ever. I wanted to bite my tongue off but I was already talking, and what's the point of holding onto feelings for him if he isn't going to be aware of them? Or the fact that I wouldn't allow myself a chance to go through with this. We're both adults, we can be mature without acting like a couple of awkward teens.

I know myself, not telling him would be worse than telling

him.

"I'm just gonna go ahead and say it," I paused, taking a deep breath, gathering all the courage I can muster, throwing my pride out the window. I finally met Reiners eyes, and this time I held his gaze.

Reiner nodded, a small act of encouragement to get me talking, or maybe he's just curious. I could see the confused look on his face.

I placed a hand on the counter, bracing myself as the words rolled out of my mouth. "I think I'm *attracted* to you. I think I've been feeling that way for a long while now, but you were so mean and rude I managed to convince myself that I wasn't. And it worked — it worked for a while but then I was stuck with you for two days. You were nice to me, *so nice* to me."

His eyes softened as the words left my mouth. Whatever look this may be, I pray for anything but pity, but I could already feel myself relax a little. I was right, telling him would help make me feel less dense.

"You took care of me. You cooked for me, I was sick. *No one takes care of me when I'm sick.* and I know you probably aren't even feeling the same way about me, but I'm attracted to you Reiner. I wish I wasn't but I really am." I paused, catching my breath, *"attracted to you."*

Reiner is standing so still I'm afraid he's frozen. Or perhaps I scared him. Either way his face was blank — not a single emotion in sight, I don't know if he's just too shocked to react. Maybe he thought I was deranged. You give a woman shelter and she manages to develop *sexual* feelings. Yeah, I guess that can be a little mortifying.

I had to salvage this situation somehow, but somehow talking more seemed like a bright idea.

I took a step forward, Reiner and I were only at arms length. "I know you're saying it was an act of *kindness*, And even if you were doing this out of the kindness of your heart that would just be *cruel and heartless* because your actions did nothing but mess with my head."

There was a knock on the door and the little bubble around popped. Reiner was at least relieved of the interruption. When I didn't move, the knock on the door grew louder.

I huffed, "hold on that must be Hayley, I'm not done with you yet." I pointed a finger at him, "I'll be back." I really wish I didn't sound as threatening as that sentence came out.

I pointed for him to stay there one last time before I walked towards the door.

The last thing I'd want him to do is to escape this conversation, leaving all my thoughts unanswered. Oh, I do think he'd love to do that. To exit the room without saying a single word. It's his favorite game to play.

"Hayley, honey did you surviv-" I swung the door open, excited enough to see Hayley, only it *wasn't* Hayley.

"God, *Leil.* You're okay."

My brows furrowed, as I stared at Luke. he truly looked a mess. I refuse to believe he was all that rattled on my account. "Of course I am, *Luke.*" I finally answered, after that long painful pause. *It was just rain.* I can't stop thinking about how I *never* thought of him during the storm. I never worried for him — and here he is *worried* for me.

He pushed himself inside my house, hugging me in the process. This is unexpected, so unexpected. In fact I want to send him away. *Right now.* Because Reiner is in the kitchen waiting for me to get back to him.

"I'm just so glad to see you okay," he squeezed my shoulders one last time.

"Yea, I'm glad you're okay too." *at least that wasn't a lie.*

Luke pulled away, and he has those same *hopeful* brown eyes he has every time he proposes for us to get back together. It's never good. I used to like it then, but it's not working right now.

He smiled, so I smiled. A painful, *forced* smile. "The storm made me realize a lot of things." He began.

Oh no.

"I missed you so much, did you miss me?"

"Luke—"

His hands cupped my cheeks, and I felt like I'm suffocating. Drowning under the wrong touch. Luke's hands no longer feel familiar on my skin, instead they felt foreign.

The guy is still cradling me, struggling to see all the signs of discomfort. "I know, I know. But we can work this time." He pushed his face forward a little, and I pulled away just in time to prevent us from kissing.

"Luke?!"

When I finally broke free from his touch, I backed away.

Standing several feet away from him. Luke looks like the small action broke him. Almost like he couldn't believe I was denying him of me.

He shook his head in disbelief, "I thought—"

I raised my hand up, stopping the explanation from leaving his mouth. *You should never think, but should always ask.*

I wrapped my arms around me, "please leave, I'll call you later."

He's embarrassed. And I feel so guilty to ever cause him to feel that way, but the blame is not entirely on my shoulders. He was only thinking of him. Like he always used to. He thinks if he wants me, *then I must want him too.*

"Really Leil, I didn't know—"

"I'll call you later, Luke."

He nodded, and I closed the door — after locking the door behind me, I turned around only to find Reiner a few feet away from me. And I curse myself for ever forgetting that he could've eavesdropped.

I hung my head low, "How much did you hear?"

"All of it."

Oh. Reiner never struggled with being Honest. It was one of the few things about him I found aggravating. All I could do was nod and swallow the embarrassment. My cheeks grew hot by the second.

In less than an hour I managed to embarrass myself in more ways possible than I would believe I could ever. First was my weird attraction confession towards him for reasons God, knows what —

and now this? Him witnessing the most out of character moment my ex has been.

Just when I figured it was time to say something because I was awkwardly standing by the door. Reiner beat me to it by taking a few steps forward, closing the gaps between us.

Right now he's staring at me, like the first time he ever met me. His face strained. So many unpleasant emotions, and I just knew whatever's coming out of his mouth won't do me any good.

He sighed as his shoulders tensed, "Soleil, I suggest we forget everything you said."

That was his proposal? To forget about it?

I frowned as I shook my head, "no, I don't want to do that." him asking me to just try and forget about all the things I confessed might just be one of the cruelest things he could say in this situation.

"Soleil, please." He took another step forward and my heart was full all over again. Ready to leap out of my chest of course.

"Please tell me that I haven't been imagining all of this, it wasn't all in my *head* right?"

He cupped my cheeks, and my skin was hot, and I'm destroyed, shattered, *ruined.*

His skin is becoming my own. I can feel the weight of comfort his single touch has over me. This whole infatuation has gotten even more dangerous for me. Everytime I grant him another second with me, his power over me grows stronger without even my knowledge of it.

"Soleil, let's *please* forget it."

My shoulders dropped as I swallowed, embarrassed, disappointed. "*Sure,* okay. I'll pretend like this never happened."

Without a question his hands dropped so quickly one could only guess my skin burned him. Reiner didn't spare me a glance. He was too busy reaching for the door behind me — in such a hurry to leave.

Frankly, I've been embarrassed far too much this morning to even care to allow myself to feel more embarrassed — besides some fucked up voice in my head is doing a damn good job at convincing me that this was exactly what I deserved.

I wiped my cheeks, it was wet and foreign. Something I forgot I was capable of doing. I couldn't even cry at my dad's funeral, but I'm crying because the man I'm *so* attracted to isn't reciprocating those same *dirty* feelings for me.

I should laugh at myself. *This is laughable.*

I fished my phone out of my pockets. I know I should be updating myself with all my assignments but I can't help but to look for comfort the only place I can get it. I released a soft breath — I felt free. My heart is no longer tugging to be near anyone. This is good, I should be grateful.

I'm doing us both a great favor — I can't imagine starting *anything* that would possibly end well with Reiner. So, In a way I should thank him for saving me from his complications.

Calling Luke is me following his orders, erasing everything that was built in those last three days.

CHAPTER ELEVEN

Reiner

A SLOW WIDE GRIN spread across my face after closing the door, but it was quickly replaced by a frown when I was reminded of my answer. *I asked her to forget about it.*

At that moment, the second she told me she was attracted to me, all I wanted to do was to take her lips, to seal her confession, to prove to her I felt the same. But I couldn't just do that, I come with too many complications, too many warnings. In a different world where I wasn't who I am right now and Soleil still wanted me the way she does now… she would not be so disappointed with me as much as she is right now.

For selfish reasons, I want her to keep trying, to keep reminding me. Maybe then, I'll lose all of my self-control and cave in, somehow make it all work.

The reminders of my complications killed all of my hopeful thoughts when I saw Noa's call pulled into my driveway. Today is the first day we've had an almost clear day and she's already at my doorstep.

Her eyes locked with mine as she watched me walking around the little fence, obviously coming from someone else's house. She glanced at the house then at me with a careful look in her eyes, she said something then smiled and her back door opened as Anna hopped out.

"Daddy!" she screamed before she rammed me. I laughed as I caught her, the wind was knocked out of my chest but it was worth it. She climbed around me like she always does as she giggled.

Noa's heels clicked before she came into view, too afraid to stand on the grass so she stood near her car. "Don't kill him, he's all you've got." she said.

I secured Anna over my shoulders with a grunt, "don't worry, Princess. Daddy's strong."

She screamed when I pretended to almost drop her — her embrace tightened, "mom will be very mad if you drop me!" she laughed.

I laughed along with Anna catching a small smile on Noa's face, she looked at us like she always used to when we were to-gether. It ruins my mood sometimes, to think about all we had — how much she destroyed. All we could've had, like this moment could've been different.

My throat went bone dry as the humor in me faded, my smile replaced with a frown, and I think Noa caught on too because she shifted, fixing her bag over her shoulder as she cleared her throat.

"We should go inside, it's getting chilly out."

"Noooo." Anna whined when I placed her back on the ground. She took my hand, frowning but I only smiled because she's not getting to me this time. Her cute little face scrunched up into what I'm guessing is an angry face.

"Once I win my next wrestling match, you'll be my mule for a day."

I frowned, "a mule? Why not a horse?"

Noa laughed, only a few steps ahead of us, eavesdropping. "Mules are better than horses, more *tamed*." she glanced back at me over her shoulders.

"Yeah, they don't run away when they hear a branch snap." Anna added.

"Ah, so you guys have been learning about… *mules*." I won't question it because it is… educational. I think I might be a bit bummed that I was out of the mule loop.

Anna tugged my hand, "I want one for christmas."

I laughed, using my free hand to ruffle her hair, "not a chance." all the hope in her eyes faded and she took a few steps closer towards Noa. I can only guess she's reporting me to HR. I'm standing my ground this time.

The door was already unlocked when Noa opened it, and I followed her inside. She held Anna's hand while they went off to the living room to discuss a mule matter. I followed them closely, leaning against the doorframe with my arm crossed, eavesdropping.

"I told you to butter him up first." Noa shook her head with a small smile. Even she couldn't take this seriously.

Anna's head hung low as her shoulders sagged, "why can't you tell him?" she attempted to whisper very horribly. In fact they were both bad at whispering. Only Noa was pretending to be bad, she was doing it for my sake. Entertaining me.

As if she could read my thoughts, her eyes met mine, and she winked at me. I didn't react, but I watched her tuck a stand of her brown hair behind her ear as she crouched down to Anna's level.

"Daddy doesn't listen to mom anymore, but I'll try." She smiled.

Anna smiled, "really?"

Noa nodded, "yeah, I'll talk to him," she cupped Anna's face into her hand and brought her head low as he kissed her forehead, "now go get some ice cream and feel better."

I smiled at the scene, watching Anna make a run for it. Once she was out of the room, my attention was back on Noa.

"She's not getting a mule, or a pony, or a horse. We don't even have a stable, or any land."

Noa held her hand up as she stood closer in front of me, "I know, Reiner." she sighed, running a hand through her hair, "But she's a seven year old who watches too many cartoons."

I nodded, "she won't understand, she'll just hate me. Great."

Noa smiled, "you're adorable, but knowing Anna she'll change her mind about her christmas gift soon."

I don't know what to make of the first part of her statement. I don't want to be adorable. Not to her at least.

I sighed, "you? The drinking?"

"Wouldn't you like to know." she said flatley.

"Actually, yes. I would like to know if you've been drinking or not."

"Oh, fuck off." Noa rolled her eyes. Already walking away from me. "You always do this, Reiner. I was just trying to be nice and give you Anna for the rest of the week because I know with the storm recently you've been missing her."

I followed her closely, with my voice kept in a hushed tone, "Yeah, very nice of you, but I don't trust you anymore Noa, so I'll always have questions."

"Well guess what, we're not together anymore and I don't owe you answers to the parts of my life you're no longer involved in!" she practically screamed the words, and we were too close to the kitchen, where Anna was eating ice-cream. I glanced at Anna, watching Noa fidget in front of me.

I grabbed Noas' arm, harshly pulling her outside the house as I closed the door behind me.

"I just ask if you've been drinking. That affects Anna, which is my concern."

"Jesus Christ, Reiner, No. I haven't been drinking, or sleeping around because I know you wonder about that too. I'm with Tony."

I frowned, "yes. I'm well aware you were completely *sober* when you slept with him."

I didn't realize I was still holding her arm until she pulled herself away from me. Angry at me. Somehow, everytime we have a disagreement, she's always the one mad at me. I'm in the wrong.

Even after she cheated, she was mad at me. *Angry that I walked in.*

Noa placed a hand on her hips as she raked her hair with her free hand, "I'm gonna go now." she mumbled, "enjoy your time with your daughter." she said as she made her way to her car.

It sounds like a threat everytime she says those words. It scares me to think that one of these moments might be the last time I see Anna. Because at Any moment, if Noa feels like it, she'll disappear.

CHAPTER TWELVE

Soleil

"FORGET ABOUT REINER, he probably had an erectile dysfunction anyways."

"Hayley!" I gasped, holding back the laugh I so wanted to bark out.

"It wouldn't be a surprise." She shrugged.

I lightly shook my head at her. Reiner might be old but he's not *that* old. I told Hayley all about the highlights from my embarrassment. And she did nothing but relieve me — she made light of the situation which was all I needed.

I did my part, it's embarrassing but now I don't have to wonder about him anymore. I know where his head's at. I do wish the moment was a lot less embarrassing, but I think I just need to keep my mind off of it.

Hayley pouted, staring at me with mischief in her eyes. "His loss." she whispered, wrapping her arms around me as kissed my cheek.

I groaned, pushing her weight off of me with a small smile on my face. "It's not *that bad,* I think I just wanted to hookup."

"Oh." she frowned, "Josie is literally only a few minutes away, why didn't you just... pick someone?"

I cringed at her wording, she made the guys that hang out at Josie's sounded like a bunch of prostitutes. I'm pretty sure half of the guys that hang out there are there to pick up girls, but still. It sounded very wrong.

"I didn't want just *anyone*. . . I wanted Reiner, and there was a storm, smarty."

Hayley nodded, "Okay, this was an easy fix, why didn't you just..." I watched her rub three of her fingers together, but I couldn't understand what was happening until she used two fingers and pointed at her vagina.

I gasped, catching her hand, covering it with mine as I shook my head. "I was at his house!"

Hayley only stared at me, then blinked, "sooooo?"

"Oh God." I laughed as I covered my face with both hands, "you have no shame Hayley." I muffled the words out through my palms.

She only shrugged as she stood up from the couch, "I say let's go to Josie's and drink our weights away."

"Josie's open already?"

"Leil, I don't think they ever closed."

124

It's been a week since the storm happened. Weirdly enough I haven't seen Reiner since. I've been in the house because college closed due to storm difficulties, but we go back on Monday though. I've mostly been stressing about all the internship papers I've been catching up on, almost none of the pay, but it was expected — my decision wasn't finalized.

I got back to work almost immediately only because they needed help with the cleanup and I always needed the extra money.

I visited Hayley and I've been stuck on her couch since. With a lot of things off my mind I manage to do half of the assignments, I just need a statement because I am a journalist and not everything on the paper can be based on my opinion.

With school opening back up on Monday, I really need to secure myself an interview with the woman from the accident.

"I'm thinking of interviewing the woman and her lawyer, and you should interview the other woman and her lawyer." I propped myself on the couch, facing the kitchen just to catch a glimpse of Hayley.

She groaned, her head hanging low, "I just wanted to get drunk." She stared at me, "why can't we get drunk?"

"Because it's Sunday, and we have no one to drive us back home." I paused, "let's not forget the fact that we have a lecture tomorrow morning."

"Yeah whatever, what about Luke though?"

"What about him?"

Hayley fixed me a look, filled with warning and disappointment. "you were talking to him this morning."

"We hooked up." I blurted out, "before I came to see you."

She shook her head at me as her tongue clicked, "back to the rabbit hole you go."

I huffed, my shoulders sagging as I placed a hand on the couch — caressing the surface, too nervous with the topic. "It's not a rabbit hole. We're *friends.*"

"*Special* friends."

"Ew." I cringed, "It sounds so perverted that way."

Hayley did a *'duh'* face, "I think it is."

I rolled my eyes at Hayley before turning around facing my computer again, sure I had a fallout. I was embarrassed by the way Reiner rejected me, so I ran to the one person I knew that wouldn't reject me.

Immediately after it happened I felt guilty, I almost cried — I didn't because I knew it would bruise his ego, and we're not to-gether anymore. I don't want to be the one to console him. I told him it was truly our last time and reminded him that it doesn't change our friendship.

Luke and I have been talking regularly ever since, he's been texting me any cringe meme that makes him think of me and I do the same. It's working. We might finally just be friends.

"We're just friends Hayley." I grumbled out, and this time even Hayley doesn't seem to care to comment on it.

CHAPTER THIRTEEN

Soleil

THE ASSIGNMENT IS DUE IN JUST A WEEK. I still haven't got a hold over the woman who's been in the accident. Hayley interviewed the other women last week. I feel like I'm the only one so behind like this.

I ended up in my kitchen not so long ago, with my thoughts scattered all over the place. I forgot why I ever stepped foot in my kitchen. I finished the paper leaving out only the parts that's supposed to involve statements from the woman and her lawyer — I think I came out here for a celebratory drink?

I still had some of the beer Reiner left here from weeks ago — I couldn't drink enough to raid a whole pack of beers, and I do hope these beers didn't come with a close expiration date. Today though, celebrating was in order. I finished-*ish* a paper that I've been ignoring for days. The hard part is over. I only have to go through the interview.

I wanted chocolate right now, but I doubt I have any. I checked everywhere in the kitchen where I could've possibly hid some for a quick grab but nothing. No chocolate, just beer.

I popped the beer can open and before the rim of the beer could touch my lips there was a knock on the door — I doubt it's Hayley because I just spent a whole weekend with her mopping over Reiner. I don't think she wants to hear me speak anymore.

I took another sip at the bitter beer anyway before placing it on the counter wiping my hands over my jeans in the process. The bitter taste of the beer grew to my liking though.

I opened the door, greeting the last person I expected to see. Reiner. He's in his casual clothes, a suit. His casual clothes seem to just be suits and ties that are way too loose. His hair disheveled. For whatever reason he looked stressed — very stressed. The dark circles around his eyes were more than visible, and he somehow made it all work. He seemed very *well-put-together* for someone who isn't.

Reiner sucked in a breath, seeming pleasingly overwhelmed. "Hi." he nearly whispered the word.

I wanted to roll my eyes because he *confuses* me. *Aggravates me.*

"Hey."

"One of my clients just called and my daughter is here, but her babysitter isn't available. I don't know anyone else to ask." Reiner, Reiner. Always so serious, he never fails to get to the point of any conversations — no going around a bush, no coaxing.

"Wow." I mouthed the word. I blinked as I placed a hand on my waist, "are you asking me to *babysit?*"

"I'm asking very *nicely.*"

He must really think the world truly does revolve around him, that everyone is supposed to bend backwards whenever he wants something.

Like now, the way he asked left me no room to negotiate. He got his answer before he even knocked.

It's not like I'm busy, and I'd be an ultimate bitch for saying no to him when weeks ago he was the nicest person on earth to me — I guess right now, that's who I wanted to talk to. The better —*nicer*— version of Reiner that seems to exist only inside of a bubble, outside of the real world.

I sucked in a breath as I nodded, "of course."

Things are moving so anxiously fast there's no room for awkwardness.

"Great, just come over. Anna's watching TV right now, and I won't be gone for long. The door is open, make yourself at home."

Before I could even get a word in, Reiner had already reached his car. I released a small breath as I walked back into the house, grabbing my phone off the counter. I walked back outside, closing the door behind me.

I didn't know why but I figure knocking on the door was far less creepy than just walking up on her saying *"yeah hey, I'm babysitting you while your dad is gone."*

I prefer waiting behind the door, unless of course she was

raised to not open the door for strangers when her parents are gone. But of course she wasn't raised that way because the little angel opened the door.

I smiled at her when she stared at me confusingly. He didn't tell her he'd leave before rushing off to my doorstep?

I smiled softly, "you weren't supposed to open the door."

Anna gave me a confusing look, "but you knocked."

I showed myself in, "yeah, I know, but I could've been a killer. Reiner never said anything about the door? Stranger danger?"

She laughed as she closed the door behind me, locking the door. "Did you just call my dad by his name?"

I faked a gasp, "oh my God, I did, didn't I?"

She laughed again as she came into view, "it's okay, you can't call him dad either."

I nodded at that because that is *very* true. Not after the ways I thought of him. I followed Anna with a heavy breath, lately all of them seem to belong to Reiner.

"Seriously, Anna, don't open the door for strangers, okay?"

"You're not a stranger." she said.

I blinked, "I'm not?"

She moved her body a little as she fought her way to sit fully on the couch. She glanced at me, "you're dad's neighbor."

For some *crazy* reason I had hoped Reiner talked about me, *outloud. . .* to other people. Crazy, *crazy* thoughts. It was even crazier that I care about little things like this considering I swore I didn't care anymore. I got rejected and I was being a gracious loser.

"Yeah, you're right." I fixed her a serious look, "but don't open the door for anyone else okay?"

"Cross my heart." her lengthy little fingers motioned as she crossed her chest with her index.

"So I'll be babysitting you while your dad is gone."

"I know."

"He told you already?"

"Yeah, he said he'd go get his cool neighbor."

I bit back a smile, this is so stupid because I'm feeling like a teenager all over again, "He thinks I'm cool?"

She laughed a little, a small smile. "No, I'm sure he just said that so I would behave."

Kids man, so brutal.

"Will you behave?"

"Will you be cool?"

I tried to shrug nonchalantly but it looked like I was pushing something off my shoulders, "*I am* cool."

I was not cool.

Reiner got back home and caught me trying to dispose of a pot of burnt brownies. Anna suggested we bake, she and her dad had bought the ingredients for a while now, they just never cooked it.

No wonder.

I was an idiot for agreeing to bake. I could only cook a few things or just pre-heat already baked foods, like pies.

The smoke detector was blasting through the house. Even Reiner was alarmed because he was in the kitchen in an instant. I could already imagine the disappointment — he left me with his daughter for less than two hours and I nearly burnt his house down.

Reiner grabbed one of the towels from the apron — which was on me. I forced a small smile on my face when he looked at me, "I'm so sorry."

"It's fine."

I watched him vent the smoke detector until it stopped screaming, I never realized Anna was laughing until the house fell silent and her laughter filled the room. The camera in her hand was pointed at me.

She insisted on recording the whole baking process, and I complied with that too. It was entertaining talking to the camera like it was a live audience.

Anna never stopped filming until her dad crouched to her level, waving at the camera. "What did you have Soleil do, Anna?" he said through a soft smile as he leaned forward, kissing her cheek.

My heart couldn't handle all of this. I've never hung out without anyone older than me for so long I forgot how mature people could truly be. By just this small interaction I could confidently say Reiner is a better father than half of the fathers on planet earth.

"We tried to bake brownies." Anna said.

Reiner stood up straight, examining the messy kitchen, "yeah, I gathered that."

My head hung low in shame, I should've known better than

to trust myself.

"Soleil." Reiner called out.

My brows shot up as I looked up at him, the small smile on his lips died when he noticed the dull expression on my face. He tilted his head to the side examining me.

"It's just a mess," he said in a soft tone.

I nodded, I pushed my body forward grabbing the plates on the counter, and Reiner was quick to lend a hand — memories from the night we were in this very kitchen drinking wine tortured me.

We were so close then, *we are so close now.*

Anna closed the camera, setting it on the edge of the island table, "I'm going to watch TV." she said.

"Okay, honey." Reiner pushed the camera more onto the table as he turned back to face me and handed me the rest of the plates.

I placed them on the sink, rinsing them to place them in the dishwasher. Reiner was moving behind me, wiping down the counters. I could feel it when his elbow brushed against back. Or when his arm brushes against my shoulder.

He drove me insane.

Alas, he spoke. "Thank you."

I cleared my throat, "it's nothing."

★·☆·★

After cleaning up I thought he'd kick me out but he hadn't yet. Instead, we made uncomfortable small talk.

I knew he said to forget about my confession but how could I when I was the one humiliated.

My eyes were glued on his face, his perfect, *perfect* face. Even with his hair all shaggy agaisnt his forehead he still looked *perfect.* Even with the dark circles under his eyes he was *still* perfect. Reiner was easily the most *gorgeous* guy I've ever seen.

Jawline so defined it could cut.

Reiner stared at me like I stared at him and it confused me so much. He studied me, *noticed* me.

I shuffled around before finally forming a thought.

"Anna wrestles?" I asked, I already knew the answer because Anna told me already and because the first day I stepped into his house I snooped and noticed the schedule on his fridge which held a wrestling match for Anna.

Reiner nodded like a proud father, looking over his shoulder just to peek at Anna in the living room. "very good at wrestling."

"Anna!" he called, the smile still glued on his face.

There was this constant happiness that radiated off of him and I know the source was Anna. *It was so pure.*

When Anna came to the kitchen, Reiner tugged her towards him and they both instantly smiled, I almost felt left out.

"Tell Soleil how good you are at wrestling."

Anna's eyes flashed with something that looked a lot like mischief. "I got a wrestling match coming soon, but my dad refuses to practice with me." Anna looked at her dad with guilty eyes hoping to trip him into agreeing.

His eyes softened with amusement, "I'll crush you." Reiner

said, his eyes pleading with hers.

"I'll do it." I offered. It was very random, "Yeah, I used to wrestle too." I paused for a second, "I can't exactly wrestle you Anna, but your dad will do."

"Really?" That seemed to grab both of their intentions.

"Yeah, I was always good enough." I mumbled, as the only memories filled my head — I wouldn't go out on a limb and say I truly enjoyed wrestling but there were times when it was *fun*. Last time I wrestled I was a sophomore.

I pushed my shoulders back, and looked at Reiner in the eye, "I can take you." I challenged.

Reiner raised a daring brow, "I'll crush you."

"I'll survive."

"Soleil—"

"What's wrong?" I smiled lazily, "are you scared that I'll win?"

"No—"

"Chicken!" Anna butted in. And she placed her hands under her armpit imitating a chicken as she made the noises. I smiled at Anna joining her in the mockery.

"Fine, let's wrestle."

I stared at Anna before offering her a high five. We were both smiling like two idiots following Reiner into a room I didn't even knew existed until now. The room was nearly empty, but there were a few toys around and a weight scale on the floor, along with a few small dumbbells on the floor. The huge mat on the floor was what took so much space — this room was designed for Anna, for her to practice.

"I'll be the referee." Anna blew a whistle and I almost went deaf.

I smiled in triumph as I rolled my sleeves up a bit, bouncing on my legs. It felt as if I was getting ready for a boxing match, but I was simply getting my blood flowing as Anna and Reiner moved the mat to the center of the empty room.

We stood in the middle of the mat. And Anna blew the whistle again, this time Reiner and I shook hands before circling each other.

This felt ridiculous, because Reiner was tall and large he could easily reach for me if he wanted to but it seemed like he wanted to make me suffer.

Without me remembering my brain seemed to be doing a fine job so far, I lightly slapped Reiner in the head and he dipped low seconds later, one of his knees was close to the ground. He was trying to get an opening to body slam me to the ground. But whenever he reached for me, I swat his hands away.

We locked eyes as we circled each other again, something in his eyes that kept telling me to forfeit — I was not a sore loser but towards Reiner I would be.

When I got lost inside of my head for a little longer than usual Reiner reached forward and actually got ahold of me as he wrapped both of his hands around my shoulders. I tried to stand my ground and tried not to move, but the man was so big his weight was fighting mine to move. And I was struggling to stay in the simple position.

I reached forward too and wrapped my arms around his neck

as I pulled his weight down a little. Anna blew the whistle and we both pulled away quickly. I tried to catch my breath because Reiner actually did have the muscles to crush me.

He didn't look out of breath, for the most part he just looked bored and *flustered.*

The whistle was blown again, and we reached for each other almost too quickly — in the same position Reiner added a little more force into his actions and pulled me down closer against him. When he finally dipped low, I dipped with him and he flipped — *us*— to the ground.

His large hands landed on my shoulder before I could process anything he flipped me around pushing me against the ground as he pinned me backwards. I tried to wiggle out of his hold, but he held me tighter, leaving me with no space to wiggle. I couldn't budge an inch. My chest heaved.

Annas' voice was faint as she counted from five to one. I could barely pay attention — overlooked by a thousand tiny little cells in my body going crazy over a human touch.

Reiners' body was on top of mine and his mouth was so close to my ears I couldn't seem to breathe.

"I won." He whispered.

I swallowed, biting back down the unsettling feeling in my stomach. Reiner was still pinning me down, his legs were wrapped around mine and the bastard was only using one hand to hold both of my hands above my head.

A cocky grin spread across his face, flashing me his cute dimples. I was way too into him to let him hold me down like this for this long.

"Ow, ow, ow!" I cried in pain under him.

His brows furrowed, his grin was instantly replaced by a look of care on his face, "shit."

His body propped on top of mine as he made a move to get off and I launched myself forward and pushed him on his back on the mat, flipping myself over him as I straddled his lap. I held both of his hands next to his head, and I knew he was allowing me this win right now because there was no way in hell where I could actually pin him.

Reiners' blue eyes pierced through mine, and I watched his eyes trail down from my face to my neck, down to my chest — my breathing seemed to have quickened, matching his. His nose flared and his jaw clenched. His eyes seemed to remain glued to the part where I was straddling his lap.

"This doesn't count," he swallowed, "Anna already blew the whistle."

I leaned forward and my chest met his as I smiled, *"sore loser."* I mouthed.

"Cheater." He mouthed back.

And it hurt like hell talking to him like this knowing that my body was burning for him, and he didn't feel a fraction of what I was feeling. I wanted to remind him that we were not supposed to be this close but I remembered we were only doing this to entertain Anna.

Anna blew the whistle again, gaining our attention. I pulled back a little and finally got off of him.

"You crushed me." I groaned.

"I said I would." He said as he stood back up. Reiner offered me a hand and I blinked a few times before I found the courage to place my hand in his.

The second my hand touched his grip tightened — Reiner let out a ragged breath as he stared at our hands. He cleared his throat before he pulled me up in one swift motion. I was rammed into his chest, and his scent clouded my head.

"Dad won, but it wasn't a fair match." Anna frowned as she shook her head at Reiner.

At least someone was on my side.

"I second that."

"In all fairness I never thought it was a good idea." Reiner added.

"You should come to my match on friday—"

Reiner cleared his throat, "Anna. . ." he glared at her.

My lips formed into a thin line. Everything felt awkward.

"Oh, I'm working on friday." I shuffled, "and I have to get home soon. . ."

I could tell when the fun was over, when the music stopped and everyone headed home. This is it, the music stopped playing, the party was over. Things were starting to get awkward again, and it was my job to prevent it from getting too bad — I was the only one suffering the consequences anyways.

"I- uh, I'll walk you home." Reiner offered.

I pulled my lips into a thin line, "I live right next door."

Reiner closed his eyes, then let out a ragged, tiring breath.

Too exhausted to even fight me on this. *"Soleil, will* you just let me walk you home without any protesting?"

My shoulder dropped, "okay." It was tiring to argue with him when all I wanted to do was the opposite.

"Okay." I mumbled. Staring straight ahead because it was better than staring at him.

CHAPTER FOURTEEN

Soleil

"THANKS." I whispered under my breath once we reached my house, I opened my door and expected him to do a 360 and leave but he didn't. Instead I heard his footsteps right behind me — on my tail. This is very much possible because this is Reiner we're talking about.

I crossed my arms over my chest before turning to face him. Reiner sucked in a breath as if the sight of me really did something to him like he does to me. I don't think I've ever seen Reiner outside at night. Under the moonlight, when his blue eyes become dark. I'm annoyed at myself because I'm beginning to realize I've given him too much power.

I've never been shy about my feelings, so I never thought of the consequences that would follow after confessing to him.

"Soleil." he whispered, taking another step towards me.

I tried not to react when he used my name the way he did. With memories from minutes ago, goosebumps were crawling over my skin, my head was spinning with too many possibilities. All of this suffering, just because I've developed a stupid infatuation with him, and being near him made it worse than it already was.

Reiner fucking confuses me, one minute hes nice the next he's telling me how much he doesnt like the idea of being my friend or the fact that he doesn't eve seem to like me as a person. He's hot and cold and it sends me all the wrong signals.

"Reiner. . ." I began to speak but I was quickly silenced when he grabbed a couple strands of my hair with two fingers, just staring at them intensively. My lips remained parted as I studied the look on his face

His eyes finally met mine, and he seemed to be dazed, *hypnotized.*

"You're *all* I think about." He whispered, moving closer towards me. The space between us was barely there now.

My body froze as my brows furrowed. I want to break our eye contact and look away, to finally breathe, but he has me hypnotized, anticipating his next few words.

I audibly gasped when his hand dipped into my hair, his thumb aligned against my jaw as he tilted my head back. *Holy shit.* Reiner clenched his jaw before releasing a breath.

I swallowed, "what are you doing?"

His eyes dipped to my lips for a split second before he could find my gaze again. His eyes softened and my whole body melted.

142

"Just a taste." he whispered, *"please."*

I tried to speak but I was at a loss for words, but I could tell he understood the ways my body trembled for him. Only then, his soft lips met mine.

The moonlight shines over us, but it felt like the light brightened when Reiner kissed me. Something straight out of a movie. His lips felt soft against mine, fragile. All the knots in my stomach tightened. I pushed my body closer against his as I held his bicep. His breath grew short as his lips pressed against mine, this time harder.

I have to stop myself from squirming. Our kiss felt like what every first kiss should feel like. Soft delicate skin, blissful embraces, racing heartbeats, jolting concoctions of emotions — and I wanted more.

Reiner pulled away a little, his forehead against mine, our lips seconds away from meeting again. I closed my eyes as my breath hitched, too nervous to even look at him. Everything with Reiner always feels unsure, and I didn't want to scare him off now that we've just shared a kiss.

His other hand cupped the other side of my cheek and my eyes snapped open, meeting his. He looked so soft, I wanted to feel his face too. Everything is soft about Reiner under the moonlight.

"It's *difficult* to talk to you because you're all I think about." He said those same cruel words again, and the world is spinning. I have nothing to hold onto.

"I am *attracted* to you.'

wasn't that good news? Then why did he say it like I just ruined his favorite suit.

I wrapped both of my hands around his arms as I shook my head, "we don't have to define anything right now."

Reiner only pulled me closer, stealing all of my oxygen in the process. I wonder if he feels exactly what I feel for him, a bunch of feelings I can't push away, I can't ignore them. They demand to be felt. There's a pause between us and I don't know why.

My whole body is screaming; *KISS ME AGAIN!*

My lips parted as I released a soft breath. Reiner is looking down at me with soft eyes, he's calm and quiet — his eyes flickering from my eyes to my lips. I am burning under him, my skin keeps catching on fire under his touch.

Luke who I've dated for months never managed to ignite me the way Reiner. A single word, a single look, a single touch will set me on fire — if I'm not careful Reiner's touch might become my kryptonite.

I closed my eyes as I leaned my head into his hands, getting lost in the soft touch. It's the small things like this that confuses me the most.

"Don't do that." He tilted my head back as my eyes snapped open. He smiled as he looked into my eyes, "I think the worst thing you could ever do to me is not looking at me." He brushed his lips against mine, kissing me again.

I was still so confused by his statement when he kissed me, but my thoughts vanished hearing a groggy groan vibrate through his lip. This time our kiss was more desperate.

My little wildflower heart was beating too quickly, too excited

— welcoming this fresh new wave of feelings. *Needs.* I want him more than I've ever wanted anyone.

This is *cruel. This feeling, it's cruel.*

His lips were so soft against mine, my body was immobilized and I couldn't move. Reiners' hands cupped the back of my head as he kissed me. Slow and desperate. I move in sync with him, kissing him as desperately as I can.

His tongue brushed against my lower lips, once. . . twice. He was asking for an entrance. I opened my mouth a little and Reiner wasted no time to push his tongue into my mouth. I clutched his shirt, fisting my hands each time his tongue brushed mine. The soft sweet actions make me go crazy — it's like I've never been kissed before, at least not like this.

I seemed to gain mobility again when Reiner pulled away just a little and I never realized I was holding my breath until I was gasping for air.

"You said to forget." I whispered, tilting my chin up, meeting him in the middle, our lips only a hair away.

He grinned, flashing me his dimples and my eyes softened at the sight. "You can forget if you want." He said.

"I just want you to remember this."His head dipped lower and his lips brushed against my cheek, his head dipped lower again until I felt his breath fan over my jaw and collarbone. I stopped breathing when I felt his lips on my neck.

Soft, warm and wet. His lips alone made me feel millions.

Reiner's lips are on my neck — he laid a sweet soft kiss until I felt his teeth graze my skin a little. My hands jumped to his shoulders for support, my eyes fluttered closed and the sensation curled all the way down deep in my spine. *Down between my legs. . .* My heart was threatening to jump out of my chest.

I've felt hundreds of kisses but never one like this.

He let out a breath and his hot breath hit my neck causing me to shift my weight, my skin growing sensitive. Reiner slowly pulled away kissing the side of my lips — when I turned my head to really kiss him, Reiner pulled away.

Fucking tease.

I looked up at him through hooded eyes, hungry for anything he's willing to offer.

This time Reiner swiped my lower lips with his thumb, his eyes glued on them — the painful expression on his face was so much more pleasing. I came alive under him. Nothing else mattered but this moment. This felt like breathing, something that comes naturally, without any complicated thoughts or other complications. It feels almost too natural to kiss him.

Reiner kissed my lips one more time, a small peck. "Fuck," he let out a soft sigh, kissing me again, "you taste better than I imagined."

I smiled like some half-wit teenage fool, "you imagine kissing me?"

Reiner smirked, leaning his face closer to mine again, "and more." He said before he kissed me again.

And more? The words were stuck in my head. I wanted to define more, solve for more, find out what was more for him.

What is more?

My thoughts froze when Reiner sucked my tongue and a sultry moan escaped my throat. Reiner *whimpered* hearing that sound.

Fucking whimpered.

Jesus Christmas. We were still outside, in front of my door.

I pulled away and I couldn't keep count on how many times we've each had to break away from our kisses. "You wanna come inside?"

He nodded, watching me open the door with heavy eyes. When I stepped into the house I was glad Blue wasn't present to witness this, let alone stop it from happening.

He took a few steps forward, eager to have his hands all over me, leading me backwards until my back hit a wall. I gasped when Reiner kissed my neck, attacking me with kisses. I hung my head back a little giving more space as his kisses trail my throat. Leaving me short of breath. My stomach is twisting from too much excitement.

I raised a hand up, tangling it in his hair, the other one fisting the hem of his shirt. His finger dug into my waist as he slipped his hands under the back of my shirt, pulling me closer against him.

I moaned, feeling the way his cold fingers felt against my back, his fingers digging deeper hearing the small sounds leave my mouth.

Reiner took my bottom lips between his teeth, coming back in for a sloppy kiss, his hands grabbed mine as he placed it under his shirt. I gasped in his mouth feeling his muscles under the shirt, so taut. I want to run my tongue over his muscles, to taste him in a whole new way.

His lips trailed kisses from the side of my lips down to my neck — his hot breath tickled my skin until I felt his lips next to my ears. Reiner licked the shell of my ear and a shudder ran down my spine as released a soft sigh.

"Touch me." He moaned, trailing his kisses lower down my collarbone.

I leaned forward a little, flushing my body against his. I kissed him, my eyes glued closed as I kissed his collarbone, leaning forward even more. I ran my hands under his shirt, hitching it up.

I dipped low nearly on my knees as I stared at his perfect skin. I laid a kiss on his hip bone, and Reiner let out a ragged breath cupping my chin forcing me to stare at him. I held onto his sweatpants, and I know one tug and it'll be down.

I licked my lips, kissing his V line, trailing the kisses up to his abs, and Reiner can't breathe properly, his chest is rising and falling — cursing words under his breath, I'm not paying so much attention to his words to make up the words. I focus on his breathing the fainty moans that leave his mouth.

"Soleil. . ."

I liked hearing my name on his lips. I love it. I looked up at him, eyes filled with lust. Reiner crouched down taking my lips in his — I moaned in need as I thrust my tongue in his mouth, earning a growl from him. His hands are on me again, under my shirt — riding higher and higher.

Reiner pulled us up, his hands grazed my breast just a little, enough to tease me.

I pulled away a little, breaking the kiss, our kiss only a hair away. I'm breathing him as much as he's breathing me. "Touch *me*." I whispered.

I want his hands everywhere. I want him to feel me *everywhere.*

Reiner groaned, his lips meeting again. His hands are back under my shirt, but he's still so hesitant to go further. I huffed sagging a little, I can't help but feel disappointed when he's always so hesitant to touch me. I groaned in his lips in response but he bites my lower lip to keep me from squirming my way out of his hold. Reiner sucks the small part soothing it as his soft apology.

"You want more?" He moans in my mouth, his hands riding up my bra as he cups me. My back arches in response, eager to lean forward. His fingers twisted my nipples, earning a moan out of me, Reiner swallowed the moan as he kissed me deeper.

I nodded without a second thought. *I want more."* I repeated back, pushing my head back a little to catch my breath. I want to hold onto something, but he's all I have, the wall behind me is barely holding me up.

Reiner kisses my neck pulling my shirt higher, but it never leaves my body. My half-exposed chest was falling and rising as I watched Reiner stare at my breast with hungry eyes. He released a breath, his chest falling and rising, his hair now disheveled.

"Fucking *gorgeous*." he whispered the words like torments, his head dipped low, his lips meeting my breast, taking my nipple in his mouth. His other hand kneaded my breast.

My hands flew on his shoulders, holding onto him as he bit my nipples, a moan escaped my throat as my brows furrowed in both pain and pleasure because Reiner sucked my nipples to make up for the pain after, soothing me with a small apology.

Reiner looked up through hooded eyes and it's the *sexiest* look on his face. I wish he was lower, on his knees. Kissing something else.

"That sound you make," he whispered under his breath, leaning forward again, biting my nipple, my nails dug into his shoulders, earning another moan out of me.

"When I do this…" He continued, clearly amused, but when he sucked my nipple the same one he bit earlier when I whined, it's the best combination of pain and pleasure, my head spinned, and my body melted as I forced my legs closed.

Reiner grinned, "I love it."

I opened my mouth to say something snarky but there was a knock on my door. I nearly jumped out of his arms —but I only stood up straight, staring in the direction of the door as I pulled both my shirt and bra down.

I looked at Reiner but he can't seem to meet my eyes, he's staring straight ahead at the direction of the door. Dread filled my body. *Was he regretting this already?*

I cleared my throat, pointing at the door. "I should—"

Reiner only nodded as I walked away, when I opened the door two sad eyes greeted me. Two red sad eyes and I immediately felt guilty.

Before I could call for Reiner, he brushed past me with an apologetic look and I understood.

Reiner kissed her forehead picking her up, "I'm sorry I was

gone for so long, were you scared?" He asked.

"Mommy called," Anna sniffed, "she got mad at me again."

Reiner glanced at me and I offered him a small smile, I can't exactly hold this against him. His daughter is sad and I'm horny those are two categories that cannot be compared.

"It's okay." I mouthed.

He nodded at me turning to face his daughter again, "will some ice cream make it better?" He asked.

A small smile formed on my face as Anna nodded at him.

Reiner looked back at me as he smiled, Taking a few steps away from my house with Anna's head resting on his shoulders "Good night, Soleil." He said.

"Good night, Reiner." I closed the door with a half-satisfied smile on my face. *I could still feel his lips around my breast.*

Deep down I think I shouldn't have invited him inside. I think we should've left things less messy, it should've been just a kiss. But right now, I'm glad I invited him inside, just disappointed our time was cut short. Who knows how far we would've gone if Anna didn't walk in.

I can't wipe the tiny smile off my face because Reiner Kline kissed me under the stars — he took all of me with him, and left me with nothing.

CHAPTER FIFTEEN

★·☆·★

Reiner

★·☆·★

"WHY CAN'T I COME WITH YOU?" Anna attempted to whisper. But her voice bounced in the empty church.

I smiled, pinching her cheek as she scrunched her nose. "It's
gonna be a grown-up talk."

She frowned, "when are you gonna stop saying that?"

"When you're a grown-up." She huffed, almost close to stomp-
ing her foot, but I'm glad she didn't. I glanced at the old lady that
stood only a few steps away from us. I sent her a curt nod when
her eyes met mine.

"Until then, you have to stay with sister Jane for a while." I
whispered. Anna glanced behind her, staring at sister Jane who
couldn't be no more than seventy-something.

Anna looked at me again with a small pout, "please hurry."

I pressed a kiss against her forehead. "I'll be quick, princess."

I sat in the reconciliation room facing toward the altar, away from the priest. The little window between us was merely showing faces. I was always glad about the privacy. I could only make out his silhouette to know he's there.

I waited in silence until he finally spoke. "In the name of the Father, and of the Son, and of the Holy Spirit." His voice boomed through my ears, feeling me up with a new sense.

"Amen." I mumbled. Reaching for my necklace kissing it with my eyes closed.

"May God, who has enlightened every heart, help you to know your sins and trust in his mercy,"

I released a small breath. "Forgive me Father, for I have sinned. It's been six months since my last confession."

I tilt my chin up, my hands clasped together over my thigh. "Truth is, I'm not even sure why I'm here." I let out a stiff laugh and somehow the silence between us intensified.

The priest cleared his throat, "well. . . have you been feeling like you've done something wrong?"

I swallowed, I've *done* something wrong. It's no longer a feeling anymore. I kissed a girl when I was nowhere ready in life to kiss one. It was reckless and *good*. I liked it a lot, which is why I think it's so wrong. I was almost too greedy with the kiss, if Anna hadn't interrupted — who knows how far things could've gone.

I can't help but want her closer — to be closer to her. I looked in her direction the first day she moved in and I haven't been able to look away since. I noticed her, in so many ways I shouldn't.

Then I didn't think any of this would mean any harm until I lost control and allowed myself to touch her.

Now I've got a taste, I'm not sure I can stay away.

"I kissed a girl." I mumbled.

There was a huge sigh coming from the other side of the booth, and I can understand why because saying something like that at the age of thirty-two sounds both childish and ridiculous. But I'm not here to classify it as my sin because I'd do it again if I went back in time to *attempt* to change things. I just want to talk about it, get it off my chest. Feel less guilty.

It was selfish of me to kiss her knowing there was no room in my life for her. Between trying to keep Anna in my life and the constant battle between Noa and whatever issues she comes up with, my hands are full. Because with Noa there will always be a big fight about everything. It's always the World vs Noa.

My life is a road that seems to destroy everything that passes through it. And it was selfish of me to drag her into it.

I sighed, running a hand through my hair. "I've always been able to control my thoughts and actions but when it comes to her all I want to do is please her, any way she allows me to."

I cleared my throat, finding new thoughts to speak through, "I'm asking for guidance on how to take her off my mind. She's all I think about."

I could hear the dry sound of his clothes when he twisted his head in my direction, "son, are you here for permission to have sex?"

I let out a strangled cough, "of course not father." I sighed, "but my mind is flooded with so many sinful thoughts."

It's almost like self-torture. I can't stop, but I didn't want to anyways. The memories play over and over, the sound of her voices — the sound of her little —*noises*— I can't stop thinking about any of it.

I want to touch myself and get off just by the sound of her voice. I want her to watch me touch myself, begging me for a taste. Oh, the sweet privilege to hear her beg — my memory of her soft skin, the way her hands felt on me — the ways my hands felt on *her.*

"Like what, Son? Confess and set yourself free of them."

"I want to hug her." I mutter in silence. Staring ahead, focusing on just the smell of her.

To feel her. Her mouth, I want to feel it. Wrapped around my cock. To hear her gag, tapping my thighs, tears rolling down her cheeks, but she'll love it so much she wouldn't want to stop. Her pretty curls would look so good wrapped around my hands. I'd love to have her on her knees.

"I want to kiss her again."

Lick her. I want to memorize every inch of her with just the tip of my tongue. I want to taste, have my head trapped around her thighs — her hands in my hair pulling at it, I want to moan in her pussy and have her gasp from the vibration. To have her clasp her legs close around my head, then I'd pry it open because I'd be enjoying myself too much to stop. I want to find out how her body works, how much she can handle until she *breaks* — how wet she can get before reaching climax. I want to know how desperate her moans can really get — I so desperately want to get drunk on the sound.

"I want to be closer to her."

Be inside of her. I want her nails on my back. I want her to claim what could possibly be hers. I want to hear her tell me how she likes it, and how fast I can go. How deep she wants it, how rough, how soft. I want to...

"I want to worship her."

To Make her feel so pathetic for ever wanting my touch when I'm done with her. I want her to cry under me from too much pleasure, I want her to beg me to stop when I know she really doesn't want me to stop. I'd kiss away her tears giving her my all. *Fucking her into oblivion.* To scream my name so much she loses her voice.

"To protect her."

Ruin her, stain her of my touch. I want her to look for me in every other man who dares to touch her — to compare because no one will ever be enough after I'm done with her.

"God, I want her. . ."

In every single way and it's making me sick.

Forgive me father for I have sinned. I'm struggling to trap the predator within. The screws of the cage are becoming undone, and I know soon he'll be set free. Soon I'll hunt for her. Soon I'll take her and I'll never let go.

"That is all, Father."

A light snore was heard from the other side of the booth, my shoulders sagged, "father?" I called out.

Nothing but faint snores responded back to me. So I knocked on the wood, "father?"

"Oh yes," he began clearly, still pulling himself from the short nap, "you must resist the temptations that test your mind." I'm positive he didn't hear me say anything.

"Now, son. Say your prayers."

I acknowledged the penance and agreed to perform them by reciting an Act of Contrition prayer. The priest finished the confession by saying his final words. "The Lord has freed you from your sins. Go in peace."

"Thanks be to God."

★ · ☆ · ★

"So I was wondering if you would come to the party I'm hosting this Friday and you know. . . bring *Soleil.* Your neighbor Soleil." Ian clarified.

He barged into my office to deliver this irrelevant piece of information. He thinks he's smooth, inviting me to his party — something that's never been done before— just to benefit himself with the presence of Soleil. He thinks just because I'm a single man going through a rough divorce I would fall for this trick.

My jaw clenched, I don't know his intentions towards Soleil, and I'm not interested in finding out.

"So I finally got an invitation to one of your famous parties and you want me to bring my neighbor." I said flatly as I straightened my spine.

"C'mon man, when you say it like that. . . " Ian frowned, tilting his head to the side.

I looked away, staring down at the papers displayed in front of me. "I don't think she'd be into it, she keeps to herself." Just the thought of having her anywhere near him or anyone else in that matter repulsed me.

"How would you know what her scene is?"

"I don't know. But I'm sure partying with a bunch of strangers wouldn't be so fun. Besides I've never been invited to one of your parties, I feel like a Trojan horse. "

"I'm inviting you right now."

I raised a brow, "but I can't come without Soleil right?"

Ian sighs, "I never said that — I simply *encouraged* the idea."

Before he could say anything more, I spoke again. "Sure Ian, I'll think about it."

Ian left my office, with a smile on his face. I've known him the longest in the firm. He's also the only one who managed to keep his sanity, going on about every case with a cheerful smile on his face — it's strange but it keeps his clients happy.

My —recent— client however, refuses to follow the rules. Simple rules that are created for her benefit. She is currently being harassed by mobs of college students with nothing better to do but to write a paper. None of them has the decency to approach my client in a professional way.

Poor Lynn answers every question in the book. I informed her to keep quiet but she insisted on declaring it'd be rude. Clearly it's been her first accident where she could possibly sue for thousands.

This case might be the lightest I've had in a while now, we're all just waiting for the hearing date and I told Lynn to hang tight but she's busy overwhelming herself with random college students with zero class.

I rolled my chair back a little as I leaned my head back. I'm exhausted, beyond exhausted. The whole process with Noa will be over soon then I'll stop stressing because I'll have full custody of Anna, and Noa would get regular visits like she wanted — I'm just waiting on the papers to get back to me.

But I can't help but feel the possibilities of losing Anna, like she'd get ripped away from my arms. Seeing her two or three times a week is only heartbreaking. It's getting harder and harder to say goodbye to her, this morning I wanted more time with her before dropping her off.

I remember how bad it was when we were going through the divorce, when Noa had full custody of Anna and I'd get once a week —*under supervision*— visits. Like I was the one who wrecked my marriage. Noa commits adultery and I'm the one paying for her infidelity — in the eyes of the law the mother always seems fit until proven otherwise.

I've worked so hard to put it all behind me, and I might finally get the only thing I wanted out of all this — Anna. It stresses me a bit knowing even after all this I might not get full custody. And I'd be forced to watch my little Anna get raised by her mother and some guy who isn't her father.

Noa got selfish and I'm paying the price.

CHAPTER SIXTEEN

MRS. ROBERTS AGREED to meet with me for an interview, so I was not completely doomed. The assignment was looking easier and easier to get done — in fact I could have it done tonight, good enough to turn it in.

All I have to do today is be there and ask a bunch of relevant questions, take a few notes and be polite.

I glanced at myself in the mirror. I think I'm dressed like a journalist, they always look like this on TV anyways. Jeans and a blouse, it's always the same so I figure why not join the club and blend in.

I was skipping my morning class for this interview because Mrs. Roberts has this really tight ass lawyer she told me about and I couldn't afford to be late.

I washed my hair last night. It was like an impulsive decision, it just happened, I never detangled it, now I have no choice but to shove it into a bun. I thought I'd have time to moisturize and detangle it this morning but I woke up late — courtesy of hitting the snooze button one too many times.

★·☆·★

I was running fifteen minutes late.

I skipped my hair routine and I'm still running late. I'm late but at least I could parallel park. It saves me another ten minutes from scouting the neighborhood for an open parking space. I parked my car in between the other cars, it was the closest available parking space to the house address I was following on GPS.

I swung my door open, shoving my laptop into my purse. Fifteen minutes late is better than showing up an hour late, I did good enough. At least I believe that, I don't have to explain myself or anything.

I rang the doorbell, adjusting myself because I sort of jogged in front of the house. Before I could raise an arm to sniff myself the door opened and a middle aged lady was saying good morning.

"Hi, Mrs Roberts, My name is Soleil Walsh, we spoke on the phone—"

"Of course I remember, you have the sweetest voice."

I smiled at the lady, "thank you, and it's a pleasure to meet you." I stretched out a hand, offering a handshake. "I'm also sorry I'm late."

The lady shook my hand, welcoming me in. "happens to the best of us."

I smiled adjusting the bag over my shoulder, as I followed her inside. When we reached the living room and the world seemed to have stopped when those two blue familiar eyes glared at me and my breath was caught in my throat.

Reiner wore a black suit, with a midnight blue tie. No designs, just the simple color. The color went so well with his eyes. He looked edible. *So gorgeous.*

My brows furrowed as I tilt my head to the side, finally putting two and two together. I stayed quiet because Reiner was quiet. I followed the lady to the couch, watching her and Reiner sit down, not so close to each other. But I was obviously the odd man out because I was sitting on the opposite couch.

It felt like I was the one being interviewed.

"Soleil, can I call you Soleil?" The lady began.

I nodded, my eyes finally finding hers, "Yes."

"This is my lawyer, Mr. Kline," she pointed at Reiner and my eyes followed her finger to him. Reiner's eyes were glued on me. But I only nodded at the lady pretending to go along.

"He saw fit that he should be present during the interviews because of a few certain questions."

I slowly nodded with an awkward smile on my face, "I have no issues with that." I clarified.

The room fell quiet when I started to dig things out of my bag. I opened my laptop typing in my password, I looked up nervously at the sets of eyes staring at me.

"The questions aren't that bad." I whispered in silence, more to myself I think because the silence was deafening.

When the screen finally loaded, and my form of questions popped up, I released a shaky breath. Mrs. Roberts is staring at me like this is boring her out and I don't mind because this is pretty boring — but Reiner is staring at me like he can see my thoughts float above my head.

He's constantly reading me, paying too much attention. If anyone who doesn't know him catches him staring at me the way he stares at me they'll think he's planning a whole vendetta against me.

I cleared my throat, setting the laptop on the cushion next to me, "I'm sorry to do this before we start, but could I use your bathroom?" I asked the lady.

She only nodded as she pointed in the direction of the bathroom, "it's the first door on the right."

I nodded, standing up on my feet, and I could feel his eyes sharp on me — watching my every move, the uneasy feeling in my stomach made me feel more self-conscious to not slip and fall as I walked closer and closer to the bathroom. Does he think I'm going to search the house or something? Holding eye contact with him was never that intense. After our kiss it changed. Everything did.

Mrs. Roberts was back to talking to Reiner, I couldn't hear what they were saying because I was getting further and further away from them as I made my way to the bathroom. The easier it was getting for me to breathe.

The second I walked in, I locked the door behind me, grabbing my phone from my back pocket shooting Hayley a text.

Me: guess who's the lawyer.

Hayley answered me almost immediately.

Hayley: the Queen of England!

Me: Not funny. It's fucking Reiner.

Hayley: NO FUCKING WAY. . . WHAT?

Me: Did you know?

Hayley: Nah I would've told you, beside I didn't go into all those details in my interview.

Hayley: Is this the first time seeing him after the hot steamy kiss?

Me: Yes, and the kiss wasn't steamy or hot.

Hayley: Is that why you're so nervous around him?

Me: Hayley I need your help!!!!

Hayley: Just be a professional, soon this will actually be your job, so start treating it that way, and come over tonight and tell me all about how it went. Promise not to get you drunk!

Me: I love you.

Hayley: I love you more!

I closed my phone and shoved it back in my back pocket,

Hayley is right this will actually be my job soon, so if I can't handle this little hiccup then I won't be able to handle anything at all.

I'll walk back out there with a polite smile on my face, and I'll be a professional. I'll try to forget about the fact that Reiner had his lips around my nipples two days ago and we never talked about it after.

I sucked in a breath, running my sweaty palms over my jeans. It's not that bad. It won't be that bad. I'm sure the second we start talking about a car crash all of the sexual tension will fly out the window. It has to, it really has to because I need to get out of taking this final and this is the once in a lifetime chance.

I opened the door making an immediate turn just to run into a hard chest. I pulled back a little with a hand over my forehead.

Reiner stood in front of me, hands in his pockets, blue eyes staring down at me, he took another step closer to me and the wall I've been building started melting again.

I blinked up at him. Waiting for him to speak first because he's the one who followed me into the bathroom.

"What are you doing here?" His voice clipped short.

I rolled my eyes, "oh don't flatter yourself, I'm here for the interview."

"With my client?"

I thought about a thousand ways to answer his stupid question but I settled with one simple answer.

"Yes."

"Oh." Was all he said under his breath, somehow he managed to make that simple sound so disappointing.

He seems to be doing just fine meanwhile I'm going crazy with the memories he engraved in my head, I'm fighting all these needs I never thought I'd have to fight. How much I don't want his hands in his pockets right now, I want them on me.

I want the same view I had two days ago, him nearly on his knees, staring up at me with those pretty blue eyes, my breast in his mouth... a sight that could make any blind woman jealous.

I shuffled, "should we talk about—"

"No." He cuts me off, turning away from me. I watch his shoulders flex with almost every step he takes, biting my lips at the sight.

So much for being a professional.

I walked back into the leaving room, and I pulled out my phone placing it on the coffee table, I had the voice recorder on. It's smarter that way, just in case I miss typing in something I can always go back and listen to the interview.

"I hope you guys don't mind that I'm recording." I said as I looked up at the both of them, Mrs. Roberts' eyes found Reiner's seeking some sort of approval because when Reiner sent her a small nod her answer was clear.

"Not at all." she smiled.

I smiled back, "before we began I just wanted to ask, how are you?"

Ms Roberts whole face lit up as she awed, glancing at Reiner who couldn't help but smile back. "You're the first one to ask, dear. All the other students just went right at it."

I pouted, "I'm sorry to hear that."

"Oh it's fine. And I'm doing great, very happy it was my car that got the most of it."

"Is the other person covering the damage or will your insurance cover it?"

"They will be paying for all the damage." she replied back.

I nodded, scrolling on my laptop, looking for questions for us to finally begin. I decided to shoot with the big guns, it's what professor Daniel taught us, if they're gonna get mad, this is the time. "How much are you suing for?"

"Don't answer that," Reiner cut her off just in time to glare at me, "Do you have any relevant questions?"

I nodded, spacing to a different question on my laptop, "of course."

"In your words, could you please describe how the accident happened?"

"Their car came out of nowhere, I was turning under a green light, I had the right of passage. They were speeding to make a yellow light that was gone too soon, and the crash happened, it took the back of my car, let's just say I was glad to be driving an SUV."

I finished typing as I looked up at her, "I'm so sorry to hear that."

She shook her head, "you don't have to keep apologizing, dear."

I nodded, "were there any injuries?"

Reiner shook his head, "don't answer that."

The questioning went smoothly after Reiner made it clear that he wouldn't have the lady answering any questions regarding money, or who caused the crash, or any injuries for that matter.

In conclusion Reiner made it his life mission to prevent me from getting any answers besides the fact that everything is going smoothly and they might get a court date soon, and they plan to keep it on the low as much as possible.

I truly hope he didn't rob me of this and he treated everyone else this way — because I wouldn't put it past him to actually do something like this out of spite. I stood up, shoving my laptop in my bag. I had already said goodbye and thank you to Ms Roberts, and I'm satisfied enough to know I can work with all of the information I got.

"Ms. Walsh, before you leave, can I have a word?"

I paused all the shuffling to look up at Reiner confused on why he's calling me by my last name but then I remember we've been pretending to not know each other all morning.

I threw my bag over my shoulder, nodding in his direction. I grabbed my phone on the coffee table, shoving it in my back pocket. Standing quick on my feet to follow Reiner because he was only waiting for me.

I noticed he didn't have his briefcase when he walked me to the door and I realized he might stay a little longer, which would be his job — in a way.

I stopped by the door, turning to face him "you know back there I was just doing my job?"

His hands reached over my head, his eyes bright with amusement and my mouth parted when he pulled a lint from my hair, showing it to me as he spoke, "I know. And I was only doing mine."

I stared at him dazed by the small action, Reiner is somehow calm right now. His face is relaxed, his hair neat. His body at the perfect composure. He looked almost at peace until he clenched his jaw.

Reiner cleared his throat, shoving his hands into his pockets, "Ian invited me to a *party* this friday."

I stared at him, unsure of what to do with that information, "okay…"

"He also invited you too."

My brows furrowed, "me?" I whispered as I pointed a finger at myself.

He nodded, "yes."

"Is this an office thing or a personal party he invited you to?"

"I'm quite positive it's personal, he is very *selective* with the invites."

I nodded, "and he invited me too?" I'm still trying to make sense of it.

"Yes." Reiner answered under his breath. "I told him you wouldn't be into it but he didn't believe me."

I smiled, "I think it's weird because I don't know them, I only know *you*."

His face softened, "I told him that too."

"Are you going?"

"Only if you are," he paused, his eyes dipped to my lips, but only for a second. "I also think it's weird to be partying with a bunch of strangers."

I swallowed, "so we're going to a party this Friday."
Why not? *It's free food, might I add.*

CHAPTER SEVENTEEN

Soleil

"SO, REINER INVITED YOU TO A PARTY?" Hayley asked as she snapped for the bartender's attention.

"Not Reiner, *Ian* invited me."

Hayley shook her head, "No luv, Reiner did." she said through her fake british accent. She's drunk, utterly drunk because she only does the accent thing when she's drunk.

I rolled my eyes at her, taking a sip of my club soda. One of us has to be sober tonight and Hayley already proved that it won't be her. I know something's going on with Hayley because I know she doesn't get drunk this often.

She parties, but she's usually far more responsible about it. She's been drinking so often lately. If I didn't know her I'd say she's an alcoholic.

"Hayley," I began, tilting my head towards her, "what's wrong?"

She flashed me a drunk, half lopsided smile, "Absolutely nothing, mate."

I frowned, "please stop with the accent, some might think it's offensive."

"How can I help?"

"Can you get rid of my dad?"

"What?" I frowned, "I didn't know he was back in town."

One of the first few things Hayley and I bonded through was shitty parents. I had an absent mother but a shitty present father. And Hayley had a dead mother with an alcoholic father who skips town the second he gets a paycheck leaving Hayley to fend for herself and her two sisters.

Community college is barely free, she goes to class as much as she can, and works as much as she can, she's been doing good on her own, she was happy, her sisters were healthy.

Her father however, always comes back, for more money, for more drinks, for anything he can sucks out of their life. The same story over and over again. He promises he's getting better, drinking less, going to AA — and he just needs some money to support himself.

Hayley fell for that trick five times, I fell for it once.

"Yeah he was back after the storm, I thought he'd leave by now, but he's still around."

"Why didn't you tell me before?"

"Because I thought he'd leave by now, but last night he crashed on my couch and I don't think he'll leave this time."

My heart shattered hearing her broken voice as she slurs out her words. I don't know what to say. My father was forgetful and neglectful, but not an alcoholic.

I leaned closer towards her, wrapping my arms around her, shooing the bartender away because I've decided Hayley had enough drinks for tonight. I waited for her to relax into my arms before speaking again.

"I struggle enough to take care of my sisters, but I refuse to take care of my angry alcoholic father."

I wrap my hands around her because I have nothing to say at all, my touch could possibly be greater comfort than offering a few words.

Hayley sniffed, wiping her eyes as she pulled back to stare at me, her eyes red from both the tears and the alcohol, "At least *yours* is dead, mine hunts me every year sucking money out of me like some blood sucking vampire."

I nodded, pulling her back into my arms, "we'll get rid of him too."

I drove Hayley home, made sure she got into bed and drank enough water. Bernie, her father, was nowhere in the house when I got there, her sisters were already in bed, or at least in their rooms because the whole house was dark and quiet.

CHAPTER EIGHTEEN

Soleil

I ENDED UP INVITING HAYLEY to the party with me. It would be easier to be in a house full of strangers if I knew at least two people. Reiner saw it best that both me and Hayley rode with him. He said it'd be simpler with one car.

I told myself that I was dressing nicely for Ian's sake. I'm not stupid, he only invited Reiner to get me there too. I fell for the oldest trick in the book because I love food, *good food*.

God, I could still taste that dry ass chicken Reiner cooked.

I didn't go too crazy. I wore a simple pink dress. I figured it would be hot because they'll be grilling, and all that hot air will just be around. Unlike the other day — I actually had time to do my hair today. I'm happy to say I'm having a good hair day but I know the second it gets hot, it'll get frizzy. I don't know what to exactly expect but it isn't much because it's been a long time since I've engaged with crowds of people.

Going to the bar doesn't count because I always follow Hayley around like a lost puppy, even at work I sometimes beg Mara to take the bigger booths. I choke when I talk to a crowd of five or more people at once. My words blend in with each other and everything I end up saying is a disaster.

So hopefully tonight I won't need to follow Reiner around like a weird little puppy. There'll be music, good food, I'll be busy. Really busy. I used the *carmex* on my chapped lips, before grabbing my purse ready to pace the room.

"You really like him." Hayley mumbled from the edge of the bed.

I forgot her existence entirely. Were waiting on Reiner who had to take care of a call before we headed out.

"I don't know." I mumbled. This was the first time that I *didn't* deny it.

"He has a kid."

I frowned, staring at Hayley, she wore a crop top, long jeans with her hair hanging beyond her shoulders. We've playfully talked about Reiner a lot but this was the first time she looked genuinely serious.

"Is that supposed to scare me?"

She shrugged, "maybe it should, because he doesn't come with *just* a kid, he comes with a whole family, a pass and a future."

I scoffed, "wow. What makes you think I don't know that?"

Hayley dragged a hand through her hair, at least trying to

find the right answer. I'm not even sure where all of this is coming from.

"Listen, I just don't want you to get dragged up in his drama, okay? His separation with his ex-wife is still fresh. And I don't want you to feel like you have to compete with her because it's impossible to."

I deflate a little. She's only worried for me.

I smiled, "weren't you the one who was advertising to jump his bones?"

She laughed, "that was before you *actually* started liking him."

Again, "I don't know."

I tried my best not to act excited in front of Hayley when Reiner knocked on my door. He's wearing a plain white shirt with khaki pants, he's dressed like a soccer dad. I almost felt bad for him but he pulled the outfit just fine.

His eyes raked my body, taking in my exposed leg with a heavy breath. I try to force on a smile because I don't know what he's thinking.

I want to know what he's thinking.

"Ready?"

I nodded, watching Hayley walk past us, a suspicious smile on her face. I swallowed, pinning my attention on Reiner again. "Yeah."

Ian lived in a really deserted area and I'm starting to wonder how rich those fuckers at the law firm actually are. Reiner had to call from the gates to get entrance. When we pulled up in front of the house my jaw was almost on the floor.

Ian's house is big and open, it looked like a better version of the Cullen house from twilight. I climbed out of the car, closing the door behind me — still staring at the house in awe.

The smoky smell of the grill filled my nostril, it smells like ribs, good barbecued ribs. I turned to Hayley with a smile on my face, she was already smiling at the smell of food too. Reiner glanced between the two of us, confused but he only gestured for us to walk forward as we made our way towards Ian's house.

Ian opened the door seconds after I rang the doorbell. A bright smile on his face, his locs are down this time, they are so beautifully brown, which complimented his skin. I flashed him a smile because unlike Reiner Ian seems to be very spirited.

"You guys made it!" He chirps, his eyes wandering off to Hayley, doing a double take, a long one.

"I'm sorry, I didn't think you'd mind if I brought someone else."

He shook his head with a laugh, his eyes still glued on Hayley. "The more the merrier!" He flashed us a cocky grin.

Ian led us to his backyard where the music was blasting loudly and I realized he must have soundproof walls because I didn't hear any of the music until he led us here.

A good amount of people are there. It's big enough to be counted as a small gathering. I took one look at who's grilling and I decided I'd be eating well tonight. Ian walked around introducing us around to his friends, and it was no surprise that Reiner knew some of them.

I ate up to two plates of food, ditched Reiner in the middle of it and I found myself hanging out with Ian and Hayley. I learned that Reiner is the best in the offices but he's picky with cases because of his schedule and responsibilities. Ian however is single, childfree so he gets as many cases he can handle.

Ian is charming, funny, and sweet. It feels like he's a person I was supposed to meet a long time ago. Right now I'm laughing so carefree, listening to the things his friends are joking about. And Hayley can't stop staring at Ian, I want to drag her into a corner and have her tell me everything she's feeling, but I don't instead, I do my best to help her start a conversation with him.

When I glance at Reiner he seems to be doing just fine in the small group he's hanging around. Nursing a small beer in his hands. When his eyes catch mine he clenches his jaw and looks away before I do.

Tonight he's tense, but carefree. He laughs from time to time. But his whole composure is still defensive. He stares at me so strangely, I pretend not to notice. Hours and hours have gone by and he's avoiding me as much as I'm avoiding him. We still hadn't talked about what *almost* happened. I think he doesn't want to, but I'm not interested in forcing him too, even if I do want to finish what we started.

I laughed when Ian leaned in closer whispering something in my ears. Some corny joke I didn't fully understand but I'm laughing to be polite. Not too much, just enough. Hayley though, she laughs gracefully. I think it's cute she took an interest in Ian.

I looked at Reiner when he cleared his throat, clutching his keys, walking closer towards us. "Soleil, let's go." This is the first time he's acknowledged me ever since we stepped foot into Ian's house. His eyes are sending daggers to Ian.

I frowned, "what? I wanted to hangout a little longer." I looked at Ian and Hayley at my side, but he was smiling at me. Reiner glared at the both of us, his jaw clenching.

"I need to get home right now, and I'm your ride home so let's go."

"Hang on a second." Hayley mumbled.

I made a move to follow him but Ian butt in. "I can give you guys a ride," he said.

I smiled up at him, taking a step back again, "okay—" Hayley and I said in unison.

"Not necessary, she already has one, now let's go Soleil." Reiner cut me off, taking a step forward. For a split second I thought he'd grab my hand and pull me towards him, but he didn't — I'm not entirely sure why I'm disappointed that he didn't.

I frowned at Reiner. And he fixed me a look, his eyes sent a clear warning. I looked back at Ian offering him an apologetic smile.

"Thank you for today, I really had fun." I smiled at Ian, leaning in as I wrapped my arms around him. I thought too long about shaking his hands so I spontaneously went in for a hug. I'm almost surprised by how fast his arms wrapped around me.

"Anytime." He whispered in my ear.

Hayley did an awkward wave and it took Ian entirely five seconds to mimic her wave with a small smile on his face.

"See you monday." Ian sent a curt nod at Reiner — Reiner grunted in response, turning on his heels.

Reiner cleared his throat, clearly so eager to get back home. I followed Reiner through the slide doors back inside the house trying to keep my voice in a hushed voice because the house is so empty I might have an echo.

"You don't have to be so rude all the time, you know." I whisper-yelled.

Reiner glanced at me, "I'm sorry, when would be the appropriate time to be rude?"

"Are you guys about to fight over this?" Hayley laughed, but her laugh fell short with all the tension in the air.

I rolled my eyes, still trying to understand his stubbornness. "The only reason I'm going home with you is because I didn't want to embarrass you in front of your friends."

His voice fell flat. "How generous of you."

"Very actually." I grumbled under my breath as we made our way around the car, and I was quick to open the door, throwing myself in the passenger seat, fighting to put the seatbelt on me.

Reiner got in the car in silence, turning on the engine, and I was instantly grateful at the AC blasting the cold air at me. My body sinked into the cushion, the small feeling of relief washing all over me.

Hayley closed her door, "please don't make this uncomfortable you guys."

It's like we didn't hear Hayley in the car with us, Reiner was determined to get his point across. "They are not my friends." He deadpanned. Driving away from Ian's *Cullen* manson.

I scoffed, "Oh yeah I forgot, you don't *make friends.*" I mocked.

Still holding that grudge. I don't care about how many times he kisses me, I'll still remember the fact that he closed a door on my face when I offered him a pie, or how he told me he didn't want to be *my* friend multiple times. He never seems to fail in reminding me.

"Just admit it." Hayley blurted out, her voice annoyed.

"Admit what?" Both Reiner and I hissed out.

"You were jealous."

Reiner went silent.

Hayley sighed, probably content with the silence that finally came. For the next few minutes, it was Hayley that talked because she was giving directions to her house. I wanted to apologize to her for the outcome of all of this but Reiner was still in the car, and it felt awkward to talk in general.

I only said bye when we dropped her off. The tension in the air between me and Reiner only multiplied now that we didn't have to worry about anyone else around us.

"Ian is not the married man *type.*" He finally spoke.

"And *you* are?"

Reiner looked at me, then looked back at the road. He seems

to be thinking about that question for a while probably wondering how to answer it — the correct ways of answering it.

"I was. *I can be.*"

What's that supposed to mean?

Reiner can be a married man. So he says, the same man who refuses to properly communicate, he tiptoes around his feelings and feeds on others feelings — acts clueless on the way he acts... that same man is the type to be married? *He's doomed and I'm cursed.*

CHAPTER NINETEEN

REINER FOLLOWED ME at a close distance towards the house — neither of us said anything, but the second I stepped foot inside of my house he was inside too, right behind me, he even closed the door behind him too. I rolled my eyes as I flipped the light switch on.

I turned around, kicked my shoes off — glaring at Reiner as I placed a hand over my waist. I sighed when he didn't say anything, he just stood there glaring at me back, but in a brand new way — a way that I can't explain.

"What are we doing, Reiner?"

For a second I thought he wouldn't say anything, I expected for him to snap out of it and pull an Irish exit, but he simply shrugged, "I want you Soleil. I want you so bad it's taking everything in me to not touch you whenever I'm around you." He took a step closer to me.

I shook my head, "you can't keep doing that, Reiner. Fucking stop it. Make up your mind, *please.*" I sneered out.

I swallowed my frustration, "don't mind-fuck me," I whispered. "You want me? Act on it, and if you don't... Tell me." I looked up at him, biting my lips in the process.

Reiner was quiet when I walked closer towards him, "it's your turn to say something now." I whispered.

His large hand reached for my cheek as he softly brushed his thumb against my skin, his eyes glued to the place he was touching and my eyes were glued on him, watching his sharp jaw clench.

My chest heaved as his fingers reached my lips tracing the outline of it. I remained quiet, anticipating his next move. I released a soft breath as I parted my lips open.

Reiner slowly pushed his thumb in my mouth, as he wrapped his free hand around my throat. I took the chance and sucked his thumb as he pushed it further into my mouth. His eyes softened as he met my gaze, but the second his eyes flickered down my lips to see our lewd action something dark flickered in his eyes.

I gagged when his thumb brushed my throat and a satisfying groan left his. I wrapped my hands around his as I softly pulled out his thumb in my mouth, sucking it on the way out.

His chest heaved as he swallowed, the guilty look on his face, "I'm sorry." He whispered.

My heart fell, "w-what?"

"Soleil." He breathed and before I could say anything, his head

dipped low, his lips meeting mine for the first time — catching my lips with such hunger.

Reiner tasted so sweet and soft. I liked the taste of him so much, I felt like I was high. My head spinned with too much contact with him, my skin was on fire yet I craved for more. *I want his hands everywhere.*

He wasn't timid about the way he touched me, I've been touched a handful of times before by shy guys, insecure guys, and the ones who had no idea what they were doing — but Reiner was different, he was sure about the way he touched me, confident. I liked the way he tilted my chin back, telling me he wanted more of my mouth, or the way his tongue swiped over my lips, begging for entrance.

My flimsy hands gripped the hem of his shirt, the warmth of his body pulled me in like a sleeping spell. I wanted to run my hand through his hair but I was too dizzy to try to move any of my limbs. It's amazing how my lips moved in sync with his. I am drunk by just one kiss.

My skin felt like it was on fire. I am alive under his touch. I pushed myself up on my tippy toe desperately trying to match his height. A groan left my mouth when I couldn't and one of his hands circled around my waist, that part of me was awake too now, burning under his touch.

I took his lower lip in between my teeth in hunger, my head spinned as I felt the sensation when his hand around my throat gripped a little, making me feel dizzy. When I released his bottom lip his mouth took mine again — his tongue invaded my mouth.

185

A moan escaped his throat and I wanted to hear the sound again, I wanted to feel the vibration of his moans in my mouth again. And I was willing to do just about anything to hear it again.

When I worked the courage to move a hand up to his hair, Reiner pulled away from our kiss. His eyes found mine, they were so soft and guilty I wanted to cry. I reached up to place a light kiss on his soft lips but before I could do so the hands on my waist pulled me back down.

I wanted to touch him so badly, I felt like crying.

"What's wrong?" I whispered.

His eyes smiled before the smile could reach his lips, a soft apologetic smile. "You're so good," he whispered, like it was a bad thing.

My gaze dropped to the floor, "I'm not that good, you know. . ." I frowned.

His head dipped down with a smile, his lips brushing against my ear, "You are." He whispered. A low growling sound.

I shuddered, because I wanted his hands on me more than I have ever wanted anything in my entire life. *Everywhere. I want him everywhere.*

"I've never voted, I laugh at kids falling, I write in books, and I am almost the cheapest person alive." I confessed, hoping to prove my case.

I leaned closer towards him. "Reiner," I whispered his name, almost like it was too forbidden to be spoken about, "I'm not good."

He ran a hand down my back, "you've never voted?" He whispered against my lips.

"Never." I paused for a second, "is that like… *horrible?"*

He smiled and it was the most sexiest look I've seen all night, "no, it's just frowned upon."

I stayed quiet, unsure of what to say next, his hands were still on my waist drawing small circles on my back. My hands were on his shoulders, griping on him like he might disappear.

Reiner brushed his nose against mine and let out a painful sigh as his eyes darkened, "you have *no idea* how bad I want you."

I smiled, almost too sweetly, "show me then."

The sentence seems to hit all the right buttons, because Reiner kissed me with a purpose. His lips were creating sparks of fire each time his tongue greeted mine. His hands that were nicely settled on my waist were now on my ass, gripping them, forcing moans out of my mouth.

He pulled away again, his face was still so close to my face. Reiner grabbed my hand as he placed it against his groin, my eyes bulged open as I gasped, feeling the outline of his cock through the pants.

It's like he stopped breathing all together, his nose flared as he closed his eyes for a painful second — I licked my lips as I made an effort to stroke him through his pants but he only pulled my hand away, holding it behind my back as a short groan left his lips.

One of my hands is being held behind my back and the other one is gripping on Reiner's shirt for support. I looked up at Reiner, his eyes clouded with lust.

My brows crunched as my eyes softened, I want this so bad

the wait is killing me. I made a move and stood up on my tippy toe just to reach his height and kiss him but he moved his head an inch higher. An unsatisfied moan left my mouth — I pulled at my hand behind my back —which— he was still holding.

His grip on my wrist tightened, and I swallowed, stopping my movements altogether. Reiner dipped his head low, his mouth came into contact with mine but he was still not kissing me.

"Did you feel how bad I wanted you?" He whispered against my lips, and my eyes were glued on his lips which are so close to mine — teasing me.

I nodded, then swallowed as my eyes found his again, "yes."

I released a breath as I moved my body closer to his. My skin felt hot, hotter than usual. "Any thoughts on how to solve that problem?"

He offered me a slight grin, "I can think of a few."

It all happened so fast, my hand moved quickly. unbuttoning his shirt, sliding my hand across his chest, feeling every single muscle. *And oh the man had muscles.*

Reiner pulled my shirt over my head, his lips latched on my neck the second the shirt went over my head, sounds were coming out of my mouth, foreign sounds. And Reiner was breathing like he was struggling to breathe.

"You are," his head dipped low facing my chest as he kissed my breast through the laced bra, *"breathtaking."* He smiled.

I released a strangled breath, feeling his lips through the thin lacy material. Reiner finally let go of my hand and placed both of his hands on my waist, pushing my chest in his mouth.

I moaned as I wrapped my hand around his neck. The feeling of his wet tongue flicking my nipples through the bra was teasing me to the brink of tears. I was already failing to control my squirm under him, but when he pinched my nipples — I jumped with a loud moan.

He laughed, kissing my nipples again, "you're perfect. So responsive."

I moaned, holding his head in place as he kissed my nipples through the bra, "thank you." I whispered.

Reiner was taking his time with me, he didn't seem to care about the fact that my bra was still on, I'm not sure if he even remembered that part. His hands were bruising my side, his whole palm is digging into my skin, branding me. His touch *demanded* to be felt.

"*Reiner,*" I moaned, finally pulling his head back up.

He brushed a sloppy kiss against my lips as he lifted me up, the action was so swift I gasped, clutching onto him for dear life — Reiner sat me on the kitchen counter.

His cold finger slowly traced my spine and I nearly folded. The single action had me arching my back. His fingers finally reached my bra and without a second thought they were off.

Reiner pulled away, kissing my face, *my lips.* He placed my hand on his chest as he stared at me — his own breath irregular, and I could feel my body doing the same. Reiner's head dipped low, so low. He kissed my breast again, this time they were bare, and the sensation was even better.

He smiled, this big bright smile. "You're so beautiful, taking my time with you hurts a little." He gripped on my waist, flushing my body against his, "I am going to ruin you in *every way* possible."

A threat like that sounded like a pleasurable promise.

"Awww Reiner, you're so full of yourself, what makes you think that I won't be the one ruining you?"

A deep chuckle vibrated through his chest, I frowned at myself because I couldn't get a glimpse of his dimples — my frown vanished when I felt his hand ride my thigh, I've never been more grateful for shorts.

His fingers felt calloused against my skin, and I could feel his breath fall over my nippled as he cupped my pussy through the jeans, I nearly jumped out of his arms feeling the roughness of his touch.

I gasped as I gripped his shoulders, Reiner groaned, rubbing his hands through my jeans — the friction of it was sending pressure down straight to my clit. I rolled my head back as I moaned, closing my legs a little.

"Fuuucckk." I dragged the words. Reiner only pried them open as he grazed his teeth around my nipple as a warning.

Reiner kissed his way up to my chest as he rubbed my clit through the jeans while I muffled my own moan, feeling his breath tickle my skin, "please stop squirming," he sighed as he kissed my lips, biting my lower lip in the process.

"you're making it really hard to control myself." He whispered.

I moaned, almost audibly, "I can't." I whispered. I really couldn't stop squirming because it has been a long time since I felt this good and the only thing that came off so far was my shirt and bra.

I pushed my body forward, pulling Reiner closer against me. I kissed his neck as I panted, still feeling his fingers through the fabric of my jeans.

This pleasure feels so different yet the same, it's rough but it feels better.

Reiner pulled back a little as his free hand cupped my face, he tilted my head up as my brows furrowed, my insides squirmed as I bit down a moan, Reiner was staring down at me and I didn't want to look too vulnerable right now.

"I am dying to *taste* how wet you are for me." He whispered. His words went straight down my spine, making the hairs on the back of my neck stand.

"What?" I choked out.

"I *want* a taste." He repeated as his face came closer towards mine, *"can I?"* He kissed my lips, a sweet short kiss.

I swallowed, losing my own voice in the process as I nodded.

His fingers hovered above my jeans buttons as he stared down at me with an amusing look on his face, "Soleil, it's too soon to lose your voice." Reiner smiled, a cocky look on his face that I'm growing to like.

"Yes." I replied.

His fingers finally worked, unbuttoning my pants. I was suddenly aware of so much more now, how bright the kitchen light was. The possibilities of my front door being unlocked. But all thoughts seemed to have frozen when I felt Reiner's fingers brushed over my pussy.

He ran his fingers through my pussy feeling the wetness of it as I gripped on his shoulders from the sensitivity of it, his touch felt like a billion right now.

"Reiner, please." I moaned.

He pulled his hands away from me, groaning under his breath as he hooked his fingers on the waist of my jeans shorts.

"Lift your hips," he mumbled in my ear. I released a breath as I pulled myself up a little, lifting my hips high enough for him to pull my pants down. Leaving me in my underwear.

And it wasn't fair how he was fully dressed and I was half naked under him.

"This isn't fair," I breathed.

Reiner looked up meeting my eyes, as he smiled taking my lips in his as he kissed me, my eyes fluttering closed again as I felt myself go deeper under his trance. I managed to forget about what we were talking about, or what I was talking about.

I do remember I wanted him naked, I wanted to feel him. I reached for Reiner running my hand under his shirt as I felt his skin under mine. How soft and hard he was, I felt how defined his abs truly were as I moved my hand all over his chest, earning a moan from him.

I hummed in satisfaction. Reiner pulled away a little and I missed his touch almost completely, but I watched him through hooded eyes as he trailed kisses from my chest down to my stomach, his eyes were pinned on me, the lust in them clear as day. He wanted me to see what he'd do next.

My chest rose and fell, my breast slightly moved in the rhythm. My stomach couldn't settle down on what to feel when Reiner laid a kiss on my hip as he hooked his fingers around the hem of my underwear, moving it only a little. And it was enough for him to tease me.

I moaned when Reiner kissed under my belly button, his hands reached up to grasp my breast as he pushed my body backwards. I held his arms as I laid flat against the island table. The counter felt cold against my skin and I groaned at the feeling.

I felt hot all over, my body craved so much and Reiner was moaning right above my pussy sending the vibrations down to my spine. He kissed me so teasingly and he moaned like he was the one enjoying it.

I gasped as I jerked forward, feeling Reiner lick my pussy over the underwear, his tongue lapped at it. My fingers were tangled in his hair as I pushed his face closer, right where I needed him. I closed my thighs around his head as I moved my hips in a rhythm that felt good, a rhythm that had his tongue lapping over my clit, sending all the right frictions.

I moaned when Reiner pried my legs open, his hand pinched my nipples before pulling down my underwear. I propped myself up just in time to watch him pull my underwear off.

I tried to reach for the underwear but before I could grab it Reiner pulled it away from me.

I tried to reach for him again, but I was too slow, "give it back." I said in a stern voice, I felt ridiculous because I was fully naked on a kitchen counter trying to put on an attitude.

"No." Reiner argued.

I sighed, as I crossed a hand over my chest and Reiner's eyes were quick to follow my movement, his eyes darkened when I covered my breast.

"Please, give it back." I whispered.

Reiner shoved my underwear in his pocket, smiling up at me, "no."

I groaned, tilting my head back thinking of the many names I could call him, "you perverted— *oohhh...*"

I moaned, and my head snapped in Reiner's direction as I looked down at him... on his knees kissing my pussy, and I lost my mind when his tongue lapped as he licked me.

I gripped on the edge of the counter, moaning breathlessly with my legs thrown over his shoulders as he kissed me in a whole new way. His eyes dripped with lust and the sight of him only encouraged me to chase my high.

I moaned, grinding myself over his lips, when he went lower his nose brushed over my clit, my body shuddered.

This felt better than anything I've ever felt or experienced before, and I'm pretty handy with my vibrator, but this — this is different, Reiner kissed me and licked me like it had nothing to do with me — like he wasn't doing it for the sake of my pleasure but for the sake of his.

Just when I thought it couldn't get any better, his fingers circled my clit retreating back to my entrance, Reiner pulled away to look at the mess he made, his face wet, I'm all over him. Reiner smiled at the mess, gazing up at me as he tapped two fingers against my pussy.

He released a breath, staring at my pussy, "you taste like *heaven*." He whispered, leaning down to lay a kiss over my clit.

Spoken like a true sinner.

I clamped my legs shut around his head from sensitivity. A satisfied sigh left his lips when I moaned as his hands pried my legs open. Reiner pushed a finger inside of me and my back arched in response as I closed my eyes.

"I Know I shouldn't be doing this right now..." he started to speak, and I could hear the sound of his voice, but it was hard to make up the words he was saying when all I could think about was how good his fingers felt inside of me.

He said I tasted like heaven, but his touch is my key to heaven, when touches me, when tastes me, when he feels me — the feeling of it all sends me straight to heaven.

Reiner pushed a second finger inside of me, his other hand reached forward to push my stomach flat on the surface — to have access to go deeper with his fingers.

"But how can I stay away when you taste that good, and sound this good?"

I wanted to say something to him, to answer him, to encourage him but I couldn't. I was too lost — too high on the feeling of his fingers pumping in and out of me. *Slower, deeper, rougher.* The rhythm switches from time to time.

I was focused on chasing my high. My thoughts were filled with the images of Reiner on his knees. He looked so good, his hooded eyes dripped with sex.

Reiner kissed my thigh, a soft sweet action that was supposed to sooth me. "Can you take one more?"

"One more?" I gasped, slightly horrified as I snapped my eyes in his direction.

His thumb circled my clit as he pushed in a third finger, my brows furrowed as I felt the small sting, my lips parted as I panted. Reiner slowly moved his fingers inside of me and everything other than this feeling seemed to be overruled by one, pleasure. That's all I was feeling.

I let out a breathy cry when Reiner moved his fingers faster inside of me, like he could feel how close I was by just paying attention to my body language. My stomach curled as I squirmed under his touch. I could feel my wetness drip down my thigh and I could hear the sound of it when Reiner moved his fingers inside of me.

"Are you okay?" He cooed as he rubbed my waist with his free hand, soothing me as my breathing increased and I focused on the pleasure.

I nodded, "mhmm."

"Soleil, look at me, please." His voice was deep, laced with a warning. His fingers move faster, and I can't seem to cope.

I finally found the courage to look at him, my eyes found his, heavy with needs. I wanted nothing more than to close them again as I felt a heavy feeling of pleasure wash over me.

Reiner kissed the inside of my thigh, "how are you doing?"

I wanted to laugh at his question but I couldn't. I felt too good when he curled his fingers inside me, causing me to grip around him. Reiner grinned at my immediate reaction, and I knew he knew what he was doing because he was amused. *Asshole.*

"Reiner, I'm close," I moaned.

"I know baby, *I know.*" He cooed as he thrusted his fingers inside of me at a faster pace, his thumb circled my clit as he pushed me over the edge.

My head felt light, filled with the light euphoric feeling, my stomach painfully settled as I bit my lips, my eyes locked with his as I came around his fingers. Reiner still stroked me at a calming pace as he helped me chase my high. My body still trembled against the cold counter as I tried to catch my breath.

Just when I thought it was over I felt Reiner's tongue all over me, lapping over my sensitive pussy, licking my wetness, his fingers still inside of me as he licked and kissed me.

"Reiner..." I moaned, tugging at his hair, desperate to get him away from me because I was too sensitive.

"Hold still for a second," he whispered.

I panted, focusing on not moving, and instead just staring at him. Reiner pulled his fingers out of me, shoving them in his mouth with a satisfying moan as he licked his fingers clean. I moaned at the sight as I tried to fight the smile that was tugging on my lips.

With the same wet fingers that were in his mouth, Reiner tapped my pussy, *"good girl."*

I held my breath when Reiner stood back up, he kissed my forehead and I frowned, scared he might leave me. I wrapped my legs around him, trapping him in between my legs and Reiner chuckled, wrapping his arms around me.

"I wasn't done with you yet, sweetheart." He said into my hair.

My shoulders sagged in relief, but that feeling was quickly washed away when he ran his hands down my back. I was quick to push his shirt off his body, Reiner laughed at my eagerness as he helped me pull his shirt over his head.

"Why are you wearing so much clothes?" I groaned.

When the shirt was finally off, I pushed him away a little — taking a good look at his body. Reiner's hands were resting on my waist and the second I moved to hop off the counter, his grip on my waist tightened around my waist, securing me in case I would fall.

Reiner paused, "I don't have a condom on me."

"I got it." I chirped.

Reiner slowly unwrapped his arms around me, allowing me to hop off the counter. I moved around the kitchen fully naked, and I tried my best not to think of it much. I opened a different drawer as I fished out a small box of condoms and handed it to Reiner.

Reiner frowned as he took the box from me, "Soleil, why do you have a box of condoms in your kitchen drawer?"

I shrugged, "I don't want to get pregnant by random guys from the bar."

"What?"

I laughed, "Kidding, I bought some the other day and I keep forgetting to put them in my room." I mumbled as I flushed my body closer against him. Reiner hummed as he opened the box of condom.

I ran my hand over his shoulders, feeling his skin everywhere. Reiner released a ragged breath when I kissed his chest. He's breathing like just the feeling of me touching him everywhere like this is painful.

He stared down at me, watching me admire him, my hands moved themselves down his body, all the way down to his belt. Reiner leaned down to my height and his lips connected with mine. He kissed me deeper this time and I felt all of his needs. Bottled up in just one kiss. I thrusted my tongue in his mouth as I pushed myself up a little, meeting his height a little as I undo his belt.

I tugged his pants off, I could only guess their pooling over his legs now. Reiner lips left mine, kissing my neck and shoulders as I shoved my hands inside his boxers, feeling his erection.

"Fuck, Soleil. . ." Reiner moaned over my shoulders as I stroked him through his boxers.

I winced when I felt his teeth graze my shoulders, but I didn't stop moving my hands, in fact; I pulled away from him a little as I lowered myself on the ground, just to connect my lips with his cock. My tongue welcomed his taste as I licked him, his eyes widened as he shuddered under me. I tugged his boxers all the way down, meeting his pants on the floor.

"Soleil, please—" He panted.

I took him in my mouth, tasting all of him at once. A moan ripped out of his throat as he wrapped his hand around my hair, pulling my head back a little.

"Soleil. . . I won't last long in your mouth."

He pulled my hair a little, not enough to make me wince, "next time baby, because right now I can't hold on forever, and I want our first time to be inside of you."

I groaned, pulling him out of my mouth, sucking his tip one last time. "You taste so good." I whispered, watching the string of saliva that connected my lips with his cock break.

"Don't say that." He groaned as he pulled me up.

Reiner wrapped his arms around my waist as he turned me around, bending me over the counter, my ass out, all for him.

"That you taste good?"

Reiner stayed quiet as he ripped open the condom, the sound of the plastic tearing had me pushing myself against him just to feel his size against me.

I shuddered when he laid a kiss on my spine, as he wrapped his hands around my waist, and I took the opportunity to speak again, "Because you do taste Reiner, you do. And I'm dying to suck you off,"

"Fuck, Soleil. . ." He thrusted inside of me. Quick and desperate.

I moaned as I gripped the counter, feeling him inside of me. So full.

"Do you want to take all of it?"

I frowned, "you're not all the way in?" I know Reiner was gifted, but I didn't think it would be this much of a thing.

He only grasped my waist, kissing my shoulders, "not yet, baby." He whispered. "Not yet."

We both let out a low deep moan, as he slowly pushed inside

of me. I have to really hold on to steady myself because the second he moved my knees buckled, too weak to handle his thrust.

I moved my waist a little, meeting his thrust in the middle and a whimper rolled off the tip of his tongue as he thrusted in rhythm, fast and quick.

"Oh fuck, this feels good." I moaned.

Reiner moaned, taking me in deeper, as his fingers dug deeper into my skin. And my head was filled with air — losing all my senses, going crazy over one single feeling.

Reiner touches me like I've never been touched before, he made me gasp and moan, he reached places I didn't know existed. I felt good — *too good*, and I could only hope he felt just as good as I felt.

He sounded both desperate and out of breath as he moaned and whimpered. Reiner stretched his hand over my chest as he cupped my breast, kneading them, caressing them.

Reiner moved his free hand over my clit, circling it. The sensation sent sparks down my body. My toes curled when his thrust slowed, his rhythm was slower but still rough, he made me feel all of him.

Reiner squeezed a handful of my ass, "stop doing that."

I moaned clenching around him again, "what?"

"That." He argued.

I couldn't help it, I was close. So close. My body was close to shutting down, the feeling spread all over my body. I was high on those crazy sex hormones, and Reiner was fucking me, helping me chase my high.

I panted as I came around him, his thumb was still over my clit as he circled it, the overstimulation had me trembling under him, still trying to handle his thrust.

Reiner groaned, "fuck."

His release wasn't too far away from mine. Reiner leaned over my shoulders panting in my ear as he chased his release and I moaned because I was sensitive all over.

When Reiner pulled out, I felt my cum drip down on my thigh. I shuddered when Reiner used his fingers to trace the cum on my thigh, I turned around to find him already staring down at me in awe, completely under a sex spell.

"Such a mess." He mumbled, gesturing at my cum over his fingers, his eyes found mine as he shoved his fingers in his mouth, licking them clean.

I've never wanted to suck his dick so much until now. I shook my head, "we should recover."

He smiled before he kissed my lips very softly, "sure." he mumbled as he handed me my shirt, and I pulled it over my head.

I could feel the awkwardness rise between us. Reiner in general is a very closed off person so this was probably a lot for him. I didn't want to make him feel even more uncomfortable. I moved around him as he buckled his belt.

"You don't have to stay if you don't want to, but I have cold pizza we can heat up."

His eyes met mine the second his shirt went over his head, "do you have beers?" He asks in return.

"Yeah, I'll just wash up a little, there's a bathroom down here

202

too if you want to use it." I pointed at a door in the corner of my house.

After I washed up, I changed into different clothes. I heated up the pizza as Reiner waited in the living room — I also made sure to wipe the kitchen counters with bleach. I hummed a tune that might not even be a real song as I plated our pizza — still clearly high on endorphins.

Each plate had three pizzas. I wasn't sure about Reiner but I knew I was hungry — I was hungry way before we even had sex, so the hunger only intensified.

His eyes widened when he saw both plates of pizza in my hands, "we're eating all of that. . . after all of that?"

I nodded as I took a seat next to him before I passed him a plate, "exactly, that was kind of a lot right?" I glanced at him.

He shrugged as he passed me a beer, "I enjoyed you."

I bit my lips as I tried not to break into a smile. Instead, I took a bite out of my pizza. "I enjoyed you too."

We sat in the living room, we ate reheated pizza in silence. The TV was on some random channel and we were sitting in perfect silence. The awkwardness between us melted slowly, then all at once.

CHAPTER TWENTY

Reiner

MY BODY ACHED, every single string in my muscles were sore. I fluttered my eyes open, finding myself in a deeply uncomfortable position on a couch that wasn't mine. . . No wonder why I'm so uncomfortable. And the fact that half of Soleil's body was over mine, still, I wasn't complaining.

The first thing that came into view was her, she slept peacefully and I thought it was unfair — with the sun bathing her whole face, her skin glowed under the light. Saying Soleil was a sight for sore eyes would be an understatement. She's simply *enchanting*. I moved her body as slowly as I could, until I was completely on the edge of the couch. I pulled my body up. Sitting on the edge of the couch.

I can't describe Soleil's beauty, my thoughts simply cannot be put into words, but I could try my hardest to find words that could fit my thoughts best; Soleil is *devastatingly beautiful.*

Watching her sleep felt like a privilege, one that I haven't earned yet, one that I might never earn. But I don't complain. I enjoy how overwhelming it feels to watch her sleep.

I hope whoever does earn that privilege fights to keep it everyday, because Soleil is a girl who's worth fighting for.

My brows furrowed and a small smile tugged my lips when I noticed the purple bonnet on her head. *It's cute.* I have no memories of falling asleep, and I was definitely not awake enough to witness her make a trip to her bedroom to grab her bonnet. The silky purple fabric is nearly falling off her head, her wild curls are half out — my hands are itching to fix it for her while she sleeps, but I'm afraid the second she wakes up she'll stare at me strangely and question my presence. I was supposed to be gone a while ago but the truth is; I can't find the courage to leave.

I should've left last night, but it's been so long since I've been in this situation. I was married before, so I couldn't exactly leave my house after, and before I was married — making out with people was as far as I went. This is new. This situation, these new needs and wants. It's all new.

What happened last night didn't fulfill half of my fantasies. Her skin, I can still feel it under mine, the faint echoes of her moans are still ringing in my ears. I simply want to do it all again but so much differently, better. Softer, rougher. I sucked in a slow ragged breath when she sighed, because even that sounded heavenly.

As if the cat could hear my thoughts, Blue came into view, just glaring at me.

"I know." I whispered. I think I should be ashamed of myself but I think I'm just a little disappointed. Maybe even a little angry with myself. Angry that I've been fighting myself over this. Angry that I didn't talk to her sooner.

I ran a hand through my hair — I'm convinced that I'm supposed to feel some sort of guilt over this because I've sinned. Again and again, but I can't stop, I'm enjoying it too much. I want to confess and beg for forgiveness but strangely enough I know I'll do it again.

Because fucking Soleil might just be my new favorite sin.

I don't even want to think about the possibilities of this never happening again, pondering on the thought alone is depressing.

Soleil stirs a little and I figure that's my cue to leave, go home and sleep comfortably I guess — I've got nothing good to do, Anna is coming later this afternoon so I cleared the whole weekend two days prior her arrival, unless it's some emergency work thing I've got to do. I'm free.

Bones in my body cracked when I stood up, my body was stiff as a board after sleeping for hours on this uncomfortable couch. We barely slept on it, half of Soleil's body was on top of mine, and the couch was definitely not big enough for me to be comfortable. I glanced at Soleil for the last time with a small smile on my face, before turning to head for the door. Blue meowed, protesting. I'm not sure if he wants me to stay, but it's strange if he wants me too.

Soleil was right when she said she was a clean person, for some strange reason I'm somewhat satisfied at that little accomplishment of hers, happy that she knows how to keep clean.

I opened the door as quietly as I could, trying to create no sound at all. The second the sun shined on my face I winced at the brightness, I don't know how Soleil sleeps through this.

When I squinted to look at my house, I noticed a familiar car parked next to mine and that grabbed all of my attention, I walked around the little fence wondering what the fuck is Noa doing here so early in the morning.

The second I walked in the house, the sound of her heels clicking filled my ears. When I reached the kitchen she wasted no time to voice her thoughts.

Her eyes met mine as she scanned my body, "where the hell were you?"

"I was out for a run."

Her eyes bounced from my gaze to my pants as she tilted her head to the side, pointing a finger, "in you khakis?" Her brows furrowed.

I stared at her contemplating on continuing my lie, there was no point to it anyway. "Why are you here?"

I walked around Noa, her brown hair flowing over her shoulders, she smells like daisies as always. I used to love that smell, but nowadays every time I interact with the scent I feel a bile coming up my throat. I'm starting to like the smell of lavender.

I opened my fridge, fishing out a water bottle still waiting for the most brilliant explanation Noa comes up with because I would love to know what the hell is she doing in my house this early in the morning. And I want to kick myself because I keep forgetting to change the locks, along with the security codes.

Noa's lips formed a thin line, her brown eyes rounding on mine, "Anna is upstairs in her room sleeping, she couldn't shut up about spending the weekend with you. So I bought her a little earlier than planned." She flashed me one of her killer smiles. I *so* used to be a sucker for those.

"I hope you don't mind because I have plans with Anthony."

Ah, Anthony. God forbid she actually wanted to grant her daughter a simple wish without gaining her own benefit out of it.

I raised both brows, "what's your play Noa? Really." I leaned against the counter crossing my arms over my chest. "You don't want to give me full custody, but you want more alone time with *Anthony*."

She slowly shook her head. "No. Me and Anthony just haven't settled in yet— he's not used to Anna yet, and I'm giving him time."

"Not used to Anna?" I scoffed.

"It's not like that at all, he's processing."

He should've processed sooner, like before sleeping with a married woman.

"You'll see soon, he's very- wait what's in your pocket?" She pointed.

Shit. Soleil's underwear. I never noticed the little ball it made in my pocket until now. This. I don't know why I actually took it.

I shrugged, "what does it matter?"

"It doesn't." She paused, staring at it a little longer. "Whatever," she wavered.

"And the custody papers?" I asked.

I know Noa, I married her. I was in love with her once. I made her happy once, I was enough once. She's a decent mother, but somehow in the middle of all this she's punishing me.

"My lawyer's still going over them."

"Hmm." I hummed.

★·☆··★

Anna woke up the second Noa left the house, and I made a mental note to schedule an appointment to have my locks changed. The last thing I need is to have her barge in the house whenever she feels like it.

I moved around the kitchen watching Anna grab some ice cream, coming around to sit on the stool next me.

"Don't you think it's too early in the morning for ice cream?" I smiled, teasing her.

She gapped up at me, "will you tell mom?"

"Never." I laughed.

"Daddy?" Anna called out.

My eyes softened a little, "yeah?"

"Are you and mom getting back together?"

The question took me by surprise. The last thing I wanted was to confuse her. I made sure to never spend any time with Noa when we're all together because I read that could confuse her about the dynamic of our family. And I managed to talk to Noa to let me keep her on the weekends so she can have some sort of stability and the time to acknowledge that her mother and I have separated.

She's only seven so it's understandable that she might have hopes that we'll be a family again, which is why it's hard for me to answer her question.

I took a few steps towards her, pulling her into my arms as I waddled us to the living room, her ice-cream still in her hand.

"We'll always be a family, you mom and I, always." I kissed the side of her head pulling her closer against me on the couch.

"It'll just be different this time, we'll share our precious time with you, and mom will be with Anthony, and dad will be with someone else. . . hopefully." I smiled a little, unsure of how she's taking all of this.

"I won't be away like last time mom and I won't go away?" She took another spoonful of her ice cream.

I held her tight, "no. Nothing like last time will happen this time, okay?"

"Okay!" she beamed. I ruffled her hair with a smile on my face as she reached for the remote, already fixing her hair.

I walked into my room, immediately awed by the sight of my bed. But taking a shower would benefit my sleep in the long run.

I closed the door behind me, stripping out of my clothes. I walked inside of my bathroom turning on the shower. Almost immediately thoughts about last night playing over and over in my head again. I grabbed my khakis fishing out Soleil's underwear.

I stared at the small lacy dark blue fabric. I try to imagine how well it looked on her. Blood rushed down my cock at just the thought. I groaned, throwing both the pants and the underwear in the clothing bin in my bathroom before climbing in the shower. I know I can't keep it, it would be ridiculously weird to give it back now after all of this but I definitely don't want to throw it away.

I wrapped my hand around my swollen cock, fisting it from the base. I used my thumb to spread the precum over the tip of my cock, I moaned at the sensitivity. I placed my hand over my head against the wall, leaning forward a little as I stroked my hand faster.

The thoughts of her hands replacing mine fills my head, I want her to join me in the shower, to stare up at me with those desperate brown eyes, her hair wet — her dark curls sticking against her nipples. Her plump lips are so alluring.

I want her hand wrapped around my cock instead of mine. I want her to moan at the sight like she could possibly feel what she makes me feel. I want to inhale her moans, begging her to move her hands faster. I moaned, chasing the euphoric high.

I'd want her on her knees for this next part, tongue out happily ready to taste me. I'd tap my dick against her tongue to tease her. I groaned disappointed by the harsh reality, I want her here in the shower with me. Right now.

I want her to moan the second I shove my cock down her throat, I whimpered at the thought, my eyes rolled back as I felt myself grow sensitive. I pumped faster, chasing my high. I whimpered as my hands worked sloppier than before.

I leaned my head against the shower wall, the water cascading down my back as I came, watching my seed get drained by the water.

I sighed, disappointed by my own actions. I shouldn't be acting like this, it's ridiculous, even when I was with Noa I was never *this* horny.

I grabbed my green loofah and squeezed the bottle of body wash on the loofah. Soaping the little fabric. Lathering it against my skin.

When I got out of the shower Anna was screaming for me behind the door, about how she wanted to go to the park. And I had no choice but to hurry and get dressed.

I got out of my room, Anna already calling for me downstairs.

I grabbed my keys on the counter opening the door letting Anna go out before me. I held my breath when I noticed Soleil, watering her plants with that hose again. I can still remember when I walked to her the first few weeks she was here to warn her about my fresh cut lawn and how irritating it can be to skin, she turned around with the hose in her hand drenching me with water.

The memory is still fresh in my mind.

"Soleil!" Anna shouted, calling out for her as she ran through the grass to meet her near the fences.

"Anna!" Soleil raised the hose a little before acknowledging it in her hand she glanced at me as she placed the hose down. Something about how enthusiastic she interacted with Anna almost made me smile.

Her hair was wrapped around in a scarf. Her face glowing, from what I'm hoping, happiness, she hadn't looked at me yet, I wanted her to look up and meet my eyes just to decipher all that

I'm feeling Reiner. I feel beyond overwhelmed. I want to wrap my arms around her, to welcome her scent. I miss her in my arms.

Soleil grinned, "how's my favorite seven year old?"

Anna beamed, staring up at Soleil, her eyes twinkling, clearly satisfied with her. "aren't I the only seven year old you know?"

"Maybe, but you're still the favorite." She smiled, "how are you?"

"Good! I just had Ice cream."

That works too I guess.

"For breakfast?" Soleil scrunched up her nose with a wide smile.

Anna nodded, "Dad agreed not to tell mom."

Soleil smiled as she looked up at me, *those eyes.* Those *enchanting* eyes.

"Reiner." she spoke, this time directly to me.

"Soleil." I replied.

Her lips were formed to a thin smile, to what I'm hoping is a *sincere* smile. She looks like she wants to tell me a million things but I understand in the presence of Anna we can't exactly talk about anything complicated.

"We'll talk later." I mouthed to her.

She only nodded, staring at Anna who was making her way back to the driveway ready to climb in my car. I offered her a soft smile as I followed Anna into my car.

CHAPTER TWENTY-ONE

Soleil

"NAH, I'M SAYING THESE PEOPLE will get the best customer services of their lives and they will have the nerve to tip you five dollars after billing it on a credit card, and it was like a family of six dining, both parents present."

"I hear you." I huffed, filling up my tray getting ready to skate to the last table I'm feeding tonight.

Half of the employees here depend on the tips. And half of the customers we get here don't tip. Some just can't afford to tip, which I completely understand, but some have you work extra to please them only to be rewarded with a two dollar bill. I'm surviving just fine, so I don't complain as much as everyone else. Other people have kids, siblings, even parents to take care of — I just have me and sometimes Hayley.

I skated towards the table, placing their drinks in front of them — their third refill this evening, but they look like they're getting ready to go so I'm no longer complaining.

I forced an awkward smile on my face when I noticed the man's eyes linger on my chest a little longer. I shifted moving back a little with the tray under my arm.

"Should I bring you guys the check?" I asked the wife specifically because the guy was still too busy staring.

She smiled up at me, "yeah, sure. I think we're about done."

I gave her a small nod, wasting no time to turn around so swiftly I bumped into a hard chest, the tray slipping under my arms, falling on the floor with a small thud. I cursed under my breath, bending down to pick up the tray, but the person in front of me was quicker than me.

I reach for the tray but he's hands laid on top of mine, "I'm so sorry." I mumbled.

"Don't be."

My brows furrowed recognizing the familiar voice. So sweet and careful. I looked up to meet those soft, soft brown eyes that often bring me comfort.

"Ian?"

He smiled, "Soleil?" He's teasing. Making light of the situation.

"I don't know." he shrugged, "I thought we were saying each other's names."

I took the tray away from him. "Har har."

"Hardy har har." He added.

He grinned, his locs were now in a low ponytail, but he left four single locs in front of his face. His eyes are raking my body, taking me in. And fun enough for me today was the day I thought was best to wear some washed out shirt that shows half of my cleavage.

"Fun seeing you here." He spoke again.

"I work here." I bit my lips.

Ian only nodded, staring at me and I opened my mouth to say something but a small person crashed against my leg, hugging them so tightly I had to take a wider step to find balance.

"Anna, hi." I patted her on the head, ruffling her hair a little. Before I could even question the situation, Reiner's body came into view.

Blood rushed through my face and settled on my cheeks as they burned. The second his eyes found mine, I swallowed, clutching on the tray. I'm still on the clock, I should get them a table — I should also bring the other family the check they've been waiting for. I looked over my shoulders only to find the husband still staring at me.

I offered him a small uncomfortable smile, when I turned to look at the two grown men in front of me I found them both staring in the direction I was staring earlier. Ian cocks his head to the side mumbling something under his breath. Reiner. Well, his gaze hardened but he looked calmed nonetheless.

I cleared my throat, gaining their attention again. "I should get you guys a table."

"Lead the way." Ian chimed in.

I made a move to walk only to remember Anna was still around my leg. It feels like I missed a few chapters because I still haven't been able to understand our relationship. She took a liking to me and I still don't know why.

"Anna." Reiner called out, holding out a hand for her to take, and without a second thought she grabbed his hand, finally freeing my legs. Ian smiled at her watching Anna find her way back close to her father.

I gave them a booth, the first one in sight. I didn't want to spend more awkward seconds making small talk about useless things with them. I wanted to be home.

Tomorrow the winner of our little assignment gets announced and the verdict for the accident also gets announced. Due to Reiner being the lawyer, I managed to have so little information on the case, he never gave me any details, he just didn't look bothered at the topic at all, which could only be good news for him. It just proves he's a great lawyer.

I'm not exactly holding my breath for those results, my chances to win are way too low. I've been sort of distracted, and with classes almost over so soon I have to start thinking about *other* jobs. Ones that sometimes don't pay, but help me look good on paper. I want to be home, in the comfort of my sheets. So I am beyond grateful to know that my shift is nearly over and the fact that I won't have to awkwardly serve them. I'm sure Mara will love this though.

After they each took a seat, I spoke again. "Someone will assist you guys shortly."

Before I could escape, Anna tugged at the apron, grabbing my attention. "Soleil! Sit with us!"

The pained expression on my face couldn't be described, but I'm trying so hard to appear collected. I looked up from Anna's hopeful little face, to Reiner's which held zero emotion. Like he didn't just hear the sentence that left his daughter's mouth. And Ian is fighting a smirk, he's entertained almost as if he was the one who proposed the idea first and whispered it to Anna.

I awkwardly laughed as I shook my head, "I can't I—"

Ian tilted his head as he stared at me, "a few minutes, we won't keep you for long."

I deflated a little, "uh, sure. I have a few minutes until my shift ends and I'll come sit with you guys."

I stared in disbelief when Ian gave Anna a high five. Still shaking my head I skated away, feeling their gaze on me.

The second I reached the back room I let out a devastating breath. Mara skated towards me, snatching the tray away from me.

"Did you get me a table before your shift was over?"

"One that tips well too." I said as I walked around her looking at all the tabs before finding the correct table number, I grabbed the check and stuffed it inside a little tab.

"Yeah, booth number six." I mumbled.

Her brows furrowed, "I didn't know we had booth numbers."

I stared at Mara, "we don't."

"Huh?"

"It's Reiner again, just spot him." I said before leaving the room, skating back to the last table I've been serving tonight.

Mara's faint voice was heard when I left something about me liking Reiner.

I placed the check on the table, sliding it to the wife, "Here's the check. Sorry it took me a while."

I kind of felt bad because they did sort of see everything happen. The whole bumping into Ian, Anna screaming my name as she hugs my legs… Reiner just standing there. His hair was messy today, and he looked tired, so tired.

"Yes, thank you."

I blinked a few times when I heard the wife's voice. Dragging me back to reality.

I sat next to Ian because Anna was already sitting next to Reiner — and because I figured it'd make more sense to slide into the booth next to Ian. but now I'm starting to regret it because each time he laughs he leans closer towards me. And the guy's always laughing. Whether it's about something silly Anna said or something he said.

I searched my brain for any conversation starters but Reiner keeps glancing at me, his eyes sometimes venture to Ian, who's constantly brushing his shoulders against mine each time he laughs.

Reiner cleared his throat a little, "thank you for joining us on such short notice, Soleil."

I shrugged a little, "it's no big deal."

It was kind of a big deal — see, I wanted to be in bed right now. It's nearly nine, and the one time I wanted to work extra hours had to be the night where Reiner and his daughter *and Ian* wanted to have dinner. But I haven't had dinner yet so I'm not complaining too much.

I stared at Mara when she came over our table to serve us. A small smile was plastered on her face — one that was not for the benefit of the customers, but one that was meant to taunt me. I was fighting the urge not to laugh the second her eyes met mine when she asked us for our order.

Her voice never sounded so weird.

Anna tugged her father's arm down, grabbing his attention as he leans towards her offering her his ears so she could speak freely. A small smile washed over his features, as he nodded at whatever she was whispering in his ears.

When he pulled away he stared at Mara, "a kids mac n' cheese will do just fine for Anna."

Mara nodded, writing down the order.

When no one said anything next I figured it wouldn't hurt to suggest something. "We can do that family bowl of spaghetti." I looked at both Ian and Reiner waiting for them to voice their thoughts.

Ian shrugged, "I don't mind."

Reiner nods, staring at me. "Yeah, sure we can do spaghetti."

After taking our drinks, Mara disappeared from our view. Skating away.

My gaze shifted to Anna who was too busy staring at her screen to even feel the awkwardness in the air. I didn't even notice when she grabbed her iPad. Her blonde hair curtained the front of her face. But conversing with her is the only way to save the dead atmosphere around us.

"How's wrestling going?"

A beat passed and I realized Anna probably didn't hear what I said, but Reiner saved me from the embarrassment by nudging over her shoulder.

"Anna, Soleil's talking to you." He nudged.

Anna looked up, her big blue eyes meeting mine. "Yes?"

"How's wrestling going?" I repeated my previous question.

"Good!" she smiled, "I won my last match."

"Atta girl!" Ian clapped his hands, his shoulder brushing against mine as he high five Anna.

I smiled at their little interaction, it's always nice to see the ways guys interact with kids — it says a lot about their personalities.

When Mara placed the big bowl of spaghetti in the middle, it was almost like second nature for Reiner to grab my plate and fill it to the rim, handing me this big plate of spaghetti. I smiled, taking the plate from him. Unsure if I'm even capable of eating this monster plate.

Ian smiles like he's paying attention to what's happening, but I don't know what's happening. All I know is that Reiner served me this big plate of food before anyone else touched it. It's like he memorized how much I eat. Maybe he did because he did feed me when I stayed at his house over those few days.

"Thank you." I smiled at Reiner, my mood shifting at just the sight of food. It's strange because I see food all day when I work, but it never fails to cheer me up.

Small talk, I need to make small talk. I stared at Anna who

was bussy scarfing down her mac N' cheese, I needed to make really small talk. I looked at Ian at my side who was plating his own food now. It feels so awkward around me.

My eyes bounce on Reiner again, "so…" I began, twirling my fork in the spaghetti preparing the perfect bite, "what brings you guys here?"

Reiner's eyes bounced on Anna before finding Ian's gaze. He's so still like he's taking a moment to choose the correct words to say.

"Ian's my lawyer." was all he said.

I stopped mid chewing to look at Ian at my side, who was also in the middle of taking a bite, now he's looking like a deer caught in the headlights. He shoved the spoonful of food in his mouth nodding at Reiner to back up his statement.

"And we needed dinner." Ian added.

I hummed while taking another bite of my food. Reiner keeps staring at me and each time he does this uneasiness settles in my stomach. And if I don't chew carefully enough I might end up choking. I shifted my foot under the table just to brush my feet against his a little because he was right in front of me.

His shoulders sagged a little as he released a small breath, taking the first bite of his shoes as my foot rested against his. Just the shoes touching.

Ian nudged my shoulder, "I keep forgetting to get your number."

My eyes widened as I sipped on my water watching Reiner's hand clench around the fork as he twirls it around preparing his next bite of spaghetti.

"Yeah sure, just give me your phone."

I punched my number into Ians phone feeling Reiner's hot gaze on me the whole time. Watching me hand back the phone. Watching me laugh when Ian mumbled a funny thank you.

Anna made a small squeaky sound, shoving her iPad into his chest. "Dad play for me, please."

Reiner held the iPad, "what am I supposed to be playing?"

"Roblox, I can't make it past the first three towers." She whined, "I just want to win a round for once!"

I took another bite of my food, watching them with a smile on my face. Reiner only squinted, hoping that would give him a better understanding of the game. He sighed, and his fingers moved way faster than before, but then Anna sighed, very loudly. Almost gasping in horror.

"You didn't even make it past the first tower, dad." She frowned.

Reiner pulled his lips into a thin line, "can't we do this another time, Princess?"

Anna only shook her head, passing the iPad in my direction, "try it Soleil. It's *Tower of* a word I'm not allowed to say." She air-quoted the last part.

Reiner shook his head, "don't air-quote. You know it's a bad word and why you're not allowed to say it."

I nodded, wiping my hands with a napkin as I pushed my plate away a little, I finished chewing as I swallowed, "and the goal is to get to the last tower?"

"Yes, and you have to get there before a new round starts."

I grabbed the huge iPad, "is this what everyone is playing now?"

She nodded, "a lot of my friends made it to the last tower."

The game is confusing, the way to navigate, the obstacles, they make it hard to get past the first tower, but I managed to make it past at least six towers. I forgot to ask Anna how many towers to expect but I was so concentrated, just talking would throw me off my game.

"Almost there!" Anna whispered, my fingers shook and Anna's avatar fell off the thin wood I was slowly walking on earlier. I grimaced as I glanced at Anna, I had no idea when she came over to my side so her voice took me by surprise.

"Sorry." I whispered, handing her back the iPad. Anna didn't say anything; she only extended her small arm and handed the iPad to Ian.

"It's your turn."

Ian only grinned, rubbing his hands together, obviously ready to outplay us.

Anna leaned over the table, basically leaning all over me, "can I sit next to Ian, please? I want to see."

My brows raised at her request but I said nothing to protest, even though I know changing seats with her would have me sitting next to Reiner.

"Yeah, okay." I moved my body slowly out of the way, watching her replace me in the seat as I awkwardly faced Reiner, taking Anna's previous seat.

Reiner tensed as he released a heavy breath, leaning over the table as he switched Anna's plate and mine. Sure enough, Ian and Anna both looked cozy with the huge iPad in front of them, no one was complaining. I picked up my fork again, taking another bite.

"At least you made it past tower one."

I sucked in a breath as I glanced at Reiner over my shoulder, nodding as I swallowed the food in my mouth. "Right. I'm surprised she didn't look at me the way she looked at you."

Reiner tilted his head as his brows pulled together, "how did she look at me again?"

"Very disappointingly."

He grinned, and his dimples came into view, "yeah."

I didn't smile with him. I couldn't. My chest was too tight, and my stomach was burning. I only nodded, staring at the plate of food in front of me.

"I won!" Ian erupted into a fit of laughter, his words boomed all around the restaurant but we didn't seem to mind, I was laughing, Anna was happy, and Reiner was fascinated, I think.

"Show off." I mumbled under my breath as I laughed.

"No, no, no," Anna shoved the iPad into his arms again, "go again, but teach me this time."

Ian stared at me as he wiggled his brows, "hahaha, prepare yourself to be *amazed*."

"Don't drown yourself in beginner's luck, Ian."

Ian shook his head at Reiner, finding his grip on the iPad again, "beginner's luck, pfft, I'll show you beginner's luck."

★ · ☆ · ★

Dinner was less awkward thanks to Ian who actually kept playing the game, and Anna almost made it to the last tower on her own, thanks to Ian. Reiner and I barely spoke, but we understood everything we weren't saying out loud. At least I think we did.

Ian and Reiner bickered over the check while I joked about it with Anna. In the end they ended up splitting it to save their egos. I didn't care much because I got an apple pie for dessert and I couldn't finish it all. I had to get it *to go.* So the second I reach home and I know I'll be hungry I'll have the apple pie to fill me up.

We walked out of the restaurant to the parking lot, my bag over my shoulders. I always parked out back of the restaurant to just walk through the back door and change in the locker rooms to clock in without greeting any of the customers.

Reiner was parked right next to Ian. It's been dark outside now for a while considering it's ten o'clock. Ian offered to walk me to my car because it's so dark outside — he wanted to be gentlemen.

Before I could argue with him, Reiner voiced his opinions, basically agreeing with Ian, that I should allow Ian to walk me to my car. He thought it was safer that way.

I stepped forward in front of Reiner, placing a hand over Anna's hair, softly stroking it. "Bye, Anna."

"See you at home. . ." she mumbled, she was thrown over Reiner's shoulders — she fell asleep long ago in the restaurant, and

Reiner wanted to go back home because she leaves tomorrow with her mother.

I smiled watching her yawn a little, poor thing must be so tired.

I looked at Reiner and immediately when his eyes softened and my stomach flipped inside out. "Thank you." I mumbled to him.

He offered me a smile, "it's nothing."

But he's wrong because talking to him is *everything*.

CHAPTER TWENTY-TWO

★ · ☆ · ★

Reiner

★ · ☆ · ★

I GROANED, leaning against my chair as I took the glasses off my face. Holding the bridge of my nose listening to my mother scold me over the phone. She's been calling more frequently now that I've made it a habit to pick up.

She's back on the Noa topic, it seems like she can't leave it alone. I've made it very clear that I've been handling it, but she still wants to lecture me almost everyday as if talking my head off would speed things up.

I don't blame her though, I used to be just as angry as her. But my anger faded once I realized what really happened — that Anna was taken away from me, the results of my own wife cheating on me. For that while, I was lost. Half hope, half despair. Work kept me busy throughout the day but not so much at night, so I kept working too. I only slept whenever I was passed out over my desk, or when I dozed off in the shower — overworked myself to the point thinking was no longer an option.

Things got better gradually. I tortured myself less because I figure it'd never truly help. I worked out more, kept myself busy but on a healthy level I was almost happy once, when the office threw me a birthday party, it was nice, even if they did thrash my house and left the mess for me to clean. It was nice though.

I tapped my fingers over the table, "mom, I have to go. It was really nice catching up, truly."

"No, Reiner I'm not done, have you heard from your father?"

I shook my head, finally sitting up "not in a while, no." I whispered, "what's up?"

She only sighed from the other line, "nothing, I just haven't heard from him in a while is all."

"Ah," I nodded, "well, he's still in the honeymoon phase with Connie, and you know dad, he'll call when he wants to talk."

I could hear mom laugh a little over the phone, it wasn't a happy laugh, she sounded stressed. "You sound like him a lot, you know."

I shrugged, unsure of how to respond to that.

"Don't let Noa take another chance at happiness away from you again, Reiner. You don't deserve any of all of this."

Ian walked through the door, a folder in his hand, probably another case for me, or perhaps his own case for me to look at.

"I won't mom, and I really have to go this time, we'll talk later." I hung up the phone before she could even protest.

"You know it's rude to hang up on your own mother?"

I pulled my lips into a thin line, "in that case, I'll make sure to make a note and apologize later." I placed my phone on the corner of my desk, I extended a hand out and Ian placed the folder in my hands.

Ian stuffed his hand in his pockets and I could almost hear an uncomfortable comment coming from the tip of his tongue, "you and Soleil?"

And there it was.

I flipped the folder open, not sparing him a look. I've known Ian for a while now, so I know for a fact that he won't be afraid to step on someone else's foot to get whatever it is he wants. I knew he liked Soleil, I just never thought he'd actually take the interest.

"Me and Soleil?" I repeated the question.

He shrugged. "I don't know man, you two seemed pretty cozy the other night."

"we barely talked." I deadpanned.

"Could've fooled me."

I glared at him, "do you want my help on this or not?"

There was an awkward expression on his face but he stayed quiet, allowing me to look through the papers of his case. I want to feel bad about the awkwardness between us now, but I didn't feel ready enough to acknowledge it. So I did the best I could in helping him.

CHAPTER TWENTY-THREE

Soleil

THE MUSIC at Josie's blasted through the speakers. It always does. I sat on a stool near the bar, waiting for Hayley who was supposed to meet me here to celebrate winning our little assignment. She gets to skip those final exams. I've been waiting for a little over an hour now. I sent her two texts. They are both still unread.

I think her passing the assignment was more beneficial for her than it would be for me. Her habit to occasionally hike is the only thing that could keep her sane besides alcohol but now she'll have a free semester. She was only taking two classes anyways.

Ben the bartender, also known as our local creep, was now standing in front of me. Seriously no matter how many complaints he gets, he still gets to keep his job. It's been only me and Hayley complaining anyways so I guess no one cares. It's his words against ours, besides, our photos are hung on the wall of *"wasted beyond repair"* so what do we know?

Ben being a good looking guy didn't help either.

"Where's thing one?" Ben asked as he wiped the glass in his hand with a towel.

"Just shut up." I groaned.

I've had a long day today, classes felt so long. I had to work an extra shift, and Hayley has been MIA all day. Dodging my calls, not answering texts — I was surprised she even agreed to meet me here given that she found out she won the assignment through me.

On our first Halloween together we thought It'd be funny to dress as *thing one and thing two,* we ended up at Josie's, got really wasted and danced on the tables, our pictures were taken, and ever since then, Ben has only been acknowledging us as *thing one and thing two,* but I truly think that night has sealed our friendship.

Our pictures are hung high up on the wall in this bar, so high up the *wasted beyond repair* wall, among a bunch of other photos. A monstrous photo of the both of us. So waisted.

I placed my elbow on the counter, hanging my head low as I traced my scalp with my fingers, I can't do much more than that. The second I run my fingers through my hair, it'll get stuck.

I sent Hayley another text because I was growing impatient here, it was nearly nine, I could be at home right now, passed out on the couch or better yet, asleep in my bed. I've been waiting for more than an hour. I know I could probably just drive to her house, but it's so late at night. Well it's not late, I'm lazy.

I huffed as I fixed my posture again, chugging my club soda before leaving the ten dollars change on the counter, I could literally hear my wallet cry out to me the second I pulled ten bucks out. I'll go home and try to call again, and if she doesn't pick up I'll go to sleep and drive to her house tomorrow.

I closed my car door as I clutched on the car keys in my hand. When I glanced at Reiner's house his light in the living room was on, it was dimmed but it was still on.

I shook my head, the more I thought about it the more I realized how much of a bad idea it was. The steps I took towards my house grew smaller and smaller. I was fighting the urge to not follow my bad idea — because clearly the better idea was just to walk inside my house and pass out on the couch with the TV on.

I sighed before I curved my house, going around the little fence. And within seconds I was standing in front of his door. I rang his doorbell as I pulled out my phone to check the time — it was kind of late, around nine late, I supposed that could be super late for him.

I shoved the phone in my back pocket, I pushed the pieces of hair that fell in front of my face, and the door opened. And he was dressed too casual for someone who's going to bed soon. He wore blue jeans, and black shirt that fitted him like a second skin. His hair was messy, tangled like he's been playing with it.

Reiner looked at me, then around me like he couldn't believe or understand why I was standing here this late.

"Hi." I finally said.

"Hey." He whispered back.

I took a deep breath, because I could smell his cologne this far away from him. And I kept forgetting the fact that I was supposed to stick with a specific perfume so I could have my own scent like he does. I smell like lavender, my hair smells like it after each wash, my soap smells like it, even my clean laundry smells like lavender. It's not a fancy scent, but I know I smell like it.

Reiner moved his body out the way as he opened the door a little wider, "come in."

I smiled as I moved past him, taking a step inside the house. I didn't want to invade and just marched into his living room. I wanted to be invited to do so — so I stood in the middle of the room as I waited for him to catch up.

The door clicked after he locked it. I turned around, holding his gaze as he walked closer towards me.

"Congrats on the case."

"Thank you," he hummed, his gaze shifting away as he slowly nodded.

"And you, did you. . .?"

I shook my head, "nope."

Reiner walked away, signaling for me to follow him. "You don't seem too sad about it."

I followed him into the kitchen, "the person who won, needed it more than me." I looked around the kitchen, everything was neat and tidy but there was a wine bottle on the counter.

I watched Reiner open his cabinet in silence, his back muscles flexed with the action. I swallowed, blinking a few times watching him pull out wine glasses, and suddenly my heart was functioning so much better than before because this was an invitation to stay a little longer.

He turned around, tipping the wine glass towards me, "wine?"

"Yes, please."

Reiner smiled as he grabbed the already opened wine bottle. He poured the first glass and handed it to me before he poured himself a glass and we made our way to the living room. The TV was on a sports Olympic channel and two familiar pairs of figure skaters were dancing on the ice. I was surprised to say the least but I didn't say anything, instead I just sat on the couch next to him in silence.

I sipped my wine as I glanced around the room, "where's Anna?" I'm surprised she hadn't come down to say hi yet, unless she's asleep already.

"Her mother picked her up a day ago." He took a swing. "I don't know, sometimes I think Anna's having a hard time— this must be really confusing for her."

Reiner barely talked about himself, it was already hard enough for him to even try to engage in conversation just to be polite — I never thought he'd willingly share anything personal without me prying.

I swallowed as I tapped the wine glass, "because of the separation?"

He closed his eyes but the exhaustion was still there, "that and everything else."

I turned my body towards him as I lowered my glass, "I'm sure she did have a hard time from the beginning but from what I can tell you've been showing her stability, and that goes a long way, Reiner. It helps her understand the situation."

He brought the glass to his lips as he took another sip, "stability." he repeated.

I nodded, "yes, kids dream a lot, they have a lot of hope too, and it's harder for them to see the way you see things, so showing her stability after a hard separation helps establish the situation. It shows her the reality of things without leaving any room for hope."

He nodded as he took a deep breath, "so she's not feeling neglected. That's good."

I raised my brows as I swallowed, turning away from him a little. It was my turn to take a swing from my alcoholic drink. I know what being neglected looked like, and I know what feeling neglected felt like. I've seen the way Reiner interacts with her, I've seen the way he loves her, so I hope he can stop torturing himself with the thought that she might be feeling neglected because she isn't, not by him at least. The situation is hard, but he's doing the best he can.

"Reiner?"

"Hmm?"

"You're a good father." I said sincerely.

Reiner tilted his head back as he laughed very softly, his eyes met mine for a second and he laughed all over again. The one time I wanted to give honest advice and help cheer someone up I managed to screw it up.

I frowned, "why are you laughing?"

He bit his lip as he suppressed the rest of his laughter, "the irony of it."

"Which is?"

"People only say *'you're a good father'* when the person is obviously struggling at being a parent."

I shook my head with a slow pause, "no. . . I don't think there's any irony in this situation. It's not how it works."

"Right." He drank the rest of his wine before placing the empty glass on the coffee table.

I stared at him as he ran a hand through his hair before he finally stared at me intensively. "I'm sorry we haven't talked at all, I know I promised you we would talk about it and we haven't."

I shrugged as I placed my almost empty glass on the coffee table next to my phone and keys. "There's nothing to talk about, really. We hooked up, it was a mutual decision and I don't think it's something to apologize for."

"I wasn't apologizing for sleeping with you," he smiled, "that would be a *lie*."

"Oh."

My thoughts stopped a little as my heart raced. The wine was finally working, but it wasn't working fast enough. I sighed as I felt this new wave of emotion washing over me.

"But we really can't let it happen again." He said.

"We shouldn't let it happen again or we can't let it happen again?"

He smiled, "we can't let it happen again."

"What is that grin for? You can't say it like that with a grin, Reiner." I laughed, "I refuse to take you seriously right now."

"What? No, this is a slight smile," he pointed a finger at his face, "I wouldn't call that a grin, it's barely a smile."

"You're awful."

He tsk, "you sure about that?"

No, he was not awful but I refused to understand his protests about us not hooking up again, because it was the only thing I could think about right now. In fact I want to let it happen as much as possible. I want him to change his mind, to take it back — to realize how much we should keep doing what we both really wanted to do right now. Another bad idea popped into my head, but with the wine coursing through my veins it seemed like a good idea at the moment.

"You're not *that* awful. . . you're a great kisser."

My memories of the first time we kissed played in my head, the soft feeling of his lips against mine, the tenderness of our kiss, it was passionate and rushed. *It was perfect.* And I wanted it the same way every single time. My skin tingles at the thoughts. Whenever he touched me he was always sure, his touch was never timid, his thoughts might be hesitant but his actions were sure.

"You're such a *great* kisser," I said, climbing into his lap. I raised my hands up to cup his face. His hands were at his side, he didn't dare to lay a hand on me — his legs however spread the second I reached his lap. I was sitting comfortably, enjoying the way his face was flushed.

Heat crawled to his cheeks, his ears turned the lightest shade of red. And I loved this so much it should be a crime.

"You look so handsome when you blush." I whispered as I

leaned closer towards him. I watched his eyes bounce from mine to the corner of the room.

Without even thinking I laid a soft kiss against his neck, listening to the way his breathing quickened, his chest heaved a little. He was suddenly tensed under me. Shifting.

I lifted my head to take a look at him, to look into his eyes, those blue eyes that held so many dark desires. One look at them and I know his head was swimming with dirty thoughts. I licked my lips, watching him swallow, his Adam apple moved with the action. I couldn't settle in his lap, the way he stared at my lips was doing things to me, so I tried to move as little as I could.

Reiner placed both hands on my waist, and it felt like I let out a heavy sigh, because his touch finally came, he steadied me on his lap, his eyes nervous. "You're drunk." He coaxed.

"After one glass of wine?" I wanted to laugh, because if I was anything, I was horny — I was horny, not drunk. I was feeling a little bolder than before, however I was still not drunk, not even tipsy. The wine only gave me courage to act out on my true feelings. The wine intensified my needs.

But Reiner wouldn't stop pushing the topic, always so hesitant. "Maybe, who knows your tolerance?"

I frowned. "Well, it's not that low."

Reiner shrugged a little, the corner of his lips twitching up to form a small smile. It's the cutest thing I've ever seen. I wanted him to do it again, but it'd be strange to make such a request.

"It doesn't matter how many times you touch me, I'm *never* fully satisfied." I smiled up at him, my confidence going higher by the second.

"I'm a glass half full kind of girl."

"Hmm," he mummed.

I leaned forward as I trailed kisses on his neck, he was still hesitant to touch me or maybe he just didn't want to touch me — if that was the case I wish he would say something because I felt ridiculous. It wasn't like he hadn't seen me naked or fucked me before.

I was bored and embarrassed, so I made a move to get off his lap with a heavy sigh, but before I could shift, Reiner's hand on my waist tightened — preventing me from getting off completely. My brows furrowed, my hands on his shoulders as I looked at him.

His glossy eyes darkened, "keep going." He instructed.

I huffed, "Reiner. . ."

"*Soleil.*"

My name was dripped with sex coming from his mouth, the sound was enough to drive me crazy, I wanted to hear it again, and again, and again. I wanted nothing more than my name coming out of his mouth.

I grind myself against him, shifting forward, I moved my hands from his shoulders and pushed them down. . . under his shirt. My skin grew hot as I felt his — I could feel his fingers slipping under my shirt, slowly. Teasingly.

"What do you want, Reiner?" I whispered against his lips, only a hair away.

I gasped when he grabbed a fistful of my ass, "*You.* Just you." He groaned before pushing his head forward, connecting our lips.

Hell froze each time we kissed. Flowers bloomed in my stomach, goosebumps rose on my — it felt like the first time every time. The rush never disappeared, and I loved the feel of the rush. When my Brain stopped working, it was filled with thoughtless thoughts, unfinished needs. My lungs went on autopilot because I kept forgetting how to breathe each time his soft lips crashed against mine.

My tongue sought for his first, taking entrance the second he moaned in my mouth. I sucked his tongue doing that same thing he did before, it drove me wild the first time. His hands were riding my shirt up, desperately trying to tug it away. I laughed into his mouth as I pushed my body away to take off the shirt.

My shirt was off and far away in a corner of his house. Reiner leaned forward and shoved his face into my chest, kissing my breast through the bra. I pulled his head away, taking his lips into my mouth again.

Reiner sucked my bottom lip for a mere second and I moaned in his mouth, he was slowly taking back control of the situation and I didn't care anymore because this felt too good. He cupped one of my tits, kneading it in his hands. I was squirming under him, moving back and forth until I felt a hard bulge under me.

His erection was hard to hide. Reiner trailed kisses from my cheeks to my neck, tattooing me with soft kisses, I fluttered my eyes closed, whimpering as I felt his lips over my collar bone, his warm breath fanned over skin.

This felt like flying, and other things that felt better than flying. This feeling was better than hot apple pies. This was better than everything else I considered good.

I moaned, moving his shirt up and took it off his body — I threw it in that same corner my shirt landed. The necklace around his neck came into view. I took a second to stare at his chest, so defined. Filled with muscles. I hooked my fingers under his necklace and pulled it up a little. The more my eyes lingered, his breathing quickened. I moved my hands over his chest and watched him squirm a little. His own hands were riding up my back to unclasp my bra.

I sucked in a breath feeling the heavy weight of the bra lift. The cool air met my nipples the second Reiner took the bra off.

"*Oh,* my fuck, Soleil." Reiner groaned, taking the sight of my chest.

I grind my lower half against his erection as I earned another moan out of him. "You've seen them before." I teased.

He shook his head a little, licking his lips as his eyes flickered from my face to my chest. "I don't think I'll *ever* get used to it."

Reiner's hands were on my waist again, and he tilted me back a little, giving me the full opportunity to wrap my legs around his waist, securing my fall — Reiner blew a soft cool air before his tongue met my stomach, licking his way up to the valley of my breast. I moaned, nearly shivering, feeling the small kisses Reiner left around my breast. He was kissing everywhere, but where I needed him the most.

I wrapped my arms around his head and gripped his hair. Reiner winced as he pulled away a little, his eyes were wild. Filled with amusement.

"Tell me what you want, Soleil." He asked, as he played with a smile on his face and his dimples came into view.

Asshole.

I groaned as I pushed him back a little, I wrapped my hands over my chest, shifting on his lap. Reiner brows pulled together when my breasts weren't in his view anymore.

"What are you doing?"

"I am not begging you." I stated.

Reiner tsk, and his fingers found the buttons of my jeans, "If it's a good fuck you want, Soleil. I suggest you look elsewhere, because if you allow me to fuck you again, I won't stop there."

I pulled my hands away from my chest, feeling all hot and bothered. My fingers found the buttons of his jeans too, and I unbuttoned them.

"Good." I mumbled.

Reiner's fingers brushed my pussy softly over the underwear before he rubbed my clit. My stomach tightened in the process. I let out an audible moan, my toes curled when he kept going. He leaned forward to hold my waist with his free hand, and his lips met my shoulders as he peppered my skin with soft kisses.

I was burning everywhere for him. Everywhere.

Reiner lifted my hips until there was a space gap between us, I helped him pull my pants down along with the underwear, when I sat on his lap again he wasted no time to rub my clit.

His fingers moved away from my clit as he tapped the entrance of my pussy, once. . . twice. The lewd sounds of my wetness filled the silence around us.

"So fucking wet, I love it when you're this wet." He mumbled against my skin, nibbling at it as he shoved two fingers inside of my pussy, no warnings.

I grabbed onto his shoulder gasping at his pace. So rough and punishing. His thumb was still over my clit, circling it as he curled his fingers deeper inside of me.

"Reiner." I moaned over his shoulders, because he seemed to be lost — drunk on the sounds of my moans. His eyes were closed and he was kissing my shoulders, grazing his teeth over my skin.

Reiners eyes snapped open, a new realization settled in. "Where's your phone?" He asked.

I bit my lips, struggling to keep my eyes open because Reiner didn't stop what he was doing, he only added more speed into his actions.

"Wha-"

Reiner groaned, pushing us both forward, as he leaned to grab my phone on his coffee table. Which I forgot was even there. Reiner nudged the phone towards me urging me to grab it. I huffed as I grabbed the phone from him. Still wondering what the hell am I supposed to do with it at this time.

"Call Ian."

My eyes widened, but a moan, a whimper escaped my throat as I felt Reiner add a third finger inside of me.

"Reiner?" I panted.

"You're allowing me to fuck you again, yes?" He paused to look up at me, "call him and tell him you aren't interested."

I nodded, swallowing as he thrust his fingers inside of me.

He laid a kiss against my collar bone, and his free hand grabbed a fistful of my ass, "call. Ian." He instructed.

I groaned, scrolling through my contacts, the only reason why I even had Ian's number was because he called me last night to make sure I got home safely, which was rather sweet of him.

I held the phone up to my ear, biting my lips, hoping to keep all the moans bottled up. I'm also praying, begging that he doesn't pick up the phone. But after the third ring he did pick up.

The line was silent, and I tried to settle as much as I could over Reiner's fingers.

"Hi Ian!" I faked my cheery voice. I never answer the phone like that but I doubt my actual normal voice would work.

"Hey, Soleil."

I nearly shrieked as I jumped a little, Reiner pulled out his fingers then pushed all three of them back inside me and curled them almost immediately.

"I'm sorry if I made it seem like I was into you. . ." I paused, pushing a hand over my mouth as Reiner bit my nipple.

"I'm sort of. . ." I stopped to let out a soft breath, too overwhelmed by trying to keep down all of my moans, "unavailable right now." I finished my sentence.

I closed my eyes, getting lost in the feeling, a whimper escaped my throat and Reiner looked up at me with a satisfied look, like he just won a stupid bet. His blue eyes were glistening with sex.

Ians' voice was hesitant, "are you. . . okay?"

"Good." I moaned, my eyes widened, and Reiner was beginning to laugh, so I tried to pull my body away from him, but the joke seemed to have died because his face hardened as he wrapped his arms around my waist. Trapping me in.

His fingers moved at a faster pace. I wanted to moan so bad, but Ian was still silent on the other line of the phone, probably trying to listen in to what was really going on because it was a strange situation, me calling him this late at night just to turn him down before he even got a chance to ask me.

Reiner, the asshole just loves to play territory.

I leaned forward, placing my head over Reiner's shoulder, letting out a soft sigh, but I think it was a whimper. Either way I buried my face deep into the crook of his neck, waiting for Ian on the other line to put me out of this misery.

"It's all good Soleil." Ian said over the phone.

I nodded and completely forgot how to use my words. I nodded, closing the phone. I didn't hang up, I quite literally shut the phone down. *Power off.* I didn't want to make any more phone calls so I let the phone slide down behind the couch. I'd regret it later but right now the only thing I wanted to do was moan.

"You did good, baby." He praised.

His voice was so soothing, his hands rubbed small circles on my back as my high washed over me, taking me by surprise.

I grasped his shoulders and sank my teeth into his skin, muffling the sound of my moans feeling Reiner's fingers curl inside of me. His thumb never seemed to stop circling my clit. He'd pull his finger out to tease me and slap my pussy only to shove it back in harsher than earlier.

I could feel my wetness pool over his Jean, it was running

down my thigh, just dripping out. I closed my eyes as I panted against this neck, letting out a breathy moan as I came. Reiner kept fingering me, riding out my high. But the second he pulled his fingers out of me, he hummed stuffing them into his mouth. He closed his eyes as he licked them clean.

My stomach tensed at the sight, he did it so seductively it's like he enjoyed the way I tasted. It was the sexiest thing a man could ever do.

Reiner grinned, cocking his head to the side as he took a look at my flushed face, "did I tire you out yet?"

"Shouldn't I be asking you that question?"

He laughed and his chest vibrated under me and I fought so hard to hold back my laughter. I wanted to smile at the sight because it was so pure.

"Did you just call me *old*?"

"Not in those exact words."

Reiner slapped my ass, causing me to gasp a little. "I'll show you differently."

Reiner lifted his lips, riding his pants down. He moved his hands, fishing a condom out of his pants. I gazed down at his hands watching him roll the condom on his cock. Reiner licked his lips as he looked up at me.

I moved forward, and his hands shot up to my waist, guiding me, helping me. Our forehead connected, my mouth parted open as I lowered myself down on him, feeling just the tip of his cock brush against my pussy. Reiner pushed me lower, my eyes snapped to connect with his but he was much rather focused on what we were doing.

His fingers rubbed small circles against my back as he pushed me down lower this time, one last harsh thrust — causing me to take all of him.

I moaned in delight, feeling him. I rolled my hips a little to feel more of him, but Reiners' hands tightened around my waist, and a low groan left his lips.

"Give me a second, baby."

Reiner closed his eyes like this was too painful for him to bear, like he was feeling too much at once. He let out a soft breath, finding his grip on my waist again as he moved me up before harshly pushing me back down, earning a moan out of me.

I placed a hand on his stomach as I moved my hips matching his movements and listening to his soft moans. Reiner leaned forward, closing his mouth around my nipple. I shuddered as I cried. I felt him deep in my stomach when he bit my nipple. Reiner pulled away with a lazy smile on his face. "I couldn't resist." He whispered.

His thrust grew deeper and rougher, his eyes glued to my chest, watching the way my tits bounce in front of him. That same lazy smile was still plastered on his face, and Reiner threw his head back a little, resting it on the couch as his hands on my waist moved me to a much quicker rhythm. His mouth parted open and moans were spilling out of his mouth.

I panted, barely breathing but what we were doing was so hot it should be a crime to close our eyes, I stared down a little watching his cock go in and out of me so easily. My wetness and his precum dripped out of me. I moaned when I paused to roll my hips over his, the spot felt so fucking good.

"Fuck." Reiner moaned with his eyes closed, a desperate, breathy sound.

I leaned forward as I licked his ear, "please look. . . Reiner, look at what we're doing." I moaned into his ear.

Reiner let out a breathy sigh, as he pulled his head back up to stare down at our lewd action, the mess we were making. He licked his lips as he lifted me up from the waist and his glistening cock came into view before he entered me again with a quick thrust. I bit my lips, groaning as I took all of him again, and I watched him *whimper* at the feeling.

I gasped, feeling the way his pace quickened, my head was starting to feel light, the knot in my stomach begging to be released. One of Reiners' hands traced my stomach before finding my clit. Circling it in a soft motion. So soft that I was melting. I think I stopped moving and Reiner was doing all the work.

I moaned, welcoming the familiar intense feeling. Reiner took my mouth and kissed me through my orgasm, his tongue danced with mine as his thrust grew sloppier. Panting in my mouth as I swallow his moans. My hair curtained around us, just everywhere as he kissed me.

Each time I clutched around him I could feel him pulse inside of me. I held onto Reiner while he fucked me through my orgasm until he came. Until his strokes grew weaker. Moaning under me as he rides out his high.

I laid my head over his shoulders, attempting to catch my

breath. Reiner thrusted inside of me one last time, so slow and deep it took me by surprise as I let out a shaky breath. Still shuddering from my orgasm.

"I think we need a shower."

"Shower." I repeated my new favorite word.

CHAPTER TWENTY-FOUR

Reiner

HER HAIR. She was worried about her hair. She's been standing right in front of me, mumbling a bunch of words that I couldn't really focus on because I could see her nipples poke through my shirt.

Soleil allowed me to fuck her a second time. And she was still here. In my bathroom. I managed to convince her to take a shower with me. Well I didn't do any convincing, I just suggested the idea and she was more than eager.

She wrapped her hands around her hair, trying to stuff it into a ponytail, but it was everywhere so it wasn't really working. I never thought of her hair before — I didn't think it'd be an issue.

"Reiner." She snapped her fingers as she pulled me from my thoughts.

"Hmm?" I hummed, as my eyes found her brown ones.

"Nevermind on shower sex, I can't bring myself to sacrifice my hair." She let go of her hair, letting them flow over her shoulders, her curls were everywhere, half frizzy, half defined.

"It's fine." I mumbled, smiling down at her. I was entertained by the fact that she was somehow disappointed at the small problem.

"Let's just clean up."

"Yeah, sure." She mumbled.

When I moved to get into the shower because I still had plans to shower, Soleil grabbed my hand, just two of my fingers. I smiled, a soft smile. I turned around to face her, it seemed like she had given up on her hair because it was flowing all around her face.

Brown skin, brown eyes, big hair. *A Goddess.*

"Did you have a change of heart, sweetheart?"

She rolled her eyes, pulling me in against her. My bare chest flushed against her clothed skin. She took a step back, leaning against the sink, her fingers trailed up my arms, down to my chest, my torso until she reached my boxer briefs holding onto the elastic band.

She smiled, flashing me her white teeth. So far, I've learned that Soleil enjoyed teasing me, she enjoyed taking control. And I learned that I enjoyed letting her take it. At least for a while. My hands were still dangling by my side, I was curious about what she wanted to do. I was allowing her to make the first move.

"Touch me."

It was a direct command, with no shame. Just direct.

I so badly wanted to place my hands on her hips, and feel her soft skin against mine. To reel her in against me enough to fill my head with only her scent, but I was stopping myself, just this time.

I smiled down at her, cocking my head to the side, "ask me *nicely.*"

Her brown eyes rounded on mine, no longer soft. It seems like I've hit a nerve. Soleil raised her eyebrows, challenging me so I raised mine. I wanted to touch her, I really did but I was not about to be the one to back down.

Soleil swallowed, as her shoulders tensed, her eyes wandering to the other side of the room before she could find the strength to look at me again.

"*Please*, touch me, Reiner."

She said it in a way that should probably taunt me, but I didn't care.

I almost lost my footing hearing those words fall out of her pretty mouth. I felt lightheaded and I had to close my eyes for just a second to fully digest those words. I didn't know why but the slightest thing she did or said to me had my whole mind and body react to her.

I finally found my courage and I held onto her for as long as I could. I reached forward and wrapped my arms around her waist. I pulled her forward, flushing her body against mine.

"See. . ." I began as I connected my lips to her ear and I whispered, "that wasn't so hard was it?"

Her breath hitched, as her chest rose, and I was quick to follow her nervousness. I slide my hand inside of her shirt, feeling her soft skin against my calloused fingers. Soleil had dimples on her hips. I learned that today, when I was holding onto her waist as she rode me I managed to find two tiny hollow spots. At that moment all I wanted to do was to flip us over just so I could kiss them.

I rubbed small circles around her dimples, my fingers trailed lower enough to feel the elastic band on her waist, I hooked my fingers around it out of curiosity, "when did you put that back on?" I mumbled against her neck.

It was an innocent question, really. Soleil melted into my arms, moaning into thin air, and I could almost swear I had no part in that. She wrapped her arms around my neck — I could practically feel her heart against mine.

I stopped, pulling my fingers away from the elastic string that she called underwear, I moved to pull away a little but she only hugged me tighter.

"What's wrong?"

Soleil sighed, a devastatingly long sigh. Her breath fanned over my neck causing goosebumps to rise on my skin. It was such a sensual action I nearly groaned because of all the affects she had on me.

"I want you again. . ." She whispered, *"please."*

Blood rushed down to my cock hearing those six letter words. I swallowed, feeling my erection grow harder. Soleil drove me crazy. *Everything about her drove me crazy.*

My hands were back on her waist, and I pulled her away a little and my eyes found hers. "You can have me as much as you'd like."

I turned Soleil around to face the mirror, because I wanted her to see everything I saw.

I hooked my fingers around the hem of the shirt and slowly pulled it up to her stomach and stopped there. I could see her through the mirror, but her gaze was focused everywhere all at once. When I finally pulled the shirt over her head, a nervous look washed over her face, she held my arms like I might disappear.

I leaned down, stuffing my face in the crook of her neck, leaving a trail of soft kisses against her skin, and I could feel her whole body curl with a smile. I pulled away a little, my head still rested on her shoulders as I looked at her in the mirror.

"Look at yourself, sweetheart."

I could only hope she saw herself the way I saw her. Soleil is the *embodiment* of a kaleidoscope. With each rotation you discover something new, something prettier. She is full of beautiful colors and you could never get bored — just addicted.

And with each second that flew by, I grew more addicted than before. And I don't intend on getting sober.

With heavy eyes, Soleil looked at herself in the mirror. And my eyes softened as she stared at her body. I didn't know what she was thinking, I wanted to know what she was thinking.

"Talk to me, *please*."

It took her a full second to make up her mind, to decide if she wanted to talk to me or not. But that previous look of nervousness was long gone, replaced by a whole new look. Her glossy eyes glistened with lust.

"Reiner, I want you to touch me."

I looked at Soleil through hooded eyes, "show me where."

My hands which were placed on her waist, she grabbed them, guiding them a little higher.

Soleil placed my hands against the swell of her breast, I was quick to wrap my hands around them, kneading them. If she couldn't feel my erection against her ass before, she had to by now.

I wanted to swallow her moans with my mouth but she was not facing me right now. So instead I had to settle with just the pretty look on her face. The way her lips parted for me the second my fingers closed around her nipples just to softly twist them.

She moaned, *so fucking heavenly.*

Soleil grabbed one of my hands, slowly sliding it down her stomach, and I bit my lips groaning when I listened to the soft breaths she took, the way her stomach curled when I got closer to where she wanted me the most.

I stuffed my hand inside of her underwear, my fingers sliding against the folds of her pussy, feeling her wetness — Soleil arched against my fingers just to feel more of me and it pleased me. Knowing how badly she wanted me *fucking pleased me.*

Soleil groaned, shuffling, trying to create more friction. "Reiner do something." She growled, So impatient.

She was so impatient.

"Patient, sweetheart." I looked at her through the mirror, her needy eyes rounded on mine, she licked her lips, sliding her own hand against her body.

I watched Soleil knead her own breast moaning as she stared at me through the mirror. I swear I've never witnessed something as hot as that. Soleil is so fucking hot.

I pulled my fingers away from her pussy, just to shove them into her mouth causing her to taste herself, Soleil twisted her nipple the same way I did it as she sucked my fingers. Her eyes fluttered close as she licked my fingers clean.

She smiled when I pulled my fingers out of her mouth, sliding it inside of her pussy. Soleil leaned back, and her head fell on my shoulder as she moaned when I added another finger. I don't think I'll ever tell her but I always fuck her with three fingers; because three is my lucky number.

I use my free hand to pull her underwear lower — using one of my legs to spread her legs a little wider for me as I pumped my fingers in and out of her.

I love the look on her face when I'm pleasuring her. I love how breathless she gets for me. Soleil never stopped kneading her breast for me. And I thought she should be rewarded for that. I pressed my thumb against her clit circling it in a familiar motion with a soft pace.

Her knees buckled at the action, a loud moan escaped her lips. And I had to wrap an arm around her to hold her up, keeping her legs spread for me as I massaged her clit. My fingers curled deep inside of her pretty pussy.

"You like that, baby?"

"Hmm." she hummed. Her head was still on my shoulders as her walls closed around my fingers, I smiled, kissing her skin as I slid my fingers out of her wet pussy, denying her of her orgasm. Her eyes snapped open, wild as she turned around to stare at me.

"What the fuck?" she bit out, her orgasm was still at bay.

I placed a hand against her waist, pulling her back in against me, "not yet."

Soleil stared at me then at the shower behind me, she grabbed my arm pulling me forward — having me follow her into the shower.

The second we got inside the shower, she turned the shower on, and I was about to ask her what about her hair but her lips crashed against mine. I moaned into her sweet, sweet *mouth*. I closed my eyes and licked her lips, tasting her against mine. Soleil had this familiar scent, this familiar taste, that I needed to engrave into my mind just for the fun of memorizing it.

I held onto her face as I deepened the kiss, thrusting my tongue inside of her mouth. Soleil sucked my tongue, earning a deep moan out of me. Her hands were on my waist as she pulled down my boxer briefs. The material dropped to the floor with a sloppy thud, due to the warm water that soaked it long ago.

Before Soleil could even reach for me, I pulled away, breaking our kiss as I turned her around, quick with my hands on her waist. The wetness that pooled between her thighs was enough for her to take me easily, but I still stretched my hand over my mouth. Spitting on it as I massaged the tip of my cock with the saliva.

I whimpered the second I slid inside of her wet pussy, the feeling felt so fucking good it didn't register until a second later that we weren't using any condoms this time. I pulled out, a little breathless and Soleil sighed at the fact that we were stopping again. My cock was hard, and it was poking her ass. I was aching to be back inside.

I held onto her waist as I brushed my cock against the seam of her ass, gaining another moan out of her and for a split second I wanted to ask her if her ass was up for offering. But I bit back those thoughts.

"What about the condom?" I finally spoke.

"I'm on the pill."

Good. I thought to myself, but I only hummed in response, feeling the precum dripping out of my cock.

The water cascaded down my back, and it seems like almost a week ago I was jerking off in this exact shower, moaning her name. Only this time, Soleil was here. In the shower with me, and her dark curls are sticking against her nipples.

I wrapped my hand around her throat as I pulled her back for a rough sloppy kiss, my tongue greeted hers dancing a familiar dance, Soleils' lengthy fingers wrapped themselves around my cock as she massaged the tip — playing with my precum as I kissed her.

"Soleil, place your hand on the wall."

She scoffed, "what?"

"*Please*, hold on to the wall."

I watched her flimsy fingers press against my shower wall glass and that was all I needed to see in order to grab onto her waist with half my strength, sliding myself right inside of her. Wet, slick.

My eyes rolled back, *"You feel like heaven."* I moaned, allowing a moment — allowing her to adjust.

She sighed, "Ah, Reiner."

I wasn't even moving yet and she was already moaning for me.

If being egoistic wasn't a sin, my ego would have shot up through the roof right now. I couldn't help the cocky grin that spread across my face.

When Soleil reared her ass back against me in full force, it was my turn to moan. So deep that it caused Soleil to laugh a little. And I took it as a sign, if she could laugh I was obviously not doing a good enough job.

I pulled out almost all the way just to slam back inside of her, the laugh in her throat died with a soft groan. She fisted her hand against the wall. Resting her forehead against it as she hung her head low.

I love fucking Soleil, but I love her *face* more.

So I did the one thing I've been dying to do since the first time I've had any sexual feelings towards her. I wrapped my hands around her hair and softly pulled her head back. Soleil winced as she turned her head in my direction a little.

"Fuck you," she winced, moaning at the pain.

I leaned forward, kissing her shoulders, then her cheeks, still slamming inside of her. I licked her ear, "*sweetheart*, you already are." I whispered.

My hips snapped against hers and she seemed to be matching my movements, the water fell against my back as I fucked Soleil in my shower, her moans echoed in my bathroom walls.

This was only our second round tonight and I've learned the more Soleil came the easier it would be for her to come the next time due to her sensitivity. I was not tired at all, in fact I think I might keep her up all night, maybe only allow her a few seconds of sleep before I feel the need to have her skin against mine again.

She smelled like lavender and it drove me wild. Her hair was wet, her skin, I watched the drops of water roll down her skin with each thrust. Soleil was a moaning mess under me, barely holding on. I had to hold onto her waist as I fucked her.

I was thinking of everything and nothing at the same time. I thought of how heavenly I felt inside of her, but I didn't think of the conversation that would follow tomorrow.

I smiled at the thought when she called Ian simply because the idea of sharing her with anyone else seemed like a nightmare. Soleil was not mine to claim, but I also didn't want her to be anyone else's.

I wanted to play, so I placed my thumb against her clit, circling it. A fun idea came to mind, a simple one. For me at least. I smiled as I leaned forward to kiss her shoulder. For some reason I don't seem to mind the warm water that was falling down my back.

"Soleil, baby. *Count for me.*" My voice was hoarse and deep.

"What?" she chewed on the words, barely spitting them out.

"Try to count to ten."

She whined a little when I pulled out just to slam back inside of her. The pleasure always intensified with that neat trick.

With a moan, Soleil began counting. "One, two, three, four, five—"

She gasped, when I wrapped my hands around her throat, flushing her back against mine as I pushed us both forward against the shower glass. Her face was against the glass with my hands still around her throat as my thrust grew deeper. We both let out a breathy moan, feeling my cock pulse inside of her.

I slammed inside of her, grazing my teeth against her shoulder, "start over."

"Reiner that's not fucking fai—"

"*Soleil,* start over."

My thrust grew slower, allowing her a few seconds to play catch up, with a sigh, she started counting again. "One, two, three—" she moaned, rolling her hips against mine in a rhythm she apparently liked. But I didn't mind because I liked it too. With both of our chest falling and rising my pace became sloppy again.

Without having me ask again, she started counting, *"one, two, three, fourfiveten."* The words slurred out of her mouth like a drunk person, when my thumb circled her clit again. I nearly laughed at the way she was falling apart just for me.

I remembered once saying I loved the sound of the rain. *I lied.* I loved the muffled sounds Soleil made whenever I was so deep inside of her that she couldn't even count to ten. The little whimpers that escaped her lips when I was giving her more than she could handle.

My head rolled back feeling the familiar intense feeling settles in my stomach, my thrust grew sloppier by the second, Soleil was squirming so much I really had to place a firm hand over her waist as she came around me, her walls closed around my cock. Putting pressure on my cock with every slow thrust.

I was a whimpering mess coming inside of Soleil, completely bare. I thrusted a few more times to ride out our high, shuddering over the overstimulation.

"Fuck. . ." She groaned, pulling her body upward when I pulled out. And I second that statement.

I finally turned to the shower, grabbing the green loofah soaping the material before brushing it against her skin. Her eyes were nearly drained, and I almost felt guilty but then I remembered how much fun we were having seconds ago and it seemed worth it.

I kissed her forehead and pulled her closer against me as I washed her skin, "you did so good taking me." I mumbled as I pulled away a little just to lay a kiss against her lips, before she could chase for more I pulled away.

I noticed that about us, no matter how much stuff we do, we will always want more. Or chase for more. And I wish I could say that statement only applied sexually but lately I found myself wanting more than just those forceful conversations we have. I find myself *wanting so much more.* And I was not sure if that was a good thing.

When we finished, we stepped out of the shower in silence, well. . . Soleil was quiet, and I supposed being tired has something to do with it. But I stood in the corner of my room drying my hair watching Soleil slip into one of my clean shirts, it was so big it fit her like an oversized dress. And I was fighting every fiber in my body to not go over there and embrace her just to fuck her deep in my bed.

Soleil asked for two shirts, one for her to wear, one to wrap around her head. I slipped into my shorts — staring at her as she stood there because she just finished wrapping my shirt over her head.

"Do you want me to go home?" She asked. Her voice was distant and tired.

My jaw clenched at the question, I didn't think about it once, because I thought I'd be obvious for her to stay over. We were not some weird teenagers with a hookup arrangement. So I wanted to scream no, and hold onto her tighter.

"You live next door, what does it matter?" I replied, my answer seemed pretty logical and not at all weird.

"Okay."

Okay? No disagreement, I watched her climb into bed, *my bed.* She turned the lamp off, staring off into the darkness but I'm pretty sure she was waiting for me.

"Aren't you sleeping?" She asked as she tugged the sheets over her body.

"Hmmm."

I climbed into bed, *next to Soleil.* I was nervous for whatever reason. I wanted to reach for her, to kiss her goodnight, but instead I settled on my side of the bed and forced my eyes closed — drifting off to sleep.

I slept. I dreamt of a field of lavender.

The doorbell was what woke me up. I sat up straight, staring at Soleils' body next to mine. Memories from last night surfaced and I could feel my whole body flush. I wished to stay in bed longer but the doorbell rang again.

I ran a hand down my face before I climbed out of bed and reached for a shirt as I glanced at Soleil one last time, she was still under the duvet, sleeping peacefully.

I opened the front door, greeting the last person I wanted to see. Though, I was glad I changed the locks.

"Noa, Hey." I winced feeling the sun shine on my face.

"Morning to you too, I'm surprised you're not up already. This is the first time in years that you slept this late," she paused to stare at me — she reached forward dusting off my shirt with a few pats, "everything okay?"

I wanted to roll my eyes because I couldn't remember the last time she genuinely cared about my feelings — or was even aware I had any for that matter.

"I'm fine, Is Anna here?"

Anna is our common ground, she's our one and only topic, so for her to show up here so early in the morning, unannounced and without Anna is definitely not a surprise but it's still unpleasant.

"I needed to talk to you about Anthony—"

"Reiner?" a soft voice called out.

Noa's eyes rounded on mine and I could practically see the whole murder scenario she had planned for Soleil. My jaw clenched as I stood in front of her way, still preventing her from entering the house.

"Is someone in there?"

I raised a hand, "give me a second." I whispered, and before she could say anything I closed the door behind me. And instantly

I smiled at the sight of Soleil. She was already halfway down the stairs in a shirt and her underwear.

"Is everything okay?"

"I- uh," I don't know how to explain myself because I've never been placed in this situation before. I scratched the back of my head, "my ex-wife is here."

"Oh, *okay*. Well, I'm not hiding." She shrugged, "I am half naked though, and the rest of my clothes are still on your living room floor." She rubbed her eye, yawning in the process.

"Can I borrow one of your shorts?" She tilted her head to the side as she stared at me, "it's too early to wear tight jeans."

I was still stuck in this trance because how could she be so calm about this? Maybe I'm having a hard time because I know Noa and she doesn't. Soleil just seems tired, not angry or irritated — just tired.

"Reiner?"

"Yeah of course, let me grab you one."

Soleil had to roll the shorts three times in order for it to stay on her waist. I think they look sexy on her. I think I'd be able to enjoy her like this so much more if Noa wasn't waiting for me behind the front door — I was hoping she'd take the hint and just leave, but I was reminded by her essence when the doorbell rang again.

Soleil pulled her lips into a thin line, "you should let her in soon though, it's pretty cold outside."

I grimaced, "do I have to?"

She nodded, "yeah I think you do."

Her eyes softened — at that moment I just wanted to wrap my arms around her, so I did. I stretched my arms and wrapped them around her waist. The smell of her —*lavender*— filled my nostrils, and it took less than a second for Soleil to wrap her arms around my neck, stuffing her face in the crook of my neck.

She pulled away a little to search for my eyes, "Reiner I won't say anything really, I just think we should be able to handle this like a couple of adults and not teenagers." She cupped my face, "we did *nothing* wrong."

"Would you go on a date with me?"

Soleil blinked a few times, biting back a smile, "what?"

"Allow me to take you out, *please*." I've learned how much Soleil loves that six letter word. "Tonight." I added.

Soleil looked away, I could tell she was flushed because she couldn't even look at me. She sucked in a breath backing away from me a little, "yes." she said.

I smiled pulling her into my arms again, and she squeaked, probably surprised by my display of affection, but if I'm being honest whenever I'm near Soleil it is beyond difficult to keep my hands to myself.

"I'm gonna get my stuff to go, Blue is probably really worried." She mumbled as she made her way to the living room.

I finally opened the door with a tight look on my face. Noa's mood had changed for the worst, this time she didn't wait to be invited in — she shoved me out of the way and walked right inside the house with wide eyes.

I closed the door and made a face that could easily be translated to *please don't say anything* — knowing Noa, that would be too much of a task for her.

Soleil didn't say a word to Noa when she walked past us, she told me she had nothing to say to her so it would be weird to come out and talk to her. I walked Soleil to the door, Noa was in the living room mumbling things to herself but I couldn't care less because like Soleil said, we didn't do *anything* wrong.

Soleil turned around to face me, she looked very amused, "where are you taking me tonight?" She bit her lips as she smiled.

"Somewhere, but I want you to be surprised."

She lightly shook her head at me in amusement, like I said something funny — but I really didn't. "Whatever, Reiner. See you later."

I closed the door with a grin on my face, and the smile was instantly wiped off the second I heard Noa's voice.

"How long has that been happening, huh?" She said through a fake chuckle.

This situation felt a lot like a shitty, awkward sitcom.

"I mean are you seeing other people now?" She ran a hand through her hair, "I should know if you're seeing people."

"I'm seeing her." I paused to stare at Noa, "Noa you have no say in my life anymore, if any of the topics you think of doesn't revolve on Anna I suggest you keep them to yourself."

It took me a while to even try to get myself to be open to the possibilities of seeing someone else — and I know nothing is guaranteed, but for some reason I feel like I could at least try this thing with Soleil.

"Reiner..." Noa began as she took a few steps closer, "I was here because I wanted us to try again, you were right this thing with Anthony wasn't gonna last." out of frustration she let out a heavy sigh.

"I mean—" she sighed, "He doesn't have a job *job*, or a 401k. This thing with him was fun, I mean... really fun."

"Thanks for reminding me how much fun you had."

"No, I mean realistically speaking here, him and I won't work in the long run, but you and I have something going, Reiner."

I pursed my lips into a thin line, "You're about six months late, but thank you for at least considering me as your last choice."

Before I could go up the stairs, Noa spoke again, "You're not even gonna consider the idea for Anna?"

"Don't you dare bring Anna into this, you never really considered her from the beginning did you?" I snapped, "did you think of her before sleeping with some other guy who wasn't me. Did you think of her when I begged you to stay?" I took a deep breath, trying not to frown how easily it is for Noa to ruin my mood.

"Don't talk to me about considering Anna, and please get out of my house." I said as I went upstairs.

The longer Noa and I interacted, the more I realized the person I married completely disappeared, the person I fell in love with is gone. She just woke up one day and disappeared.

CHAPTER TWENTY-FIVE

Soleil

AFTER LEAVING REINER'S HOUSE I took care of Blue and had plans to stay home until it was time for work then my date with Reiner, but Hayley was still AWOL on me. She wasn't picking up, or calling back, she wasn't even reading any of my texts — it's been days since I talked to her, the only solution was to see her myself.

I took a shower and threw Reiner's clothes in the load in the laundry machine before I dressed myself — having his clothes could be a good excuse to just show up at his house again.

The drive to Hayley's wasn't long, but the amount of time they're taking to open the door was too long. I've been knocking for what I think felt like three minutes. No answer. I've also been calling Hayley non-stop. No answer.

When the door finally opened it was neither Hayley or one of her sisters. It was her father. I slowly pulled out my phone from my ear right on time when it went to voicemail, I hung up as I suspiciously stared at Bernie.

"Soleil! It's about time you came around here, I've been asking Hayley to bring you around, but you know Hayley."

Oh, I know Hayley.

I saved my breath, breathing around the stench of alcohol was too strong. Bernie smelled like a whole bar. Maybe a lot stronger.

"Hey Bernie." I moved past him to get inside the house.

On my way in I picked up a few things from the floor — I do this a lot when I get here. Whenever I see a mess my urge to clean it up almost automatically kicks in. Last time Hayley got angry with me for doing this — I ended up rearranging a few things that ended up confusing her.

"Hayley?" I called out.

"She's out with Isa." Samie's voice boomed from the living room.

Samie is one of Hayley's little sisters, she's only fourteen, and Isa is the youngest, she's eleven. I'm a little mad now because this whole time I've been thinking something was horribly wrong but she was just actively ignoring me.

I moved around the kitchen, already fixing a few things — I figure if I'm going to kill time while I wait for Hayley might as well do something productive. I should honestly be at home studying for my exam tomorrow, but I barely have time today to do so because I have a date later with Reiner.

Samie shook her head at me, watching me clean cautiously. "Hayley's gonna be so mad when she gets home."

"How is she?" I asked as I sprayed the counters before I wiped them clean.

Samie is on the couch, playing sims on the PS4 barely paying attention to me, "she seems fine to me, I mean she's doing the best she can, but Bernie's a real bummer." Samie said.

I nodded at that before my face formed a confused look, "wait why aren't you in school?"

"It's exam week, and the only exam I had to take was only two hours long, so early release basically." she explained.

"Lucky." I mumbled.

Seems like everyone's exams are going smoothly. Hayley gets to skip her exams meanwhile I haven't studied shit. Bernie came into view, and somehow Samie noticed him — we both groaned unison.

"Why don't you go hangout with your groupie friends, Bernie? Crash with them while you're at it." I smiled at him.

Bernie rolled his eyes barely walking into a straight line, he took another swing of his *drink*. "I'd much rather hang out with my daughters."

I shook my head, "I don't think they would agree."

He took a few wobbly steps forward, taking a seat on one of the stools, "what happened to you, Soleil? You used to be sweet."

"That was before I wasted two-hundreds dollars on you." I bit back.

"Whatever, just try to tell Hayley she needs to find a new job, we're starting to run low on things."

"Shut up, Bernie." Samie bit out, causing Bernie to roll his eyes as he hopped off the stool making his way down the corridor.

My brows furrowed, because if Hayley lost her job she would've told me. Right? I would've helped her look for a new one, or just supported them while she looked for a new job.

"What the fuck is Bernie talking about, Samie?"

"Nothing." she grumbled, pulling the headsets over her head at the same time the front door opened.

I stood in the kitchen, leaning against the counter because I was trying to figure out why hasn't Hayley told me anything yet. If I ever made her feel like she couldn't tell me anything then I need to know because I want her to be able to count on me when she needs help or something.

I want her to be able to at least try to tell me things — she had to be drunk in order to tell me her father was back in town. Which made our friendship kind of look like a joke.

"Remember what the dentist said, Isa. No warm food until a few hours." I watch Hayley whisper to her little sister, while she takes her backpack off her back.

"SAMIE WE'RE HOME!" she yelled as she looked up and her eyes met mine. I offered a soft smile, which she barely returned.

"Hey, Hayley." I moved forward wrapping my arms around her for a brief second before I pulled away.

"Hey Isa!" I ruffled her hair a bit but she only gave me the stink eye as she fixed her hair. I keep forgetting she's getting older and she doesn't like it when I do that anymore.

After Isa left the kitchen I turned to Hayley, raising two brows, "What's this I hear about you losing a job?" before she could speak I spoke again.

"I was a little worried Hayley, I've been calling non-stop."

Hayley sighed, running a hand through her raven hair, "I got into a fight with Bernie, and I had a tantrum like a child and broke my phone, it's at a shop right now."

I huffed, frowning a little, "you could've told me, and if you ever do need help, Hayley I could—"

"I don't want your handouts, and I'm not jobless. I'm pretending to be, just to get Bernie out of the house."

"Why not just kick him out? I mean really? You've created an actual ploy to get him out of your house." I blew out a breath, "like yeah, let's torture him by limiting him of food or beverages while he's broke, that'll show him." I said sarcastically.

Hayley sighed as she rolled her eyes, "do you have any better ideas?"

I frown a little thinking about the Bernie situation. "Can't you just get a restraining order against him?"

"It's a long process and I don't even think we can get one against him."

"It's worth a try."

"Why can't you leave it alone, Soleil? I don't exactly expect you to understand the situation but I'd at least hoped you'd try you know? I said I was handling it, just trust me."

I awkwardly nodded, "right, I'm sorry I cared."

She sighed, "no, I'm sorry. I know you care, I just get stubborn when it comes to depending on people."

"Ahhh, no I get it."

No, I really understood. Depending on people is probably one of the most dangerous things a person can do, because they could just leave anytime and you'd have no idea how to take care of yourself without them. *I don't understand dependent people at all.*

Hayley looked around the kitchen nodding along. "Usually I'd be mad that you cleaned for me, but I'm so tired, I'm glad you cleaned.

I smiled, "good thing you don't have an exam to take tomorrow."

"Oh yeah!" She laughed.

CHAPTER TWENTY-SIX

Soleil

REINER PULLED ME A CHAIR, he pushed it back the second I sat down. He sat in front of me, there was a spark in his eyes as he stared at me.

I scanned the room, I've never been here before, mostly because I don't go to fancy restaurants to eat by myself, but even when I was dating Luke we only went to the movie theater occasionally when a new movie came out — we usually just ate where I work at.

I smiled, "this is nice, piano music instead of Ed Sheeran."

The lights were dimmed here. Fancy piano music played in the background, unlike where I work. They have Ed Sheeran on nonstop, and he's great, but after a while it starts to feel like I'm being tortured. Here the piano or the violin is very soothing to my ears, I didn't even know places like this in Minnesota.

Reiner raised his brows, definitely unsure of the situation, "is Ed Sheeran bad?"

"He's kind of like the concept of eternity, it's nice but after a while it's boring. No one should be forced to listen to one artist forever."

"That does sound awful," he grimaced. "I can have the music changed for you right now if you'd like."

I shook my head immediately, "no, no, this is nice, really nice."

He's in a suit, I'm in a dress. We're on a date. This is perfect.

"Good."

A waiter brought two glasses of water with lemon and mint and just left. I eyed the water suspiciously, I've had lemon water before, I've just never tried it with the mint. I pursed my lips into a tight line as I grabbed the glass of water before I took the world tiniest sip.

I placed the glass of water down as I cleared my throat, "so. . . is this what you usually do?"

"Do what?"

"Hook up with people and take them out to fancy dinners later because you felt bad?"

His jaw clenched as he lowered his tone, "we're not here because I feel bad. In fact I don't regret sleeping with you at all."

I smiled so big my cheeks hurt.

"Why are you smiling?"

"I was messing with you about the whole *you're taking me out because you felt bad*," I air quoted, "but you like me." I taunt.

Reiner opened his mouth to speak, but a different waiter came over to our table.

"Good afternoon, my name is Scott and I will be your server for tonight."

"Hey Scott, thank you for serving us tonight." I said as I took the menus from his hand and handed Reiner one.

"I'll be back in a few minutes to take your orders." the waiter said.

"Hmm." Reiner hummed.

I opened the menu the second the waiter left, as I read my options. I'm a little picky when it comes to fancy foods in fancy restaurants — but Reiner's large hands pushed my menu down just to gain my attention.

His blue eyes seared into mine. " Soleil, we had sex. Multiple times, how is liking you still not established?"

I shrugged, "you never *said* it, and I mostly thought we were having some fun."

Half of the times I've been kissed, *(specially on New Years)* none of them meant anything. I'm positive anyone can kiss anyone as long as they find them some sort of attractive. So when Reiner kissed me, I wasn't completely sure it had anything to do with me. He could've been lonely, or maybe he just wanted to get laid.

He lightly shook his head as he finally opened his own menu, with his face hidden behind the menu, Reiner spoke again, "you're not the *worst* company in the world, Soleil."

I smiled, picking up my own menu. My heart was nearly out of my chest, desperately trying to fly into his hands, "you're not so bad yourself, Reiner."

When the waiter was back again, I already had something picked out. Reiner was more than eager to force me to order first, a smile was on his face the whole time — then he ordered, I was completely dazed. Staring at him with a smile on my face because I like hearing him talk.

He doesn't do it very often, so when he does I don't like to miss a second of it. It's strange because he's a lawyer, his job is to talk non-stop.

We kept small talk light, he talked about a few parts of his childhood, which he didn't tell me much about because he just told me ever since he was little, he liked the idea of defending people who needed it. He went on to tell me his days in college — claiming he was a nerd, whore glasses, still wears them. I don't know how to wrap my head around Reiner wearing glasses, just trying to picture the sight has me clenching my thighs shut under the table.

I know he's religious, but I kind of thought he was just born into it, but it was his choice, he found his way to build a relationship with God.

The more he talks, the more I realize how much of a mystery he's not, he just keeps to himself — he talked less unless it was his job. And I wonder who made him quiet.

I ended up avoiding any topics that involved my childhood. I was playing it safe tonight — it's our first date. I don't really want us to start talking about deep stuff, because the second we fall into that rabbit hole only one of us will be struggling to climb out. So

I told a few safe college stories.

I learned that Reiner doesn't have any siblings, he was born in Canada, both of his parents are alive. His mother still lives in Canada, he talks to her mostly, but after his father remarried they talked less because of the honeymoon.

"What got you into journalism?" He asked.

There are so many different ways I could answer this question because I've been answering it so many times I lost count, usually I've had to debate whether to lie or tell the truth. When people are just trying to make conversation I lie, because I know they don't want the truth. I tell them I've always loved writing as a little girl, I watched the news a lot. Read a lot of magazines or newspapers. Whatever was believable. I've never told anyone but Hayley the version I'm about to tell Reiner.

"My dad was a non-fiction writer. He published those kinds of books no woman would ever want to read." I let out a small dry laugh.

"Either way, he was really good. Made good money too. And writing was sort of a bond for the both of us. Except I never really wanted to write books in general, fiction or nonfiction." I explained.

"I liked gossip better, or just helping people to tell their version of the truth, or at least the version I see."

It's true. People sometimes do gruesome things to keep the hard truth buried because they're selfish. Whatever has the power to hurt them has to be gone. I like to discover those truths, even if right now all I've done is write about a local car accident. And I know I probably will never write about a murder scandal — but I'd like to think along the way I'll do better things to help people feel heard.

The waiter came around the table just in time to bring us the order, and another waiter next to Scott rolled a cart that contained the wine Reiner ordered a while ago.

A *sterling vineyard,* first bottle edition.

We ordered the same thing, well Reiner ordered what I ordered. But somehow I was the only one struggling to cut my steak. Reiner on the other hand was cutting his steak the most delicate way possible like he was trying not to cut it too harshly.

Still struggling with my food, Reiner reached for my plate taking it away and before I could say anything he swapped it with his — his nicely cut steak. I smiled at him, watching him cut the abused steak that used to be mine.

"Thank you." I mumbled.

He nodded, "I'm sorry about my ex-wife by the way."

"It's fine," I wavered, my shoulders tensed at a thought, "I'm not in the middle of anything right?"

Reiner shook his head, swallowing the food in his mouth, washing it down with wine. "No, uh. Noa cheated on me," he said.

I gripped on my utensils because it would be very inappropriate to drop them at a time like this, instead I slowly placed them down and I reached for my wine and took a sip as I waited for him to decide if he wanted to keep talking about it or not.

"I've honestly always known that she was but I didn't have any proof so I just decided to move forward and hope for the best because we have a daughter together and I really wasn't thinking of myself at all."

I was still quiet, I figured the less I talked the easier it would be for him to talk. My only plan was to do nothing and just be there.

Reiner laughed, and it felt forbidden because I could tell that he's not about to crack a joke. "But then I caught her on a date, funny enough it was at the restaurant you work at."

I pressed my lips into a thin line, "must've been a cheap date." I awfully tried to make a joke, but I guess it wasn't so bad because Reiner gave me a half smile.

"Me and my colleagues go there for lunch as much as we can because it's the closest restaurant to our firm." He paused, his eyes refusing to meet mine. I don't know why he felt embarrassed to tell me this, but I don't want him to feel that way at all.

"And they saw what I saw. Which made the situation so much more humiliating. Noa was very shocked, I don't know why though because she knew I went there for lunch often. I didn't say anything though, I just left and went home."

My heart breaks for him. I placed my hand on top of his on the table, when he flinched I tried to pull away. Reiner was quick to grab my hand again as he intertwined our fingers. My heart, my poor heart. It was overworking right now. His warmth is coercing through my skin. I can already feel the goosebumps rise on my skin.

I regret wearing a spaghetti strap dress.

"That same night because of Anna I forgave her and I was

ready to find a new way to move forward with her. I had divorced parents and it wasn't so great so I didn't want Anna to go through that at all."

His voice was low, but he was speaking loud enough for me to hear. The way he tells me the story breaks me — he says the words like he's never actually said any of that out loud before. Ever.

"Noa agreed, said she'd stay, but the next morning she was gone with Anna. Two weeks later she mailed me divorce papers." Reiner used his free hand to grab his wine, taking a good swing at it.

"I saw Anna less and less, honestly I recently gained some sort of custody with her which is why I'm allowed to see her and have her home with me. In these custody battles the mother instantly has the upper hand no matter what the situation is because it's her words against mine, and in this society who do you think they'll believe?"

"That's horrible." Those two generic words were the only thing I was able to come up with. I wanted to say so much more, to do so much more, but I didn't know how.

"Ian said he's getting close to finding something that'll be good to use in court."

I squeezed his hand, "I hope that he does."

Reiners stared at our hands, he smiled. "Thank you for listening."

I smiled, and I felt so ridiculous because I couldn't remember smiling so much in just one day. "Thank you for telling me."

"And I do apologize if I ever seemed rude to you in the beginning, I was stuck in this whole mess with Noa, I wasn't able to see Anna, barely talked to her on the phone — I was stressed, that day you brought me the pie was the day I had my first phone call with Anna that lasted three minutes." Reiner said.

Well that explained a lot. Now I felt stupid because I assumed so many things, I was angry for all the wrong reasons. And I resented him for such a long time.

Reiner finally started eating again, so I pulled my hand away, eating too, "there is so much to say to your daughter in so little time, and there's also the fact that I just hate pies."

I paused mid chew, "why?"

"Well, when I was a kid, I threw up once after eating a pie, and my brain convinced me that if I ever do eat a pie I'll have the same reaction."

"Oh."

The more he explained himself the more stupid I felt. I stayed quiet, eating a little faster than him because I think the steak hardened a little when it's no longer hot — and it's not hot anymore, barely room temperature.

"What about you, I'm still guessing on how you got the house next door?"

That question pinned my attention, I nearly choked on my next words, but I washed the food down with wine, this whole entire time I didn't think telling him about that story would ever be necessary.

"Tell me your best guess."

"Since you're a journalist, you saw something you weren't supposed to see and before you could write about it the people offered a shit ton of hush money. And you took it and bought the house next door to mine the second the man who used to live in it died." He pursed his lips into a thin line, "or it was an inheritance."

I laughed, because it was pretty good, "the first guess had a lot of scandal, but the second guess was more accurate." I sipped my wine, "the guy who died in that house was my father and he left me the house."

"I'm sorry."

"Don't be." I paused at the thought. I played with my food for a second before realizing for the first time in years I want to say the words out loud.

I looked up at Reiner who was already staring at me. "Sometimes I thought my father resented me because he and mom were very happy until I came into the picture, I mean I was such a bad thing she left."

"Soleil, you're *not* a bad thing."

I frowned, "I know, but sometimes. . ."

"Soleil." He whispered, this time it was him who grabbed my hand and Intertwined our fingers again. I stare at our hands then at him. "You are *not* a bad thing." He said.

I smiled, nodding with his statement as I took the last bite of my steak.

★ · ☆ · ★

"You're intoxicated, I should walk you home." I laughed, pull-him in his driveway.

"We live next door, and if anyone should be walking anyone home, it should be me because I've had one glass of wine, and you've had four." He said pulling us to a stop.

He raised four fingers in front of me and something wet fell on my forehead. My eyebrow furrowed when I looked up at the sky. It was never starry tonight but I didn't think all these clouds would show up so quickly. It was slow at first but then the rain began to pour in a matter of seconds, the air grew colder too. I squinted my eyes at the sky watching the rain pour.

A dry chuckle escaped Reiner's throat, "we really shouldn't be surprised, we live in Minnesota, the weather is so fucked up, next few weeks we might get snow."

I stared at Reiner. "Really?"

"Yeah."

"What? Summer is just about to start! It was snowing all January." I tried to frown but I couldn't. I think the smile on my lips might be permanent.

I tilted my head back a little and I watched the rain fall. I've always loved the rain. The feeling of it, the sound of it, the smell of it. Everything about it.

"This is amazing, I had a fun time tonight, and now it's raining, the rain is really beautiful."

"You're beautiful." Reiner blurted out.

I laughed when his eyes met mine, but his hands cupped my cheeks, and I stared at him, really staring at him. His hair was starting to get wet. The rain is pouring down on him and somehow it only made him look mesmerizing.

His eyes are the darkest shade of blue, his lashes are wet and curly, his narrowed nose brushed against mine. He was breathing so hard I could hear it, and I'm sure he could hear me breathing too — with the rain pouring so hard, it was hard for us to catch our breaths.

But I wasn't completely sure the rain was the only reason why I was struggling to breathe.

"You are so. . ." his breath was caught in his throat. "You are so beautiful Soleil." His eyes searched mine. His cold hands were still on my cheeks, and somehow it was the only thing keeping me warm.

I stood on my tippy toes and connected my lips with his. My whole body ran hot, my spin straightened. I pulled away a little, just so he could come back for more. Which he did, instantly. He connected my lips with his again. I wrapped my arms around his neck, deepening the kiss with my tongue, Reiner wrapped his arms around my waist, pulling me in closer against his body.

My stomach curled the second his tongue massaged mine, his hand cupped the back of my head, his fingers threaded my hair. Which I could only guess was wet. Really wet.

Reiner pulled away, breaking off the kiss. I trembled from the lack of warmth. Reiner ran his thumb over my lips, and my eyes were bouncing from his fingers to his eyes. I parted my lips almost immediately when he came in for another kiss as he thrusted his tongue inside of my mouth.

This time the kiss was delicate, like he was savoring me. He kissed me softer, more passionately. More desperate. He kissed my top lip, then my bottom lip, thrusting his tongue into my mouth again. Licking it, sucking it.

I gripped his shirt, I wanted him closer, so much more closer.

"Maybe you should come inside, you know get desert, you like pies right?" He whispered against my mouth.

"I have an exam tomorrow, and I have some studying to do." I let out a breathy laugh before pecking his lips, "but nice try with the pie though."

He laughed as he tilted his head back, "yeah it was worth the try."

The rain was still falling around us and I caught a glimpse of a wild Reiner, one that I'd like to see again for a second time. He let go of me, and I walked around the little white fence and walked toward my house.

"Soleil!" He shouted over the rain.

I turned around, the water drenched me to the point that I might finally slip in these heels and fall.

"Good night!" He shouted

I smiled, already trying to process how wonderful today has been, "good night, Reiner!"

CHAPTER TWENTY-SEVEN

Soleil

"MARA PLEASE, Tony isn't here today, and I'm stuck covering deliveries."

Mara fixed me a look, "delivering sucks, but we've all been there, it's your turn now."

"C'mon if you were asking, I'd trade places with you in a heartbeat."

She tilted her head to the side and her gaze was sending daggers, "no you wouldn't."

My shoulders sinked, "I wouldn't but I would if you begged, and I'm begging." I pouted, I pulled my hands together as I crouched to her level.

I hate delivering, all the driving around — the anxiety I go through trying to get to the right place, smelling the food while

I starve. It's no fun. And Reiner was right, the weather here is beyond fucked up. It's so cold outside you could easily freeze your nipples under six layers of coat — and I don't get it because everyone is more than comfortable with just one layer of coat.

I want to stay in, where it's warm. Where the lovely customers are at.

"She can't because she's serving a table that actually needs her." Sylvia butted in.

My head snapped in Sylvia's direction, "what?"

"My table speaks Spanish only."

"Mara is not a walking translator. Shame on you for not hiring more people who speak Spanish. How do you expect to serve other diverse customers?"

"That's why we hired Mara in the first place!" Sylvia groaned, throwing her hands around.

"So you only hired Mara because she can speak spanish? I think that's rather racist."

Mara laughed as she shook her head, Sylvia only frowned, "you can't just throw the word racist around just because you're not getting what you want."

I wrapped my arms around myself, "I just don't want to do deliveries."

"Then just quit." Sylvia shrugged.

I groaned.

"Yeah, so stop pestering me or Mara, because you have deliveries to make."

I sighed, staring at Mara skate away as she stuffed her little notepad in the pocket of her apron. I slowly turned my head in Sylvia's direction who was already staring at me — waiting patiently.

"Fair warning, we might get a few angry calls later today." I glanced at Sylvia as I made my way to the back rooms to change because I have deliveries to make.

I changed my outfit in the locker room, and grabbed the car key on my way out. Sylvia was kind enough to help me place all the orders in the car. And I had to wait about five minutes for the car to warm up because I couldn't stop shaking.

So far I've made two deliveries, both deliveries were for two groups of teens too lazy to drive to the restaurant themselves. But I can't stop thinking about the fact that my last exam was this week — the big one. If I pass, I get my bachelors degree, I become a real journalist, simple as that.

Everyone is already looking for an internship, or a solid job — I haven't even applied anywhere yet. Professor Daniel wrote me a letter of recommendation and I intend to put it to good use, but I'm paralyzed with fear, or maybe I'm just not ready yet — whatever it is, I want to be ahead of it.

I pushed my thoughts in the back of my head as I focused on the road, but that didn't work long before I started thinking of Reiner. I thought of his voice, how soothing it was —*it is*— I thought of his face, how gorgeous it is, and how much he uses his eyes whenever he talks to me. I was starting to think of him too much. I took a slow breath, shifting in the car seat. I think I need to *stop* thinking about him.

The last order was kind of close to the restaurant which pissed me off a bit because why not just drive to the place yourself when you're so close? I was so pissed it took a solid minute and a big logo to remind me that I'm driving to Reiner's law firm. I was about to deliver food to him and his colleagues.

I sighed as I turned off the car, looking at the heater longingly. I'm missing the warmth already as I stuffed my body into my coat.

I went through the double doors expecting a big fuss but security allowed me to walk right in there because I'm a delivery boy. He thought I was a boy. With the cap on and the uniform fitted me like it would fit a boy, and the fact that I had a coat on.

The second I walked in the room, two guys who seemed to be waiting by the door clapped, jumping off their seats, " foods here!"

The other guy eyed me up and down, "you're not Tony."

My lips formed a tight line, "no, yeah— uh, Tony called in sick today I'm covering for him." I clarified.

"Is he gonna be okay?" David asked.

I didn't know Tony had a whole law firm swooning over him, go Tony — I guess. The tips must be nice as well, I can bet.

"Yes, it's just a bug I think." I smiled, opening the huge bag as I pulled all the smaller brown bags out. I moved out of the way just in time for everyone to grab their order.

The only bag left was for Reiner who was nowhere in sight. I didn't recognize anyone until Ian came into my view. He grabbed his food and made his way towards me.

"Soleil." He greeted me with a half smile.

"Hey Ian." I mumbled, there was so much awkwardness between us.

He shoved his free hand into his pocket, "Tony's kinda famous around here."

I nodded as I laughed, "I can tell, and I'm sure he'll be back like tomorrow or the next day."

He nodded, "sure."

"Ian, about the weird call, I'm sorry if you—"

He raised a hand, "no, you made yourself *pretty clear*, and I understand." He said as he offered me a soft smile.

I blew out a breath, grateful that I didn't get the chance to make things more awkward between us. I smiled too as I looked around the room, "Where's Reiner?"

Ian pointed to a room down the corridor, "he's in his office, you'll have to bring the food to him — knock first though, he hates being interrupted."

I nodded as I clenched the brown bag in my hand. Today I realized I didn't have his phone number and I never realized how weird that was. We've done so much, but I think the fact that we're neighbors neither one of us has ever thought we'd need it, it didn't seem important.

I tried not to think about what his reaction to all this might look like. I mean it's not like I've planned all of this myself, it's all just a horrible coincidence. Reiner will be surprised, that's for sure — but I wonder if he'll be at least a little happy to see me.

My stomach dropped as I stood in front of the door. I felt excited but stupid at the same time. I felt stupid because I was acting like some teenager who's going to a football game too nervous to look at all the hot jocks.

But I am excited to see Reiner. I fixed my hair under the cap, as much as I could anyway because I already went through a struggle to put the cap on in the first place — so there's actually nothing to fix, if I take it off, my hair would be a mess.

I knocked on the door and just in cue his voice chimed in, "come in."

Reiner was very focused on his papers when I walked in, so focused he didn't bother to lift his head to even look at me. Reiner was in a proper white dress shirt, his suit was hung on his chair. The closer I walked towards his desk the more I thought of saying something, but my brain kept coming up short. I was simply staring at him — he had his glasses on, and God. He looked too good for his own good. I shuffled a little because I had to adjust myself as I finally cleared my throat.

"Hey Tony, just place the food anywhere on the desk for me, anywhere you don't see paper." He instructed.

He thought I was Tony because he hadn't lifted his head once to look at me. I stared at his desk with a grim look on my face — there was paper everywhere on the desk.

"There's paper literally everywhere." I mumbled under my breath as I looked around the room for a second desk or a half plant table.

His head snapped in my direction, his brows furrowed, probably laced with confusion. He looked at me, then blinked. Reiner adjusted his glasses. His whole body flexed as he leaned back against the chair with a small smile on his face.

"Soleil." he whispered my name quietly. "What brings you here?"

"I'm covering Tony's shift, he called in sick."

"Oh." He stood up, coming around to the other side of his desk to meet me, he grabbed the bag of food from me, "I can do that." He whispered.

"I was doing it just fine before." I laughed.

"No, I got it. I'll make room on my desk for it." He said as he walked away with the bag of food. He stacked a few papers and moved away a few folders as he made room on his desk for the food.

Before I could open my mouth to say something he beat me to it. "Do you mind staying for a while?" He looked at the time, "can you?"

I nodded like some lovestruck idiot. I thought after sleeping with him the awkward nervousness would go away, but it didn't — I just grew comfortable with it.

I cleared my throat to speak because Reiner was still waiting for a verbal response. "This was my last stop, so yeah I think I can stay for a while."

"Good, let's have lunch." He pointed at the chair in front of his desk.

I stared at him then at the chair he was pointing at, "okay." I mumbled. I don't really remember what the hell Reiner ordered — I'm not sure if I ever looked, but I know I'm hungry. I wasn't complaining so much because he ordered a burger, who would have thought? Reiner handed me the burger as he opened a salad bowl.

I shook my head as I pushed away the burger, "you eat the burger, I'll take the salad."

He stared at me, "do you *want* the salad?"

I frowned as I stared at the bowl in his hand, "no."

"Okay, eat the burger. I don't mind."

"I do." I grabbed the little pack of cutlery and opened the tiny plastic bag as I took the knife out of it. Reiner watched me cut the burger in half with a slight smile on his face. I placed the smaller half on his plate as I licked the mustard off my thumb.

"There, now eat." I pushed the plate towards him.

Reiner raised a brow, "what about the soda, who's getting it? Because we don't have another cup to do half and half."

I shrugged, "oh, well. We've kissed like ten times already, we can share a drink, or we could just use different straws." I said as I held up another unopened straw.

"I was messing with you."

"Oh." I nodded as I leaned back in my chair, grabbing the burger, stuffing my mouth with a bite.

It was quiet, I was starting to enjoy the food until Reiner started talking again, "and the salad? Will we share that too?" He began.

I groaned as I tilted my head back, "shut up."

When my eyes found his again, boring into them. There was this new glint of happiness in them. There was something peaceful about the way he looked at me. I didn't know how else I could possibly describe the soft look on his face — Reiner looked happy. Or content, or the least *satisfied*.

He makes it really easy between us, it's easy with him, even when we don't say anything I feel comfortable — nervous but still comfortable. We developed this dynamic, a safe bubble.

I grabbed a napkin and wiped ketchup off my fingers. I placed the napkin on top of the brown bag after. Reiner grabbed my hand before I could pull away, he traced my fingers before he held my hand completely.

He looked at our hand and frowned, "Why are you so far away?" He leaned back against his chair as he tapped his thigh, "come *here.*"

I swallowed, "I'm okay."

Reiner fixed me a look, "Soleil, come here. I won't bite." He grinned, "okay *I might* but I bet you'd like it."

My shoulders sagged as I stood up. I walked around the table, and the second I was at arms reach Reiner grabbed me by the waist — forcing me down on his lap with a tight hug. I tried to hug him back but the man was holding me so tight I couldn't budge, so I settled with my head on his shoulders.

Finally, when his grip on me loosened, Reiner dipped his head low as he kissed my neck, "I miss you." He whispered against my skin.

I shuddered as I struggled to let out a dry laugh, "but—" I paused, taking a breath because Reiner hitched the collar of my shirt down just to kiss my collarbone. I swallowed, "I'm right here."

"I know."

Reiner pulled away a little, sliding my food in front of me and I guess now I have to awkwardly sit on his lap to eat. Reiner hasn't touched his food once, instead his hands are all over me as he took my coat off my back. I shuddered as the cold air brushed past my skin, still it's so cold.

Reiner used his hands, moving them up and down to warm me up, "you're cold?"

I struggled to take a bite of my burger because Reiner held me so close. "A little." I mumbled with a mouth full of food.

"Mhmm."

Reiner leaned forward as he laid a kiss on my cheek and I closed my eyes, smiling at the small action. With all the things I learned about Reiner, this is my favorite — he needs the physical touch, he *craves* it — it pleased him, even the smallest touch has him almost satisfied.

He brushed his lips against my ear, *"I'm hungry."* He whispered, nearly groaning in my ear. His lips brushed against my neck as he nibbled on my skin, and he was quick to use his tongue to soothe the pain.

I tried to make a move to grab him his half of the burger, but he wrapped his arms tighter around my waist, "not for *food.*"

I froze as heat crawled on my cheeks. I'm also engrossed by the fact that I have a mouthful of greasy burger in my mouth while Reiner whispered dirty things to me. The butterflies were blooming in my stomach at this point.

I frowned and took another bite of my burger, "but *I'm* hungry too,"

Reiner smiled and kissed my cheek as I chewed on my food, holding me tighter, stuffing his face in the crook of my neck. I closed my eyes as I felt his breath fan over my neck.

"I could feed you something else if you'd like."

My eyes snapped open as I turned to look at Reiner — he looked at me with those daring blue eyes and pretended that he didn't just whisper the most filthiest thing in my ear. My breath hitched, and now I no longer wanted to eat, so I swallowed the rest of my food, but my throat was still parched.

Reiner placed the straw against my lips, and it took me less than a second to wrap my lips around them — drinking the content. I pushed the soda away when I was done, and Reiner placed the cup back on his desk — I was still staring at him, waiting for him to say something along those same lines again, so I could take him up on that offer.

Reiner stared at me quietly but I could feel the way he slipped his finger under my shirt just to circled my waist with his thumb. My eyes almost closed as I felt his cold fingers against my skin.

I melted into him, my eyes softening as I cupped his cheek, and I know my hands probably smelled like burgers because I only wiped it but Reiner kissed it anyway.

I stared at his lips, so pink and full.

Reiner's eyes searched mine because I'm pretty sure I zoned out, thinking about *other* things, "are you—"

I dipped my head low, laying a soft kiss against his lips. I knew my mouth tasted like a burger but I wanted to know what he tasted like, so I pulled away a little and came back for another soft kiss. Reiner didn't do anything, he only kissed me back because he was following my lead — I could still feel his finger under my shirt only now, I felt more than a single finger.

I laid a kiss on top of his lips and licked his bottom lip after — asking for entrance, which was given almost immediately. Reiner tasted sweet, not like mint or anything else that was refreshing, just sweet. His mouth had a faint flavor of cherry. His tongue was soft, deep into my mouth as it grazed mine.

I tried to move myself on his lap but he only held me tighter in place, both of his hands were under my shirt now, just feeling me everywhere.

I brushed my lips against his as I laid a kiss on top of it again and left him chasing for more as I kissed his cheek, his jaw, under his jaw. I trailed kisses near his ear, almost breathless because of how much I was squirming on top of him. I was starting to feel him now, under me.

His erection alone had my head spinning.

I pulled away a little, staring into his eyes as my fingers found the buttons on his shirt. Reiner leaned back in his chair, his hands on my waist as he shifted my whole body on him — I was straddling him completely now.

I licked my lips as I unbuttoned his dress shirt. "I wanna *taste* you next." I said.

I tried to catch my breath the second Reiner pushed forward attacking my neck with kisses.

I groaned softly as I pushed his shoulder, "Reiner. . ."

"*Soleil.*"

I hummed as I took off his dress shirt — ignoring his heated gaze because he wanted me to be the one naked right now. He wanted me to be the one who's shirtless, not him. But I wanted him in my mouth so badly that I didn't care about what he wanted right now.

"God, Reiner—" I took in a breath, staring at the muscles on his chest, "God." I whispered under my breath again as I dragged my hands over his chest — still not used to this.

Reiner took the hat off my head and it wasn't until he did it that I remember I still had it on. I tried to protest but Reiner caught my hands and held them both over my head as my chest heaved.

He smiled as he leaned in closer before biting my jaw, I groaned and wiggled as I tried to loosen his grip around my wrist but he only held me tighter.

"You are like nectar." He whispered as he lowered my arms again, but his grip on my wrist was still tight. "Sweet and viscous. *My sweet, sweet nectar.*" He kissed my lips, a quick sweet kiss that left me melting.

I sighed, "I want to touch you now."

Reiner used his free hand to lift my chin up, "stop using God's name in vain."

Really? Reiner never fails to entertain me. He has done *beyond* sinful things to my *body*, said so many *filthy* sinful things, yet — this, using God's name in vain *can't* seem to fly over his head.

I nodded, "*okay.*"

He kissed me again as he released my hands in the process. His tongue was quick to explore my mouth exploring all over again, tasting me as I kissed him back. Reiner moaned in my mouth, doing that little thing we do to each other — he sucked my tongue, moaning as he held me closer.

I hummed into his mouth as I ran my hands down his chest until I found the buckle of his belt. I pull away from the kiss, trailing kisses down from his neck to his chest.

Reiner was squirming under me, like he was feeling too much all at once. I removed myself off his lap, sliding down to my knees. Reiner parted his lips with a sigh as he watched me through hooded eyes, a heavy possessive look on his face.

I unbuckled his belt and unbuttoned his pants as I pulled them down as I catched a glimpse of his V-Line. I smiled as I stared up at him on my knees, too excited to have him in my mouth.

Reiner sighed before he lifted his hips gracefully as he manspread, "fuck, Soleil don't smile looking up at me like that." He groaned.

I pouted as I trailed an innocent finger on his V-Line, "why not?"

Reiner leaned forward as he crouched to my level, he cupped my cheeks, kissed my lips and tsk, "it makes me want to *fuck* you so hard that the whole office would hear how *heavenly* you when you're being pleasured."

I sucked in a breath as I clenched my thighs.

He kisses me again, quick and soft, "I don't want them to hear you because then they would want a taste of you." He paused, still holding my cheeks, he licked his lips, staring down at me.

"I share a lot of things, Soleil, but you're the one thing I'll never share. *Not ever.* Not even if I wanted to."

Before I could process all he said, Reiner kissed me again. This time is longer, rougher. He squeezed my cheeks in the process — deepening our kiss with his tongue. I moaned into his mouth and that had him moaning into mine. I stopped for a second to catch my breath, while Reiner kissed my cheeks, the outline of my jaw.

"So *possessive*." I mumbled under my breath.

"You like it." He whispered before leaning back into his chair — staring down at me again as he waited for me to make a move.

I sucked in a breath as I allowed myself time to process. Reiner smiled as he looked down at me. *His dimples* showed again. God, the dimples.

Reiner tilted his head to the side, "well?"

"Shut up." I groaned, sitting on the heels of my foot. I placed my hands in his chest, the previous hazy thoughts floating back to me again.

I kissed his hips as I brought the pants lower down — exposing more of his soft skin. A moan rolled off the tip of his tongue as I licked his v-line shuddering under me, his whole body was hot. The adrenaline was fueling the both of us.

I pulled his boxers down and his erection came into view. Reiner is so incredibly gifted, I still couldn't wrap my head around the fact that I've taken it before.

I licked my lips by just looking at the tip, the veins all over his cock was art, I could almost feel them by just looking. I sighed, audibly — I wrapped my hand around his cock, and his whole body jerked forward the second my hand came into contact with his erection.

"You're so pretty." I mumbled, still staring at his erection.

"Don't. . ." he shuddered, his breath caught in his throat. His voice shook with the words. "Don't say things like that."

I hummed, staring up at him as I took him into my mouth, tasting his tip, twirling my tongue around it. Reiner clenched his jaw, staring down at me with lustful eyes. He's holding back I could tell — I want him to touch me while I do this. To help me do it better, the way he likes it.

I pulled away a little, "you can touch me, you know."

His face softened a little but not long enough before I took him in my mouth again, deeper this time, pulling him out just to spit on his cock fisting my hand around the places my mouth couldn't reach.

Reiner moaned as he placed his hands on my head and pushed my head deeper and I took him deeper. There was an instant gag because Reiner bucked his hips forward as he pushed his whole cock into my mouth. Tears blurred my vision, a single one already rolling down my cheek.

Reiner moaned as he pulled out of my mouth a little, giving me only a few seconds to breathe. There was a string of saliva that connected from my lips to the tip of his cock. Reiner grinned at the sight, staring down at me in adoration.

"Baby, you feel so good." He hummed as I licked the bead of precum off his cock. Pumping the rest of him with my hand.

I massaged his balls, earning a moan out of him. I loved this, I loved making him feel this good, it pleased me — it turned me on. Right now my underwear was positively soaked and I was trying so hard not to shift because I just wanted to relieve myself a little.

Reiner whimpered as he came into my mouth, groaning and squirming, holding my head in place as his thrust grew sloppier, filling my mouth with his hot load.

I swallowed with a delightful groan and looked up at him, a small smile on my lips because I've been dying to do this ever since he fucked me in my kitchen. Reiner seemed to be proud of me too because he pulled me up with a sloppy kiss, tasting himself on my mouth.

"You deserve a good fuck, don't you think?"

I nodded, words stuck in my throat as he flipped me around and laid me over his desk, as he stood and kicked his chair back. Reiner lowered himself on his knees as he took off my pants along with the underwear. Kissing the back of my thighs, having me do a shaky dance on his desk.

His kisses hitched up higher until I felt his finger brush over my pussy, coating his finger with my wetness.

Reiner hummed in satisfaction, "look at how fucking wet you are, you liked sucking me off?"

His tongue soaked up my wetness as he licked my pussy. I shuddered in response. "Fucking nectar." He whispered as he lapped his tongue over my clit.

I squirmed over his desk in response. I wanted him to do more, well, more than he was already doing, but he was too busy teasing me.

Reiner lightly slapped my pussy as he gained my attention again, "Soleil, *baby* I know you're really sensitive right now, but stay with me, please."

I nodded as I tried to stick with his voice but Reiner finally pushed two fingers inside of me and a moan ripped out of my throat. Reiner kissed the back of my thigh as he pumped his fingers in and out of me, his thumb was playing with my clit as he circled.

The sound of my wetness filled the room along with the sounds of my moans.

I pushed my ass more, grinding my hips against Reiners fingers, I wanted more. So much more, "one more." I moaned, it was a desperate moan.

Reiner tsk slapping my ass as he pushed in a third finger inside of me, probably smiling.

"such a fucking slut."

Reiner circled my clit a little faster causing me to groan, "my pretty baby is so spoiled getting fucked with three fingers."

"Mhm-hmm."

"I can't have you coming around them though." The second the words left his mouth, he pulled his fingers out.

I let out a ragged breath, I couldn't speak because I was shaking. Reiner kissed my hips twice before he stood up. Once on my left hip dimple, once on my right hip dimple.

He stood behind me as he positioned himself in front of my entrance. I could feel the tip of his cock pushing against my pussy and I trembled, completely ready for him. "Soleil, hold onto the edge of the desk." Was all he said as he allowed me those few seconds to hold onto the edge of the desk, and the second he witnessed my hand stretch for the edge of the desk — He entered me with one rough thrust.

I moaned in delight, feeling my cheek brush against the cold desk, I closed my eyes, feeling his hands on my waist as he pulled out just to slam back inside of me again, moaning as he kept a normal pace. Each thrust is different from the other.

Rougher, slower, softer, faster.

"Fuck. . ." he let out a desperate breathy moan. His thumb made small circles against my waist — his apology for the few rough thrust.

The knock on the door snapped me back into reality, my body tensed but I couldn't stop myself from moaning. 1 Reiner tensed on top of me, but he didn't stop, he seemed rather annoyed than scared of getting caught.

Reiner leaned down and his mouth leveled next to my ear, and I could practically feel the smile on his lips as he talked to me, "you wanna answer that for me?"

"Are you crazy?" I hissed.

"A little." He hummed as he nibbled the shell of my ear. "But don't worry, baby. No one will know that I have you mewling under me. So long as you behave."

I shuddered with his words as my stomach tightened. I shouldn't feel this food when he talks like that to me.

"Yes?" Reiner answered.

Reiner placed a hand over my mouth thrusting harsher than he was before we both heard Ian's voice. He leaned down — licking the shell of my ear, "please, be quiet. *Be good.*"

I nodded, swallowing my moans as I felt him pull out just to slam back inside of me again. I bit the inside of his hand as his punishment after he thrusted into me that harshly. He wasn't making this easy.

Reiner groaned, placing his thumb over my clit in response. "How can I help you today, Ian?"

My eyes rolled back, as I struggled to keep my voice down. Reiner was fucking me like Ian isn't behind the door — telling him about a super boring case — I didn't really pay them any attention as I gripped the edge of his desk, trying to think of anything but moaning.

Reiner used one of his feet to kick my legs open wider. "Can we discuss it later, Ian? Soleil needs my help with something."

Ian went quiet behind the door before clearing his throat, "yeah sure, later."

When Ian's footsteps faded further away from the door, I reached to claw Reiner. "You fucking traitor." I hissed.

Reiner slipped his hand inside of my shirt as he fondled my breast, "I am helping you with something."

I groaned as I felt him roll my nipples against his fingers. I clenched around him, feeling his moan as he leaned down to kiss my shoulders mumbling nonsense into my ears. This feeling, I wanted it with him only. And I wanted to be the only one to make him feel this way — to have him breathless. I wanted to be the only one to see all these sides of him that no one would expect.

But Instead of saying anything I just focused on how well he was making me feel, and I hoped that I was doing a successful job pleasing him just as much.

Reiner whimpered as I rolled my hips against him, coming around him as I felt his spill inside of me. With a few sloppy thrust, Reiner pulled out of me with a shallow breath. He pulled his pants back on as he grabbed a few tissues and wiped our body liquid off my thigh, which was dripping out of me already.

I propped myself up on the desk as he pulled my pants and underwear back on. When I turned around Reiner placed a kiss on my forehead as his eyes softened.

"I'm sorry, you wanted to eat and—"

I laughed, and I guess it caught him off guard because he was staring at me like I grew a third head.

"You're apologizing after fucking me now?" *Funny. He's so damn entertaining.*

Reiner awkwardly scratched the back of his neck, obviously a little confused, "yes?"

"Please don't, I'm a little tired right now, but I have to drive back to work."

"Stay here," he wrapped his arms around me as he pulled me into a hug, "call in sick."

I hummed in his chest, holding to his warmth as much as I could. I pulled away after a while and grabbed my hat. "I can't." I whispered.

I really wish I could stay here and hang with him. But the more we interacted the more I got to know him and the more I got to know him the more I started to care for him. I won't be able to stop myself from developing feelings for someone who seems to always be there.

Being with him is beginning to look more like a dream. We both have different meanings of things, different lifestyles — I'm a mess. I am now just getting a kick-start at everything. I'm still dealing with everything in my life. Reiner already made his mark in the world. He has many, many accomplishments. Just being near him makes me feel like I'm dragging him back down.

My attraction towards him was developing rapidly. I can't do anything to stop it. Reiner is addictive. Every second I spent with him strengthened my feelings for him. I can't control any of it, but what I could do is spend less time with him.

Reiner is everywhere — before any of this he was still everywhere but now it was different.

He's everywhere under my skin.

CHAPTER TWENTY-EIGHT

★ · ☆ · ★

Reiner

★ · ☆ · ★

THE SCHOOL GYM smells like pizza and sweat. I couldn't tell why, it just did. Well, that and the fact that half of the people in here were eating pizza. On the bleachers — I always sit in the first row. I get a great view of Anna, so if anything happens I reach her quicker than I would — I also don't like having to climb the bleachers up and down when I get to a higher level.

I was a little distracted today. Every time she whipped her head around, the smell of her slapped me right in the face — *and it got under my skin every fucking time.* Whenever she was in a room, she became my entire focus. When it's just the two of us together I don't mind that at all, but in a room full of other people, it becomes a problem. She didn't ask for my attention, but she didn't have to. It was already hers.

I'm becoming this uncontrollable person when it comes to her.

Soleil smiled so hard and I couldn't force myself to look away. What happened next might've been an accident but she placed a hand on my thigh, and I sucked in a breath, blinking as I swallowed. My eyes fell on my thigh, watching her hand grasp around my thigh in excitement — some sort of reflex.

I managed to pull my focus at the center of the gym again. I noticed Anna was winning this round, which only explained Soleil's excitement, she tried so hard to contain herself it was almost too amusing to witness. I smiled to myself when she cheered on behalf of Anna. She immediately grew quiet when she realized no one else was cheering and clapping, mostly because they didn't care about Anna's match, they only cared when it was their kid winning. Soleil, however, did care and that's all that mattered to me.

Anna invited Soleil to her last match for the school year, after Noa said she couldn't make it, she thought of inviting Soleil. I don't know why but that alone made me feel anxious.

I tried not to think of Noa as I paid attention to the match, they were both tied, so whoever scores the last point wins.

"Excuse me."

My head whipped in the direction of the deep voice that boomed behind us. At first I thought the man just wanted to get by because Soleil was sitting on the edge near the little stairs in between, but the closer he got I realized what exactly was about to happen.

The guy crouched a little, trying to talk to her as privately as he could, and I found myself paying more attention to them than the match in front of me.

"Are you the babysitter?" He asked, a smug smile on his lips. I nearly rolled my eyes, but I am a patient man, I'm very curious to see him *try* to flirt his way into her life.

Soleil laughed, shaking her head, "no uh—" she froze as she turned to me for an answer. I smiled.

She could've lied. She could've said anything she wanted to — but she didn't. She turned to me for an answer, she wanted me to decide.

I glared at him, "do you have a kid here?"

He must, it'd be weird if he didn't. But I wanted him to feel uncomfortable.

His eyes landed on mine, flicking back to Soleil again, and I could see the hesitation in his eyes. He's not so sure but he knows I was trying to stop whatever he was trying to make happen.

He smiled, "yes, she's wrestling yours."

What a coincidence.

Soleil looked at me and smiled as she turned to face the guy again, "sorry, but Anna has this one in the bag."

He lifted his head to stare at them, the girls were still slowly moving around each other. "I thought so." He hummed.

Soleil stopped looking at him, her attention was back to the center of the gym, and I casted the guy a glance, a smug look on my face — I just couldn't help it, she didn't show an *ounce* of interest towards him. I'm not sure if she even noticed he was flirting or even trying to make a move. The guy only shook his head disappointed, maybe a little pissed that I was there at all — but he left anyway.

Fucking punk. If he wanted his dick stroked he should've tried one of those fucking dating sites.

The problem with us is we never talked about it. We could go for rounds after rounds and she gets dressed and leaves like nothing happened, a small satisfied smile on her face, we only went out once, we hugged and kissed — we still haven't talked about whatever the fuck it is we're avoiding.

The other day after having her on my desk she avoided me a little, I know she didn't think I noticed but I did. She is avoiding me. She's here right now, but for Anna. Whatever it is she's trying to do — I want to shut it down, and I know I can give her the clarity she needs. I just need one true moment alone with her, to have her somewhere where it wouldn't be easy for to leave me.

She's not entirely a secret, I don't want her to be. I just wanted to talk to her about it, to at least get an idea of what she wants. From the beginning my warning to her was that this wouldn't be just a *'fling'* — it's not.

I may not have an answer for her or my feelings but I sure as hell don't want to be stupid and figure it out without her.

Her knees brushed against mine, setting my skin on fire as I crawled out of my head just in time just to notice Anna won the round. I stood up, clapping as she smiled in my direction. Soleil stood next to me — clapping.

I leaned down, leveling my lips next to her ear, "we have to talk." Even so far away, I can hear the little breath she takes, how uneasy she felt.

How much I affect her.

When Anna came to our side, she hugged me. She held me tight and the sweat on her face made an imprint on my shirt. Soleil smiled as her eyes bounced from me to Anna. And I don't think I've ever considered this bit until now, only because I never thought that far, but me and Anna come as a package deal. She can't have me without having Anna.

"Did you guys see that?!" She exclaims, flashing us the little metal she won a few minutes ago, but I didn't expect anything less.

"I saw it!" Soleil chants, offering Anna a high five. Anna didn't hesitate to slap her hand, a bright smile on her face.

"You did good, Princess." I said as I ruffled her head.

The smile on my face froze, my skin grew cold when I spotted Noa in the crowd as she made her way toward us. I released a small breath. I had zero intentions of keeping her away from Anna — I would never rob her of her mother, but even so, her presence still taunts me.

The second Anna spotted her mother she ran towards her, and Noa did so little to match her energetic embrace. The flowers in her hands had a better clutch in her hand than the one hand she was using to hug Anna.

"Congrats, baby." She whispered as she walked toward us.

Soleil shifted uncomfortably, but her face gave away nothing. There's this small generic smile on her face that looks so unnatural as she smiled to Noa, and I'm guessing that's for Anna's sake because she is the only one here who has no idea what's happening.

Even Noa tried to smile.

"Hey, Noa." I mumbled.

"Reiner." She stared at me, not wasting a second, she went straight to the point. "Can we talk for a sec?"

My brows shot up for a sec as I glanced at Anna. Noa frowned as she handed Anna's hand to Soleil. "We'll be back." She said.

I stared at Soleil apologetically, my eyes softened but she sent me a small understanding nod. I smiled at Anna who had already started talking to Soleil. I rolled my shoulders, so tense just by the idea of talking to Noa alone. I can never know what she'll say.

I followed her near the food stands, where the smell of popcorn grew stronger. Lots of people are still nearby but they're all scattered — talking to each other, and the other half was trying to leave. Either way, where we stood granted us a little privacy.

I crossed my arms over my chest, "talk."

Noa rolled her eyes as she walked closer towards me, "I thought a lot about the other morning. I've decided to give you a second chance to come around."

"What?" *Second chance to come around? How much do I have to be?*

"I'm saying, it's time we work through this, go to therapy like you offered before."

A dry laugh escaped my throat, and my face hardened. "Noa, we're divorced." I stated, flatly. "I wanted us to try therapy six months ago."

With Noa nothing should ever be sugar coated because then she'll use that as another window to get whatever she wants, so I always have to be clear, and straight.

"Yeah, but we can start over again."

This time a blink, I looked around a little. *She's truly delusional.*

"Noa, this isn't one of those situations where *'the marriage was bad for us'* — you cheated, left me, *took my daughter,* came back *months* later and you think a start over, or a therapy session will slap a band-aid over this?"

She stared at me dumbfounded, and I hope she didn't think therapy could fix this —*her*— because it can't. And she's fooling no one but herself.

Anger washes over her face. "Who do you think they'll believe, huh?" She snapped, and I could tell what was about to happen.

"A picture perfect fit mother. Or some guy having some sort of mid-life crisis fucking an 18 year old?"

My jaw clenched as I took a step forward before narrowing my eyes at her, "Soleil is fucking twenty-three and you were an unfaithful wife." I whispered harshly, Noa might've forgotten we're on school grounds, but I didn't.

"Good thing that's not on paper right?" She smiled in defiance.

"If you truly want your daughter to have a father figure in her life, fucking breakup with that young gold digger in the making." She spat as she turned around to leave.

My jaw clenched, as I caught her arm, pulling her back against my chest, "don't you *ever* fucking call her that." I spat as I released her arm before I walked away. My skin was hot.

A fucking ultimatum. She's using Anna as leverage. I wanted to know why because I'd understand if she loved me, and wanted me back — but she's only trying to keep me around simply because she didn't want to be alone, and the second another man shows her half of the interest she wants, she'll disappear again.

Noa feeds on the attention, she loves it. Which is why I loathed myself in the beginning of all this mess, maybe I didn't give her enough of it from the start and the need to search it elsewhere was what caused all this. But I reminded myself everything I did was for her and Anna. I wanted them to be happy and healthy. I always made sure I had time for them. I stopped blaming myself a long time ago when I realized Noa was just selfish all along.

I ran a hand through my hair, my eyes scanning the gym — my chest heaved when I spotted them near the popcorn stand, Anna was grabbing a bag of popcorn from the guy running the stand. Soleil caught my gaze before she looked away.

It took me only a few strides to walk towards them, and as Noa appeared again, obviously ready to take Anna back home. I held Anna, but what seemed different was the way I watched Soleil try to shrink herself — she's trying to seem less and less invisible under Noa's eyes.

My brows furrowed as I stared at Noa who's only staring at me and Anna waiting impatiently, but I could tell Soleil no longer wanted to be here.

I cleared my throat, "I'll see you later, Princess. Call me before going to bed, yeah?" I laid a kiss on her forehead, watching her go as I fixed my posture again.

Noa sent me a small smile, not daring to even look at Soleil as she took Anna's hand, making their way out. Soleil turned hot on her heels and before she could follow them out I called her name.

"Soleil." I called out. And I could see her shoulders sagging before turning around.

She wasn't smiling, her eyes were glistening but it was not happiness. She looked away, before she sniffed, wiping a hand over her face. She looked at me again. My brows furrowed as my eyes softened.

I don't care anymore, I took two steps towards her and she took one back, breaking my heart in the process. Something was bothering her.

"What's wrong?" My voice softened as I took a small step closer towards her, this time she stayed in place as she released a slow breath.

She stared at me before she looked away for a second, "I'm just tired, I want to go home." She stated.

"I have a trailer, I usually go on the weekends when I'm free. . . *sometimes.*" I added, "I want you to come with me this weekend." I nodded, "come with me this weekend."

Her big eyes rounded on me, growing curious, "I thought we needed to talk?"

"We'll talk there."

CHAPTER
TWENTY-NINE

★ · ☆ · ★

Soleil

★ · ☆ · ★

I HAVE THE HICCUPS, it just wouldn't go away. So now, each time I laughed I had a near death experience because of my hiccup. Hayley thought it was funny, so when she laughed I laughed again because she has this horrible contagious laugh that makes people laugh.

We were having drinks at Josie's. At first it was Hayley, Samie and I — Samie had not been injecting any alcohol, I'm not even sure why she was tagging along in the first place, but she was here. Mara joined us way later, she came here for a drink after a horrible date with some guy named Dante. And Samie's face has been flushed ever since. I think we all know she has an innocent crush on Mara by now.

I wanted to drink, to drown myself in it. I wanted to be completely gone when I left with Reiner for his trailer tonight. It didn't look so good because I was trying to get shit faced in the middle of the afternoon even though I'd probably sober up before eight.

I agreed to go with him, I don't know why I did, but I did. So he and I are spending a whole weekend away in his trailer, in the woods, *somewhere.* He mentioned something about privacy and stuff we needed to talk about — if I wasn't so attracted to him, I'd start questioning his choices but I like him so damn much.

"No mopping allowed!" Hayley slurred out.

She was obviously already drunk and I was still on my first drink, and Mara was nursing what I think is a club soda. At least we could count on her to drive tonight.

"Yeah Mara," I chimed in even though I was the one frowning. "FUCK DANTE!"

She laughed, her cheeks flushed after realizing I yelled *fuck Dante* which grabbed the attention of half of the guys in the room. I didn't know they were all so sensitive about the name *Dante.* Hayley laughed then I laughed — Mara and Samie stared at us with a strange look on their faces. Hayley was drunk, that was her excuse, but me? I was still sober. *A sober asshole.*

"This is sad." Samie whispered over Mara's shoulder.

I nearly rolled my eyes because I knew what she was doing. She was trying to appear calm and mature when she was the actual child here. Mara barely laughed as she shook her head at us.

"Oh, did Soleil fill you in?" Hayley chirped as she pinned her attention on Mara.

I groaned, nearly sliding down the chair. I grabbed my drink and took another sip — wishing the earth would swallow me whole right now.

"No. . ." Mara casted me a glance, "what's up?"

I shrugged as I took another sip.

"She's going to the woods with Reiner for the whole weekend." Samie blurted out.

"Pfft, not the woods," I butted in, "just his trailer."

"which happens to be in the woods." Hayley added and I groaned.

Mara stared at me, "*ay*," she tsk, "pero, you said no right?"

I shrunk in my seat again, this time I drank all the remaining alcohol that was left in my glass. How could I have said no? Reiner stared down at me with those needy blue eyes of his, and I was already falling apart because of what happened before that — and he said we needed to talk, which was very true.

"His eyes were very scary when he asked." I pouted.

Hayley pointed at me, "yes, I've seen them before! So blue, so scary."

Mara stroked her dark hair, her fingers tangling in her curls. Samie was lost looking at her stroke her hair and me and Hayley were so entertained by the little school girl crush, we nearly exploded with laughter. I *completely* understand why Samie would crush on my sweet Mara though.

"Why are you getting drunk?" Mara nudged her head in Hayley's direction, and Samie instantly frowned.

I just wanted a little alcohol to take me off the edge, to make me less nervous so I could be in the same room with Reiner without ripping his clothes off instantly. Yesterday at the game. I felt him watch me watch the game — and that only deepened the weird unwelcome feeling that grew in my stomach.

Hayley however is just getting drunk, for no reason at all. She does that sometimes. And I'm guessing Samie hates it.

Hayley only shrugged, "to get drunk?"

Her answers sound awful really, given her family history with alcohol — she knows she's not a drunk, I know she's not a drunk, but everyone else would easily think so — even Samie. I noticed.

I placed my head over her shoulder as my thoughts drifted. Mara and Hayley were talking and Samie was silent — probably because wanted to go home by now but I doubt anyone would budge if she said anything. I stayed quiet and thought about all the ways I could survive a weekend alone with Reiner.

CHAPTER THIRTY

Soleil

ONE OF THE COMPANIES I applied for emailed me back, possibly offering me an internship but I was too scared to open the email. I slammed my laptop shut the second I received the notification. I have to start off somewhere but the fear of not getting accepted was nearly choking me, so maybe it was a good idea to go away for the weekend — I'll leave my laptop behind, that way I won't get tempted to open the email.

I shoved two Pijamas in the bag. Yeah, I could wait till Sunday afternoon. I huffed as I fished out long pants from my drawer, his trailer might not have AC. I have to at least prepare for that. The weather is getting colder and colder by the day. I ended up packing so many clothes it felt like I had to switch my outfits every hour. I thought about unpacking some but they were my back-up clothes.

I'm not always so lucky with nature.

I understood why the bag wouldn't zip. After packing my shampoo and endless other amounts of hair products there was barely any room left for my toothbrush. I groaned and shoved it in my tote bag — which was already filled with face care products.

"Fuck." I grumbled under my breath as I checked the time. I have less than thirty minutes until Reiner comes knocking for me and I know he will because he's big on punctuality, so on that note he might be coming in fifteen minutes. So I made a small sacrifice and took out the bottles of shampoo.

I took out a few clothes I deemed unnecessary, making the bag lighter and easier to zip. I took the bonnet off my head and I packed it too.

I patted my clothes and ended up stuffing my hair into a high bun. The second I sprayed perfume on myself there was a knock on the door, and my shoulders sagged. That's not usually my re-action to spending time with Reiner but something changed now and I have to find a way to bring it up this weekend, not tonight, that would make the rest of the trip awkward, so I'll wait tomor-row night. I didn't know Reiner was coming so soon, so I was glad I dropped off Blue with Hayley yesterday.

I grabbed the bag and made my way downstairs to open the door for him because I can feel his knocking growing impatient. I opened the door, taking his entire body in.

There was a chill that came when I opened the door. It wasn't caused by my nervousness, but by the wind. It was cold and windy out. A small smile on my face as I stare at him. He looked kinda ridiculous with that *legendary whitetails* jacket he had on. But out of the both of us he was obviously more prepared than I was.

"It'll be cold out there. . ." He said as his eyes scanned my body.

I knew it would be cold out there. That's why I packed all those heavy clothes and that's why I had my own ridiculous coat over my back. But I only nodded as he took my bag from me, leaving me with the tote bag to follow after him.

"Are you allergic to anything?" He asked as he glanced back at me over his shoulders.

I shook my head before I spoke, "none that I'm aware of."

"Hmm." he hummed.

Apparently the woods weren't so far away from us, because after just about twenty minutes of driving we arrived, well we arrived after he made a scary turn into the woods — pulling up to his trailer in the middle of nowhere.

Reiner's trailer didn't look so bad on the outside, it seemed clean and even the set up on the deck looked nice. The uneasy feeling in my stomach only intensified as I stepped out of the car. A whole weekend with Reiner doesn't seem like something I can survive.

Just a day with him is too much to handle, and I'd run away everytime, but I can't run away now. He had me right where he wanted me. I was stupid for agreeing to this. *I'm fucked.*

★ · ☆ · ★

Reiner dropped our things inside, and the trailer was even more modern than I could've guessed it to be, and bigger too. And he did have a heater. There were no personal Knick knacks inside but I wasn't surprised to see how tidy and clean the place was. It smelled just like him in here.

I followed him deeper inside the trailer as he led us to the back, and I stared at the single bed in disbelief. Granted, it wouldn't be the first time we shared a bed, but this would only make not touching him the more difficult. And I really didn't want to touch him this weekend.

Well, I do and I'm a liar.

I opened my mouth to protest but nothing came out, instead I glanced around the room. Reiner only turned to stare at me and looked around the room, clearly bored.

He tilted his head as he shoved his hands in his pockets. "There's nowhere else for me to sleep, unless of course you want me to camp outside."

I shook my head, "the bed's fine."

Why did I agree to this again? I can't remember. Something about his eyes and how he tilted his head — he stared at me like if I said no he would crumble. I like that look a lot so I said yes, and now I'm stuck with him alone in the middle of nowhere sharing one bed.

Reiner dropped my bags on the bed and moved towards me again. I swallowed before realizing he wanted to go back out there to grab his bag. I released a small breath as I moved out of his way, feeling his shoulder graze mine.

I am losing my mind here.

When Reiner left the trailer, I just stood there for a second before I walked in front of the bed and opened my bag before closing it up again. I was kind of out of it. I blew out a breath as I stared at the TV on the wall, positioned perfectly in front of the bed. God, this place was so nice and modern.

I reached for my phone in my back pocket to send Hayley a text.

Me: Hey, I'm here in the woods, there's electricity, TV, food, I don't think he brought me out here to kill me, it's too nice to commit murder out here.

Hayley texted me back almost immediately.

Hayley: Have you watched any movies??? This is how it always starts, he probably already has a secret underground bunker ready for you...

Me: lol, not funny. Anyways I'll send you my location.

I sent Hayley my location, the signal was still spotty but I was able to send the text. I closed my phone and took a seat on the bed.

I clasped my hands over my lap as I stared at them. It's not too late, I could tell him I feel sick and have him drive me back home, but whenever he's so close and I try to tell a lie, it backfires so quick because of the way he stares at me.

I sighed under my breath as the door of the trailer clicked open. My eyes scanned the empty trailer before I noticed Reiner in front of me.

Reiner dropped his body on the bed as he sat next to me and I could inhale his whole aroma, this whole time I've been trying not to throw myself in his arms. I've been trying not to stare too much because his hair was starting to grow a little and for some stupid reason I wanted to thread my fingers in his hair — I wanted to offer him a haircut. I'm no stylist, but I've been trimming my hair for as long as I can remember and I am more than capable with a pair of scissors, but I keep my thoughts to myself.

I was trying not to notice the dimmed look in his eyes whenever I avoided looking at him. He's like a boy who's been denied fun at a party and he has to sit there at an empty table and watch all the other kids run around — I'm right here, and I made him feel like he's only allowed to stare at me.

Reiner blew out a small breath, "would you be my girlfriend?"

"I accidentally overheard your conversation with Noa the other day." I blurted out, "I didn't mean to, Anna wanted popcorn, and you guys were near the stands. I didn't stick around to listen to the whole conversation but I did hear the part where you had to choose between me and Anna." I explained.

It took me a whole lot to not cry that day. Not because I was sad and I wanted Reiner all to myself, well I do — but I felt guilty for ever placing him in that position. His life was already complicated as it was, he didn't need anymore complications. I think it's okay to let him go, Reiner was never mine to begin with. From the beginning we never established the rules of whatever this is and I think that's where things went wrong.

Reiner sighed as he ran a hand through his hair. I tried to keep quiet because he said we needed to talk — I wonder if he was ever going to bring that up.

"Is that what's bothering you?" He asked. His voice was soft and uncertain.

I turned to face him, "Isn't it bothering you?"

It should, I think it definitely should. I can't even imagine being on the verge of losing a kid, and the only thing that would be standing in my way is some. . . *girl*.

Reiner tilted his head to the side, staring at me curiously and I felt ridiculous because I could tell that I was the one putting up a fight against us. I didn't want to. I really didn't. The more I thought about it — the more I focused on deciphering my feelings for him, the more I understood clearly what they truly meant.

I've only just realized I'm beginning to fall for him.

I've never felt this with anyone else before, and I don't ever want to. I wanted to keep the way my skin grew hot every time he entered, how my stomach twists whenever he laughed at something I said. I'm always nervous around him, not because I'm scared but because of the thrill I feel, liking him was thrilling. I was attracted to him the second I laid my eyes on him, the spark was there. I was too blind and childish, and he was. Well, Reiner was at a different place then.

I couldn't tell him though. I couldn't. I'm scared the second he allows me to touch him, he'll figure it out. He'll decipher it through my eyes. I wanted to rip pieces of my heart out and hand it to him, to beg him to keep them for as long as he wanted — and I couldn't.

Stupid heart. Why didn't you fall for Luke?

Reiner said something before but, I wasn't paying attention, my eyes were glued to his hand on the bed — the same one that was involuntarily shifting closer to mine. "I stopped paying attention to Noa a long time ago, and I have my faith in Ian." He said, the answer left his lips so easily, almost as if the second he was given the ultimatum he had his decision made already.

My eyes drifted to the corner of the room, "this feels *wrong. . .*" I began, "I'm a distraction." I shook my head a little.

Reiner moved closer towards me as he hooked his finger under my chin, turning my face towards him. I casted my eyes down, refusing to look at him.

"*Soleil look at me,*" his tone dropped, and my skin grew hot. Everything in me suddenly ignited.

I think I've seen all sides of Reiner by now, until his possessive sides grow. Reiner is always confident, closed off but confident. You can feel it drip off of him the second he enters a room, but I'd never tell him.

I turned to look at Reiner, meeting his blue eyes. I let out a small breath as I felt his eyes drill holes into me. Before I could cast my eyes down again, he harshly held my chin, grabbing every ounce of my attention. His finger on the bed brushed against mine, and the urge to close my eyes and feel his touch became primal.

"Watching TV while I work is a distraction, Soleil. . . You're.
. ." he let out a small shy breath as his fingers lost their grip on my
chin.

I watched Reiner run a hand through his dark hair with a
troubled look on his face. He was holding so much back he looked
troubled. But I nodded anyway, pretending to understand the un-
spoken words between us.

Reiner started a bonfire. He suggested it, and I just went
along with it. We sat in those camping bag chairs, across from each
other a little — unlike me who didn't think of food at all, Reiner
brought food. I settled for some nice marshmallows over the fire
while Reiner sipped his beer while he monitored my every move.

I tried not to think of our conversation from earlier in the
trailer. How I felt. *How I was currently feeling.*

I stayed quiet as I twisted the marshmallow over the fire.
Reiner *simply* had woods already chopped from his last trip here.
Of course he did. At home I would've been in bed right now —
crying in my own bed forcing myself to get over a guy that I'm not
sure was ever even mine to begin with. I'd force myself to sleep,
after a few scoops of ice cream.

Instead I'm here, right across from him. I get to watch his
face glow under the firelight and my chest tightened by the sight
because I wanted to crawl on his lap and hold his face in my hand
while he gives me one of those big dimpled grins he only does for

me — sometimes Anna, but he only ever smiles at us two.

Reiner shifted in his seat, and I could still see the strained muscles under his jacket flex a little, and I averted my eyes away, feeling the familiar fire between my thighs ignite. It only ever does for him. I swallowed, growing uncomfortable in my chair.

It wasn't dark outside, sure the woods seemed scary, but we're not so close to them, we're on an open field where the only thing I could do is look up. I tilted my head back gazing at the stars. The sky was dark blue and twinkling with so many stars, I could see my breath in the air whenever I exhaled because it was so cold out. But I've been suppressing my shivers for so long — I think I've got myself adjusted to the cold weather, that or I've frozen my bones.

A small genuine smile tugs at my lips, and for the first time in a while — I've thought about my father. He was nice. . . *sometimes.* Very forgetful, he forgot me half of the time. He was always busy, projects after projects after projects — I suppose now I understand why even he couldn't stand a heartbreak. For some reason, I wish he's up there, in the galaxy, that he became some strange ball of hydrogen and helium. *Hoping that he was now a star. Shining the little light left from him on me.*

My smile grew bigger when I closed my eyes and just listened to the way the branches broke, how the leaves wrestled with the wind, the crickets sang their own song. It was a little peaceful out here. I could smell the fire, the woods. The air was crispy cold, a little too harsh when the wind blew, but it felt nice when I sucked in a breath and now I understand the light smell of Reiner I could never decipher. He smelled like. . . *here.* Nature, the woods, everything.

He shifted, and I turned to look at him curiously because he was so close to speaking again.

"I started coming here after Noa left, it was the only place she didn't taint." He said as he sipped his beer, "I've never been here with *anyone*." He said the last part quietly.

I wanted to say something, to at least joke about the fact that I thought he was an ax murderer. But I couldn't bring myself to form any words right now, I was not even sure of what to say to his previous statement.

I stared at him as a shiver ran down my spine, I pulled the marshmallow away from the stick shoving it into my mouth as I shivered — and this time he caught it.

"You're cold." he stated, moving his body as he took off his jacket, Reiner left his chair and made his way towards me.

"Oh, I'm fine, Reiner—"

He pushed the jacket over my shoulders and my body sank into the chair with warmth, his jacket worked wonders. And I felt bad. I stared at him, he had on a long sleeve shirt that fitted his body more than I wish it did, but I doubt it was doing him any justice.

I stared at him when he sat back in his chair, sipping his beer and I'm guessing his body was enough to keep him warm because he didn't seem fazed at all.

"Thank you." I mumbled loud enough for him to hear.

He sent me a slow small nod, still studying me. And I guess I should be more wary about the way I act around him because he's a lawyer and he's been reading people — it's his job.

"It's beautiful out here." I sucked in a breath.

"Yeah. . ." he nodded, glancing around, *"peaceful."* He added. His eyes rounded back on me again, and I could feel the shift, "Soleil, really. . . what's happening?"

"I tell you I want more, and you tell me. . . what?"

I could tell he was serious about this. I know he won't drop it unless I finally make a choice — I'm afraid he won't allow us to sleep unless he deciphers each and one of my emotions. *He wanted us to talk about it.*

I closed my eyes for a second and wrapped my arms around me as I laid the stick on my lap. I huffed, breathing out watching the air out of my mouth come into view. My gaze flicked on the grounds settling there, it was less scary than looking into his eyes. I always seemed to drown in my own pool of emotions everytime I looked at him.

"Reiner. . ." I began, placing a hand on my forehead. My eyes stinged, and I hated the fact that I'd started crying in front of him for reasons he could never know.

I heard movements from his chair but I didn't look, but then I felt his hand on my lap. My shoulders shook with a small sob, when Reiner knelt in front of me, trying to grasp my hands away from my face, but I didn't want him to see me like this so I hurried and wiped my eyes.

His eyes softened when he looked at me, he placed a hand on my cheek and I let out a soft breath as I leaned into his touch.

His eyes were filled with emotion, a strained look on his face, his jaw clenched and unclenched, "are you crying because of me? You don't want to be here? Because I can—"

I shook my head violently, swallowing, "no, I want to be here with you."

I do. I really do.

His hand caught the other side of my face, now he was holding my face with both hands as his thumb brushed a tear away, "then tell me what's hurting so I can try to make it stop hurting."

I wrapped my hands around his wrist, my brows furrowed as my eyes softened, "I like you so much. . . I'm *scared.*" I whispered.

His whole face lit up with my words, and a small smile formed on his lips. Reiner cupped the back of my neck with his hand as he pulled me down a little, laying a kiss on my forehead, *"baby. . ."* He cooed as he scooped me into his arms.

I gripped his shirt as I felt his muscles flex under me. Reiner was now fully kneeling on the flow with me in his arms, hugging me so tightly my whole body ran hot. His mouth was leveled near my ear, so I felt his slow breaths. And it sent shivers down my spine as I held onto him tighter.

"I like you so much," he began, "it *terrifies* me." He let out a slow breath, and I circled my arms around his neck, my face stuffed into his neck, feeling my tears dry near his skin.

I pulled away a little to look into his eyes, Reiner looked at me curiously in his arms as I smiled, "so you want more?" I asked and my voice was small.

"So much more." He breathed as he kissed the side of my head, then my forehead, then he pushed me into his chest again. Hug-

ging me like I might disappear.

I let out a small moan, melting into his body, and Reiner's whole body tensed — and I love that reaction so much it should be a crime. He does that everytime. Always so surprised. This time he was the one to pull me away a little, his eyes flickered on my lips, then my eyes, back to my lips again as he licked his.

I licked my lips, my arms still wrapped around his neck as I pulled him down a little, my lips parted, releasing a small rush of air into his mouth, not intentionally, I think the tension was filling up all the room around us, and everything was so much more tense and. . .

I pressed my lips against his, tasting cherry. His lips part for me as I dart out my tongue, exploring his mouth — tasting more of cherry when his tongue moved with mine. I wanted to know why he tastes like cherry everytime we kiss but the kissing usually leads to more, and well. . . I always end up too drained to care to ask.

Reiner swallowed the small groan that left my mouth as he wrapped his arm tighter around my body, one of his hands reached the back of my head, tilting it a little as he deepened the kiss. *Moaning into my mouth.* My fingers threaded his hair, gripping at the roots of his hair, earning a few small groans out of him.

I slipped my hand under his shirt, feeling his muscles flex under my touch and Reiner pulled away from the kiss, almost too overwhelmed, staring down at me as I moved my hands under his shirt. My chest heaved, still breathless from the kiss because Reiner always managed to steal all of my oxygen.

"I think this is more." I whispered, *breathless.*

His nose flared as his eyes darkened. I bit my lips, a new version of Reiner awaits and I couldn't wait to find out. Reiner moved me in a swift motion as he stood up with me in his arms, I laughed, wrapping my hands around his shoulders. My head tilted back a little and he didn't miss it as he latched his lips against my throat.

I winced at the small bite he made but he only sucked my skin harsher — he licked the sensitive skin, and I knew that it would surely leave a mark. Reiner Kline gave me a hickey. . . *I wonder if that's under the terms of more.*

Reiner almost couldn't get inside the trailer because he was too busy trying to strip me on the way there. My back hit the door as he locked it, my hands were on his shoulders, he managed to pull off both his coat and mine. Kissing me after like it was some sort of reward.

"Tell me again," he kissed me again. *Soft, quick and rushed.*

"Hmmm?" I hummed, moving my arms under him, fighting his muscles as I pulled the shirt off his back, and Reiner moved me away from the door, my legs were still wrapped around his waist as he dropped my ass on the counter in the small kitchen.

Reiner breathed, still breathless as he shoved his face into my neck, "tell me you like me," he ordered. His words tickled my skin.

My eyes roomed his bare chest as I ran my hands over it, hungry for more as the wetness pooled between my legs. "I like you." I whispered. My breath was getting caught in my throat.

Reiner pulled away, staring into my eyes, his hands planted at my side on the counter, "how much?"

I leaned in and kissed him, *"so much."*

Reiner pulled my shirt over my head, his eyes dilating as he took in the sight of my swollen breast. My nipples poked through the laced bra. Reiner hands darted out as he grabbed my breast feeling the weight of them with a soft sigh.

He kissed my breast through the laced bra as he hooked two fingers under the waistband of my leggings, pulling them off — Reiner pulled back just to pull the leggings from my feet. He took a step back as his eyes roamed my body with a heavy breath. He licked his lips, probably admiring me in the lingerie I picked out earlier.

It was for 'just in case'.

Reiner grinned, his dimples coming into view, he stalked over me as he cupped my cheeks. He licked my lips, "for someone who was acting so closed off earlier, you sure as hell look prepared for a good fuck. . ."

I smiled at him, "ah, don't be a narcissist, Reiner." I breathed out as I felt his hand cup my pussy, before he slid the laced underwear to the side, his finger gliding over my wetness. Reiner coated his fingers with my wetness before he brought his fingers over my clit, circling it.

Fuck.

"Let's face it. . ." He whispered as he kissed me, gliding his fingers against me again, this time he shoved both fingers at once, "you're obsessed with me," he breathed, my back arched as I moaned.

"Shhhh. . ." He mumbled, "take it like a good girl."

Reiner kissed me, swallowing my moans with his as my eyes rolled back, feeling my orgasm at bay already. The small sparks were there, collecting each other for a bigger feeling — I could feel myself getting ready to explode, my stomach tensed as he brought his thumb over my clit again, and I opened my legs wider for him, encouraging him to keep doing what he was doing.

Reiner was attacking my neck, my collar bone, *kissing me everywhere.* My skin was on fire. When I moaned out I gripped his biceps and I'm sure he'll have my little crescent moon shape marks on him for days. And I'm proud to give him pieces of me. Things to remind him of me. *To remind him of the things we did.*

"Already?" He mumbled against my skin, feeling my walls close around him as he pumped into me with that slow pace he knew I liked. A small smug smile on his face, I could feel it against my skin with my eyes closed.

"Asshole." I moaned out as coming around his fingers, Reiner was still playing with my pussy, shoving a third finger in there, after my fucking orgasm, the man is a monster.

He pulled away from my neck, staring at the mess between my legs as he slowly pumped his fingers in and out of me — I was still holding onto him as he circled my clit softly, earning a few raspy moans out of me.

"Fuck, Reiner." I whined.

"I love it more when I come inside of you, and I get to play with it with my cock, it makes you *mine.*" He whispered as his eyes flicked up to meet mine, as I closed my mouth, swallowing.

I moaned again and he grinned, pulling his fingers out of me, "you and your breeding kinks." I playfully shoved his chest, but the guy didn't even budge.

Reiner licked his fingers, moaning at the satisfaction of my taste, my cheeks felt hot because he acted like I taste better than anything else he ever tasted.

I stare at his bare chest, the hunger coming back again when my eyes flicker to his small silver necklace, I love it so much. I ran two fingers down his body as my hands settled at his belt.

Reiner grabbed my hands, throwing me over his shoulder and slapped my ass, and I squeaked — I'm thinking it's something about the woods that gave him this new confidence. He's all cocky — well he was alway cocky and confident, I don't know. Something's a little different.

I liked it.

I laughed when Reiner laid me on the bed, placing one knee over the bed as he pulled me towards him by the ankle, my body jolted, when his lips met my breast instantly. Pushing the bra over it. My tits bounced, coming into view, my perky little nipples were so hard and sensitive.

I moaned Instantly when Reiner took me into his mouth — I nearly choked on a gasp. "Oh, *G-fuck.*" I moaned, and Reiner shook his head a little with a light laugh. I nearly said God, and I have to keep reminding myself to not say it.

"So gorgeous," he moaned, *"gorgeous girl."* He sighed desperately as he unhook my bra with one swift movement, smiling up at me like a kid on Christmas morning.

I moaned, feeling Reiner trail kissed down to my stomach,

my hips — he purposely let out a soft breath against my skin, just to watch me jolt and a shiver ran down my spine, as I reached for him, *so needy.* My eyes searched for him as he hooked his fingers on the waistband of my underwear, peeling it off as he stood back up on his feet.

Beautiful, he looked beautiful. Easily the most gorgeous man I've ever seen. My heart was pounding as blood rushed through my ears. The hunger in his eyes still lingered as he stared down at me, still shirtless with his pants on and my mouth watered by just looking at all the *veins* near his v-line. His erection was poking through his jeans, begging for my attention. My own wetness was already pooling between my legs, in need for another release.

I propped myself on my elbow, but Reiner's hands circled around my ankle, and he flipped me on my stomach and a smile grew on my face as my hands fisted the sheets.

"Reiner," I cried.

I heard his belt unbuckle and my skin grew hot with excitement, still, I didn't want to look behind me because the feeling of not knowing what comes next was thrilling. I heard the bed dip and I felt his body against me. I let out a soft breath.

"C'mon baby." He said as he leaned down against me, his hard cock brushed against my ass. The feeling of it was already clouding my head. I let out another soft breath as he licked the shell of my ear, "get on all fours for me."

I smiled, *wide.* Pushing my body back as I got on all fours. Reiner used his knees to spread my legs wider for him, placing himself at my entrance. Moaning already feeling him against me.

His finger dug my skin as I felt him slam inside of me with one quick thrust. I gasped, fisting the sheets. Throwing my head back as he started to fuck me.

"You feel so good, baby." He moaned out, raspy and needy.

His thrusts were *powerful, punishing, and possessive.* I moaned loudly, squirming beneath him. "Harder." I rushed out.

In and out, quick and deep, so much strength. He was gasping behind me, moaning as I whined under him. His fingers were bruising my skin, burning holes on my body.

"Reiner, Reiner. . ." I moaned as I felt his finger rub circles over my swollen clit. This was starting to feel too much. My body was getting more sensitive as he fucked me harsher.

I wanted to hear him, not just his moans, but other things too. I felt my stomach tense. Reiner leaned down and kissed my shoulders — he often did this and it always clouds my head. He does harsh things to my body then apologizes for it seconds later by doing something soft, like kissing my shoulders as he pounded into me.

This feeling was becoming more primal. I wanted to possess him. *To own him.*

"Say it." I whispered as he licked the shell of my ear, "you can say it."

Reiner moaned as he thrusted inside of me again, his cock pulsed inside of me as he held onto my hips, his rhythm grew faster.

"Reiner, please," I moaned, "I want to hear it," I could feel my orgasm at bay, but I pushed it away a little as I held on a little longer.

"Fuck." He moaned as he pushed himself harder inside of me, "you want me to call you mommy?"

"Ah," I gasped as I closed my eyes. "You're a big boy, let's hear it."

"Mommy." He moaned. And I fucking melted, rolling my hips against him. Reiner pushed my head deeper against the pillow as I arched against him.

He whimpered and pulled out just to slam back into me again, earning a raspy moan out of me, "you like it when I'm a good boy, *mommy?"*

"Fuck, yes!" I moaned, reaching for my orgasm at this point.

My skin burned as I gripped onto the sheets, my mouth parted open as I panted.

Reiner let out another whimper when my walls closed around him and I felt his cock pulsate inside of me, *"just like that, mommy?"*

I couldn't even respond to him as I came and I could feel my body jerk. I smiled as my body relaxed, still shuddering each time he thrusted inside of me, chasing his own orgasm. I let out a raspy moan listening to Reiner moan as he came inside of me. My toes curled as I bit my lips, everything felt good.

His body fell on the bed, his chest flushed against my back as he held onto me, kissing my back, my shoulders. He moved next to me as he kissed my cheek, my eyes were still closed — still too sensitive to say anything. I flipped on my back as I turned my head in Reiner's direction. With a heavy breath, his hand reached in between my legs as he played with our release that was leaking out of me. I sighed, a shuddery breath. I felt his fingers circle my clit — his own chest falling and rising behind me.

Reiner touched me until I felt him grow hard behind me again, and I was ready for another orgasm. He was careful to not touch me too much because with my sensitivity I could come anytime. We stayed quiet listening to our breath fall and rise as we caught our breath.

Reiner let out a strangled breath, as he entered me again, this time, slow. His breath fanned over my lips, his eyes holding mine. I gasped as I rolled my hips against his a little, encouraging him to start moving again, but his head only fell on my shoulder as he buried his head in the crook on my neck, his chest heaved, holding himself up with one hand.

I wrapped my hands around his neck as I dug my heels against his back as I kissed his shoulders, "c'mon, baby." I whispered, my voice laced with desperation.

The feeling was too intense to put into words, but I felt it too and I wanted him to know. Something was different now, he was softer, his touch meant so much more now. The way we were holding each other was so much more different now.

"Fuck. . ." he moaned out as he finally moved inside of me again.

I moaned, as I kissed his shoulder. My nails into his back because with each slow stroke, he was reaching me deeper than before, he made me want so much more. Reiner's tongue traced my neck, kissing my skin — causing the hairs on the back of my neck to stand. A shiver ran down my spine. He kissed my jaw and stroked me at a slow pace, I learned his rhythm and rolled my hips against his.

Reiner gained control of the situation again, groaning as he kissed my jaw, my cheeks, then he took my mouth, softly. Biting my bottom lip as he thrusted his tongue inside of my mouth, my eyes were glued shut feeling his tongue caress mine. He moaned into my mouth as he deepened our kiss, stealing my air supply in the process.

I squirmed under him and his necklace dangled, a moan rolled out of my mouth,. I was hungry for more. I clawed his back, trying to push him deeper — trying to crawl under his skin, for some reason this wasn't enough, it didn't feel close enough.

"Reiner."

"Hmm?" He hummed as he shifted over me, he trailed his hand down on my stomach and rolled two fingers over my clit, I trembled — I held him tighter

"No, Soleil." He hummed, leaning forward as he kissed my lips, "let's see those pretty eyes, baby."

My brows pulled together, whining — fighting the tight knot in my stomach, I opened my eyes and his face came into view, a smug smile was on his lips.

"I want you to look at me while I make you come." He whispered, his blue eyes seared into mine.

"Oh, God."

Reiner's fingers circled my clit in a quick fast pace, the pleasure of it was so intense I wanted to scream.

"What did I say about using God's name in vain?"

I paid him no mind as I felt him move in and out of me in no rush, just slow and deep, my toes curled as I dug my heels deep against his ass, feeling my eyes roll back. I could lay in this bed and fuck him for eternity if that was what he wanted — it would be enough for me.

We came together this time, holding each other's eyes, riding out our orgasm with slow strokes, when Reiner pulled out he slapped his cock over my clit and earned a whimper out of me as he glides his cock against my entrance, making a mess with our fluids that was leaking out of my pussy, he kissed my shoulders, then my lips.

He used his finger, coating it with our mess, "it makes you *mine*." He mumbled under his breath, looking at me as he stuffed both fingers into his mouth. Pushing them into my mouth after licking them.

I moaned with his fingers inside of my mouth, as he pulled them out just to give me a soft kiss.

I think maybe it was an hour. I don't remember, but after we cleaned up late. Reiner even changed the sheets because there was more of a mess than we thought. I wore one of his shirts and I had my bonnet on when I crawled back into bed, he was still naked. His dick half-hard and I was starting to wonder if he has a permanent erection — I could still remember Hayley joking about the possibilities of him having difficulties getting up so I found it pretty ironic that he can't get down at all.

Reiner held me until our breath became one. My head was on his chest and his arms were around my waist.

I poked his chest, "are you tired?"

"Why?" He asked, as he wrapped his arms tighter around my waist, his mouth was near my ear, "you wanna go again?" His sultry voice dropped an octave, the words seduced me as my stomach rolled.

I swallow, thinking about how good I felt earlier, his hot skin against mine, his smile, his kisses — I savored it all. But I shook my head and stopped myself from thinking about it for now.

"No," I whispered, "I wanna introduce you to the *Marvel Cinematic Universe.*"

Reiner groaned as he threw his head back, "that is the least sexiest thing you've ever said."

I laughed as I pushed against his chest, "don't be so excited." I said playfully, "we'll go slow and start off with *Iron Man.*" I said as I grabbed the remote that was next to the lamp near the bed. I turned on the TV hoping I could find a trace of any marvel movie anywhere.

He groaned again, closing his arms around me as he stuffed his face into the crook of my neck, "will I be rewarded for this?"

I smiled when I saw *Disney+* on the list of apps his *Roku TV* had, and then I clicked on it.

I placed a hand in his hair and played with it. "I don't know." I whispered in a low voice that I hoped came off sexy, "watch and find out."

I scrolled through the *Marvel* section, sighing as I scrolled past *Daredevil*, I still haven't binged it. I clicked on *Iron Man,* watching the *Marvel* theme rolls on screen. I closed the lamp, darkening the room completely, crawling back into his arms.

Reiner kissed the side of my head, "don't fall asleep."

CHAPTER THIRTY-ONE

Reiner

I WOKE UP ON MY STOMACH as I rolled on my side. Relief washed over my face once I realized Soleil was right next to me. She was nearly on the edge of the bed on her side — her back was facing me. I groaned, pulling her closer against me as she let out a little groan. Involuntarily she turned to her side and faced me, and her bonnet had slipped out a little, revealing her hair. I smiled to myself as I reached out and fixed it.

Soleil let out a soft breath as she breathed softly. Her long lashes were pretty. I don't think I've ever noticed it before but she has a small beauty mark on her cheek, near her jawline. A smile spreads on my face with this realization — *how come I've never seen it before?*

She's so beautiful. Beautiful. Beautiful. She's mine. *All mine.*

Mine. Mine. Mine.

My chest tightened feeling so overwhelmed all of a sudden, it's like when I'm around her it's hard to breathe — but when I'm not around her I can't breathe at all. The feeling is spreading, so much that I have to reach out for her, to make sure she's here. Thoughts of her leaving me are so much more painful than expected.

What if I'm not enough? Last night she cried in my arms because she liked me so much, it made me happy. But scared, so damn scared. I don't want her to feel like I've cornered her into a relationship she didn't ask for — I'll understand if she leaves me though, I'm thirty-two with a kid. She's just getting her life started while mine is passing by, I've done almost everything already.

I fell in love, married, worked, and had a kid. What can I really offer her?

The thought haunted me. I'll be fine if she leaves me I think, I'll just miss this more than anything because she showed me things I didn't know existed, feelings I didn't think I had the capacity to develop.

Soleil fell asleep but made me promise to finish the movie by myself — which I did. It was pretty good. Would I have watched without the threat she made last night? No.

I remember those tired eyes of hers when she barely pushed my chest, *"I'm gonna pop quiz you tomorrow and if you don't get any of the questions right I'll know you didn't watch it, and that'll be no more sex for you."*

I kissed her and I agreed. I mostly watched her sleep, but I'm positive I can pass this pop quiz if hers.

Soleil shivered a little, bringing me back to reality. I pulled the sheets on her body, staring at her as her eyes fluttered a little. My face came closer to hers as I laid a kiss on her forehead — she hummed, under my touch and she moved her body a little closer.

I get drunk by just the smell of her, even more now because half of her smells like me now. I stuffed my face in the crook of her neck and my body melted into hers — I wanted to stay here all day, under her. She comforts me without the knowledge of it.

Soleil stirs, her arm shooting up on my bicep, and I suppose she's awake now. I laid a soft kiss against her neck, pulling away as I stared at her.

"*Hi.*" She whispered when my eyes met hers, her raspy voice ringing in my ear, branding itself into my brain. *It tricked my stupid heart to beat faster.*

My eyes scanned her face, her puffy eyes, *"hey."* I whispered back. Bringing my face closer to hers connecting our nose against each other.

She smiled, pulling away a little, "I have morning breath, Reiner." She whispered the words like they were some sort of crime.

I smiled, leaving a quick kiss on her lips without a warning, a small look of shock washed over her face, "okay." I said.

She closed her eyes for a moment, smiling. I place a hand against her cheeks, soothing her soft skin with the rough pad of my thumb.

"Come on a picnic with me."

She stared at me dumbfounded, "why? It's so cold out, and there's so much more we can do in this bed," she said as she climbed onto my body. My body goes stiff as my dick twitched, hardening under her. Her eyes went wide for a second before she adjusted herself on me.

I groaned as I placed my hands on her hips, "there's this nice stream nearby and it's always nice out there, I have everything, the food, the basket, everything, I just need *you*."

Soleil stared at me, still refusing to give in, so I rolled her hips against me, making her feel my erection. I want to go by that stream today with her because I know she'll like it, she's just being stubborn. *I'll fuck her into submission if I have to.*

My grip on her waist tightened, "please?"

She sighed, shuddering under me. She closed her eyes for a second before staring down at me again. "Okay, but I'm using your jacket again, it's really nice, and you can use mine if you want." She said.

I laughed at the size of it, "I'm fine."

She smiled, leaning down kissing my lips, pulling away just to stare at me. I swear she looks better everyday. My eyes roamed her body, the shirt she had on — *my shirt.* It Covered almost everything. So I used my hands to help me see better. I pushed my hands under her shirt as she arched her back under my touch.

I might not have to fuck her into submission but I'll fuck her anyways.

When Soleil brought her face down again, I leaned forward just to kiss her again, this time deeper.

★ · ☆ · ★

"Reiner, can we please just go back inside?" She huffed. My hand in hers as I dragged her through the woods, we're so close I can hear the water stream.

I glance back at her, "Aren't you supposed to be excited about stuff like this?"

She made a cute scowl with her face, her brows furrowing as she tried to tug her hand from mine, but I held it tighter. "That's sexist. *A*: it's cold outside, and *B*: it's fucking cold."

"We're almost there." I mumbled, wrapping my hands tighter around the basket as I dragged her near the stream, the smallest sunlight coming into view. Today was cloudy so we didn't get that much sunlight.

I let out a breath, watching it go with the wind, the water looks so peaceful flowing by. I've been meaning to take Anna out here, maybe fish. She'd like it — I should've taken my phone with me after all she would've liked this view.

I turn to look at Soleil as the wind blows, her hair flying with it. She winced at the cold air, her nose going up a light shade of purple, and I wonder why she lives in Minnesota where we get snow and rainstorms for summer instead of the sun. I place the basket on the floor pulling Soleil closer to me. *Stubborn little thing.*

I ran my hands up and down her arm trying to get her body warm even though I can see her shallow breath in the air. I kiss her forehead, "you'll like it, just give me a second."

She groaned when I turned away, knowing I was her only source of warmth made me smile.

"We could've been in bed right now."

I shook my head as I walked closer near the stream, "are you still mumbling under your breath?"

"No. . . but it's true, *we should be in bed.*" she mumbled the last part under her breath.

I set up the stuff near the small calm stream, the rocks were so nicely flat it wouldn't be too painful sitting on them, although I did offer to put more than one layer of covers on the floor but Soleil protested, keeping two covers to herself claiming she's cold. But before everything, she forced me to stand out of the way to snap a picture of the set up.

I supposed it was nice, I made us sandwiches back in the trailer, and only packed fruits, and a bottle of wine. *Soleil liked it so I liked it.*

I kissed her on the cheeks, "can we please sit now?"

"Oh sorry," she huffed, stuffing her phone in the basket, "I'll send you the photos if you want."

"Sure." I mumbled.

I watched her sit down, right in front of me. At arm's length — and I find myself itching just to pull her body against me. I don't know what's happening to me but I want her touch all the time — I took whatever she offers. I became a version of myself I could hardly recognize.

Maybe I should see my priest this week.

I watched Soleil reach for a bush of flowers that was near the stream, probably curious. "Don't touch that, it could be poisonous."

She casted me a look over her shoulders, rolling her eyes in the process as she plucked out a branch, the little purple flower blooming at the top. I watched Soleil curiously as she brought the little flower to her nose, her face remained stern with no signs of emotions.

Soleil handed me the flower, I shoved another grape in my mouth and grabbed the flower from her hand. I stared at the little flower, then at her. I brought the little purple flower to my nose with my eyes still glued on Soleil. *Nothing.* The thing smelled like nothing. I shrugged and placed it near the basket.

"It smells like nothing." I mumbled.

Soleil only nodded as she opened the basket taking out the wine glasses, along with the wine. I popped another grape in my mouth staring at her still as I shewed.

"Do you like flowers?" I asked.

"Yes, but I hate *red roses.*" She looked up to meet my eyes but I stayed quiet, waiting for the explanation.

She shrugged, "they're awesome, but it's everyone's choice. And when a guy buys red roses it's like they didn't put *any* thoughts into what you'd possibly like, he just went along with what everyone else likes."

I nodded, "what do you like?"

She smiled, wide. Pushing a strand of hair off her cheek, *"food. But if you're asking about flowers, then *Begonia.* They bloom very beautifully."

My chest shook with a hearty laugh, because knowing Soleil — I know it's true.

I unwrapped one of the sandwiches and handed it to her as she handed me a glass of wine, and I'm wondering if it's too early for wine because it's barely the afternoon and we're out under a foggy weather about to drink wine by a river.

We sat in silence, well almost — the river was running very calmly, and Soleil was nearly shivering. I was starting to feel bad for dragging her out here. It's not that bad out so her shivering is really an issue. I grimaced when she let out a soft breath, her hands were shaking — struggling to take a bite of that sandwich, but when she finally did get a bite, she looked up, almost embarrassed offering me a sheep smile.

I moved closer a little, draping the blanket over her shoulders, grabbing her legs — placing them on my thighs, her shoulders sagged at the new found warmth. Yeah we can't stay out here too long, she's so cold she might get sick. But I don't think it's exactly normal to be this cold under this light weather.

I ran a hand over her thigh, providing as much warmth as I could, watching her body melt under my touch. "Soleil, are you anemic?" I questioned, because that would make so much more sense now.

Because this isn't the first time either, back in my office, she was freezing under all those layers of clothing. Her hands are almost always cold — she can't stand the cold, her body can't handle much of it.

She thought about it for a second before shrugging, still chewing — I reached in the basket fishing out a water bottle being careful to not knock the wine along with the glasses, I opened the cap of the water bottle and handed it to her.

Soleil smiled as she took the water from my hand and took a sip, she swallowed, staring at me again, "I don't know." She answered.

"Well you might have a low iron, which would explain why you're shivering right now."

She shook her head and took another bite. "I'm fine, I just hate the cold."

"Hmm." I hummed, grabbing my wine glass again, drinking as little as possible.

Soleil turned to look at the River, watching the water run smoothly, and I was stuck, too mesmerized by her beauty to even care how well the water looks.

She sighed, pondering, "I think this is the *nicest* thing anyone has ever done for me."

I frowned, "this is merely nothing sweetheart, trust me, I thought more of me than of you." That wasn't true, but this was basically nothing. Anyone can do this. I find it hard to believe that —*this*— is the best anyone has ever done for her. I don't always do grand gestures but lately I find myself willing to do —*try*— anything just for the sake of Soleil's happiness.

Her happiness became my own. Whatever she feels, I feel it too.

"I've only ever dated one guy, his name is Luke. We met in college, —*we were*— I was stuck in a relationship that wasn't going anywhere, we didn't have anything in common, half of the times I think he only dated me because he wanted someone with a pretty face," she paused for a second to meet my eyes, "at least I think so."

I opened my mouth to say something but nothing came out, instead I finally looked at the River. The water was so clear I could see the fishes swim alone, only a couple of small ones swam in groups. I used to have a group, my family. I was once foolish enough to believe it was my forever — even before everything went down, something was dying. Parts of me that never got a chance to feel alive.

Then our family fell apart, I swam alone for a while, I hated it. I was miserable, but I was willing to push through because of hope, —Anna— and now that I've met Soleil, I don't ever want to allow myself to be alone, *to swim alone*. The parts of me that were dying came alive the second she walked into my life.

With her, I'm new. *Better.*

"I've only been with Noa." The words fly out of my mouth, shocking me in the process.

We erased the awkward confessions with a few kisses, Soleil climbing into my lap knocking the wine bottle near the rocks as it spills, I laughed between each kiss because it amuses me how badly she *always* wants me.

She apologized for the wine by sliding her tongue into my mouth, caressing it with an erotic kiss. Her hands in my hair tugging and pulling as I gripped onto her hips, holding her in place as she tried to grind against me.

I broke the kiss a little panting against her neck as she kissed my jaw, my cheeks. I felt so *overwhelmed* under her touch. She touched me so softly, I was melting. I held onto her because she was my only source of gravity, she's the only thing that made sense to me. I held on hugging her tighter as she held me. My head buried in the crook of her neck as she rested her shin on my shoulders, the both of us catching our breaths and listening to the sounds of the river.

This must be what it feels like to fly.

When we walked back to the trailer, it was nearly four in the afternoon, we stayed by the river longer than planned. Soleil ate half of the food in the basket, and force fed me the other half, I ate just to entertain her. It keeps her happy. So it made me happy.

I listened to her talk about journaling and how excited she was to start the internship program she applied for — she talked about the things that interested her the most and whenever she went quiet waiting for me to speak, I said something stupid and boring and urged her to keep talking because I liked watching her talk. She used her hands a lot, and when she laughed she moved around, laughing for so long she went silent but you could still tell she was laughing.

I found that entertaining.

Soleil let go of my hand making a run for the trailer and I shook my head as she disappeared into the place. I followed her inside shortly placing all the things back where they belonged. A short clean up was in order, but that didn't take me long — soon enough I washed my hands making my way back to the room.

I grabbed my phone from the bed, with plans to check on Anna but I only ended up frowning at all the miscalls from Noa clicking on her name just to call her back as I stepped out — walking past Soleil in a towel as she headed for the shower.

CHAPTER THIRTY-TWO

"REINER YOU WERE RIGHT, it was nice out."
I shouted as I pulled his shirt over my head, the door slammed
closed and I jumped a little. The harsh sound took me by surprise.

I pulled my leggings on, watching Reiner storm in the room,
grabbing his keys. My brows furrowed as I stepped closer near
him, his chest was heaving up and down, breathing in a harsh
rhythm. If I had to guess, I'd say Reiner's pissed right now.

I've never seen him angry. *Ever.*

Even when he was closed off or seemed *"mean"* he was never
really angry just. . . closed off, and grumpy in a way that would
keep you away from him.

I pulled my sweatpants on as I stood behind him, watching
his back flexed as he ran a hand through his hair, "Reiner what's

wrong?"

"Grab your things, I'll drop you off at home."

"What?" I whispered, "why?"

"Soleil, just grab your things and I will drop you off home."
He paused, shoving his phone in his pockets, turning — not to
face me but to walk away. "We're leaving." He announced.

It wasn't a suggestion, it was something that was already decided before I even got a say, still I didn't complain as I grabbed
my things in a hurry shoving them inside of my bag. He's angry,
something was very wrong.

I place a hand over my forehead stopping to look around for a
second. Little as yesterday, Reiner dragged me inside of his trailer,
my bag in his hands, kissing me the second we walked in — now
I'm packing alone as he slammed his car door shut outside. Just
an hour ago we were making out by the river where the world
revolved around us.

When I stepped outside with my bag in my hand, Reiner was
already in the car — the car was already on, he was only waiting
for me. I tried my best to walk faster.

"Soleil, let's go!"

I nodded, coming out of my trance as I walked faster to reach
his car. I climbed into his car and dropped the bag near my feet as
I closed the door.

"Reiner, will you tell me what's wrong?"

He didn't look at me. He said nothing. He only drived.

I squinted as Reiner pulled up to my driveway, the whole car
ride had been stressful and now I'm staring at Luke on my porch

just standing there. I think Reiner noticed him too because he cast me a harsh look. At least he's still in the mood of being jealous.

I didn't know what was going on, but I wanted to. I wanted him to tell me so I could try and help in any way that I could. All I knew is that, he stepped outside after getting a phone call, came back inside slamming doors. With this insatiable urge to get rid of me entirely.

He was making me feel unwanted right now and I didn't like it.

I made a move to remove my seatbelt but stopped when a bright idea came to mind, I could almost see the lightbulb turning on over my head. Instead of getting out of the car, I sat still, getting more comfortable, "I'm not getting out of the car until you tell me what's wrong."

Reiner didn't seem to like my idea. He groaned as he scratched the back of his neck, "Soleil get out of the fucking car. I don't have time for this shit."

I raised two brows, disappointed — shame on him for thinking it would be this easy. "Whatever it is must be serious because it got you swearing like a sailor."

His jaw hardened as he stared at me, "I'm serious."

"So am I." I pushed, "tell me what's wrong."

He tapped his fingers on the wheels, impatient. He wanted to be somewhere else and now he's probably contemplating on just driving there with me in the car, *fuck it right?*

"That phone call. . ." My eyes flicked from his hand on the wheel to his face, "who called you?"

Still, he didn't say anything, he only ran a hand through his hair — *stressed so stressed.* I'm surprised he hasn't exploded yet. His face was strained, his eyes were uncertain.

"Why can't you understand-"

"Understand what, Reiner? Just tell me, tell me and I'll understand." I snapped.

"I don't want to be near you right now, get out of my car!" He leaned closer towards me as he stretched his arms and opened my door. "Please, go home." He whispered the last part, avoiding my eyes as he spoke.

I shivered feeling the cold breeze brush past my exposed skin, I nodded as I hopped out of his car and I stared at him.

"Why are you being so immature about this? Just tell me what's wrong, tell me who called at least." I pleaded.

His nose flared as he thought of an answer to feed me, maybe he's thinking of lying. And what if he does lie. . . why would he lie? I've never given him any reason to.

"*Noa.*" He hissed, "Noa called and she was in an. . . *accident* with Anna." He nodded in disbelief and my heart crumbled, watching him place a hand over his mouth, shocked he got to say those words. The words alone are choking him. I climbed back in the car, devastated by the news.

"Are they–"

He shrugged, "I don't know."

Oh, Anna.

He let out a harsh breath, "the doctors said she was intoxicated." He finished his sentence, scoffing to himself in disbelief.

"Ohmygod," the words came out of my mouth like a train, "Anna—" I choked, my voice cracking mid sentence. So I swallowed, took a breath. I shook my head, my voice softening, "I don't think you should drive, let me drive, instead." I extended my hand out waiting for him to hand me his car key.

"I don't want *you* there." He mumbled. His eyes were bloodshot red already and I was trying to figure out when he cried, was it outside of the trailer before he yelled at me to pack? or was it all those times he ran a hand over his face?

I swallowed, "Reiner—"

"I'm going to check on my wife and kid alone, Soleil."

My eyes darted away from him, stinging. *"Ex-wife."* I mumbled. There was a pain in my chest, it was indescribable. It felt like someone had pushed a knife right into my chest and the blade cut right through my heart.

He didn't look at me when he said these next few words, but I wish he did. Just to see how much they ruined me.

"I can't handle any more *distractions*, I have to keep a clear head for them."

I swallowed as I felt a quick tear run down my cheek, hot against my skin, so hot I forgot how cold it was outside. I shivered after the thought, wiping my cheek with the back of my hand.

"You said I wasn't a distraction— you—" I choked.

I needed a second to find a way to breathe again. "Reiner, you're trying to push me away. That's fine if you want space but don't start saying things that you *won't* be able to take back."

This was me trying to tell him he's allowed to have space. That was his escape. He's allowed to be hurt, he's allowed to cry and be angry, but he's absolutely *not* allowed to ruin this for us because of a brief moment of anger.

He only shook his head as he ran a hand through his hair nervously, "I'm so sorry Soleil but you were right. *You are a distraction*, and I'm sorry for ever making you feel like you weren't."

"What?" I pulled my arms under me — hugging myself from the chilly air that's trying to wrap itself around me.

Now my heart was torn beyond repair.

Reiner ripped the fourth layer of my heart, now I'm all bare. Just bleeding out. My love for him is hurting my heart. I was trying, I was trying so hard to slap a few bandages on it and just hang in there, but I could only handle so much. Couldn't he hear what he was saying right now? If he wants to go to the hospital alone, I'll let him, I was only worried for his safety and I just wanted to be able to wait for him to come back home to me. But he was saying so much stuff. *Too much stuff.*

He cleared his throat ready to repeat his sentence again, "you—"

"I fucking heard what you said," I bit out, "I can't believe you were about to say it *again*."

His eyes softened, "Soleil—" he called out, his voice soft, smooth as butter.

I shook my head a little, anger flashing through my eyes, "you know, I really wish you found that out sooner."

Reiner looked away, "me too, but I guess it took me this weekend to realize that."

"Okay," I mumbled, wiping my eyes so quick and fast I think I might've cut my skin, "this is wasting time, you have to go now." I mumbled as I made a move to get out of the car because I refused to spend another second near him just to hear him say words that made me feel useless.

Reiner grabbed my elbow, and I grimaced, ripping my arm away from, his touch still lingered on my skin. *Still familiar.*

"Do you *ever* fucking touch me again." I hissed.

Reiner's eyes only darted to my porch, staring at Luke who was still by the door, one leg against the wall, staring at us intensively. I'm surprised he hadn't interfered yet, "Soleil, whoever *he* is. . . send him away."

I scoffed, nearly laughing at his audacity. I could feel the tears at bay but I tried my best to keep them there as I leaned forward a little, staring at Reiner like I was about to tell him my deepest darkest secret, "you're an asshole and I mean this sincerely Reiner. . ." I paused, *"go fuck yourself."*

The second I hopped out of his car, the tears were pouring as I released a shaky breath. I was hurting not only from the nasty things he said but because he's driving away with half of my heart in his hands and doesn't even know it.

I immediately felt guilty but I couldn't go back and apologize too much has already been said and I have to find a way to convince myself that I wasn't the one in the wrong here. He was the immature one, not me.

Still I was trying to figure out how fast everything happened. I was willing to take a few blows and be there for him, because I did understand that he was having a hard time. But he only kept pushing and pushing — he's scared right now, so scared which is why I felt guilty for being hurt in the first place, I should be the last thing he has to worry about right now. We went from wanting to be more to being *nothing* at all.

I keep forgetting that Luke was around so it was a little alarming when his face came into view when I reached my front door. "*Please* tell me you didn't hear all of that." I groaned as I pushed the key into the keyhole.

"Are you okay?" He asked as he pushed himself off the wall, coming at my side. I could smell the pity radiating off his body like some cologne.

I sniffed a little, a hiccup catching my breath, "I'm fine Luke, just go home." I mumbled.

"I don't think you should be alone right now."

"Whatever." I mumbled, too tired to have another worthless argument so soon. I stepped inside of the house, pushing my shoes off my feet only to realize my bag was still in Reiners car, so was my phone. I don't plan on seeing him again, not so soon, but he has *my phone*, my clothes. *Fuck.*

So I cried, I had a breakdown, nearly falling down on my knees but Luke caught me in his arms, allowing me to cry on his shoulder.

I cried because of the nasty things Reiner said to me.

I cried because he ripped out half of my heart and took it with him.

I cried because of the fact that I'm so worried for him.

I cried because *I love him.*
I cried because I am *in love* with him.
I cried because I'm stupid.
Stupid, stupid, stupid.

CHAPTER THIRTY-THREE

★ · ☆ · ★

Soleil

★ · ☆ · ★

LUKE FORCED me to go out today. He's been hanging around a lot lately, well I've been hanging around, considering I've been at his place, Blue and I have been staying with him. *He said one week of sulking was enough.*

I think so too, I should stop sulking and feeling guilty about the way everything went down, but everytime I try to I am reminded that Reiner was the first guy to ever make me feel good about just being near him — *existing.*

He always wanted me close, whenever I was near him, I wasn't ignored, not even a little bit, maybe for the first time in my life I got too much attention — I got lost drowning in it, unconsciously I learned how to live in it — I adapted and got used to it. Now the water's gone, and just like a fish I'm choking on land, searching for water even if it's a single drop. *He's gone.*

"If she wants to cry all day, *let her.*" I heard Hayley argue, her voice was a low harsh whisper.

"Not if it's eating her away." Luke hissed.

"It's called a process dumbass."

"It's been *three weeks.*"

I never realized it was ever that bad until Luke said it outloud. I know I've been. . . But I didn't think it was ever *that* bad.

Hayley sighed, "exactly, you should give her a lot more credit than that, the fact that she was willing to even come out here." She gestured to the restaurant.

"We both know she did that just to please me."

"Then you should be pleased."

I took my seat at the table, and both of them immediately went quiet. Hayley didn't like the fact that I was staying with Luke, and she argued for me to go home with her everyday instead — but Luke allowed me to do things I know she wouldn't. Like to not say anything and just let me cry, alone.

Luke is a guy, he's simple, crying makes him uncomfortable. Hayley however, will hold me while I do it.

Hayley looked at me and her eyes softened, at least with Luke his pity is laced with annoyance, which I understood. But Hayley was treating me like a baby, and the more she stared or treated me that way I'll always want to cry. *I don't want to keep crying.*

"Say the word and we'll go home and watch people skate." She placed a hand on mine, and I smiled as I shook my head.

"No, Luke is right, it's been too long and I have to start acting

372

normal again — my internship starts tomorrow."

She scoffed, "when has *Luke* ever been right?"

"My internship starts tomorrow." I repeated.

"Does that mean you'll be going home?"

I stared at Luke, waiting for him to answer for me. I was only ready for the internship because I have no choice but to be. Life didn't completely suck because tomorrow I'll start working for free as a junior editor. I'd rather sneak away to cry in the bathroom rather than to waste the opportunity all together.

Luke sighed as he stared at Hayley, "no, she's not ready."

I nodded along with him, frowning at the disapproval look on Hayley's face.

"So what? Are you her new lapdog now, the Jacob to her Bella."

"Hayley, stop. Please." I mumbled.

She only sunk herself in her chair and went quiet as she grabbed the menu.

I turned to Luke, "I'm sorry."

I should be considerate, he's been nothing but kind to me. I've been crashing at Luke's place since he witnessed the mess Reiner and I created. I don't know why but he suddenly became my clutch. He doesn't touch me. Not like that anyway. Hayley's not so happy about it but I'm trying not to invade her space.

I know Reiner has been going on and off at his house, I also know Anna's okay, just a bruised rib, and a fractured wrist, which she was healing safely, with Reiner as her advocate I can only guess how he must be going above and beyond just to get the right care

— Noa's also great, only a few scratches. It's kind of a small town and the rumor was; Reiner lost it to her at the hospital. Yelling and yelling. And Ian became his new bestfriend because of the situation now. Reiner was getting custody faster than ever. Drunk driving with a child does a lot.

I was happy for him. He deserved his daughter all to himself. I wanted to go see Anna, and I will. I just need to figure out a way to not cry the second I see him.

Luke said he asked for me once but that only made me cry so Luke stopped telling me about his encounters with. I got my phone and clothes back, Hayley had to get them for me because Reiner refused to hand them to Luke.

Three weeks without him feels like three centuries.

Three weeks without him *sucked.*

I missed his voice.

His smell.

His smiles.

Those dimples.

I missed him.

"Why do you think we never worked?" I asked Luke once. We were sitting in his living room, the window curtains were opened a bit.

He said, *"we were not enough for each other, we would never be enough."*

"Why?"

He stared at me, his brown skin shining under the moonlight, *"you never made me feel alive."* He mumbled, as if it was a new realization. He stared at me and asked me the same, *"did I ever make you feel alive?"*

I swallowed as I shook my head.

"*Leil*. . . Leil?" Luke called out from a distance, pulling me out of my thoughts, "have you figured out what you wanted to eat yet?"

Luke is handsome, he's kind and passionate about things, it sucks sometimes realizing he wasn't the person who made me feel alive. Sometimes I wish he did — and I wish I could do the same for him too. But the universe flipped a coin and pushed me into the hands of Reiner, and for while I was happy, then another coin was flipped, it landed on the wrong side, the universe took back what it once gave me.

"Soleil, what are you ordering?" Luke asked again, his voice laced with worry.

I nodded, "I'll have whatever Hayley's having." I haven't glanced at the menu yet, so I was settling for Hayley's food.

Luke stared at Hayley, "you sure you want a salad?"

I nodded.

I dreamt of Reiner again. He apologized, Anna was okay, he held me close. *I woke up crying.*

★ · ☆ · ★

The first week of my internship went fine, maybe even great. I wasn't sure — the paper publishing house was great, I haven't been able to write a piece yet, I've only been able to edit, assist and shadow other people, which actually makes sense because it's an internship after all.

I was back home the second I started my internship. It would be too much of a hassle to keep going back and forth — Luke still checks in on me, we have dinner occasionally. Well, he showed up to my house uninvited — he's convinced I crumble every time I see Reiner.

The whole process was a whole withdrawal, but I'm doing better now, I'm moving on — I don't cry as much anymore but it's still painful when I see him, mostly because I still feel guilty for pushing him, but if that's what pushing him looked like then I guess I was right to do it.

Better to know what I was dealing with now than later.

I closed my car door shut as I dropped my keys inside the bag. I walked inside of the hospital without a purpose because I didn't know the room Anna was staying in or anything.

The second I mentioned the name Kline, the receptionist gave me directions to a private floor in the hospital I didn't even know existed. The elevator door opened and I searched the halls for the room number and when I saw there were only two rooms side by side it made everything easier for me.

The door was opened, and Anna was merely awake. Reiner was at her side, sitting there just staring at his lap like he was think-ing of things that he shouldn't be worrying about. I knocked on the door a little because I was never invited, and I've felt like that enough already so I figure a little heads up would be fair instead of marching in.

"Soleil!" Anna chirped.

"Anna," I smiled, "oh, God, how are you?" I marched in as I stood at her side, I noticed Reiner, I did. But I focused on Anna.

Reiner's eyes darted on mine, finally taking me in, looking behind me — probably surprised to see me here or maybe because he was low on sleep, he looked miserable. I've never seen him this. . . tired. It's almost heartbreaking.

"Soleil. . ." He straightened himself as he ran a hand through his hair. He seemed so disorganized.

I offered him a small smile, "hey."

I stood next to Anna, staring at her — more like examining her, she's tired, but good, there's a cast on her arm, and it was decorated with signatures. I think she noticed me frowning because she explained herself.

"I'm okay, I'm going home with dad this week." She said. And I looked at Reiner for approval and he only nodded.

I smiled, "that's good, when will they take that awful thing off?" I pointed at the cast on her arm, and she only smiled as she grabbed a sharpie which was kept hidden somewhere under her sheets.

"Sign my cast." She said as she handed me the sharpie, I smiled as I took it from her — trying to find room on her small cast because a lot of friends have signed already.

"The cast comes off in two more weeks." Reiner answered my

previous question.

I hummed in response as I signed my name on Anna's cast, adding a little heart next to it.

"There." I whispered as I stood up straight, staring at the small signature, Anna smiled, content at my work.

I turned to glance at the TV that was on, "what are you watching?"

"The amazing world of Gumball." Anna answered.

I try not to pay attention too much, but I could still feel Reiner's eyes bore into me. Just staring at me, I hope he was blinking because it felt too intense.

I stayed a little longer because Anna was already half asleep, so the second she did fall asleep, I made a plan to leave, but instead of leaving I just stood there, like I was waiting for. . . *anything*, but Reiner wasn't saying anything — when I realized he really wasn't going to speak, I started walking away.

"Did you get the flowers?"

I stopped on my tracks when I heard his voice, but I didn't turn around to look at him.

I thought about it for a second before answering, "I don't know, I think Luke threw them away."

That *was* true. Sometimes the doorbell rang at home and Luke answered and walked back inside with flowers in his hands — he gave me no explanation he just threw them away, when I asked him about it he just waved me off. I had a feeling they probably had something to do with Reiner but at the time I didn't care about anything that had to do with him.

Reiner stood up from his chair. I could hear him take a few steps closer towards me until he was standing behind me. "Soleil can we talk?"

I wanted to say *no* because that answer would benefit me the most. But I knew whatever it is, it is better to be dealt with now — I think I got enough space, besides if I talk to him now, I won't have to talk to him later.

"Sure."

I followed him to the hospital cafeteria, and took a seat in front of him. He thought it was best to not speak in front of Anna while she slept.

I think we've been sitting in front of each other for what felt like five minutes — *in complete silence.* We haven't talked in so long, and with all that went down last time we did talk, it's like we forgot how to be normal around each other.

Reiner looked tired, not only did he look like he hadn't slept much, but this was the most depressing I've seen him. His eyes were slightly red, like he'd been crying, his skin was beyond pale, and I wonder how long he spent in that room with Anna. I felt bad for him, I really did — but he was only going through all of this alone because he wanted to. *He made sure of it.*

"How are you?" I asked.

"I've been worse." He let out a dry nervous laugh as he ran a hand through his hair.

I nodded, "How's um— how's Noa?"

"She's fine." His answer was clipped, and I could tell he hated the topic.

I shifted in my seat, "I'm sorry for keeping you away." Reiner shook his head, "no, Soleil— I'm."

"Stop." I mumbled as I shook my head. I grabbed my bag, ready to stand up because I refused to hear his apology. He wanted to talk and I was willing to listen to him, and try to be there for him but I did not want to hear him try to apologize.

"Soleil you have to at least—"

"No Reiner, I don't have to do anything. I don't *have to* listen to you say anymore things." I stared at him and his eyes softened, acting like my words were the cause of his pain.

I gripped my bag, "your wife and kid needs you right now and I don't want to keep *distracting* you." I bit out, and I could understand why that sentence was easy for him to spit out — it was kind of fun to say.

"*Ex-wife.*" He corrected.

I raised two eyebrows at the irony, "hmm." I hummed, turning around to walk away.

Reiner grabbed my arm as he dragged me into the nearest closet in the hospital and the second he hushed us inside, he moved me against the door. I pulled my arm from his grip.

I looked around the small closet which was obviously the janitor's closet, and I grew irritated because why on earth was it unlocked?

He was close. So close, he was causing something inside me to thaw. It wasn't fair, he was cornering me into a room, where he knew he would easily have the power. I didn't like being so close to him because it made it harder to resist him. My eyes softened for a second, a mere second that I counted but that's all he got from me until I found a way to build up my newfound confidence. My anchor is the anger he left in me that night.

My chest heaved as my eyes snapped up at him, "what?" I hissed.

His brows furrowed, maybe a little shocked by my tone but his eyes softened when he said, "I miss you."

I blinked, I only blinked. "Okay." I whispered and my stomach twisted as I lied. I wanted to leave this closet and get some fresh air because being near him was too overwhelming. There's not a button where I could just turn off everything and be unaffected by him.

Reiner leaned down a little, searching my eyes. I kept thinking if I kept pushing myself against the door, I might melt into it, but it didn't work. And Reiner was still staring down at me. . . waiting. I think he wanted a different response.

"Don't you miss me?"

"No." I answered firmly. My eyes flickered down to his lips as my chest heaved, "yes." I spoke again. I shook my head when I realized my answer.

"No." I said again.

He only stared at me intensively, "hmm."

His face was close, impossibly close. I stood still like a robot when he leaned in closer. I'm scared if I squirm he'll take it as an invitation to touch me, and I know the second he does, nothing else will matter. I will lose my ground and all of my morals, I wouldn't care about my self respect. I'd be more than willing to allow him to humiliate me some more. So I stood still and tried not to budge because it was the only way I could prevent all of that from happening.

"Reiner. . ." I began.

His lips hovered above mine, *"Soleil."* He whispered back.

He kissed me, shy and hesitant. I didn't move when he pressed his lips against mine for a second time. A quick peck. He was waiting for me to deny him. But I didn't. Instead I stood there like an idiot, and took whatever he was giving, even if it was for one last time.

I parted my lips, my hands were still at my side as I kissed him, tasting the faint taste of cherry. I missed him on my lips much more than I thought. So I took. I thrust my tongue into his mouth and he moaned into mine in surprise. Reiner cupped the back of my neck, kissing me harder, the sound of our faint breath filling the small crowded closet.

Reiner smiled against my lips, a single tear falling down his cheek, he kissed me again, this time harsher just to assure himself that I'm still here. He pulled away, his eyes glistening and I wanted to laugh at him because there was hope in his eyes, he actually thought a rough kiss in the hospital closet would mend things.

"Hmm." I hummed. He was smiling, I was not. He was starting to catch on because his smile dropped.

"What?" He whispered.

"Nothing, I felt nothing."

Liar, liar, pants on fire.

Reiner ran a hand through his hair and he took a small step

back as he wiped his eyes, "what are you talking about?"

I stared at him as I ran a finger over my lips. I closed my eyes before speaking, "when you kiss me I used to feel excited, but when you just kissed me now. . ." I opened my eyes and they bore into his with zero interest.

"*Nothing.*" I whispered, watching the colors drain from his face.

"I felt nothing."

Half of it was true, my body was hot and warm and I was more than willing to keep kissing him. But my heart— it was broken, it felt borrowed. *Not mine.* Kissing him brought me more pain than happiness. I didn't feel complete like I used to, and I missed the feeling.

Reiner scoffed, cupping my cheeks with his hands as he stared at me, my brows furrowed a little because I expected him to just take my words and get lost.

He only shook his head, *"liar."* He whispered accusing me in a soft tone.

I blinked as I tried to look away because I'm scared if he stares at me for too long he'll see right through me.

"So when I do this. . ." he leaned down, laying a kiss on my shoulder, right against my collarbone, my body tensed, the hairs on the back of my neck stood straight at his attention. Anticipating for more, and I have to stand there and pretend like none of this affects me.

He kissed the same spot again, pausing, blowing hot air against my skin while I clamped my mouth shut and my jaw hardened.

My stomach was creating knots by the rough tension building around us. If I stick around for too long, I'll forget how to stand, *I'll forget everything.*

"You don't feel anything?" He asked in a low sultry voice. *It's really not fair how sexy he can sound.*

I shook my head not trusting my voice.

Reiner laughed as he lifted his head up to meet my eyes, his dimples came into view. "You wanna try looking at me while you give me a clear *vocal* answer?"

I cleared my throat as I stared at him, and I could practically feel myself melting into the door. I opened my mouth and nothing came out. Only a shallow breath.

"Stubborn little thing, you're such a liar." He laughed to himself, but I know half of him is already doubting whether or not I am really lying. I can see the small panic in his eyes.

"I know you're lying but it still hurts, you know?" He pulled his lips into a thin line, "so please, admit it, baby." He mumbled, "tell me you miss me."

I shook my head, a small smile on my lips. "It doesn't matter, I'll get over you."

His face softened, "Soleil, please. . ."

I shook my head, trying to stop him because I know his apology will hit me like a train. Reiner cupped my face in his hand again, staring down at me, his eyes glistened. And I wanted to forgive him. I really wanted to but the reminder of what happened hit me.

"Soleil, I'm so fucking sorry. I am, and I miss you, so much."

His voice was soft, pleading with me. I can see the tears pool in his eyes already.

I can only shake my head because what happened wasn't really a *one time thing*. Noa will always be in his life and Anna will keep getting hurt because kids get hurt all the time and I don't want to become this *thing* he pushes away every time he feels the need to, choosing Noa over and over again, just because I allow him to crawl back again and again. *I can't.*

"I take everything I said back." He said firmly.

I shook my head, "you can't just take it back."

"I can and I do." He squeezed my cheeks, "baby, I take it back." Another tear fell down his cheeks, this time another followed very quickly.

"I take it back." His voice cracked.

I tear rolled down my cheeks, I no longer wanted to be near him, everything I felt earlier completely vanished — locked away, *I lost the key.*

I turned my head to the side because I didn't want to see the longing look on his face, "Reiner, please get off of me."

He lets out a soft sigh, taking his hands off of me, but he can't seem to shut up, "Soleil— *please*— I'm sorry, I'll make it up to you I swear," he chanted the words as I opened the door, leaving him behind in the crowded closet.

'Make it up to me' — This wasn't a birthday dinner he missed. How could he possibly make it up to me? *He lost my trust. He lost me. Everything is broken beyond repair.*

CHAPTER THIRTY-FOUR

★ · ☆ · ★

Reiner

★ · ☆ · ★

EVERYTHING was quiet at night. When I'm out there in the woods, I stare at the stars. I listen to the logs scream as they burn in the fire, the smoke tries to be one with the sky, but it can only get so far, the trees dance with the wind, crickets made a different version of music that I couldn't understand, frogs complained at the sounds the crickets made, but everything for me was peaceful. I took in the stars, I relaxed.

Here in the hospital, it was haunting, every now and then a cart strolled by, doctors whispered, not about their patients but about their personal lives, and still so weird to me to be constantly reminded that they have one. We've been allowing flawed humans to decide how to save a life for over centuries now — with all the time in my hand now, and with every second I spend in the hospital, I find it weird.

The only music that filled my ears now was the beeping sound of the monitor, but the faint breaths of Anna put me at ease, staring at her sleep felt better than staring at a starry sky, except I couldn't relax, I could only worry. This place haunted me. *I hate hospitals.* Everything about it. The smell. The dull colors. The doctors.

I tried to think of something good, a memory but I thought of Soleil. How I've ruined her, all the cruel things I said. I replayed the situation over and over in my head and as much as I'd like to beat myself up over it, I got the same outcome every single time.

I was happy. I got a phone call, it was Noa, she wasn't making any sense, she sounded in pain. I was worried for her. Even when I didn't know what she'd done to my Anna I was still worried for her. I told her to calm down as I made my way out of the trailer. I politely asked her what happened the second I stepped outside.

"Reiner," she cried. *"Reiner, I'm sorry. I'm so sorry. Our little girl. . ."*

I remember freezing in place, the world was hanging over my head right then and there. It felt like if I moved it'd crush me. I didn't say anything because I was so scared if I asked, then the bad news would come, and I didn't want to hear the bad news, I wanted Noa to say nevermind — that she was just being jealous and then I'd smile and shake my head and crawl back into bed with Soleil, I'd hug her tightly because Noa called and I didn't want anything to do with her.

No, reality got so much worse.

"Anna's in the emergency room, and I can't see her either because

so am I. We. . . got into a car accident."

Still then, I was worried. For both of them.

"I think I was a little tipsy Reiner, I am so fucking sorry, they won't tell me how she's doing. Reiner I'm sorry,"

She kept telling how sorry she was, that her head was hurting, she was really sorry.

I couldn't yell at her. Could I? She was hurt too, in the hospital. God knows how bad her condition was. The only thing I could think of was how much Noa meant to Anna, which made me care so much more.

"I'm on my way."

The rest of what happened was almost a blur, all I could remember was the fact that I was angry, so angry at Noa but then I didn't think it'd be fair to be angry at her. Only because I didn't know how light her injuries were, I thought she was worse, really worse. But I was still so angry, and Soleil was there, and I needed something to *ruin, someone to blame* and I couldn't yell at Noa, but *she* was there.

She wanted me to communicate but I wanted to be at the hospital — instead I said a bunch of things, I made her feel small. *I did those same things Noa has been doing to me for years.* Now I'm here wishing I could've done things differently knowing that I really wouldn't.

I ran a hand through my hair, as I tried to find a new way to breathe because being with her was the easiest way to breathe. My lungs were closing in on me the more I reminded myself about the possibilities of losing her forever.

I'm an asshole, someone who taints every little good in their life. I didn't deserve her at all, I *never* did.

I don't remember crying at all. But now my head rested on the edge of Anna's bed as I cried. I had all these feelings I've been trying to keep away from escaping — but now when everything was quiet, they came out and haunt me — they forced me to feel the pain I caused her in just thirty seconds.

I opened my mouth for half a minute and ruined everything good we'd built. Half a minute, thirty seconds. It seemed like plenty of time now but it was only *half a minute*. That's how long it took to make her cry.

I saw the look in her eyes when she said she would get over me, I trust that she will because she was so determined. I'm not so hard to miss. I had one good thing and I ruined it, I snuffed the light right out of her. I saw it, even after telling her things after things — she tried to stop me, to make me take it back. Everytime I tried to blow the candle she lit it up again until I snuffed it out completely. Still she stood there for one second waiting for me to apologize to take it back. *I didn't.*

Why didn't I?

The tears stingged as they spilled. It was all so overwhelming.

"Dad?" Anna's soft voice startled me a bit.

I looked away a little to buy me enough time to wipe my eyes, "Hey, honey."

Anna stared at me like I was an alien, probably confused because I've never cried in front of her — I don't think she knows I'm capable of crying too, "is mom mad?" She asked.

I only shook my head.

She rubbed her eyes, yawning in the process, "then why are you crying?"

"I did something bad, I was really mean."

"To who?" she asked.

"To Soleil."

Anna frowned, "but Soleil is *so* nice. . ."

I sighed, "I know."

Anna offered me a small smile, "tell her you're sorry and she'll be friends with you again."

"It's not that simple Anna, Soleil is a special friend, it's harder to get her to be friends with me again." I said.

"Is she special like mom's special friend Anthony?"

I thought about it for a second before answering, "*more* special than that."

She gasped, "she's your girlfriend?"

I laughed, feeling my cheek dry a little from the tears, "who told you about girlfriend?"

"Jennie at school has a boyfriend."

I shook my head as I pointed a finger at her. *"Don't be like Jennie at school."*

"Jennie also got a new mom, if Soleil becomes your girlfriend again, will she also be my mom?" There was hope in her voice, and it overwhelmed me. I don't think she understood what any of this really meant.

I shook my head. "It doesn't work like that."

Anna pulled her lips into a thin line, "dad. . . when I'm sad after losing a match, you always buy me ice cream and it makes me feel better. You should buy Ice cream for Soleil too" Anna smiled.

"I'm not sure that'll work."

I wish it could though.

"Then do whatever makes her happy." Anna tried to scratch her cast but it was too hard, she was scratching a lot. And I wondered; *when did my little girl get so wise?*

"I want pudding, not the ones here, those are yucky." She stuck out her tongue and made a nasty face.

I laughed, "I'll get them tomorrow."

"You can get them now," Noa chimed in and I turned to notice her by the door and now I wondered how much of the conversation she heard.

She was discharged only two days after the accident, a few stitches on her forehead. So now this bandage was there, covering half of her forehead. There's only so much I say to her nowadays. I got full custody over Anna two weeks after the accident, the whole process was quick because of the accident — so for some twisted reasons I should be grateful for the accident, thank it for handing me my daughter.

Noa cried, and I couldn't tell if it was because she could no longer use Anna as leverage or because she was actually sad to let go of Anna. But she still would get visits, whenever she wanted — it was only up to me to allow Anna to stay with Noa. It would take me a few months to allow that to happen.

We barely speak. I yelled at her that day mostly because I was on edge and because she needed to be scolded — either way after that, we didn't speak much anymore, there's this guilt in her eyes everytime she looked at Anna and I was glad. She should feel guilty because she almost—

"It's fine." I pressed my lips into a thin line, "I'll get them tomorrow." The last thing I wanted was to leave Anna alone in a room with Noa.

The second I looked at Anna she frowned, still struggling to scratch her arm under the cast, but she couldn't.

"Reiner, she's in the hospital. The safest place she'll ever be, you can go buy pudding." Noa argued, as she stepped into the room and her heels clicked.

"I thought being with you would be the safest place for her but I was wrong so excuse me for being hesitant on your judgment."

I don't think Noa's a bad mother. There's a lot of moments that could define her as a bad mother, but when she interacts with Anna, there's nothing but love in her eyes, so it's her actions that clouded my judgment. But I also didn't think she was the best version of herself for Anna. But that's just Noa, she'll never be the best version of herself for anyone, she was only enough for herself. She's selfish. Until Anna came into our lives I never realized it because I've never asked for much. I only started asking for Anna.

She lets out a low breath, "fair."

"Daddy please," Anna's eyes pleaded with mine, and I ran a hand through my hair. She was in pain right now, she wanted to scratch but she couldn't, and if the pudding would put her at ease, I should get it for her.

She's in the hospital, she can't leave. *Noa can't leave with her.* I grabbed my coat on the chair and a sigh escaped my lips, and I looked at Anna, "go to sleep." I pointed a finger at her.

She nodded with a small smile on her face. I stared at Noa who was already by her side, stroking her hair. She looked at me but I looked away as I checked my pockets for my keys.

"Do something that makes her happy." I was reminded of Anna's words as I looked at the pies in my passenger seat.

She loves pies.

I stare long enough to watch her hug that same guy I saw on her porch weeks ago goodbye. And my jaw hardened as my knuckles went white. I pulled up in my driveway only a minute ago, and before I could hop out of the car her lights went on and I was curious — only to watch her hug some guy.

I released a breath as I watched her wrap her arms around herself as she watched the guy leave.

Soleil's eyes bounced on my car, and she stared for a few seconds and I was scared she could see me, but it was pitched black out and I have tinted windows, so she glanced at my car one more time before she closed her door.

I was not ready to give up Soleil anytime soon. She's the only person I allowed myself to be selfish with, so even told me to *fuck off*, I won't. I'll keep crawling back until she takes me back.

I want to be the only guy to make her smile, to earn her moan. I want to be the one to prove myself worthy of her.

The second Soleil opened the door, I was swept away — buried deep in heaven with the soft smell of lavender. I sighed in her presence because I could finally breathe again. It was night and the moonlight was my only source of light — even then I could see how beautiful she looked.

Her eyes rounded in on me, "Reiner, what are you doing here?"

I was a little disappointed, she had no reaction towards me, only irritation. I wanted to pull her into my arms but it felt like she'd slap me from trying. So I tried to smile even though my heart was completely torn apart. *I smiled.*

"I was grocery shopping because Anna's coming home soon, and she loves pudding. I had to get her pudding."

She stared at me before she looked around me, "and now you're on my. . . porch?"

"Yeah the apple pies were on sale, I thought you'd want to know."

"Reiner it's *midnight*." She said flatly, her voice was clipped short.

"Yeah, I brought you some," I pointed at my house, "it's at my house now but that's why I'm here." I nervously laughed, because I felt like a fucking teenager again. "They were on sale and I brought you a couple."

I said that before, right?

She offered me a small smile, but it wasn't genuine. "Thank you." she said.

And I guess I should've gone back to my house to grab her the pies, but instead I took a step closer toward her — her breath hitched. I don't think she knew about the small gasp that escaped her mouth when I took another step towards her.

Soleil gripped on her door like she was ready to slam it shut in my face at any time, but she didn't. At least not yet. I took another step forward, now she was only at arms length, she was so close yet so far away. She was staring at me — and there was a war in her eyes, like she didn't know what to do with me yet.

Her brown eyes come alive at night, under the moonlight.

She stood up straighter, as she tried to act like I didn't affect her at all and I thought it was cute. It really was. I just know she wished she could control her breathing around me, and that little satin pajamas she had on told me all I needed to know. I could see her nipples right through the material, they got hard as a pebble the second she heard my voice.

I took one last step, invading her space completely, "Soleil."

"Hmm?"

I leaned down as I grazed my lips against her ear and I could feel the way she held her breath.

"I miss you."

She sighed, "you keep saying that. . ."

"Because I *do* miss you."

Soleil turned her head to meet my eyes, our faces were so close I could feel her breath. "I miss you too." She *finally* admitted. It felt like the fucking sky opened up and I flew right into heaven.

Soleil took a step back and the hole in the sky started closing up.

"But you hurt me Reiner, you *really* hurt me." She wrapped her arms around herself. Her eyes were glossy again. Talking to her hurts because every time I was around she cried.

It hurts me when she cries.

I'm a fucking asshole. I don't deserve her. I never did. But I could try. I'll try really fucking hard.

"What can I do to fix it? Tell me what to do, Soleil and *I'll do it.*" I pleaded.

She took a step closer as she placed a hand on my chest and my whole body melted, I almost closed my eyes as I felt her touch again, it felt like fucking years. I wanted to hold her. I wanted to so badly, I was going crazy.

My happiness was short-lived when she gently pushed me out of her house. I never realized I was helping her push me out until she started closing the door a little. I was too focused on the way her hand felt against me to pay attention.

"Good night, Reiner." Her voice came off sad. So sad I felt like punching myself because she was too nice to do it for herself.

Before the door closed all the way, I placed my hand over it, "what about the pies?"

She smiled, small. Very small. "I'll get them tomorrow."

I sighed as I ran a hand through my hair and walked toward my house. The same advice Anna gave me earlier rang through my head, hitting me like a bell. I had an idea. It's probably the only thing that could change her mind. It's such a bad idea, it's perfect but it's so fucking complicated I'll need a lot more help. I wondered after what happened how many people I could possibly sway to be on my side — even if it's only to benefit Soleil.

If I think it's the only way to get Soleil to even look at me like she used to, It's worth a Fucking try.

And I'll try. I'll try like hell.

CHAPTER THIRTY-FIVE

Soleil

"WHY ARE WE IN HERE AGAIN?" Hayley mumbled as she used a pen to get rid of the spider webs over her head.

She was referring to the weird closet we were in. The one I use to store all of my boxes after moving in — also the closet I use to store all of my fathers' belongings. It's not much because I kept his furniture. It was the papers, his books, his clothes. I couldn't donate those things.

"Mara wanted a few empty boxes, I told her I'd bring her some." I answered her previous question.

The light in this room was weak, but with the door wide open it helped a little.

I grabbed a half filled box as I glanced at Hayley. "You can empty the boxes that don't have much in them." I said as I grabbed what looked like a shirt out of the box. I stuffed it in a trash bag and coughed in the process because of the dust.

"What's all this stuff again?"

"My dads."

The room fell silent after I spoke because we never talked about my father — well, *I never do.* I remember the second I moved in here I boxed away half of his stuff and donated it, the other half I kept because I felt like they were too personal to give away. I kept them in this small cramped room for his sake.

I managed to empty three whole boxes. I didn't know how many boxes Mara wanted but six boxes will have to be enough for her because I didn't want to stick around in the room any longer — waiting for the ghost of my father to say *boo.*

I turned to look at Hayley as I reached for the third box, fighting to shove the stuff in the bag.

"Leil." she called out.

I sighed because I was expecting Hayley to offer her help, but she only stretched her arm, handing me an envelope with a questioning look on her face. "I totally wasn't snooping, but this had your name on it." She handed me the white envelope, well the color was beginning to fade anyways.

I stared at Hayley as I took the envelope from her hand. I've only been in the room a handful of times. After packing his things away I decided I'd never touch them again. So it made complete sense that I missed this envelope.

I gripped the paper with two fingers, staring at my name on the center of the envelope. I'm just about 110% sure that it was my fathers handwriting. *Soleil* was written in cursive. *My father loved writing my name in cursive.*

He said it looked more like me. It looked pretty.

I flipped the envelope so quickly and tore it open. These must've been my fathers last few wishes. And if this was about his funeral he was almost a year too late.

I gave him a funeral. *I'm not a monster.* It was a nice service. The minister and I will live long enough to remember it. It's something my father would've wanted. At least I thought so. I wasn't close enough with my father to know exactly the kind of funeral he would've wanted. The second I left for college, he moved away and bought this place. We fell into a pattern of only talking *twenty one words* a year. With just one phone call.

I released a breath before scanning the page full of words before pinning my attention to the top of the paper again.

Dear, Soleil.

My sweet Soso. The last time I called you that, you were three. I stopped when your mother left because it reminded me of the sound of her voice. It was also what she used to call you. I didn't want to be reminded of what was gone, I know I told you she left before you even turned one. It made things easier, it made you ask less questions. Sorry about that. Your mother left and she didn't want to be found, and I didn't want you to have any desires of chasing her, or finding her. So I worked hard, and made enough just to offer you everything you could possibly need.

I controlled everything from how much to tell you, or how much of the pieces of your mother you should be allowed to witness. I did everything I could to erase her out of the picture completely. There was only one thing I couldn't control, Soso. You. The more you grew the more you resembled her — the more you looked like her, the more you reminded me of her, and you always knew how I felt about the reminders of your mother. I never loved you any less Soso, you were and always will be my little girl. I'm sorry my heartbreak robbed us of a better relationship, I could've been a real father, I could've loved you more, spend more time with you. But it's in the past now, isn't it? That's why I use words like "I wished," or "I could've," those are words of regret, the way to speak of the past. I am writing you this letter hoping to explain why I've always been so distant but it only made me realize how much of a coward I truly was — I still am because I'm alive and well right now and instead of reaching out to you I've managed to convince myself that this letter will be enough, that you're doing well as it is — that this will upset you. Soso, I do not know when I will die, but I am sick. And my last wish is for you to find this letter hoping it's able to explain the reasons behind my cruelty. I am leaving you the house along with everything else I have left — make them all yours. Make the world yours. I'm sorry I didn't have the courage to become yours. The father you wanted.

With love,

Corbyn.

My eyes rounded back to the top of the letter and I released a slow breath finally feeling the tears roll down my cheeks. I wiped them quickly as I turned the other way around before Hayley noticed anything. I stuffed the letter back in the envelope, folding it before shoving it in the back of my Jean pocket. This letter would be the only thing I'd be reading for the rest of this month. *I could tell.*

My fathers' words are haunting me now.

Part of me.

I'm sorry I didn't have the courage to become yours.

Make the world yours.

"So what was it?" Hayley asked as she dragged a box.

I didn't want to tell Hayley about the letter, mostly because I was scared that she would want to read it.

"My father left me notes, encouraging words about the way I should be spending his money once he's dead." I lied.

"Control freak, now I know where you got that from."

I hummed as I walked out of the room with a few boxes in hand. I followed Hayley who was currently struggling with her boxes because she didn't fold them well enough.

I was still thinking of my father. . . the letter. In the letter he said he was sick. He never told me. One night eight months ago, I received a phone call. It wasn't any saved number but I picked up anyway. It was the police who had found my fathers dead body after someone filed a complaint about his sudden disappearance. It took everyone a whole week to realize he never stepped foot in or out the house and a strange smell was oozing out.

My father had a seizure in his sleep. *He died alone.*

I didn't know. I would've never known.

"Say Leil, how much do you miss Reiner?" Hayley asked, coming at my side with a subtle suspicious voice.

I blinked as I fought my way out of my head. I sighed, "I don't know, I miss him an average amount."

"If he didn't say those things would you have stayed with him still? Like right now?"

"With a strong possibility, yes."

"Do you love him?"

I stopped in my tracks, "why are you asking me all these questions all of sudden?" I didn't like the game she was playing.

"Is it annoying that he lives next door?"

"Hayley, spit it out. Why are you meddling?"

She frowned, "I'm not, I won two raffle tickets a week ago, and it's a trip to *Vancouver*."

My brows furrowed with curiosity but I remembered that this was Hayley. The same person that went on random hikes and called it a mental health day. So really anything was possible for her.

"That's nice." I mumbled, "which one of your siblings are you taking?"

"You."

"What?"

"Think about it, Soleil. It's only a three day trip, meaning; *three whole days away from Reiner*." She dropped the boxes on my kitchen counter.

I frowned. "I'm always away from him."

"Cut the shit, he came back home last week and every time I came over, I see you staring longingly through his window, waiting for him to show up."

"Hayley. . ." I darted my eyes away from her because what she said was partially true. Some part of me was still waiting for Reiner to show up on my doorstep because if he kept doing that — eventually I'd take him back.

Hayley placed both hands on my shoulder and her eyes rounded on me as she spoke, "take the three day trip with me, clear your head, have some fun and fuck a few nice Canadians and get Reiner out of your system."

"Hmm." I hummed. But it was more like a scoff.

Hayley smiled as she lifted a brow, "what do you say?"

"Do I really have a say?"

She took her hands off my shoulders as she checked her phone before texting someone, "You don't. We're leaving tomorrow afternoon, the tickets are expiring the next day."

"Hayley." I bit out. If she harassed me sooner about this I could've been more prepared. Before I could ask Hayley who would take care of her sisters while she would be gone she already disappeared out the door. Leaving me alone in the house.

I didn't chase after her because I had to drive to the restaurant today to drop off the boxes for Mara, and apparently shop for a three day trip to Vancouver. I was beyond thankful for my ability to not waste my vacation hours because I could easily just call off for the next three days.

I pulled the letter from my back pocket and opened it up

again, just to read it all over. I kept reading the same sentence over and over again.

Make the world yours.

Those words were strange coming from my father because he never made me feel enough. It was always like I was never completely enough for him, like I was always the afterthought. Everything that was checked under incomplete.

He loved me.

In the letter, he said it. I could finally cry over his death because he finally allowed me to.

CHAPTER THIRTY-SIX

Soleil

HAYLEY ONLY HAD A BACKPACK and that deeply concerned me. This morning I was prepared for her to show up with luggages, lots and lots of them. But now we were in line to get on the plane. She only brought a single backpack.

"Are you buying clothes in Vancouver?"

Her head snapped in my direction, anxious. "What?"

I pointed at the backpack, "you only brought a backpack, so I'm guessing you'll buy more stuff over there. . ."

"Oh," she laughed, "it's only three days."

Her words flew over my head as I glanced at the luggage I'll be dragging the second the line moves.

I sighed and faced forward, passport in my hand as I waited for the line to move. We were flying in the afternoon because Hayley didn't want to arrive in Vancouver while it was night over there, so we thought it'd be best to take a late afternoon flight

Hayley nudged my shoulder as she grabbed my attention, "did I tell you you're flying first class?"

"We are?"

She nodded as she grinned like a madman.

"Remind me again, what kind of raffle did you win?"

Because whatever she was doing, I wanted to do it too. No one just wins a first class trip to Vancouver. But Hayley only laughed and took the first step the second the line moved as she checked her phone with each second that flew by.

First class was nice. I didn't know where else to compare it, I've never experienced it before so I could only think of it as *nice*. I kept glancing out the little window like the plane might take off in the middle of boarding, a small smile was on my face because this might be a good idea after all.

Hayley was right, I should put myself out there, have a little fun and *maybe* fuck someone new. The idea was still not completely on the table but the idea of doing it didn't sound so bad.

"I feel like I'm over Reiner already." I smiled as I turned to look at Hayley.

She was checking her phone as she ran a hand through her hair before she looked up at me. She laughed, but it was a nervous laughter. She checked her phone again and my face fell flat. Now I know something was up, her knees were bouncing, she looked like she was trying hard to keep her mouth shut.

I didn't know how much longer I could pretend and act like

she was not hiding something. She was glancing around anxiously — like she stole something.

"Did you. . ." I leaned forward a little because Hayley was sitting in the chair in front of me, "did you. . . steal the tickets?" I asked.

"I won't be mad, I swear." I whispered. I won't, it's too late for that now, we made it this far, it'd be incredibly stupid to do anything about it.

Hayley rolled her eyes as she shook her head, "no. Soleil I didn't. . . steal the tickets."

My brows furrowed as I grimaced, because if she didn't steal the tickets, something else was wrong because Hayley was anxious. Mousy, jumpy. Waiting for, apparently. . . something to happen.

The flight attendant spoke, telling us to buckle ourselves — I twisted my body, pushing until I heard the small click, I turned to look at Hayley again, "you're not gonna be like this the whole trip are you?"

She shook her head as she stood, "I'll be right back."

I frowned, "the plane is about to take-off?"

"Yeah. . ." Hayley pointed behind her, "just. . . bathroom."

My mouth parted open as I tried to say something but nothing came out.

Apart from worrying about Hayley's behavior — I was excited to see what Hayley had in store for us. She said it was a surprise, she wouldn't tell me anything, not even where in vancouver we would be staying. For all I know we could be staying at a two star motel.

The second announcement went on and Hayley was still not back, the plane will start moving in a few seconds. I glanced in the direction I saw Hayley leave, waiting for her to come back anytime. She's been in the bathroom for a while.

I shifted in my seat feeling the plane move. The second we get in the air I'm going to find Hayley because I was really worried. I didn't know how but I felt it, all of it. I snapped my head in his direction — pulling my brows together when his body came into view.

He stood by the door, his formal black suit hugging his body. His hands were in his pockets, this. . . *look* on his face. His face was clean shaven, his hair neat. His blue eyes were as vibrant as ever. *Reiner looked good.* It was even worse because I'm sure he knew.

"Soleil." He mumbled. His voice was stern, full of determination.

All the air in the world was now clogged in my throat, I opened my mouth, closed it. My eyes were wide, like a deer caught in the headlights. My heart was pounding against my ribcage — I'm scared he'll notice how nervous I am, so I breathe. I tried to relax.

That didn't last long, I panicked again, I started unbuckling my seatbelt as the plane moved. In just a quick second his hands flew over mine, preventing me from doing so. My chest heaved as I felt his cold hands close around my wrist.

The plane took off, defying all laws of gravity. Pushing his body on top of mine in the process — forcing me to lean back against the chair. I honestly hoped he'd crush me, that way I wouldn't have to survive whatever comes after this. But Reiner caught himself, his chest heaving in front of my face as he gripped the armchair keeping himself steady. I closed my eyes, smelling him for just one second, feeling the same warmth I used to feel every time he was around me.

When I opened my eyes and looked up, Reiner was already staring down at me, a small smile was on his lips as he pushed his body back up. I'm pretty sure the plane settled a while back but I didn't say anything, I just stared at him and took the same seat Hayley was previously sitting on.

Heat flushed all over my body as I felt his gaze settled on me, his scent still lingering around me. It's been days — *weeks* since we last talked, well, since I last talked to him. And now he was here on a plane with me, and I couldn't get up and run away.

I cleared my throat, "where's Hayley?"

I didn't know how any of this worked, there was an empty chair next to Reiner and I'm hoping that's where Hayley comes in. Reiner being here had me questioning everything because coincidences can only go so far.

Reiner stared at me, and I couldn't tell if he was thinking of lying to me or not, but he pursed his lips and he finally answered my previous question, "on her way back home."

My face scrunched up in confusion, "what?"

Before he could even explain anything the confusion started to melt off my face as I pieced all of this together. There were never any free tickets to Vancouver, were there? *I was tricked.* She said she wouldn't meddle, but she did.

She tricked me into getting on the same plane as Reiner because he somehow had her brainwashed that a conversation will solve what happened between us. She threw me down a snake pit and ditched.

"She did this." I accused, but it was meant for me more than him. It was a slow realization. I was merely talking to myself. "That traitorous bitch."

"Not all of it, she only got you here." Reiner jumped at her defense and I wanted to ask since when did they develop such a pure bond.

I scoffed, "I am so going to kill her."

Fuck a few nice Canadians my ass.

He looked away, adjusting himself in his seat. "This was the only way I could get you to listen." Reiner said as he ran a hand over his already slicked hair.

And I nodded, pulling my purse on my lap, taking out my phone and headphones. I have to survive this plane ride to Vancouver in order to buy a ticket for a plane ride back and the only way I can survive all of this is by tuning out Reiner. I can't have him talking my ears off about how sorry he is.

I've honestly heard enough of it.

I plugged the headphones in and pressed play on my playlist, tilting my head back catching one last glance at Reiner who had this annoyed look on his face. I wanted to smile at that but instead I settled for closing my eyes as *Enjoy The Silence* by *Depeche Mode* started to play. I was ready to get off the plane. The second I get back home Hayley is going to feel my wrath.

I woke up feeling Reiners cool hand on my cheek, and I was so startled I jumped back a little. Pulling away from him with my eyes wide.

He smiled, but it looked painful, "we're here."

Good. Now I could finally get up and run far, far away from him. I unbuckled my seatbelt, and stood up too quickly and everything felt fuzzy from sitting down for so long, my knees felt weak, and before I could stumble back Reiner wrapped his hands around my waist, steadying me.

He flushed my waist against his, and my hands were around his arms, pulling his closer I think. I held my breath for a second before finding my strength. I pushed him off a little as I took a small step back.

"Reiner, I'm buying a plane ticket back home."

His face fell, it was like I snatched whatever hope there was left in him right out.

"what?" He whispered.

"I don't want to spend the next three days with you." I moved around him, walking out the door, because I'm sure we were supposed to leave a while back

I didn't want to spend three days with him not because I didn't want to, but because I think I'll eventually forgive him, but then I'd feel guilty for doing so.

I could hear his footsteps behind me, quick. And the more I

walked the more I realized how long it took us to get off the plane because it was completely empty. No trace of anyone. *Every Single chair. Empty.* I could understand we were a few seconds behind but everyone in the whole entire plane couldn't have possibly got off the plane this quickly.

I started walking a little slower, but I didn't turn around, "Was it just us on the plane?"

"Yes." His answer was immediate and I didn't like the rest of his sentence. "I rented the whole plane, so the doors won't open unless I say otherwise"

I stopped in my tracks, turning to face Reiner. My anger seeped through whatever armor I had left. "I'm not a fucking doll you can place in a corner until you feel excited to play with it again." I bit out, taking a step closer towards him.

Reiner took a step back, "I *never* said-"

"Get them to open the fucking doors so I can go!"

He shook his head, once. "No." He said, "you have to at least *try* and let me fix this."

My brows furrowed as I tilted my head to the side, *"let you try and fix it."* I mocked, "I don't think you understood what really happened Reiner so let me clear things up a little for you." His jaw ticked, and he fixed his posture, standing up straighter than before, it's like he's getting himself prepared for a bunch of nasty words.

I took a small step forward, lowering my tone because I really wanted him to get this part the most so I decided to speak calmly.

"Your daughter was hurt, I get it. But that happens, Reiner. Kids get hurt, *all the times,* and I'm fucking sorry if I demanded your attention so much you missed a few phone calls, but I could've been there with you, though. And the way you pushed me away was so. . . *ugly*." I swallowed thickly, watching his eyes soften as he listened to me speak.

This felt good, saying all of this felt really good. I didn't want to stop myself from standing up for myself anymore. I've been trying so hard to blame myself for something out of my control. It was not my fault Reiner pushed me away the way he did, and I don't want him to think he could easily come back because his issues are solved, or because things got better.

That's not how relationships work.

Noa and Anna are there to stay, they are the only few people who are guaranteed to have a place in his life — and I don't want to change that, I simply wanted him to make room for me, to not make me feel like an outsider. I didn't want to be the person who's placed under the *temporary* category.

I shook my head, scoffing under my breath, robbing him the chance of speaking, "no, what you did was way worst Reiner, you made me feel like I was *worthless*, like I wasn't worth a second of your time — most of all you made me hate myself for ever going there with you. You made me blame myself for something that couldn't possibly be my fault. So *fuck you*, and if you thought a free plane ride to wherever the fuck we are was gonna fix this you're out of your fucking mind."

"Soleil I just want-"

I sighed, "Reiner, open these doors so I can please leave."

It was his turn to take a step forward, and it was my turn to take a step back. I was scared that if he took too much of the space between us I wouldn't be able to stand my ground, I looked away before meeting his gaze again.

"Soleil I know that you're mad, and you have every right to be, I did say a lot of stuff that I shouldn't have said. I know and I think I'll have to spend the rest of my life making it up to you, but right now please, I just want to tell you a few things, I feel like, I might, I don't know. . ." He took a breath, as he ran a hand over his head, but he did it so roughly, it brought back a few strings of hair over his forehead.

And I sucked in a breath, trying to find a way to focus, because Reiner was talking like he was flustered and my lungs weren't working properly. I might just start choking on thin air.

He took another step forward and for some stupid reason I was still grounded in the same spot. I looked up to find his eyes, he looked pained, restless. The whole *macho man* thing disappeared, he looked like he might start begging at any time.

Reiner's hand reached out to grab mine, but he hesitated, retreating back, keeping his hands to himself, "Soleil. . ." He began, the words caught in his throat, my lips parted, as I watched him lick his lips, the simple action felt like a sultry signal for me to stare at his lips.

Reiner looked at me, his eyes glistening, "when I'm around you, *I explode*. And when I'm not around you *every* cell in my body burns to be near you." Reiner, let out a small breath, watching me closely. Waiting for me to react, but I think I can't react because I might've just died a little. Right here, right now. By his words.

415

I don't mind. I wish to be buried here, by his words, the tears he spills just for me, I want to drown in them. I want to relive this moment everyday. I want to reach out and touch him just to tell him I feel the exact same. That piece of me dies every time I see him, knowing I can no longer have him. It hurts just as much.

I think he noticed when everything softened for him, because he took another step forward, eating all the space between us. He pursed his lips, his eyes softened. And I just stood there, my hands glued at my side. Reiner stroked my hair a little, staring at his hands, as he softly touched my hair, pushing it out of my face so gently until his hands cupped my cheeks. And I sighed, feeling his touch spread warmth down my body.

I wanted to close my eyes and feel this blissful moment for as long as I could, but Reiner was staring at me like he needed to look into my eyes to at least see what I was thinking.

Reiner leaned down a little, a devastating sigh left his lips as he closed his eyes, like staring at me hurts entirely too much.

"I am falling madly in love with you, Soleil and I don't think I'll ever stop."

I could feel his words warm my heart, nurturing it. Kissing it better. My armor was softly falling down, and soon I'd be vulnerable again. Once again. Bare in his hands. Undone by him. Only him.

Reiner opened his eyes, and I could see the tears pooling, "it pains me not telling you how much I love you. I want to tell you how entirely in love I am with you, *every second of the day.*" He closed his eyes, and the tears rolled down his cheeks.

My heart hurts entirely too much.

I wanted to reach up and kiss his tears. To tell him I miss him, to hold him. To feel happy again even if it's just a few seconds. But my arms were still glued to my side, my face was still blank. My chest was heaving as my stomach twisted inside out.

Reiner shook his head, and his thumb stroked my cheeks like I was the one crying. "I'm sorry for making you feel like a second thought, I know I've always been hesitant, making half choices, but it stops now because I know what I want, and it's you I need."

He lets out a slow breath, one that made it look like he'd been in pain for too long, and my poor heart couldn't handle all of this, "I'm *so* fucking *tired,* Soleil." He whispered. I was losing my balance again, my arms were still planted at my side. I haven't said a word, and it was weighing down on me.

There's so much I want to say, but I couldn't find the words, I didn't know where to start.

"And I'm so, so sorry that it took losing you to realize all of this, I know I'm not exactly playing fair."

"You're not." I breathed.

He smiled a little, pulling away as he stroked my cheek with the rough pad of his thumb, "you're all I want Soleil. *Please.*"

I didn't dare to say a word. I was not even sure what he was begging me for anymore. Because Reiner was crying in front of me. And it hurts to witness it.

When I didn't say anything Reiner pulled away, and took a step back.

"I wanted to show you something, I'm not really expecting

anything, I just. . . wanted to show you and then I'd let you go for good, have this plane take you back home the second you change your mind over anything." His head hung low after he finished his sentence, refusing to even look at me.

"I want to see it." I mumbled. Surprising myself.

Reiner smiled, a small satisfied smile. "Okay." He mumbled.

I didn't know what to expect but it was certainly not a helicopter ride. After getting out of the plane, Reiner led me to this helicopter which was spontaneously waiting for us.

"How'd you know I'd say yes?" I yelled over the loud noises.

Reiner looked at me as the helicopter started to move, "I didn't"

I smiled, wide. Shaking my head, but so nervous because I can feel the air blowing my hair away, the pilot said something but I wasn't really paying him any attention, I kept looking at the view then at Reiner who was only looking at me. *Smiling.*

Everything looked so beautiful, this high, *small and insignificant.* I don't know why but I started laughing, the rush was coursing through my blood and it felt so great, so I laughed, glancing at Reiner who was smiling harder and harder.

When we landed, Reiner had us pushed into a black car almost immediately — and I was so curious to see what he wanted to show me.

The car ride was shorter than I thought it would be, soon we were walking down a path that looked somewhat familiar. A huge building came into view, a skating rink — I couldn't remember why but it felt like I'd seen it before. Like bits and pieces of it — I've seen them before. Still I asked no questions, I simply followed Reiner wherever he was leading me.

I gasped when the full skating rink came into view, the same familiar one I see on TV, YouTube clips, *everywhere*. It's the skating rink in Vancouver where *Tessa Virtue* and *Scott Moir* performed back in 2010 and won all three segments. It was truly a beautiful program. It's the same everything but it was empty. I could only make two figures in the rink.

I turned to look at Reiner but he was only guiding me to the front row where I could get a better view. I'm almost freaking out, and even under the cold weather I could feel my hands sweat. *Did Reiner hire two professional Ice dancers just to perform for me?*

"Reiner?" I whispered.

"Shhh." He placed a finger over his lips, "it's about to start."

And on que, the lights dimmed, the whole place going completely dark. The music blasted to the speakers, taking me by surprise, but I stared ahead. In the center of the rink, the only place that was glowing with a small light.

The skaters started doing the short program, skating with the music, and the more they skated the more I noticed her. From her movements, the techniques she used. They were all familiar. I gasped when she went by my glass, skating in one quick motion, nearly flying into the arms of her partner.

"Ohmygod, is that Tessa virtue?!" I gushed.

Reiner grinned, content with my reaction, "I have a friend who has a friend who has another friend and I may have threatened all of them." He said.

"Reiner oh my God!" I exploded, strange happiness seeping through me.

He smiled, "I was hoping this would cheer you up a little."

I turned to watch them move like one, and everything was amazing but I could only think of Reiner. He did this for me — now I don't know what to think. Tessa retired a few years back. You can't just summon her to do a short program for a girl with a broken heart. That doesn't happen often. I could only imagine the things he had to do to make this possible.

I watched the rest of the program with a small smile on my face, constantly turning to look at Reiner but he was so focused on the program I don't think he even felt me staring.

I wrapped my arms over my chest, smiling to myself. Today has been one hell of a chaotic day but it's so close to being the best day ever. I just have to stop fighting myself.

I turned to Reiner. "You did this for me," I looked away before looking at him again. "Thank you."

"I'd do *anything* for you." He whispered, as the light slowly glowed again, "I am so devastatingly in love with you, Soleil." He sighs, looking away, literally turning his whole body away from me.

I don't say anything, I stay quiet, waiting for him to speak again because I feel like he has more to say. But I took a small step forward standing closer next to him, feeling my shoulders brush against his.

"I find it hard to even *imagine* a future without you." He admitted — His voice was small, tired.

Reiner turned to face me as he ran a hand through his hair. Messing it up, now it's all over everywhere. "I am tormented with memories of you everyday, thoughts of you filling every chamber in my head. I get drunk just by the sound of you laughing. I want you to be mine, just as much as I am yours."

My heart was pounding out of my chest, trying to find its new way home because he's where I belong. My home. My other half, *the one part of me I never searched for.*

Reiner broke my heart without me ever handing it to him. Now he's giving me his. He's laying himself vulnerable in my hands, Hoping that I'll accept him, that I'll eventually love and forgive him. He doesn't know that I never took my heart back, he stole it but I wasn't interested in taking it back. He doesn't know how much I already love him. *That I'm his.*

So I stopped trying to fight it, I took Reiners' hand in mine, staring at how perfectly they fit together, I lifted my head up to stare at him, smiling a little because I decided to give us another try. His eyes were wild and confused, but there's a small soft smile on his face.

"Take me. I'm yours." I whispered.

He stared at our hands, then at me. "What?"

"You should kiss me."

Reiner grinned, shaking his head as he wrapped a large hand around my waist pulling my body against his as I laughed. Reiner nudged my head back with his chin, leaning down a little, leveling his lips close to mine.

I was still laughing when his lips met mine, a small quick peck that left us both laughing. He pulled away, cupping my cheeks, trying again with a small peck, it felt more demanding and desperate. Reiner glided his hands to the back of my neck, gently massaging my scalp with his fingers, and my eyes fluttered close when his lips came in contact with mine again.

Soft, firm, delicate, passionate. I hummed into the kiss because this one wasn't a peck, it was a kiss, an *'I missed your lips'* kiss. I ran my hand on his bicep, holding onto him for life support. I opened my mouth welcoming his tongue into my mouth, soft and demanding.

Everything felt light and heavenly. My heart was beating for him and only him. In his arms I felt safe. I felt whole. Home.

Reiner moaned into my mouth, pushing me closer against him, like he couldn't get enough of anything that I was offering. And every small sound that I made, Reiner swallowed it. Kissing me.

When he finally pulled away, he laid a kiss on both sides of my cheeks, pushing my body against his, as he hugged me tighter, I felt so overwhelmed because it never occurred to me how much I missed him until now, how scared I was to lose him again. I see what he meant earlier, because now that he's holding me and I have my arms wrapped around his waist.

I couldn't imagine a future without him either.

Reiner laid a kiss on neck as I sniffed, my face buried deep against his chest. "I'll *never* hurt you like this *ever* again, I promise." He whispered and I sob into his arms, half of me relieved, half of me terrified.

But he kisses the side of my head, chanting, *"I promise. I promise. I promise."*

After a while of holding me while I cried, Reiner found my hand, and tangled our fingers together as he started leading me away.

"Come on, let's go meet, Tessa." He whispered with a smile on his lips.

My brows shot up as I wiped my nose, "I get to meet her?!"

CHAPTER THIRTY-SEVEN

Soleil

REINER DRAGGED ME TO HIS HOTEL ROOM — well, our hotel room. He was so confident I'd say yes to everything. I was still a bit stuck on the part where I met THE *Tessa Virtue*. She was incredibly sweet. She signed my shirt and now I was dying to take it off and just hang it in one of those glass jersey boxes guys use to store their signed jerseys.

I told Reiner about it in the elevator. He just agreed and grabbed my hand the second the elevator opened, now he was rushing us down the halls of the hotel nearly running. I swear he'd fly if he could. But I can't help but smile. His excitement was amusing.

We made a sharp turn down the hall and in just a second I was pushed against the wall. Reiner's hand cupped my cheeks as I held his hands. I leaned forward a little, I was so ready for the kiss, but Reiner smiled as he licked my lips, "you won't get any sleep tonight." He said, leaving a small peck on my lips.

I laughed a little when he pulled away, "Is that a threat?"

"It's a promise."

With that look on his face, everything in me ignited. Everything shined brighter for him. *Just for him.*

I tried to smile but his lips fell on mine searing his promise with a passionate kiss. I could feel myself float because this kiss was an out of body experience. His kiss felt like a confession, an apology. His never ending love for me. His lips were soft like feathers, such an innocent kiss, I could feel my body press against the cold wall, Reiners hand cupped my face as I gripped on his bicep.

Reiner pulled away a little and a groan left my mouth as his eyes met mine, "I miss you."

My eyes softened, "I'm right here." I whispered.

It was like my words weren't convincing enough so he looked for other ways to reassure himself. He held me tighter. He pulled me closer, his chest heaved, and I could feel how heavy everything was between us.

He made an audible sound but I wasn't sure if it was a moan or a groan, the only thing I was sure of was when his lips came on top of mine again — *I* felt like I could fucking *fly*. He stole my breath everytime he kissed me, he shared his instead. Breathing for the both of us.

He was my favorite everything.

When Reiner pulled away from me, he grabbed my hand.

And this time, *we ran.* Our laugh echoed through the hallway as we ran. The adrenaline crawled under my skin. It wasn't night, the sun was still up and the hotel was clearly busy — people who walked past us, stopped or slowed down to watch us run.

They probably thought we were fucking crazy. What they didn't know was how much we missed each other, how much I was hurting when he wasn't near. They didn't know how much we've shown each other things we thought were impossible. They didn't know how everything felt right with him.

The rest of the world was damned, it's just me and him right now.

With him everything seemed easier, being with him felt like breathing. I love the person I become whenever I am near him. So I gripped his hands tighter and ran a little faster as I dragged him with me because I was dying to get into that hotel room.

There was so much I wanted to do — so much I wanted to say. I wanted to tell him about the days he wasn't around, to tell him how much I missed him.

Some part of me was still worried that this is just the beginning of a horrible mistake, that he will do much worse in the future, that he'll kick me back to the curb the second it starts pouring — he says he won't, he says he'll try harder for us. That he'd rather have me at his side while it storms, we'll do a better job repairing the damage together.

Instead of letting my doubts win, the small possibilities of things that may never happen — I was allowing myself to be happy for once, even if it wasn't guaranteed forever. Knowing that I'd have him tomorrow was enough.

I smiled, looking back at Reiner who was only one step behind me, our hands still linked together as we ran, making one last sharp turn before reaching a dead end, just a door in the end waiting to be unlocked. We slowed down and our chest heaved. I couldn't tell if I was truly laughing or aggressively breathing — but I didn't care because It was entertaining watching Reiner struggle to find the hotel keycard.

"Oh, God, please don't tell me we have to go back down to the lobby." I huffed, running a hand over my soft laid back hair.

"After all that running?" I stared at Reiner, his side profile is sharp and defined, a small smile on his lips as he shook his head.

"I mean, have we no shame?" I continued, "Do you know how fucking awkward it'll be crossing paths with those same people we laughed at while we ran?"

"I got it," Reiner flashed me the silver card, swiping it as the light went green. I didn't know what the fuck happened, but somehow the heavy mood that was in the air earlier was killed. Murdered by a stressed Reiner looking for his keycard.

I was more delighted seeing my luggage by the end of the bed the second I stepped into the hotel room. And it was so fucking weird how it arrived before me — we ran for fucks sake. What's worse now was the fact that I didn't know what to do next. It was somehow awkward feeling the sexual tension between us rise a little.

I turned to look at Reiner, my lips pursed to a small smile, "I'll be in the bathroom. . . uh," I swallowed. I really didn't think this through.

Reiner scratched the back of his neck, nodding along, "yeah, take your time."

"I will." I mumbled as I dragged my suitcase behind me, and I was fighting everything in me to not turn around and look at him. Instead I headed for the bathroom and closed the door behind me.

It was the middle of the day, and we would obviously be hogged into this hotel room so I couldn't really change into one of my spectacular outfits. I felt stupid, but I'll still feel weird about wearing a pajama set in the middle of the day. I didn't pack any lingerie, and I don't think I'd ever be bold enough to just walk out there naked.

When I came back out, Reiner had a drink in his hand, he was obviously pacing, but the second the bathroom door opened his eyes snapped at me, and I could feel his eyes drag from my face down to my legs, he lets out a little breath as he chugged the last of his drink down his throat.

He was staring at me so intensively I felt the need to dig a hole into my own skin and hide there. Here I was, thinking I should've just walked out naked instead of the pajama set. "So?"

"Sit." he pointed at the bed.

It's the way the words spoke to me that made me listen, he wasn't trying to command me, it wasn't about control — he was just in fact losing too much control. His words were desperate. *Needy.* I listened because I was still in control.

I walked towards the bed and took a seat at the edge, feeling my ass sink into the soft mattress, it's so soft I'm tempted to just laid there for a while and just sleep, but Reiner was backing away a little until his back softly hit the door, and that was enough to remind me how much sleep didn't matter right now.

Reiner placed the glass down near a small table by the door, the same one that he had placed his silver keycard. He ran a hand through his hair, his eyes heavy. Whatever he was thinking about, it's been on his mind for a while.

Reiner leaned against the door as he loosened his tie, "did Luke fuck you when I couldn't?"

I bit my lips, "yes." The lie rolled out of my tongue so easily I could almost *hi-five* myself. I just wanted a good hard fuck and I knew getting him riled up would get me just that. . . and a little more.

"Tell me how." He said, his face was blank, his body still leaned against the door.

I swallowed because I didn't know what to say, last time Luke fucked me was many, many months ago as rebound sex and he only lasted five minutes or so — the last person to ever touched me was Reiner, I already lied, I couldn't back away now so I needed to be quick and come up with something simple. Something he'd believe.

I drew in a breath, "he made me touch myself."

I deserve a fucking Oscar for my acting.

His jaw ticked, "uh-huh, wanna show me how?" His tone was soft and curious like he was speaking to me with care.

I slipped out of pajama pants along with the underwear, sitting back down on the bed hesitant before spreading my legs open a little. I didn't know how Reiner did it, but with him I was rarely shy, just a little intimidated by him, he made me feel enough to keep me on my toes. Reiner sucked in a breath, letting out a soft *'hmm'* as he breathed. Still leaning against the door and the suspense of him prowling at me at any second was delicious.

He was so fucking sexy. It was unbelievable. And to think I'd never see this look on his face ever again was nearly a crime. The way he was staring at me almost made me confess and give in, but I couldn't help but indulge into the lie a little more. It was exciting watching him be jealous when we both knew he had no right to be.

I let out a soft breath as I licked my fingers before placing them over my clit, circling it. My body jolted and my heartbeat grew faster as I felt the rush. This felt too good already. My fingers may have been the ones pleasuring me right now, but Reiner's eyes were the true source. I moaned, feeling my muscles relax, some of the tension was already leaving my body as I touched myself.

"What else did you do for him?" His voice was demanding my attention, to stare at him. So I swallowed thickly, suppressing my moans just to stare at him. Reiner was barely staring at me, his eyes were glued between my legs, his jaw hardened, and I could see the way his pants stretched as his erection grew.

I moaned at the thought of finally having him back inside of me, how good that'll be. I closed my eyes, tilted my head back, circling my fingers over my clit before finally shoving two fingers inside of my pussy — a light moan escaped my throat, this felt too good to stay quiet, and knowing he was watching me fuck myself made this so much more fucking hot than it already was.

"Did you make those sweet sounds for him too?" His voice was playful, like he was mocking me. He was talking like he knew something about me that I didn't.

With my head still tilted back I clamped my lips shut only to pant a few seconds later because I was so close to my orgasm, *'hmmm.'* I moaned, pulling my fingers out, circling my clit with my wetness, my thighs closed around my hand involuntarily due to the sensitivity, but I was still circling my clit, falling on my back against the bed because I could no longer keep myself up.

"Open your legs, *sweetheart,* I need to see how you touched yourself for Luke."

Oh right.

I whined as I opened my legs, gliding my wet fingers between the folds of my pussy, tilting my head on the bed just to find Reiners' eyes again as I slid three fingers inside of me. I think he knew I meant it as a *"fuck you"* kind of thing because his brows shot up, impressed with me and my little defiance.

"Three fingers. . ." he thought for a second, "you were spoiled, weren't you?"

"*Hmm.*" I moaned, going faster, my eyes flickered down to his pants just to be met with his erection.

"You wanna look at me so I can see how full of shit you are?"

The question took me by surprise. And my eyes snapped back up to meet him. My stomach twisted with nervousness, but I was so close to my peak, so I didn't stop myself from going faster, moaning as I felt myself reach the stars, the blood rushed through my body as my ears ranged. My mouth parted open as I panted, my thighs closed, as they shook a little. My body trembled as I came.

I swallowed watching Reiner push himself off the wall, walking towards me. Reiner kneeled in between my legs.

"Soleil if anyone touched you, it was yourself." He softly laughed, and heat rushed down to my face, "you're a shit liar you know, I can see right through you." He pried my thighs open, and my eyes met his as ran his own fingers down my pussy.

I shuddered immediately whimpering because I just fucking came and Reiner wanted to play again.

I swallowed as I fought back a moan, "What?" My voice came out weak and desperate but at this point there was so little I could do about it.

Reiner kissed the inside of my thigh, inserting a finger inside of me. I squirmed, fighting back another moan.

"Yeah, ever since that day when you lied about that phone call, I memorized the look on your face when you lie."

"Ah," I moaned when Reiner pushed another finger inside of me. Shuddering at the sensitivity.

"Please." I whispered. I was begging for a small truce, to stop the torturing because I could already see how badly it'll end.

"I couldn't even touch myself." He spoke as he hooked his hands under my thighs — he pulled my body down fast and quick, now my ass was nearly at the edge of the bed. "Thinking of you was too much, Soleil."

I propped myself up on my elbow, sending him a look, "and who's fault was that?"

Reiner tsk, giving my pussy a light tap, *"mine,* but trust me," Reiner leaned down blowing air over my pussy before he kissed me. My chest heaved as I swallowed a moan and my fingers dug into the sheets. "That'll never happen again." was the last thing I heard him say before he disappeared in between my legs.

My body jolted the second I felt his tongue against me, hot and wet. Sending warmth down to my body, goosebumps rose on my skin, as he licked my pussy.

I didn't know how he did it, but he always knew where to touch, where to feel, where to taste, all at the right time. Reiner pushed my legs over his shoulder and I was struggling to hold myself up to watch — I wanted to close my eyes and let him take me far, far away from here, but watching him do these things was somehow even more erotic than the things he was doing.

"I missed you. . . *like this.*" I bit my lips as I curled my toes.

He hummed as he sucked my clit, "I can tell," He groaned, "you're soaking."

I moaned, but it sounded like a scream, a cry, and that amused Reiner because he just discovered a spot I liked, he chuckled against me and I could feel the vibration of his laugh right through me, my mouth parted as I pant. Feeling Reiner do the same thing again, over and over and over.

With his tongue flicking over my clit, Reiner pushed a second finger inside of me, but he hasn't been moving it — he took them right out and I groaned, feeling empty again. Those fingers that were coated with my wetness, he rubbed my clit with them, going lower as he kissed my pussy and his fingers worked on my clit. He was driving me fucking insane, my skin was hot — there wasn't anything solid for me to hold onto and everytime I tried closing my legs — because this was all too much — Reiner whined and pried my legs opened.

I'm fully convinced nothing he ever did was fully for my own pleasure or benefits.

"Reiner! — fuck, enough." I cried, feeling Reiner push a third finger inside of me. I'd been anticipating it, yet it still took me by surprise.

He kissed my pussy this time before his eyes met mine, "this must be your pressure point."

I swallowed, "my pressure point?" I trembled with the words as I tried to keep my eyes opened as he fucked me with his fingers.

Reiner nodded, licking his glistening lips that were coated with my wetness as he curled his fingers inside of me. "What drives you crazy, what ruins you completely. . . what makes you mine."

I moaned, writhing under him. Completely out of things to say. Speechless.

"I think we should get a safe word, sweetheart." He licked his lips again, "because I'd really like to know when you really want me to stop when you keep screaming for me to stop while begging for more."

I relaxed as I dropped my head against the pillow, feeling the butterflies in my stomach dance around, I turned my head away from him. "You're so fucking full of yourself."

Reiner went quiet, in fact his hands weren't on me at all any-more, "wait," I propped myself up again, "are you really stopping?"

He was still on his knees, and my feets were still on his thighs. He kissed my thighs, before removing them from him — standing up tall, and somehow he could be taller than slender-man.

I stared at him, waiting for his answer. Reiner hooked a finger under my chin, "of course not, sweetheart." Reiner smiled, "I've just found a better use for your bratty little mouth."

I laughed a little as I shook my head. I watched him undo his belt. "I thought you couldn't last long in my mouth?" I teased.

Reiner looked away, heat washed over his face as his cheeks grew the lightest shade of pink.

"Do you ever not say anything, Soleil?"

"I haven't found the kryptonite to that yet, no" I shook my head playfully.

His erection was poking through his jeans, waiting to be revealed. I was beyond excited to happily discover it, but something fun came to mind, something about revenge and the desperate need to hear Reiner beg.

I pulled away from him as I sat back straighter on the bed, and Reiner sent me a wary look, obviously he hasn't figured out what's happening yet.

"*Soleil.*" he cast me a look.

I shook my head, a small smile on my face, "beg for me Reiner, make it pretty."

Reiner bit his lips as he bit back a smile, "I adore you baby, I really do. But I want you on your knees, now."

The words made me tingle, my body reacted to it — it made me desperate. I couldn't stop reacting to his words — they triggered something buried deep inside of me and I wanted to hear the commands again and again. I sighed, staring at Reiner, before I could say anything he cupped my cheeks.

"Please." He begged, gliding his fingers down my jawline in the process.

And I knew that would be all he'd offer.

A desperate sound left my lips because I wanted to please him. I did as he asked. I dropped both knees on the cold floor as I stared up at him.

Reiner held his cock with one hand as he fisted it. I bit my lips as my heart raced.

"Hands on the floor, tongue out, sweetheart."

I swallowed as I lowered myself even more just to have my hands on the floor. Reiner tapped his cock over my tongue the second I opened my mouth and stuck my tongue out. His muscle flexed as I tasted the precum that was already leaking from him — I couldn't resist, I sucked his tip and he hissed as he grabbed ahold of my hair and fisted a handful of it.

"So eager." he moaned as he pushed himself inside of my mouth.

My lips stretched at the size of him, and I could feel him pulse too. My hands reached for his thighs as he reached the back of my throat and tears started to pool in my eyes. I looked up at him with pleading eyes, hoping he'd pull out to offer me air.

"Fuck. . ." He grunted out as he shoved himself deeper. "Soleil, you have no idea how beautiful you look right now, taking me so well. *Fucking goodgirl.*"

I moaned as I whimpered with a full mouth, and tears fell down my cheeks. I lightly tapped his thighs, as my nails dug into his skin, and his thrusts into my mouth slowed as he pulled himself out of me, rewarding me with air. My chest heaved as I swallowed my saliva and his precum as I allowed myself to inhale a large gulp of air. Reiner was back to stroking his cock with a painful look on his face that told me he was sensitive.

He leaned down as he cupped my cheeks just to pull me into a deep kiss and I'm sure he could taste himself on my mouth, but he moaned as he tasted my tongue. Taking and taking.

I pulled away from our kiss as I licked my lips, the wetness in between my legs had me trembling. I was beyond aching, "please." I whispered as I pushed him back up again as I fixed myself on my knees, taking him back into my mouth again.

Reiner groaned, loudly. And his hands found their way into my hair again as he thrusted, I sucked. I sucked, he moaned and with a stretched mouth I cried until he came then I swallowed.

"I am so proud of you, sweetheart." He whispered as he pulled me up with a kiss. Still short on his breath.

★ · ☆ · ★

"I missed you so much." He thrusted inside of me, slow and deep.

I released a heavy breath, feeling my body tense before relaxing under him again. Reiner didn't move right away, he allowed me a few seconds to adjust, but it felt like it was more for him because

Reiner closed his eyes, breathing me in, holding me just to provide himself some sort of comfort.

Reiner finally moved and hell froze, nothing else exists. *It was just us and this moment.*

I breathe in his skin, I made it my own because it became my new home. I took each harsh thrust with a whimper, every kiss with a moan, I took all of him. I gave him all of myself, over and over again, feeling better and better, my body was aching but I didn't want us to ever stop.

We were so lost in each other, the moans left his lips and flew straight into my ears, they were my reward — I made him feel great, I could hear it in his voice. His breathing, the temperature of his skin. My name was on his lips over and over again, the burning desire between us was alive and the flames would never die. I affect him in every way possible. Whatever happens next will fuck us both over, it wouldn't be just my heart at stake. I'll have him tomorrow and that was enough for me.

Tomorrow can always be our forever because tomorrows never end.

I could feel the tears pool my eyes, but I swallowed just to find my voice. "Reiner." I whispered his name like a soft prayer, begging for his attention, cupping the back of his neck, holding onto him. His eyes met mine and I could feel everything in me thaw.

There was this barrier I didn't want in between us anymore.

"Reiner." I moaned his name again. Calling out to him

"I know." He whispered, pulling his brows together like he knew what I was desperately trying to say.

He leaned down, closer and kissed my lips, "baby, I know." He kissed me again, soft and sweet while he thrust into me so harshly he rocked the headboard against the wall, a moan escaped my lip as the tears finally fell down on the side of my head and I wondered how could love be so soft and brutal at the same time.

I held onto him tighter, scared he might make a run for it. "I love you." I whispered, nearly choking on the words.

Reiner froze, stopped moving inside of me and looked down at me through hooded eyes. I reached up to push his hair back a little, cupping his face as I leaned forward a little, rubbing my nose against his with a satisfied hum. "I love you." I repeated again.

His nose flared, "baby, you're killing me here." He breathed as his mouth came on top of mine with a smile.

I laughed, wrapping my legs tighter around him, Reiner dropped his body next to mine, stuffing his face into the crook of my neck as he held onto me.

"Say it again." He whispered softly, but there was this need in his voice that made me want to hold him and never let go.

"I love you, Reiner."

When Reiner entered me again, he touched me softly, he kissed me, his hands were soft, he showered me with love. We laughed but he killed the sound of my laughs with his kisses.

Our tomorrow started today.

CHAPTER THIRTY-EIGHT

Reiner

"I THINK SHE'S PANICKING, or spiraling." I whispered into the phone, watching Soleil throw another shirt across the room. I was surprised there were more shirts.

"Does she know you called?"

"She's not even looking at me right now."

Soleil groaned, as she lifted a dress into the air a black long sleeved dress, I think it would do, but I'm afraid if I spoke right now she'd prance at me then choke me to death.

"Matthew, you're an idiot."

"Hayley I think we've reached the stage where you can call me by my first name instead of my middle name."

I quite literally heard her gag, "Eww, that's weird, don't make things any weirder. Just hand Soleil the phone."

I rolled my eyes, "what am I supposed to do after?"

"Nothing, just let her do whatever she's doing now."

"We're running a little late I don't think—"

"Shut up and hand her the phone, Matthew."

I sighed, taking a few steps forward, handing Soleil the phone, she stared at me before taking the phone from me.

Soleil lets out a slow breath, her shoulders sagged "Hayley I'm still mad at you, but fuck, I'm meeting his parents in an hour." She deadpanned.

I ran a hand over my hair because I didn't think it was this bad. My parents had been nagging me to see Anna after all that went down, and honestly letting Anna visit them all the way here sounded like a bright fucking idea. She'd be away from all the mess her mother created which would've bought me time to figure everything else out.

Noa didn't go to jail because she's privileged in many many different ways, but it was still not enough — she was stuck on patrol after paying an expensive fine, and bail. I have full custody — and it'll take a long time before I could fully trust Noa again. I still couldn't rob Anna of her mother completely.

Anna has been with my parents for a few days now, and I promised them long ago I'd go see them the second I stepped foot into Canada. My parents are divorced but they get along just fine for the sake of Anna. My father was still traveling but after the accident with Anna he wanted to see her too, so he stepped foot into Canada with his new wife, hours after I shipped Anna there.

I dragged Soleil into this stupid thing we were doing because

I figured it was time to share more of me with her — and because I wanted her to meet my parents. The shock on her face when I mentioned my parents still replays in my head over and over again.

"I forgot you have parents." I remember her saying. She exploded before piecing herself back together just to offer me an apology. *"That's not what I meant at all."* she frowned, *"I- you just rarely ever mentioned them before."*

I laughed but it was short and breathless because soon enough, Soleil crumbled in front of her suitcase, crumbling completely. Panicking about seeing them for the first time, what to wear, what would they think of her.

It was like that for a few minutes until I called Hayley. I was obviously helpless here, and that phone call lasted shorter than I expected. Soleil threw a pair of jeans over her shoulder, turning to look at me as she handed me back my phone. I took a few cautious steps forward as I grabbed the phone.

She stood up, something that could be a shirt was in her hand, "did you tell them?"

I pulled my brows together, "mhm?"

She sent me a blank stare, "Did. You. Tell. Them."

"Tell them what?"

Soleil used her free hand, wavering it around her face, "that I'm black"

I snorted, turning my head as I laughed. I didn't know whether I should reply to this comment sarcastically or not — but the sound of my laughter died in my throat when I noticed the serious look on her face, "Soleil, why would that be important?"

She frowned, shrugging — and my heart hurt a little because I could feel her closing a door on me, hiding. Shrinking. I took a step forward, wrapping my arms around her waist, pulling her against me. I kissed the side of her head, melting into her because the smell of lavender is the smell of home.

"Baby, I can't promise you that the whole world will accept us without an ounce of judgment, because there will be some people who'll roll their eyes seeing us, but I can tell you my parents are *nothing* like them and they will love you for who you are and not for what you look like."

"*Okay.*"

"Okay."

Soleil had her hair down, and it was everywhere. She turned to look at me and every curl recoiled with the action. her brown eyes shined under nothing but her own glow. Her knees are bounced, knocking against mine from time to time. I placed a hand on her knee and I could feel the bouncing slow. She relaxed a little, but not enough because her eyes were still so round and scared. She was nervous and I wanted to tell her that she had nothing to be afraid of — but as stubborn as she can be she'd always add more to it.

I smiled, wide. choking on a big wave of happiness because Soleil reached for my hand, she did it for herself. For her comfort. I watched our fingers intertwine before she pushed herself into my chest, and my body instantly relaxed against hers, welcoming her warmth.

She slowly exhaled, "anything else I should know about?"

"Anna's there."

No reaction, she simply hummed, playing with my fingers, "when did she get here?"

"A week ago."

She sighed against my chest, "at least someone I know will be there."

"I'll be there."

"Meh, it's different with Anna. You wouldn't get it."

I laughed, watching the car pull up — I did my best to get us there on time because my mother didn't fail to remind me how much trouble she went through to get us a reservation, last minute. She was excited to meet Soleil. She hasn't even met her yet, but she has a good feeling about this, so she says.

She never liked Noa. I always thought it was because we were too young, making all the commitments too fast, but I guess my mother was right about all the bad feelings.

I opened the door, stepped out of the car, dragging Soleil out right behind me. Her hand was still in mine, the cool air blowing caused the hairs on the back of my neck to stand. I could feel Soleil shake a little. I was grateful she didn't wear the dress after all. I pulled her against me, wrapping my arm around her waist and guided her inside of the restaurant.

Anna jumped out of her seat the second she saw us, running straight into me. I wrapped my arms around her whole body, hugging her, careful enough to not break her, the cast recently came off but I'm still scared that if I hold her too tight she'll break — I pulled her with me when I stood up again, kissing her cheeks as she laughed, "I missed you, little Princess."

"I miss *you*, dad."

I smiled, "I'm here now."

Anna lifted her head a little, looking over my shoulder, "Hi, Soleil. Thank you for the pies." Anna said, shyly

Soleil brows furrowed completely unaware of how to answer, she smiled, "you're welcomed."

I sensed her confusion because Anna was referring to the pies I bought Soleil, which she kindly rejected. I didn't want to trash them so I gifted them to Anna. A recovering gift from Soleil.

I rubbed Anna's hair causing her to laugh a little as she pushed my hand away, she leaned in whispering into my ear but couldn't understand her slurred words, and by the time we made it to the table she gave up and just shook her head at me.

I flashed my mother a smile, looking at Soleil over my shoulder, "Hey, mom. . ."

My mothers' blonde hair was much more golden than the last time I saw it, she must be bleaching regalary just to slow down the process of aging, my father on the other hand is graying slowly but naturally. They're only sixty-seven years old, so I'd say they're aging pretty well.

My mother stood up, pushing her chair back and my dad shook his head because he knew she was about to cause a scene. My mothers eyes bounced from me to Soleil, who was shifting uncomfortably.

"Mother, I'd like you to meet, Soleil." I said before turning to look at Soleil, offering her a small smile, "Soleil this is my mother, Brandee."

The creepy smile only widened when Soleil tried to offer a handshake but my mother only trapped her into a hug, "you my dear," she pulled away from the hug, but still held her arms, "are *gorgeous*." Mother turned to look at my dad, "isn't she Tom?"

Soleil smiled as my dad stood up, offering a handshake, "I'm Tom, and yes Brandee is right, you are very beautiful, dear." Soleil shook his hand.

"Thank you." she added.

"So how'd you get stuck with Reiner?" my dad said as he sat back down.

I sighed, "why don't you let us sit first then you can harass me, or try not to suffocate her with questions."

"Yeah, let them sit, Tom, Anna you too, come back to your chair."

The first twenty one minutes were basically just Soleil playing twenty one questions. I jumped in there when things got too personal, but my Soleil? She was a rockstar, handling all this so well. She was still so very nervous, but she was not breaking.

Mom and dad seemed to be getting along well, or maybe they've gotten better at fooling me. Mom did bring up the fact that Connie wasn't here with us, but either way I was glad — glad we're having a good day.

"What are you in school for again?" Dad asked.

"Journalism."

"Ahh, journalism, such a fickle career."

"Tom!" Mom shouted, and I glared at my dad, because I wanted him to drop that topic completely. It's none of his business what Soleil does with her life or not.

Soleil laughed, "it is, believe me it is, but I'm trying my best to sink my teeth into it completely."

"Calm down, Brandee, see. . . she was agreeing with me."

The tension thickened when the waiter came over to our table, but thanks to Anna everything cooled down when she ordered herself dino nuggets — Noa has tried multiple times to break the cycle and manipulate her into eating healthy food, but once Anna has her mind set on something I don't think anything or anyone has the power to change her mind.

I could feel the disturbing smile on my face as I watched Soleil order some sort of pasta. I wasn't really listening — everyone was talking, Anna was babbling with my parents but I could only see her, and everything and everyone faded. I was in the moment.

I grabbed her hand under the table, laying it flat over my thigh as I drew small patterns against her palm. I don't know what I was doing — all I knew was that I needed to feel her somehow. My smile widened when I felt her leg brush against mine, it was more like a small kick, a warning — asking me to stop what I was doing, to focus, something I couldn't do at the moment.

I leaned closer towards Soleil, my lips brushed against her ear and I could feel the way my body jolted at her attention with every response hers gave me, every shiver, I could feel them — I could see the way she sucked in a breath when I invade her space like this. She was always nervous when it came to me.

"I love you." I whispered, it was quick and quiet. I pulled away watching the small smile on her face widened, Soleil shook her head a little, wiping the smile off her face, because unlike me she was aware of her surroundings.

She looked at me, "I ordered for you."

My brows shot up with curiosity, I hadn't even noticed that the waiter left a while back, with a single finger, I drew a small circle against her palm, "what did you get me?"

Her eyes widened, finally understanding the signals I've been sending her, she snatched her hand away, a quick movement that made everyone realize her hand was once on my lap, "one of those creamy soups you like." she said.

I could hear my mother shush my dad as she stared at us. Obviously listening in. I didn't want to look at her yet, but I could already imagine the frightening smile on her face.

Soleil made sure to stop me from reaching for her with the small space she placed between us, and her awkward body language — I knew people in general went crazy over PDA, I do too sometimes, but when it came to Soleil I always tried to get as much of her as I could.

Anna sat on my lap as she ate her dino nuggets, and the dinner went by fast and peacefully with only a couple of questions for Soleil.

Mom refused to let me leave without dragging me to the side, and I didn't know what she had in mind — I truly couldn't tell if she'd complain about me or dad.

"You were never like this with Noa," she said. The same gigantic smile on her face.

I catched a glimpse of Soleil, just sitting at the table laughing obnoxiously loud over something Anna said. "I don't know what you're talking about."

Mom slapped my shoulder and I turned to look at her with hurtful eyes, placing a hand over the shoulder she almost misplaced, *"Ow."*

"Reiner, I *know* you." She whispered, "You were *never* like this with Noa."

I shook my head, "I loved Noa"

"This is different. . . *you're in love.*"

I smiled, finally at ease, proud of myself even.

Mom pulled me into a quick hug, because after all, I'm pretty sure that's why she had me cornered. "I adore her Reiner, in some ways. . . she calms you, even Tom saw it.

"Saw what?"

"You're happy, *truly* happy." Mom turned around in Soleil's direction, watching her play with Anna, "and it's all because of them."

Watching her play with Anna filled my body with this joy that I couldn't even begin to process. I was falling for her, *right now*, in this moment. Everyday I fall a little harder. I once thought I was in love, but now I realized the things I felt weren't even a fraction of what being in love felt like.

We regrouped again, and dad whispered something to mom

and I was still staring at Soleil — Anna was the one to break their little chat, walking towards me with a purpose, a complaint under her breath, "grandma won't give me my iPad back." she huffed.

I laughed because I saw that complaint coming, Anna always had a strict screen time when she stayed with my mother. "You're mad you're not getting spoiled?"

She turned to Soleil who obviously said something with the look she sent Anna, and Anna turned back to me, pouting her lips, then she started whining. The two were obviously scheming.

"Your puppy dog face needs a little more work."

"But dad—"

I shook my head, "Grandma's the boss."

Anna sighed, walking past me and if she thought her stiff puppy dog face would work on my mother she was in for a world of disappointment. I laughed to myself, taking a seat next to Soleil on the table.

"I think we're waiting on my pie, I have the waiter plating it in a to-go plate." she said.

I nodded, grabbing her chair, pulling it closer against mine. I grasped her cheeks with one hand leaving a quick kiss on her lips, "why do you love pies so much?"

She sighs when I release her cheeks, "my dad never bought me cakes on my birthdays, only pies."

She only stared at me when she spoke, and that was one of the million things I love about Soleil, she never held her head low.

"Because they were my mom's favorite." She finished her sentence.

I frowned a little, grabbing her hand, "do you ever want to find your mother?"

She smiled, a small sad smile, "she doesn't want to be found, Reiner, and no one should ever look for something that was never there."

"I don't miss her, I'm not sad, because she was never there, to me she's nothing, something I can live without, but to my father she was *everything*."

I released a small breath, I didn't know what to say to that, so, I reached for her and wrapped my arms around her, pulling her into my chest. Soleil didn't fight it, and we spent a few seconds like that, in silence.

"Maybe I get sad sometimes, but not for her. For my father, and the pies fill an empty void I think." Her voice was small, and before I could say something the waiter came back with a big brown paper bag.

We said goodbye to Anna and my parents when our car came around, they waited for us before finding their own car in the parking lot, and since I didn't think bringing Anna back with us because our hotel wasn't exactly ideal she'd be staying with my mother for a few more days — I don't know when my dad is getting back on the road anytime soon this week.

Soleil had her head on my shoulder for the whole ride, at some point I think she fell asleep because when the car came to a stop I had to wake her up.

She yawned, "this isn't the hotel."

"I know."

I didn't tell her we would go skating earlier because it was a last minute thing. It's something I thought would bring her mood up — after that chat about her mother she'd been. . . calm. I don't know the exact right things to say, but I do know about the things she likes.

I held her hand as I dragged her into the place, it was empty because I made sure of it — having other people around would make everything feel like a nuisance, being looked at, all the loud unnecessary laughters that would distract us both, bumping into people. It would be unpleasant.

I made sure Soleil left her guard cap on because we haven't stepped into the ice yet, she stood in front of me, giddy. Her eyes were bright with excitement. I wrapped my hands around her hair, wrapping it into a bun, which was a harder task than imagined.

"I've never skated before." she said as she placed her hand over my waist, her hair kept falling down again as I struggled to hold onto it to keep it in place with the hair-tie. With a concentrated face, I finally managed to keep her hair up in a bun.

"Me neither." I mumbled, placing her extra hair-tie on my wrist, I wasn't not even sure what she needed it for.

"Then why are we here?" she laughed.

"I got us a trainer."

Her face fell, the shock eating up the silence. I think her reactions are genuinely cute so I lay a kiss on her forehead. I hope she doesn't ask to see her hair-do — to me it looked great and that's only because I don't think I could do any better, but she could. I only hope she'd be distracted enough to forget about it.

"How rich are you?"

I took her hand in mine, leading the way, "enough."

The woman training us came closer into view, standing in the middle of the rink, waiting for us. and I wonder how we will ever get there without falling, losing our dignity in the process.

I took off my cap guards as Soleil took off hers, and she was still holding my hand like a vice, if one of us falls, we both fall. She leaned closer towards me, careful to not drag us to the ground because we were taking penguin steps, "a free lesson won't get you laid Reiner."

I smiled, "there's other ways to change your mind."

Her breath hitched and we both fell.

Soleil is a natural, I'm convinced she's just great at everything. I'm competitive so I made sure to learn as fast as I could. After many, many, *many* failed attempts I could finally stand and skate without falling, the basic forward two foot glide. I stopped there. It was Soleil who kept going, she said she'd learned a trick or two, like a cherry on top.

For her first day of training the lady was only willing to teach her how to Dip as she skated. My energy was nearly all spent, so I stood there by the pole, watching her fall on her ass — at least she knew how to fall properly.

Soleil flipped me so quickly when she caught me holding back a laugh.

Soon enough she got the hang of it, at first she started moving slowly, cautious — focused on her balance. On her second try, she was a little more confident, moving at her own pace. She just fell on her third try, but when she finally did it, there was this bright smile on her face, and I was the first person she reached for. She skated towards me, laughing in excitement, and I caught her when she leaped at me, because I'll always be there to catch her when she's ready to leap.

Soleil kissed me fiercely, laughing when I wrapped my arms around her waist, holding her tighter. She darted her tongue into my mouth, teasing mine. I smiled into the kiss, my whole body reacting towards hers.

She laughed as she pulled away, but I brought her back against me for another kiss, and another one and another one. She was laughing like crazy and I always want to see her this happy. I wanted to capture the sound of her laugh and play it on a vinyl record.

"I love you." she said. And it made me feel special to be loved by her. *Complete.*

It was my turn to smile like a madman, kissing her cheeks.

Everything about her was bright, she was the light everyone talked about — she was the light everyone craved. There was this exhilarating rush I felt whenever I was with her, when I felt that feeling I chased it. I never want to let go because Soleil is the only light I want. And I'd be more than willing to chase her for the rest of my life, and every other lifetime. She was consistent, the one thing that would never change to me. I'll search for her in every lifetime, searching for pieces of her in everyone I meet. Forever with her sounded magical. Like a dream where I'd only chase her. My starlight. I'd be chasing a starlight in every lifetime.

EPILOGUE

★·☆·★

Soleil

★·☆·★

I NEVER DREAMT OF A BIG HOUSE. The white picket fences, a pool out back — simple things I never had. A job I love, someone to come home to, kids of my own to love — I never thought that far into life, or even dreamt this far at all. I had plans to get myself a career and survive. Be lucky enough to even meet someone.

It almost felt like this perfect life was handed to me, and I don't know what I ever did to deserve all of what I've got.

My husband has been tending to my needs the second he helped me step outside of the car, he pointed at the house, meaning I had no business in helping him carry in the groceries, he only screamed for Anna— he called for her to come help. Anna was probably deep in her room, she probably didn't hear anything so I had to send her a text. But instead of finding my way inside of the house, I walked towards Reiners' direction.

I didn't say anything, I simply reached for a bag.

"Soleil, do not touch that." Reiner pointed a finger at me as he tilted his head to the side, right now he was sending me a warning, the same one he probably sent Cullen every time he entered Anna's room.

"Why not? Even Cull can do that."

Reiner sent me a blank stare, "Cullen. . . our three year old son, can take groceries out of the car?"

"If we let him. . ."

He sighed, and I could feel it. Some perfectly reasonable bullshit is going to come out of his mouth and I'll have no choice but to agree.

"Why are you fighting me on this?"

I furrowed my brows, running a hand over my forehead, "why are *you* fighting me on this? It's just groceries, Reiner."

Reiner shook his head, taking just two steps to reach me. He wrapped his arm around my waist and his hands circled my belly. "You're a planet."

And there it was. The reasonable bullshit that I couldn't disagree on. I tried to fight my smile but it only widened. The second he found out this pregnancy was high-risk everything was tripled. He was more gentle with me, more careful. I thought being pregnant with Cullen was bad, but everything only intensified for Reiner.

Cullen happened during our honeymoon, Reiner jinxed it.

I'm sure of it. We weren't even sure and he was already bossing me around.

We had Anna, we had Cullen, they were more than enough. Now Riyoh was only a few days away from being born and this precious cargo was more fragile than the one before so Reiner is always on edge, worrying so much — he never says so, but I know he is.

I sighed when he shifts to stand behind me, wrapping his hands under my belly as he lifts it a little, practically holding my belly up, it felt like he just lifted a thousand dumbbells off of me — the doctor thought him that two weeks ago, and he does it all the times, I never had to ask. Sometimes I feel like he'd breathe for me if he could.

"Our girl is coming any day now, let's get you to bed. And that means no more work."

My eyes that were closed, snapped open. "What? What do you mean 'no work'?" He had a point, of course he does, but what I was asking for didn't require anything but my computer.

I was offered, partner at the company a month ago, a few days before I was supposed to go on maternity leave. I've been working my ass off, writing articles after articles, doing interviews after interviews and only a few days before my maternity leave, I was offered partner. *Co-ownership of a newspaper company.*

This chance was one of those chances that only come once in a blue moon, and I didn't want to let it slip away from my fingers because I was a scared mother — I can do both. Worry and work, my mind is placed at ease every time I think about co-ownership of that small newspaper company. I was working just to take a few things off my checklist. I know the second I have Riyoh I won't even blink at my laptop, so if I take care of all of it now, I won't have to freak out after pushing out a codependent baby out of me.

"I'm so close to getting Partner Reiner, we're just working out the small details."

His arms around me loosened, and I could feel his body tense, "I thought you took maternity leave already?"

"That was before I found out I was up for, Partner."

"Soleil."

"Reiner."

I sighed, caving in just a little, I turned around to look at him, "I'm doing all of the typing in bed, me and Riyoh will be fine." I pressed my hand firmly against his hard chest, "Your wife and daughter will be fine."

His eyes met mine and for a split second I could see the fear in his eyes. I wish he would tell me about the part he was scared of — he never talked about it, but I tell him mine all the time just to show him he was not the only one scared about everything.

I trailed my hands to his face, then I reached up for his soft shaggy brown hair, running my fingers through it, playing with it. "We're gonna be fine, Reiner."

He nodded as he kissed the side of my head, "the second you cough, sneeze, or even groan, I'm taking you to the hospital."

I laughed, nodding as his lips reached for mine, sealing our promise with a kiss. I let out a breath feeling completely at ease. Reiner had this effect I couldn't explain or put into words. *He calmed me.*

"We should celebrate," he said.

"Yeah," I chimed in, "with apple juice in wine glasses. . . if I drink enough it'll start to taste like wine."

"You guys are so old." Anna sent us a weird look walking past us to grab groceries out of the car. Her blonde hair bounced as she moved.

"Hey, no!" I pointed a finger at Anna, ripping myself away from Reiner, "he's old, not me, I'm twenty-nine, baby." I smiled, "And he's like thirty-eight."

Reiner sent me a disappointing look when I turned to look at him, "glad you're not throwing me under the bus."

Anna only shook her head as she walked past us, granted no one really wanted to see us bicker like two children, but when it was over — when Reiner was walking us back inside of the house I was only thinking of one thing and I just had to tell him.

"Riyoh is going to be so much like Anna, I can tell. . . She won't be blonde, but she'll be a mini Anna."

Reiner sucked in a breath, "I don't think I can handle two Annas'—"

Anna was officially thirteen, a teenager. Which meant she had crushes, talked to guys in general. Idolized the toxic beauty standard, always on her phone, basically Reiner's worst nightmare. I told him it was a phase and that it would pass, but he was almost convinced that Anna might be a middle school mean girl. I couldn't completely disagree on that, but I trusted that we've raised her well. Even Noa was part of the reason why I can say Anna is going to grow up to be an incredible woman.

Cullen only realized I was home when we entered the kitchen, when we were opening cabinets and closing cabinets and that must've grabbed his attention. And when he hugged me he threw all of his body weight against me, and I'd usually have to take a step back. But I never complained because I could feel his little arms really squeeze my legs and he kissed my belly — his brown eyes shined, full of love, so pure and innocent.

"Hi baby." I cooed, my fingers tangled in his light auburn hair, "how are you my baby?"

I only asked because he had a whole mental breakdown before we left the house, and the only thing that calmed him down was the fact that Anna told him he'd be staying with her in her room — Cull loves Annas' room. I think it's her style he loves. He was clearly a fan, we thought it was cute but Anna found it annoying.

"I flushed Jeff down the toilet." He blurted out. Cullen was at that age where he just blurts out random words. He talked just to talk, and at this rate you either say something back or just nod, and I chose to nod.

Jeff is — was his Lego. He flushed his Lego down the toilet.

I leaned down kissing his forehead before he ran off to Reiner. I'd say Cullen was the exact copy of his father, apart from the ginger hair and brown eyes. It flattered me a lot knowing I was his favorite.

I watched Cullen detach himself away from me just to run to Reiner the second he came into view — Reiner lifted him up, threw him in the air and I swear, I got a heart attack everytime he did this. Cullen laughed, but my soul flew out of my body each time.

I grabbed a few things out of the bag, stuffing them somewhere in the fridge, "You know people at the daycare think Cull isn't ours— that he isn't *yours* at least."

Reiner stared at him, his brows furrowed as he turned to look at me, "Why?"

I looked at Cullen who was touching Reiner's facial scruff. He loved doing that, "why do you think?"

"He's a redhead, dad," Anna chimed in, "and yeah when it's just me and him, some people *really* stare at us."

I frowned, I didn't know *that*. Cullen's hair color brought up a lot of controversial comments sometimes, people loves to just guess, and I didn't mind when they did — it just bugged me when they have questions that has nothing to do with them or their business, instead of asking they spread it around, and the answer to those questions changes everytime someone who wasn't us answered it.

I have dark hair, Cullen has auburn hair, Anna's blonde, Reiner's brunette and Riyoh. . .? but I could see why everyone had their questions.

Reiner huffed, "yeah but stuff like this happens, and it's from my side, my mother told me she had a cousin who was ginger, this is normal. Stuff like this happens."

"Rarely." Anna added.

I nodded before speaking, finding Cullen's bright eyes, "yeah, but it happens."

"Who knows, maybe Riyoh will have purple hair." Anna said those words with a straight face, so serious we couldn't help but laugh. Even Cullen joined in, I'm not sure if he knew we were laughing at the possibility of his sister having purple hair though.

So we laughed at the thought of Riyoh having purple hair, and if she does — I just know we'll love her fiercely.

BONUS CHAPTER

★ · ☆ · ★

The Honeymoon

★ · ☆ · ★

I LOVE HIM with every beat of my wildflower heart. He loves me like his world would shatter the second I leave him. And me? I love him so much to the point where I'd push him into the water, laughing as I watched the waves take him under. Reiner came back up of course, but he took me with him.

I coughed, feeling the salty water slide its way down my throat with no filter. Reiner held my face with two hands, "you really gotta stop swallowing the water, it's not good for you."

I tried to breathe but it burned, "asshole." I mumbled under my breath.

"C'mon, I was playing fair."

I push against his chest, angry that he somehow won this game we were definitely *not* playing.

Reiners' eyes softened as he looked at me, he pushed my hair back and kissed my forehead. "Yeah, let's go." The second I nodded he turned around, throwing my hands over his shoulder as I eased my way on his back. Carrying me out of the ocean.

★·☆·★

"Reiner stop it," I hissed, "this is ridiculous, I am not pregnant."

"Yet." He added.

"This is not twilight, you're not Edward, I'm not Bella, so no I'm not pregnant just because we're having sex with no protection." My gaze sent him daggers but he didn't seem to care, "plus. . . I'm on the pill." I whispered the last part.

I swallowed, listening to the words roll out of my mouth. They sounded a little stupid once I said them outloud, I sounded like a crazy person and he knew it. It's exactly what he wanted. His blue eyes nearly twinkle as he laughs softly.

"You can hear yourself right?"

I sighed, "tell you what, if by some miracle you get me pregnant by the end of our honeymoon, I'll name the kid Cullen."

"He's gonna hate that."

"How will he, if he doesn't exist?"

Reiner smirked, "We'll see."

AUTHOR'S NOTE

This is not a fanfic.

This is me denying it.

I was. . . motivated. That's all.

Anyways, my love and gratitude goes out to all of my readers, new ones included. Without any of you, my words wouldn't be on pages right now, so thank you for fueling my imagination, thank you for believing in me, and thank you for joining me in my own world. Thank you for enjoying this book, for convincing me it was a decent enough story. This book started out with my obsession with Reiner Braun, back in January when season 4 part 2 of AOT and MAPPA's Golden boy was clearly favored. We (the fans) were very pleased with the changes. Everyone looked great, but Reiner looked extra great, and so began the edits on TikTok. They were innocent at first, but my imagination started rolling. It may seem like my Reiner and OG Reiner only seem to share a name, but they have much more in common.

ABOUT THE AUTHOR

TAMISHA KUENEE

was born in a small Caribbean island — a country called *Haiti;* she lived somewhere in *port-au-prince* for the first 11 years of her life. She currently resides somewhere in Florida complaining about the weather. She can be found planted in front of a TV consuming rom-coms, action movies, anime shows & k-dramas. Sometimes, she's stuck in a book. She loves cats, and laughs at her own jokes. She follows her imagination and doesn't confine herself to just one genre. *Chasing A Starlight* is her debut novel, living proof of her amazing imagination.

Find her on Instagram! @juicyfruitsX0

Printed in Great Britain
by Amazon

19555360R00264